HIDDEN HEIRESS

AMANDA SCOTT

The Secret Clan

HIDDEN HEIRESS

WARNER BOOKS

An AOL Time Warner Company

Jacket design by Diane Luger
Jacket illustration by Franco Accornero

ISBN: 0-7394-2719-9

Warner Books, Inc.
1271 Avenue of the Americas
New York, NY 10020

W An AOL Time Warner Company

Printed in the United States of America

To Terry and Jim Drennan,
because they are what it's all about

Author's Note

For readers who enjoy knowing the correct pronunciation of the names and places mentioned in a book, please note the following:

> Ceilidh = KAY-lee
> Dunsithe = Dun-SITH-ee
> Eilean Donan = EEL-ee-an DOE-nan
> Mo chridhe = Moe HREE
> Sleat = Slate

And now, if you've ever wondered what would have happened if Cinderella had lived in 16th-century Scotland . . .

HIDDEN
HEIRESS

Prologue —————————————————————

The Scottish West March, 1530

The flaxen-haired little girl hurried silently up the dark, twisting service stairway, alert to every sound. The servants would not bother her, but other residents of Farnsworth Tower were not so kind.

She flitted past her ladyship's solar without even peeping inside, lest her ladyship or someone else see her and give her some unpleasant task to do.

If she could get to Sir Hector's private sanctuary, perhaps he would allow her to visit with him for a time and tell her interesting tales about the days of old. Sir Hector told good stories, but even if he was not of a mind to entertain her today, perhaps he would let her sit quietly with him while he worked. He was kind, Sir Hector was, and his company was peaceful. If he had work to do, she could let her mind wander and think up stories of her own, and no one would seek her there.

She was reaching to lift the latch on Sir Hector's door when she heard quick, tapping footsteps coming up the main stairway at the opposite end of the short corridor. Recognizing the steps, the child quickly concealed herself in the shadows of a narrow alcove between Sir Hector's room and the service stairs. Maidservants frequently set their buckets and mops there, but presently it was empty.

Lady Farnsworth appeared in the archway leading from the stairs and hurried toward Sir Hector's door, thrusting it open so abruptly that the child heard it bang against the wall inside.

"You must do something about this unhappy situation at once, husband," Lady Farnsworth declared in strident tones. "You cannot allow it to continue." The door swung partially closed again, and the child crept close enough to peek through the crack, listening intently.

Annoyed by the sort of interruption he most disliked, Sir Hector Farnsworth unlooped the cords of his spectacles from his ears, then carefully set them in their appointed place on his writing table, where he could be fairly certain that if his temper became exercised—as experience warned him it might—he would not inadvertently send them flying across the room with a careless gesture. That had happened before, and he found it embarrassing to have to call for a lackey to help him find them again. Only when they were safe did he look directly at his wife.

He could certainly see her well enough with her stout body and several chins quivering with indignation. He could even see that her coif and the elaborate, unnaturally red wig beneath it were sadly disarranged. It was only small items right in front of him that he had difficulty making out. Poor vision was acceptable sometimes, such as when his wife insisted on invading his bed, but otherwise it was annoying to an educated gentleman who enjoyed an active correspondence and an interest in law as it applied at Stirling and generally did not apply in the unruly Borders.

Hoping he sounded reasonable and did not reveal in his tone the irritation he felt, he said, "With what particular situation would you have me deal, madam?"

Lady Farnsworth's heaving bosom continued to display her agitation, and the unladylike snort that preceded her reply informed him that his mild tone had not deceived her and that she was very angry indeed.

"You must write to the Earl of Angus at once, sir, and command him to abide by the agreement he made with us if he wants us to continue fostering that misbegotten brat of his."

"It would be extremely presumptuous of me to do such a thing," Sir Hector said testily. "A man of my inferior rank does not command any earl, let alone the Earl of Angus."

"Couch the matter in whatever diplomatic terms you like," she retorted, putting her hands on her ample hips and leaning forward over his table. "Just make it clear to his lordship that he must send the money he promised us for her care."

"Or?"

"Or, what?"

"That is precisely *my* question, madam. What would you have me do with the wee lassie if Angus refuses?"

"Why, cast her out, of course. Send her to the nuns if you like, or give her to some family in the village to raise. She should not be here, sir, associating with your daughters! It is not as if her mother had been anyone of rank. Angus may be her father, but her mother was a common serving wench."

"Dear me," Sir Hector said, rubbing the back of his neck and savoring the coolness of his palm against the nape. "Wee Elspeth has lived here now for nearly four years, madam, more than half her life. By now, she must look upon Farnsworth Tower as her home and upon Drusilla and Jelyan as her sisters."

"Well, they are *not* her sisters, sir, and she shall speedily be disabused of that notion if she does dare to entertain it. If Angus refuses to support her, he can scarcely expect us to do so. She is his bastard, after all, not yours!"

"Madam, I do not like to hear such vulgar words on your lips."

Her quick flush satisfied him that she retained some delicacy of mind, but her harsh tone did not alter as she said, "You may dislike the term, sir, but you cannot dismiss its accuracy. If you prefer to think of Elspeth as his natural child, do so, but it does not alter the situation one whit."

"I would remind you that Angus is presently in exile."

"Aye, and he has been in exile for three of the four years we have kept her, has he not? He paid for her upkeep after he fled the King's wrath to join Henry of England, so 'tis not his exile that prevents his sending the money he owes you."

"He may no longer have enough even for himself," Sir Hector said.

"They say he lives higher than England's Henry does, even in London, although he spends most of his time at the house Henry provides for him near York. Moreover, sir, I would remind *you* that Angus has twice managed to finance armies to attack our Borders and is said to be raising a third even now." When he grimaced, she raised her chin, adding, "Your mother may have been proud that she suffered a connection to the Douglases, sir, but I warrant even she would not support their wretched exiled chief against the King of Scots!"

"Now, my dear," Sir Hector said, feeling uncomfortably defensive for the first time since the interview had begun.

"You know perfectly well that Border loyalties are . . . well . . . flexible."

"We should more properly call them fickle," she snapped. "Still, since Angus ordered you to look after his brat, he must keep his part of the bargain."

"I shall write and remind him that the lassie requires upkeep," Sir Hector said. "Although I will not write as sternly as you suggest, mayhap a gentle reminder will not come amiss."

"Be as gentle as you like, sir, but find some way to tell his odious lordship that if he does not comply, we will turn the brat out to look after herself."

"No, I will not tell him that," Sir Hector said, reaching to reclaim his spectacles. Holding them, he idly stroked their silver wire frame with his fingertip as he added, "We will not send her to the priest or into the village. Elspeth will remain here at Farnsworth Tower."

"Then she must earn her keep. She is nearly six years old, after all."

"Yes, I suppose she must if Angus fails to honor his word," he agreed. "Now, if you have naught else to say to me . . ."

Outside the half-open doorway, little Elspeth stood as still as a mouse, listening. Upon hearing Sir Hector dismiss his lady, she turned abruptly, eyes wide, her attitude that of a startled deer seeking to bolt from danger, only to come face-to-face with her nemesis.

"Elspeth, you wicked bairn!" nine-year-old Drusilla Farnsworth exclaimed. "Listening at my father's door? Och, but you'll catch a rare skelping for this!"

"That she will," Lady Farnsworth declared harshly from the doorway.

Caught between the two of them, Elspeth stiffened with fright, but she held her tongue, knowing from experience that anything she said would only make her punishment worse.

Chapter 1 ————————————

The Scottish Highlands, ten years later

Twelve ships sailed down the narrow Sound of Raasay between the east coast of the Isle of Skye and the west coast of Kintail on the Scottish mainland. At the bottom of the Sound, the ships turned east into Loch Alsh. Despite an August morning mist rising from the loch and giving the steep surrounding hills a softened gray-blue appearance, the day promised to be a fine one. The mist dissipated before the ships came within sight of their objective.

At Eilean Donan Castle, on its islet at the east end of Loch Alsh, where the loch forked into Loch Long and Loch Duich, the first warning of danger was a shout from the ramparts.

"Ships on the loch!"

The shout echoed down the spiral stone stairway to the great hall, where the constable of the castle, Sir Patrick MacRae, sat at the high table, looking over accounts supplied to him by the castle's mistress. As usual, he checked them only to digest the information they afforded him and found no errors in her ladyship's careful calculations. He had been about to set them aside when he heard the shout.

A tall, broad-shouldered, muscular man with dark hair and gray eyes, he leaped to his feet with the agile quickness of an athlete trained to deal with crisis and ran for the stairway, shouting at two nearby men-at-arms to follow. Halfway up the stairs, they met the watchman clattering down.

"Ships, sir!"

"How many?" Patrick demanded, pushing past him up the stairs.

The man turned to follow with the other two close behind. "I lost count but at least a half score, maybe a dozen."

"How far away?"

"Not far enough," the man replied tersely. "Maybe a mile and a half beyond Glas Eilean."

"So they are still three or four miles off. How is the wind?"

"Stiff, sir, and from the northwest. I reckon we may have an hour but no more than that and probably less."

Patrick had reached the top of the stairs, and he strode through the open doorway without replying. On the crenellated walkway, he saw at once what the watcher had seen, and the sight stopped his breath. A dozen large ships sailed toward the castle, one of them significantly larger than its companions.

"Holy mother of God," he muttered.

The other three men crowded close behind him, echoing his dismay.

He said crisply to the two who had followed him from the hall, "The laird and his lady are in the village. Go at once and fetch them. Also, bring back anyone else who desires to take shelter within our walls."

"Who d'ye think it be, sir?" the third man asked as the two others turned away. "Be it them wretched Macdonalds again? It be more than a year since their laird attacked us and died here, but mayhap young Donald hopes t' take his place."

"Those are not Macdonald galleys," Patrick said. "I know of only one group of ships in the area. Those are Jamie's ships."

"The King?" A note of awe tinged the man's voice.

"Aye," Patrick said grimly. "I wish we had finished building our new horn work, so we'd have our cannon mounted and ready."

"But would his grace no ha' sent word o' his coming, sir? Folks in Portree kent for a week aforehand that he were going to visit there."

"He would have warned us had he desired to be our guest," Patrick said. "They say, though, that he is collecting Highland chiefs as hostages, hoping thereby to tame an area he fears still remains hostile to him. He has already collected Macdonald of Clanranald, Macdonald of Glengarry, and MacLeod of Dunvegan."

"But why would the King o' Scots come here? Forbye, sir, if he be collecting his enemies, he should collect Donald Gorm o' Sleat. After all, it were his father, Donald the Grim, who tried to take back the Lordship o' the Isles last year and raised an army and a fleet o' galleys against the King. Our laird remained loyal to Jamie throughout. Moreover, his own father and yours died in battle against the traitor, and it were here at Eilean Donan that Donald died."

"Aye," Patrick said, still watching the approaching fleet. His gut told him that his grace was not coming to thank anyone for ridding him of Donald the Grim.

By the time he saw Mackenzie of Kintail and his lady being rowed home across the narrow tidal channel between the islet and the Kintail mainland, the lead ships were close enough to make out their royal banners.

Hurrying down the stairs, Patrick had begun to issue orders to men in the hall when Kintail strode in with his wife, Molly, Lady Kintail, at his side.

"We saw them from below," Kintail said. "What make you of this, Patrick?"

"Is it really the King?" Molly asked.

"Aye, I'm sure it is," Patrick said, managing a smile for her. He had a warm place in his heart for his master's wife.

Turning to the laird, who had been his close friend from childhood, he said, "As to what I make of this, Fin, it can be nothing good. If Jamie and his advisors are coming here without first sending word that we should expect them, it can mean only that they did not want to warn us of their coming."

"But the gossips say that Jamie and Cardinal Beaton are collecting hostages," Molly protested. "Taking Fin would be pointless. We fought against Donald. Moreover, we had planned to spend the month of September at Dunsithe!"

"I have no answer for you," Patrick said. "One can rarely divine Jamie's thinking, but the wind has picked up, so we'll have answers soon enough."

Half an hour later, men rowed to the castle in a small boat from one of the lead ships, demanding that Kintail surrender to the King's grace. Kintail refused, albeit with respect and a suggestion that the parties first discuss the matter civilly.

Shortly thereafter, the first explosion sounded from the ships' cannon.

MacRae men-at-arms under Patrick's direction did what they could to defend the castle, but although Eilean Donan was impregnable to most attacks, its walls were small defense against cannon fire. Not long after it began, when a furious barrage threatened to bring down part of the curtain wall, Kintail ordered a halt.

"Take a boat to Jamie's ship and tell him I yield," he said

gruffly to Patrick. "Invite his grace to join us for supper and offer him a decent bed for the night."

Patrick left at once, but the first thing he learned was that he should have paid more heed to the banners, for the largest ship was not Jamie's. When he asked the man-at-arms who met him as he boarded to take him to the King, repeating the command in broad Scot when the man shook his head at his Gaelic, the man smiled wryly and said, "Ye've come aboard the wrong ship tae see his grace, sir."

"Then whose ship is this?"

"It be Cardinal Beaton's ship. That one yonder be the King's," he added, gesturing toward the second largest.

"Then I will seek his grace there."

"If ye—" The man broke off, stiffening to attention, his gaze fixed on a point behind Patrick.

Turning, Patrick found himself facing a man he knew most women would find attractive. In his late forties, he was dressed all in red, his elegant velvet doublet and trunk hose slashed with crimson silk in the French style.

"I am Davy Beaton," the man said. "Have you the authority to yield Eilean Donan to the King's grace?"

"Aye, sir," Patrick said. "I am Patrick MacRae, constable of the castle, acting at the command of Mackenzie of Kintail." Uncertain exactly how he was supposed to address Cardinal Beaton, who was said to be one of the most powerful men in Scotland—more powerful even than the King, some said—he decided that under the circumstances, proper form did not matter.

When the cardinal said nothing to indicate that he cared one way or another, Patrick added, "Kintail bids you and his grace the King to join us at Eilean Donan for supper and to spend the night if that be your pleasure. Bring any others you care to bring, for the laird would like to remind his grace that we have ever been his grace's loyal subjects and that this attack on a peaceful residence is unseemly."

Beaton raised his eyebrows. "Peaceful?"

"It was you and yours that made all the noise," Patrick said bluntly.

"Aye, 'tis true, but you shut your doors to us."

"Only after you demanded that Kintail surrender to the King's grace as a hostage. With respect, sir, one does not take one's friends hostage. You would have done better to seize young Donald of Sleat, who is your proven enemy."

"Aye, and so we expected to do," Beaton said, "but someone warned him, and he has fled. Doubtless, he will find sanctuary with England's Henry. He would not be the first enemy of his grace's to do so."

"That is true enough," Patrick said. He had never encountered England's Henry, the eighth of that name to rule there, but like any educated Scot, he knew that Henry had for years been a thorn in the side of his nephew, James of Scotland. "Nevertheless," he added, "Kintail is no enemy of the King's, sir."

Beaton smiled. "You should call me 'my lord,' or 'eminence,' Sir Patrick."

Patrick found himself smiling back, astonished that Beaton knew his title. "I apologize, my lord. I have never conversed with a cardinal before."

"I am also the papal *legatas a latere*," Beaton said.

That news astonished Patrick, for having studied at St. Andrews University, which was connected to the Archbishopric, he knew that the title Lateran Legate meant that Cardinal Beaton acted as the Pope in Scotland.

Uncertainly, he said, "Does that mean you make the decisions here, my lord, or should I still present my master's invitation to King James?"

To his further astonishment, Beaton grimaced and said, "I

am certainly not the one making the decisions today, Sir Patrick. You must render your duty to his grace, of course, and mayhap he will accept Kintail's generous invitation—if you can persuade him that it will serve his interest to do so."

More uncertain than ever about what was going on, Patrick bowed. "I thank you, your eminence. I shall go at once to his grace's ship."

As he turned away, Beaton said gently, "Sir Patrick, I am told that you are astonishingly loyal to Mackenzie of Kintail, so it occurs to me that we may find opportunity to meet again."

Glancing back, Patrick raised his eyebrows. "I do not take your meaning, my lord. Unless his grace orders me to accompany my master, as constable of Eilean Donan and Dunsithe—Kintail's castle in the Scottish Borders—it is likely that I shall remain to attend my duties."

"Nonetheless, sir, if you are ever in need of a friend at Stirling, you may apply to me."

Bowing again, but no wiser than before, Patrick said, "I thank you and hope you will not think me disrespectful if I add that I hope the occasion does not arise."

His expression unreadable, Beaton dismissed him with a nod.

Still bewildered, Patrick descended the rope ladder to his boat and told his oarsmen to row to the next ship, where after learning his mission, a lackey led him below to a cabin from which issued the sound of hearty masculine laughter.

His escort pushed open the door and, blocking the way, announced loudly, "Sir Patrick MacRae desires speech wi' your grace, an it suit ye, sire."

From within a mild voice said, "Bid him enter."

His escort moved aside, and Patrick stepped through the doorway to find two men inside a luxuriously appointed cabin. Their clothing was rich enough to make him aware that his was no longer even fashionable. Tapestry hangings covered the walls, and carpets decked the floor. A leather dice cup and a pair of ivory dice lay on a marquetry table between the two men, along with a gold wine flagon and two delicately etched golden goblets.

Although Patrick had never met the King, he had no difficulty recognizing which of them was James, fifth of that name to be High King of Scots. At twenty-eight, his grace was tall, handsome, and well built with the Stewart red hair and blue eyes. Rumor had it that he drank too much and wenched too much, and indeed, Patrick could see that the royal face and figure were puffy, and the royal complexion blotchy. He decided that his grace probably needed more stimulating exercise than spilling dice from a cup.

The man at James's side—also handsome—was younger, more slenderly graceful, and carried himself with a lordly arrogance that James lacked.

Bowing deeply to the King, Patrick waited until he heard his name spoken before he looked up again.

James smiled and said in broad Scot, "Does your master yield to his king?"

"He does, your grace," Patrick said, speaking the same language.

"Then where is he?" demanded the second man. "He should be here."

Not liking his shrill, arrogant tone, Patrick had all he could do not to reply sharply, but he suspected that the gentleman must be one of the King's infamous favorites, and Patrick was not a fool.

Carefully controlling his voice, and addressing a point midway between the two, he said, "As constable of Eilean Donan, I speak for the Laird of Kintail and yield to a superior force." Turning slightly, so that he now addressed only James, he added gently, "He commanded me to offer hospitality, as well, your grace. The Laird bids you join him and his lady at supper, with any number of your party whom you choose to accompany you, and to pass the night in a comfortable bed."

James chuckled, but the other man said indignantly, "He would see us murdered in our beds, more like. Don't do it, James!"

"Peace, Oliver," James said with a fond smile. "You know that these Highlanders have notions of hospitality far stronger than ours. In any event, the Mackenzies of Kintail have ever remained loyal to the Crown."

"I have told you and told you, James! The only safe Highlander is one you can watch every minute! Do you really believe he will surrender so meekly?"

Since it was not appropriate for him to interject his opinion, Patrick held his tongue, but he longed to tell James he had nothing to fear at Eilean Donan.

James glanced at him, his eyes twinkling. As if he could hear Patrick's silent thoughts, he said, "Have you naught to say in your defense, sir?"

Bowing again, Patrick said quietly, "Not in my own defense, sire, but for the people of Kintail, I say that all here remain loyal to your grace. In fact, sire, were you enemy instead of friend, you would still be safe inside our walls now that Kintail has extended his welcome to you. Highland hospitality forbids attacking those seeking its benefits. Our rules forbid, as well, any refusal to grant hospitality. In a fierce winter, such a refusal could equal a death sentence."

"There, you see, Oliver. Ah, but I have not yet properly made Oliver known to you, have I, Sir Patrick? This is Oliver Sinclair," James added with his easy smile. "He is my friend, and those who are loyal to me are likewise loyal to Oliver."

"Your friends are all welcome at Eilean Donan, sire,"

Patrick said, "and tonight you may be glad of a bed that does not rock at the whims of the tide."

"So I will," James said, chuckling. "We accept your master's invitation, Sir Patrick, and trust that we will never find your doors locked against us again."

Seeing nothing to gain by pointing out as he had to Cardinal Beaton that only the royal demand for Kintail's submission had resulted in the gates being shut, that without such a demand they would have opened eagerly, Patrick said nothing.

James let the silence linger for a beat before he said, "We will join your laird in an hour, sir. I do hope that he and some others within your walls also speak Scot, for I confess I have but a smattering of your wretched Gaelic."

"All within speak Scot if need be, sire. Kintail and I attended university at St. Andrews, and our lady speaks both Scot and the Highland Gaelic fluently, due to her unusual upbringing."

"Ah, yes, I recall Lady Mackenzie's history," James said. "I have heard that she is a bonny lass, too. If she has the good fortune to resemble her mother . . ."

Since Patrick's hackles rose at this cavalier assessment of his mistress, it was just as well that Oliver Sinclair said petulantly, "James, if you wish to sup with Mackenzie and his lady in an hour's time . . ." He paused, frowning.

"Indeed," James said, "we must send Sir Patrick back to warn them to expect us." To Patrick, he added, "Tell your master I am pleased to learn that he means to surrender without a fuss." With a dismissive gesture, he reached for the dice cup, and Patrick was grateful for the diversion. He knew that one ought to back away from the royal presence, but he had no memory of what lay behind him. Hoping the King's amiability meant that James was unlikely to insist on absolute adherence to ceremony, he glanced over his shoulder to see if the way to the door was clear.

"One moment, MacRae," Oliver Sinclair said curtly. "James, you cannot mean to send this fellow back before us. He and his master will likely use the intervening time to plot mischief."

"Peace, Oliver," the King said. "I tell you, we have naught to fear."

"But the Highland chiefs are all treacherous dogs," Sinclair argued. "You trusted Donald of Sleat, and look where that led. The purpose of this venture is to teach these barbarians a lesson before more of them defy you, is it not?"

James sighed, pushing back his chair. "Very well, we shall return now with Sir Patrick. Will that suit you?"

"Only if we take a well-armed contingent with us."

"Can you accommodate such a force, Sir Patrick?"

"Aye, your grace," Patrick said quietly.

"Then we will go with you now."

Seething at the aspersions cast on his honor and that of Kintail, Patrick nonetheless held his peace. He had changed his mind yet again, however, about who was the most powerful man in Scotland.

That thought reminded him of his interview with Beaton. Since duty, family honor, and friendship demanded that he do whatever he had to do to win freedom again for Kintail, having a powerful friend at Stirling might well prove helpful.

Elsewhere, and in their own time

The shadowy, orange-gold glow that lit the twelve faces in the Circle resembled that of a fire dying at the end of the storytelling at a Highland *ceilidh,* but the present gathering was no celebration. The sinister, black-cloaked shapes of the twelve were unmoving, and the glow did not flicker the way firelight did.

Brown Claud sat uneasily outside the Circle, a short distance behind his mother, Maggie Malloch, who was a member. The long silence was awesome to one who had not experienced such an occasion before, and Claud did not know why he had been ordered to attend. He did not even know who had issued the order. Maggie had simply said he was to come, and one did not refuse such an invitation, because in their world, the Circle reigned supreme.

"But why do they want me?" he had asked her.

"They've questions tae ask ye, and I've a few tae ask them, too. Doubtless they'll want tae hear what ye can tell them about our recent time in the Highlands."

"They'll no want tae hear about Catriona, will they?"

"Ye'd best hope they dinna ask ye about that parlous slut," Maggie snapped. "And whilst I think on such, ye'd best no be thinking o' taking up wi' another such, me lad. Try thinking for once wi' your brain, such as it is, and no wi' that other, less sensible bit o' yourself."

Claud did not want to answer questions about the Highland pixie who had bewitched him. Maggie never approved of his romantic adventures, but he feared the Circle would agree with her this time. What they would do, he did not know, but he was sure to fare badly. "I've no met anyone like her since we left the Highlands," he protested. "Ye've had me running hither and yon all over the Borders."

"Aye, and what ha' ye found?"

"Naught," he admitted. "I ha' searched from Angus's Tantallon all through the east and middle marches, but no one kens aught o' the wee lass we seek."

"She'll no be so wee anymore," Maggie reminded him. "There be mischief afoot, though, and I mean tae learn who lies behind it."

Her mood since had deteriorated, and Claud had taken care to stay out of her way. He had accompanied her to the meeting, though, knowing no way to escape.

The silence continued until he felt a chill slither through him. Then, suddenly, without visible individual movement, the Circle opened and straightened out, with the two black-robed members who had been flanking Maggie at each end of the line.

She remained alone, isolated, facing the other eleven.

"Stand and account for yourself, Maggie Malloch," a deep voice intoned.

Claud was not certain, but he thought the one in the center had spoken. He watched as his mother straightened, reading anger in her tense posture as easily as if she had flown into the sort of animated fury that her anger usually produced.

She stood still, but her plump body was stiff, her expression enigmatic to those who did not know her well. He doubted that anyone now sitting in judgment over her fit that category, though.

"With what am I charged?" she demanded.

"With overstepping your authority in the mortal world, o' course," said another voice. "Sakes, lass, ye canna overturn history wi'out we call ye tae order, as ye ken right well."

Amusement underscored the new speaker's voice, and Claud gazed in astonishment at the male who had spoken.

He sat one position left of center. Claud did not recognize him and wondered who he was that he dared to laugh at Maggie Malloch, who was one of the most powerful of them all.

The chap was odd-looking, to say the least, with hair that even in that golden glow was clearly dark at the roots, reddish as it grew out, and fair at the tips. It radiated from his head like rays of the sun, sticking straight out in a semicir-

cle around his long, narrow face. The face was not remark-
able, unless one counted the thin yellow, green, red, and blue
streaks on each cheek, but his dark eyes gleamed and his
smile was mischievous, as if the chap delighted in seeing
Maggie called to order before the Circle. Ornaments glinted
on his robe and in his hair, and when he fluttered a hand in
Maggie's direction, Claud saw that the hand bore six fingers, each decked with a glittering ring.

"Overstepped my authority, did I?" Maggie snapped, giving back look for look. "Since when, Jonah Bonewits, does
your authority allow you or any of these others but our chief
himself to question *my* authority?"

"Of mine own accord, perhaps it does not, though we ha'
yet tae measure your power against mine, Maggie lass," he
retorted, still twinkling. "One day we will, but today is no
the day. Today the chief agrees that ye've overstepped."

"Aye, as do the others," the man in the center said grimly.

"Be that why ye sent for my Claud, tae question him?"

"Aye, for belike he can tell us about such time as the pair
o' ye spent in the Highlands," the chief said. "It be possible
ye ha' placed us all in jeopardy."

"Pish tush," Maggie said. "We did nobbut our duty, and
we did it well."

"We'll judge that for ourselves. Some amongst us believe
ye interfered more than our rules allow, that because ye did,
ye were forced tae reverse all that had gone before. Many
were involved, and all ken too much about your activities."

"None who were involved will ever mention my name or
Claud's," Maggie said. "I stripped most o' their memories
after the event, and none o' them recalls aught but what I
meant him tae recall. It be just as it should be. I ha' done
nowt tae endanger folks in me own Good Neighbor tribe or
any o' ye in the Circle."

"Perhaps, but we have many questions for you and for Brown Claud."

She shrugged. "Ask away, but mind, the lad were in lust wi' a Highland strumpet and had eyes for little else. It be his nature, as well ye ken, the lot o' ye."

Claud trembled when all eyes turned toward him, but the ordeal proved less terrifying than he feared. It was as if he blinked and it was over, for when the chief said, "That be all, lad. Ye may go," he had no memory of any question put to him.

"One moment," Maggie said sharply. "I'll ha' a word wi' him first—in private, if ye please."

The chief nodded.

Maggie whisked to stand before Claud, saying quietly, "They canna hear what I say tae ye now, so dinna heed them, but listen well and do as I bid ye."

Still stunned, Claud said, "But wha' happened, Mam? I didna speak a word!"

"Ye did nae harm, lad," she said. "They'll keep me here a while, but I've learned summat, m'self, and I want ye off tae the Borders straightaway tae continue our search. Although Angus dwelt in the east, there be Douglases aplenty in the west, so look ye there. And mind ye stay clear o' trouble, for we've still our duty tae do."

"What ha' ye learned, though?"

"That Jonah Bonewits takes interest in what we do."

"That odd-looking, six-fingered chap wi' the peculiar hair?"

"Odd-looking he may be, but dinna underestimate him, for he wields as much power as I do, mayhap more," Maggie said. "And 'tis odd that I didna consider his possible interest afore now. 'Tis plain 'twas unnatural means hid the truth from me, and Jonah be one o' the few who could ha' done it wi'out my knowing he did."

"But why would he?"

"Because he and his ha' long served the earls o' Angus

just as we ha' served the Gordons, Claud. Bear that in mind whilst ye search Douglas country, because even in exile, Angus still rules a vast portion o' that meddlesome tribe."

Some time had passed since Brown Claud had received his instructions, and he was growing bored with his lack of success. He had been searching the west march for what seemed like eons, and he knew no more than he had ever known. As he sat on a grassy hilltop, contemplating his failure, he decided that a benevolent guardian's tasks were much more difficult than he had expected them to be.

In his youth, listening to stories told around peat fires at *ceilidhs,* he had envisioned achieving more heroic deeds, such as fighting evil beasts, subduing malevolent spirits, or saving damsels from dragons—albeit without the burden of heavy armor or a white charger to feed in between his daring deeds.

He smiled wryly at his youthful folly.

Birds chirped, clouds sailed across an azure sky, a light breeze blew, carrying a salty tang from Solway Firth, but that was all.

Claud wished he could search for adventure instead of seeking an unknown, grown-up child, but Maggie had said he must find wee Bessie and not rest until he had. Still, if Bessie had survived a dozen or more mortal years where she was, surely no harm would befall her merely because he took time out for a bit of adventure. Maggie was just angry that the Circle had dared question her; that was all.

As he let his thoughts wander, he became aware of light, tinkling, feminine laughter. Looking around, he saw no one, although the sound did not seem distant.

Curious, and certain that he would lose nothing but his boredom in the few minutes it would take him to investigate, he went in search of the laughter's source.

The sound drew him into a nearby woodland to the edge of a grassy clearing. In its center, in a circle of bright spring flowers, a feminine figure danced. She wore a pale lavender gown of a soft material that caressed her body and legs as she moved. Her hair was like fine corn silk, long and flowing softly in the breeze. Looking as light as thistledown, she danced and skipped and twirled with astonishing grace and skill in time to her own musical laughter.

Transfixed by the scene, Claud stood gazing at her. He had heard of fairies so lost in their dancing that they could hear only the music and could see nothing of the world around them. He wondered if she might be such a creature.

Even as the thought flitted through his mind, she stopped and looked at him. Despite the distance between them, her eyes were like forest pools drawing him into their depths, her attraction so strong that he walked toward her without feeling the ground beneath his feet. Had he been capable of thought, he might have assumed that someone had cast a spell. Whatever stirred him, he had no choice but to respond.

Up close, she seemed delightfully small and attractively plump with soft curves and a mischievous, enticing smile. Her face was ordinary, but her smile was magical, and her eyes drew him deep inside, as if he could touch her soul.

"Ye seem a likely lad," she said, laughing again.

Her musical voice and even more musical laughter sent a thrill through him, stirring his most sensitive appendage instantly to life.

"What do they call ye?" she asked.

He tried to reply, but managed only a gravelly grunt. Clearing his throat, he tried again. "Brown Claud. And ye?"

With another trill of laughter, she said, "I be Lucy, Lucy Fittletrot. Will ye dance wi' me, Brown Claud?"

"There be nae music, lass."

"We always ha' music, Brown Claud, but the best be when me father plays his pipes for the dancing. I can always hear his music in me head. Can ye no hear it, too?"

He shook his head. "Nay, I hear nowt. Worse, I'm a lump when it comes tae the dancing. I'd sorely disappoint ye."

"Fiddle," she said, laughing again. "Try now, do. Can ye no hear it?"

To his astonishment, he heard the merry tinkling of bells and the notes of a stringed instrument playing a lively tune. His feet started to move, and when she held out her hand, he grasped it. Before he knew what he was about, he was dancing with her in her circle of flowers as if he had done so forever.

They danced and danced until at last they collapsed in a heap on the grass. Lucy Fittletrot was laughing, and she continued to laugh when Claud hugged her and drew her close, his body leaping in response to hers.

"What brought ye tae these parts, Brown Claud?"

"I were sent tae seek summat we lost in years past," he said, stroking her soft hair and peering deep into her sultry eyes.

"Aye, sure, a mystery," she exclaimed in delight. "Tell me!"

"I canna think, lass. Touchin' ye muddles me thinking!"

"D'ye no ha' a lass o' your own, Brown Claud?"

"I do now," he said, reaching for the lacing on the lavender gown.

"Aye, ye do," she agreed, "and when ye've taken your fill o' me, I'll help ye find what ye seek, for there be nothing and nae one hereabouts that be unknown tae Lucy Fittletrot."

Still laughing, Lucy helped him untie her laces.

Chapter 2 ————————

The Scottish Borders, April 1541

"Elspeth!" The intrusive shriek rang through the hilly, sun-dappled woods.

Silence followed. Not even a bird twittered.

"Elspeth, where are you? Mam wants you, and if I have to search for you, be sure that you will regret it. Come home at once!"

More silence. No breeze stirred, no leaf twitched. It was as if every living creature in the woods held its breath, so quiet that one could hear the rushing of a burn some distance away.

Minutes passed without a sound, and the next shriek, when it came, was farther away and fading. Soon no more shrieks shattered the silence, and then at last, a small brown cottontail rabbit hopped out from beneath a bush. It paused and looked about. Apparently satisfied that the offensive intruder had departed, it turned its attention to a nearby patch of new spring grass and started to graze.

When the *chip-chip-chwee* of a chaffinch sounded from a treetop, echoed soon afterward by the chattering of a squirrel, a certain thick clump of shrubbery slowly parted in front of what looked like a rock slab, and a face appeared.

It was a perfect oval with high cheekbones, black-fringed gray-green eyes, a tip-tilted, freckled nose, and full, rosy lips. The narrow, slightly arched eyebrows were considerably lighter than the lashes but many shades darker than the flaxen hair that fell in long, loose, silken sheets, framing the lovely face.

The gray-green eyes were wide and watchful. The head turned cautiously, to the right and to the left.

The bunny continued to graze, the birds to sing.

One small, rawhide-shod foot stepped forth from the shrubbery, followed by the other, whereupon the slender figure of a young woman, seventeen or eighteen years of age, was revealed. She wore a faded, simple blue gown with a plain white apron, and if she had earlier worn the customary white coif and ruffled cap that most females wore in daytime she had mislaid both elsewhere.

Free of the shrubbery, she paused and listened, and one could see that her fine, straight hair reached all the way to her hips. Apparently realizing that the hair required some sort of confinement, she reached over one shoulder with both hands and gathered it, flipping it forward to plait it with deft, experienced fingers.

The birds continued to sing, and although the bunny had stopped grazing and seemed alert to possible danger, it did not dart away.

The plait finished, albeit loosely and showing no sign that it would remain so for long, the young woman drew a deep breath and exhaled it slowly. She would have to go home now, and on the way, she would have to think up an acceptable excuse for her tardiness. Not that any excuse would help if her ladyship was already angry, but at least Drusilla had gone away. She could be sure of that, because

Drusilla was incapable of keeping silent, let alone of moving silently enough to fool the birds and other denizens of the woods.

That she had to return was a pity, because the day was a fine one for April, and she enjoyed the solitude of the woods. Moreover, she could not be sure that Drusilla had shrieked the truth at her. The elder of the two Farnsworth daughters might easily have come looking for her without a command to do so, because Drusilla was not kind and often exerted herself to make Elspeth's life difficult, and others' lives as well. Less than a week before, her complaints that Sir Hector's falconer had dared to flirt with her had cost the man his position.

As these thoughts flitted through Elspeth's mind, a new sound intruded on the woodland peace. Although distant, it was nonetheless easily identifiable as the baying of sleuth-hounds, and they sounded as if they were heading toward her.

To hear such sounds in daytime was unusual, for sleuth-hounds generally hunted reivers, and reivers generally did their reiving by moonlight. Doubtless, someone was either training his hounds or—although the season was young—using them to hunt rabbits or deer. In either event, she decided she would be wise to leave the woods before the hounds surged into view. No animal had ever harmed her, but a sensible person left unknown dogs to themselves.

Thus, she turned reluctantly homeward, but she had taken only a few steps when, just as she sensed a presence looming behind her, a large, warm hand clapped over her mouth and a muscular arm wrapped tightly around her torso, lifting her off the ground and holding her securely against a hard, masculine body.

Kicking backward, her heel connected solidly with a shin, and she had the satisfaction of hearing a muffled grunt of pain, but her captor did not release her. Instead, his grip across her chest tightened, making it hard for her to breathe.

She kicked a second time but missed, whereupon a low voice growled in her ear, "Easy, lassie, I mean ye nae harm, and if ye cripple me, I'm sped."

Elspeth stopped struggling, realizing that further such efforts would be useless. He was too large, too strong. She would hurt only herself.

"Good lass," he said. "What lies behind yonder shrubbery?"

His hand was tight across her mouth. When she tried to twist away, he said, "I ken fine that ye canna speak, but I'll ha' your word first that ye willna shriek."

She hesitated and then nodded.

He moved his hand so that she could talk but kept it near enough to let her know he would slap it across her mouth again if she tried to scream.

When she did not speak at once, he said more urgently, "Be there a cave there, where ye were hiding?"

"Aye," she said, "but 'tis only a shallow one."

"Big enough for the pair o' us?"

"Since I cannot see you, I do not know how large you are," she said.

"Large enough," he said, and to her surprise she detected laughter in his voice. "I'll put ye down, lassie, but if ye shriek, I swear I'll throttle ye."

He set her gently on her feet, and she turned to face him.

She had known from the way he held her and the ease with which he had lifted her that he was a large man, but the reality was greater than she had imagined. He was a full head and shoulders taller than she was, which made him at least two or three inches above six feet, a height unusual among Borderers, who tended to be small and wiry. His shoulders were broad—very, very broad.

He had thick, dark hair, but where a shaft of sunlight touched it, it gleamed with auburn highlights. His eyes were stone-gray, set deeply, with lashes long enough and curly enough to be the envy of many a woman, and laugh lines at the outer corners. His eyebrows were thick and straight, like hasty slashes in a drawing. His other features seemed well chiseled, as if a skilled sculptor had modeled them. His complexion was tanned and ruddy, his beard short and well trimmed, emphasizing the strong, straight lines of his jaw. He was the handsomest man she had ever seen, and his intense, penetrating gaze stirred feelings in her body the likes of which she had never known before.

He wore the tawny breeks and brown doublet of a hunter but carried himself with an arrogance that showed he thought he was superior to most men. Doubtless, his size gave him such confidence, she decided, his size and the sword and dagger he wore at his side. Certainly, he looked capable of wielding both weapons expertly.

His voice was deep and pleasant, but his accent puzzled her. He spoke broad Scot, of course—or English, as they called it on the other side of the line—but the cadence was neither that of a Scottish Borderer nor yet quite that of an English one. Still, to her finely tuned ear, it sounded nearer the latter than the former, and although the exact line was debatable, England was close, only a few miles away.

Bluntly, she said, "Are you English?"

"Nay, lass, I be as much a Scot as ye be yourself, but we'll no fash ourselves over me antecedents just now if ye please. Will I fit into yon cave o' yours, or no?"

"Aye," she said, measuring him again with her eyes, "but barely."

"Then we'll ha' tae cuddle up a bit, I expect."

"You cannot keep me with you," she exclaimed, feeling nerves stirring to life in places she had not known she had nerves. The thought of cuddling with him was not at all distasteful but, indeed, quite the opposite. Nonetheless, she said firmly, "I must go home. Surely you heard Drusilla calling me!"

"I didna recognize that infernal screeching as anything so tame," he said. "What a heathenish voice that lass has got! Still and all, I collect that Drusilla must be your sister and 'tis rude o' me tae condemn any kinswoman o' yours."

She opened her mouth to correct him but, instead, said again, "I must go."

"Nay, lassie, I canna afford tae trust ye that far, I fear. Ye'll bide wi' me in yonder wee cave till the danger ha' passed."

With a sigh, she nodded and turned to lead the way, pausing when she reached the thick bushes in front of the opening. Clearly, the dogs had his scent, and she wondered when it would occur to him that simply hiding in the cave would not be enough to shield him.

The cave was larger than she had led him to believe, but it was not deep enough to protect them both from discovery or attack, and the dogs were drawing nearer every moment.

"Who is chasing you?"

"My erstwhile host," he muttered.

"I beg your pardon, sir. I do not understand what you mean."

"Them be English soldiers, lass, and not pleasant folk at all. Now, get ye inside," he added, this time his words a clear command. He held the bushes apart and nodded at her to go first, then followed, pulling the branches together again.

Inside, enough light penetrated the shrubbery to reveal the walls of the cave, and he grunted at the sight. She could stand upright, but he could not, and although they could sit, they would be more vulnerable to attack on the ground.

He drew his sword. "This doesna seem the best place for

concealment after all, lass. We've no retreat, and they'll easily track me here. Mayhap ye'd best leave me, after all. I'll no want ye tae suffer for helping me."

She had been trying to think of a way to persuade him to let her go, but at these words, perversely, she changed her mind. "One moment," she said, turning away. "I have something here that might help."

He made no move to stop her when she bent to retrieve the jug that some weeks before she had placed on the floor of the cave near the wall.

"What be that stuff?"

"Aniseed," she said. "Sir Hector's huntsman told me it is one thing that will put sleuthhounds off their scent. One of the local reiver bands uses it, he says."

"Ye begin tae intrigue me, lass," he said. Taking the jug and removing the stopper, he sniffed and grimaced. "Ha' ye tried it on your own hounds?"

"Not yet," she admitted. "I did think, however, that it might prove useful if Drusilla ever set our dogs to find my hiding place."

"Do I just shake it out yonder on the ground?"

"Rub some on yourself first to disguise your scent," she advised, "and perhaps you would be wiser to let me do the shaking. If someone should see me, he would think nothing of a young woman walking in the woods."

"I'll let ye, but only if ye promise to do it quickly and come back here," he said firmly as he took a large handful to smear over himself. "I'd no trust the men wi' the dogs tae act honorably wi' any female."

She did not argue with him, nor did he repeat his insistence that she return. She had a feeling that it did not occur to him now that she might disobey him. What sort of man, she wondered, had that sort of confidence in his ability to command others? Surely, he was not just a common huntsman.

He held the shrubbery aside for her, and she hurried out, going the way he must have come, toward the barking dogs. They were only minutes away now.

When she had gone as far as she dared, she shook aniseed from the jug. Realizing that the method was inefficient, she poured some into her hand and then cast it to the breeze, as if she were scattering grain for chickens.

Although trees blocked her view of the dogs, she could tell they were much closer, perhaps only a half mile away.

Backing hastily toward the cave, she scattered more aniseed as she went, taking care to scatter it heavily over the route they had taken after he captured her.

As she neared the cave, still scattering the pungent herb, she wondered if she had taken leave of her senses. She had only his word that the men hunting him were English. They might as easily be Scots, chasing a thief or a murderer, but she could not shake the notion that returning to him represented safety while remaining where she was represented danger. She had no time left to make for Farnsworth Tower. The dogs would be upon her before she could cover a quarter of the distance.

They were too close now for comfort. What if they could catch her scent on the air? Deerhounds and many sleuthhounds possessed that ability.

Running now, still flinging aniseed across her path, she saw that he was holding the bushes apart for her. Diving toward them, she stumbled, but he caught her arm, steadying her and drawing her into the sanctuary of the cave.

"Take a few deep breaths, lass," he recommended calmly. "Ye must calm your breathing, else the hounds will hear ye. Their sense o' hearing be nigh as acute as their sense o' smell."

The dogs had been baying in a rhythmic way, all making similar sounds, but that rhythm suddenly changed. They were yelping now in some disorder.

"They've come upon the aniseed," her companion murmured. "Be still now. Not a movement, not a word."

"I am not a fool, sir," she said.

Nevertheless, she was grateful to feel his large body close to hers. Big, warm, and solid, it made her feel safe despite the increasing danger outside. Her fears continued to ease only to return threefold when she heard hoofbeats and knew they announced the riders following the hounds. Chills shot through her body. She had not let her thoughts dwell on the men with the dogs.

Swallowing, she did what she had done since childhood whenever she was unhappy or felt she was in danger. She thought about something else, pretending that she was far away, in a very safe place.

The warmth of the large body next to hers made it easier than usual to return to memories of her early childhood, of a large, muscular man—her father, surely—holding her close. She basked in that warmth, telling herself that she was on the shore of a pond with her father, surrounded by woods that were a haven of safety, the only sounds those of birds and squirrels, and the occasional splash of a fish leaping to the fly that twitched at the end of her father's line.

When her present companion's hard, muscular arm draped itself across her shoulders, she leaned into it, forgetting that it belonged to a stranger, accepting its reassurance without question or comment.

Through the shrubbery blocking the entrance, she could see the dogs now, at least a half score of them, and she saw at once that the aniseed had put them off their scent. Three bunched near a tree, and feeling the body beside her stiffen, she wondered if that was where he had stood, watching her emerge from the cave.

Riders appeared, guiding their ponies through the trees toward the dogs.

"Damnation," one of the men exclaimed, "they've lost him!"

"Look up in the trees," another voice shouted. "Mayhap he's climbed one and lies concealed on one of its branches."

They were English voices, so at least he had told her the truth about that.

"As I recall, there'll be a brook or a river yonder to the east," another shouted. "Mayhap he walked into the water to cover his trail. Send the dogs along the banks on both sides, and I'll wager we'll find him again in short order."

"How far away flows that burn?" her companion murmured when the area nearby had fallen silent again.

"Less than five minutes' walk from here," she murmured back.

"And where does it lead?"

"It springs from the hills to the northeast of us and flows southwest into Annan Water and thence into Solway Firth."

"And if they follow it north?"

"They'll pass Farnsworth Tower," she said. "That burn provides our water."

"Farnsworth Tower is your home?"

"Aye."

He was silent for a moment, then muttered as if he were talking to himself, "Surely these English will not remain long on the Scottish side of the line."

Elspeth said gently, "If they have declared a hot trod, they can remain in the west march for six days."

"How so?"

Shifting so she could look at him, she said, "Well, if I remember Border law correctly, either side can declare a hot trod up to six days after a crime, and anyone chasing a criminal may cross the line as long as they are in hot pursuit of him."

"And how is it that a lass like yourself kens aught o' Border law?"

"Sir Hector frequently serves as clerk when opposing march wardens meet for Truce Days, and he has explained many such laws to us at home."

"I see. Six days, eh? Does that not mean only that they can cross the line for six days after discovering the crime, and only if they know who they are chasing?"

"Aye, but Sir Hector says that many interpret the law to mean that if they follow at once, they can search for the full six days. Did they follow you at once?"

"You mean directly after I committed my crime?"

Again, she detected laughter in his voice, but this time it annoyed her. "I do not think that felonious activity should be a matter for humor, sir," she said primly.

He chuckled. "Doubtless you are right, lass. I confess, I've been up to my ears in felonious activity for so many months now that I've forgotten how most folks view such behavior. At present, however, I care only about saving my skin."

"Your accent has changed," she said.

"Has it, then? I ha' an odd knack for picking up cadences from the person I'm speaking with unless I take care no tae let m'self," he added, his accent now thicker than ever. "Doubtless, I ha' just picked up a bit o' your pretty speech, lassie, for ye dinna talk like a common Border wench."

"I speak as Drusilla and Jelyan speak," Elspeth said. "Sir Hector is a scholar, and he taught us all to speak properly."

"Ye ha' two sisters, then. What be your name?"

"They call me Elspeth," she said, deciding it was unnecessary to explain to him that Drusilla and Jelyan were not her sisters. "What of you?"

"Ye can call me Patrick," he said. "That be sufficient."

"The men who seek you, what will they call you?"

Again he chuckled. "Ye be too wise and too full o' troublesome curiosity, sweetheart. It doesna matter what they will call me."

"It will matter if they seek you at Farnsworth Tower," she pointed out, trying to ignore the way the casual endearment stirred her senses. "I am likely in trouble already for being away so long, and if they learn that a villain is running loose hereabouts, they will ask me all manner of questions. Did I not see or hear the dogs? Did I perchance see the man?" She grimaced. "I am not a good liar, sir."

"Then you must work to perfect your skill," he said with a wry grin. "Believe me, practice makes nearly anything possible. I know that for a fact."

"Lying is not a skill that one should aim to improve," she said curtly.

He did not respond. Indeed, she thought he looked regretful, and the look stirred her sympathy. She wanted to smooth his furrowed brow, to make him smile again. She swallowed hard, mentally scolding herself as harshly as ever Lady Farnsworth or Drusilla had scolded her. Clearly, she had lost every ounce of good sense she possessed the moment she laid eyes on the villainous fugitive.

She could not hear the dogs any longer, but the shrubbery rustled. A breeze had come up, and if it was blowing from the west as most breezes did in that area, it might well blow sounds of baying and barking away to the east.

"What will you do now?" she asked when the silence began to hover uncomfortably between them.

"I must think about that," he said. "If ye be right, and them villains mean tae stay this side o' the line for six whole days, I must go tae ground somewhere. I doubt I can get by wi' posing as a traveler, wending me way north tae Stirling."

"Nay, you are too large to pass as a common Borderer. Moreover, everyone hereabouts knows nearly everyone else. Must you go to Stirling?"

"Aye, in time, I must."

"The King's birthday is in a fortnight, on Palm Sunday," she said. "Because he and the Queen are expecting a new bairn to arrive before then, his birthday celebration is to be a grand fête to celebrate the child's birth, too, so we and other Border families will travel to Stirling for the celebration. Travel will be safer for you then, I warrant."

"Aye, if I had a safe place tae stay and the fortitude tae wait that long."

Another idea stirred, but she rejected it, deciding that she had already been foolish enough for one day. Indeed, most sensible people would call her foolhardy to linger thus, chatting with a felon and confiding her family's plans to him.

"How far is it from here to Farnsworth Tower?" he asked.

"Twenty minutes," she said. "Less if I hurry."

"Will you tell them about me?"

She hesitated, knowing it was her duty to warn everyone about a scoundrel in the area. If Drusilla, or even Jelyan, found out that she had kept such information to herself, she would face dire punishment. But try as she might, she could sense no danger in the man, and over the years she had learned to trust her instincts.

"I'll tell no one," she said. "But I must go home."

"It should be safe now," he said. "Listen for the dogs, though, and if ye hear them, make for an open space, preferably one wi' a good many people about."

She nodded, and when he parted the bushes for her, she stepped past him, feeling energy from his body as she did.

Glancing up at him, she opened her mouth to bid him farewell, and then shut it again, uncertain what to say.

He smiled, revealing strong white teeth, and his eyes twinkled. " 'Ware strangers, lass," he warned.

The absurdity of such a caution coming from him made her smile back. "I'll be careful," she said.

"See that you are," he said more sternly. "And, lassie, bind a ribbon round that plait when ye get home, lest ye be punished for untidiness."

"Yes, sir," she said, automatically responding to what was a common command to her.

"And, lass . . ."

Annoyance stirred, but she paused again, forcing patience. "Aye?"

"Thank you," he said gently. "I am greatly in your debt."

"Good-bye, sir," she said, turning away without telling him he was welcome to her help, although doubtless it amounted to aiding and abetting a felon. But even with her back to the man, she could sense his strong vitality, and she did not want to leave him, not—or so she told herself—with danger possibly still at hand. Swiftly, she turned back, and without giving herself a chance to think more about what she was doing, she said, "Do you ken aught of falcons or hawks?"

A flashing grin lit his face. "Aye, I ken all there be tae ken about them," he said. "Why d'ye ask?"

"Because Sir Hector's falconer left a sennight ago, and presently Sir Hector has only one careless lad to look after his birds. You would need to know only as much as the lad knows, although it would not hurt to know more."

"I see that ye're either hard o' hearing, lass, or that ye ha' the good sense no tae believe a man wha' claims tae ken all there be tae ken, but I spake the truth. I warrant there be few men wha' ken as much as I do about birds o' prey. I were raised wi' such. Do ye mean tae hide me in a falconer's cot?"

"Ours had no cottage," she said. "He dwelt in a small chamber near the kitchen. The mews contain no residence, only perches and twig cages for the birds."

"How many birds?"

She shrugged. "I do not know exactly—three or four, I think. The lad warned Sir Hector that he might have to put one down. He said the bird bated and before he could control it, it broke two of its primaries. I am not entirely certain what all that means, but Sir Hector told him to wait a day or two."

"It means he startled the bird and in its panic it broke some feathers. Faith, though, he cannot mean to put down a gallant fellow or lass only because of that. I see that ye need me as much as I need your sanctuary, lass. By heaven, I'll do it."

"Mercy, can you repair broken feathers?"

"I can, and if ye be a good lass, I'll show ye how tae do it yourself. But how will we introduce me fine skills tae Sir Hector? I canna walk home wi' ye. 'Twould be tae shred your reputation an I did such a thing. In any event, I dinna ken what Sir Hector can be thinking, letting ye wander about at will like this."

"If you are going to scold, we will part at once and you can seek your own fortune," she said tartly. "You are hardly in a position to preach good behavior."

"So ye've a temper, have ye? Well, sheathe it, lassie, because ye willna win any fratching contest wi' me. Consider that I've only tae pick ye up and carry ye home bottom upward over me shoulder—"

"You wouldn't!"

"Would I not?" His feet were set apart, and now he hooked his thumbs over his sword belt and gazed at her sternly. A prickling awareness engulfed her, not that he would harm her but that he would carry out any threat he made.

Choosing her words carefully, she said, "It would be wiser, I think, if you were to present yourself to Sir Hector later today. If you tell him that you heard at a tavern or some such place that his falconer had left unexpectedly and that, therefore, you decided to apply to replace him . . ."

"Aye, that might suffice," he said when she paused expectantly. "Be there any other odd detail that I should ken about the position?"

She frowned. "I do not know much more about it myself."

"D'ye no ken why the last chap left, then?"

Smiling sweetly, she said, "He was impertinent to Sir Hector's daughter."

"Aye, sure, and bein' that I'm an impertinent lad myself, 'tis a good thing ye had the foresight tae warn me." He frowned, looking into her eyes as he added gently, "Now, tell me that it was yourself to whom the man dared be impertinent, and I'll have yet more business to tend before I can leave for Stirling."

His accent had altered again, but she did not think it wise just then to point that out to him. Instead, she said, "He was not impertinent to me. Indeed, I doubt that the poor man was impertinent to anyone. Drusilla complained that he looked at her oddly and insisted that he be turned off."

"That would be the screecher, would it not?"

"Aye."

"Farnsworth Tower sounds as if it harbors some pleasant folks," he said. "Almost do I look forward tae spending some few days in their company."

"Understand me, sir," she said. "I can be of no assistance to you in gaining employment there. You must speak to Sir Hector, and you must not mention me."

"I ken that fine, lass. Dinna fash yourself, for I'll no betray ye. I'll hope tae see ye again, though, so I can show ye how tae mend a feather properly."

She smiled but wondered if she had lost her senses. Doubtless, she had accomplished nothing more than the potential introduction of a murderer into the Farnsworth household. The thought widened her smile. Whatever he was, she was certain the man was no murderer. Nor was he what he claimed to be, however. She wondered if she would learn who he really was before he had to leave.

Brown Claud gave a sigh of relief. "That went well, dinna ye think?"

"Aye," Lucy Fittletrot said, wriggling closer. "Ye were that clever, Claud, but ye couldna ha' done it wi'out me."

"Aye, lass, 'twas a grand day when I found ye dancing on the green."

"But I dinna ken why ye'd want tae match the lass up wi' a man she doesna ken," Lucy said. "Seems impulsive tae my way o' thinking."

"Aye, well, but ye dinna ken all that has gone afore," Claud said glibly. "'Twas amazing and all how ye kent where tae find our Bessie when I'd searched two-thirds o' the Borders for her. The while, sithee, I ha' been keeping an eye on other parties wha' may ha' some connection tae her."

"That man Patrick be one?"

"Aye, o' a sort. Moreover, he'll look after the lass till I can think what tae do next. I'll wager me mam will be proud I thought o' that, when I tell her."

"Ah, Claud, she will, for ye be a gey clever lad," Lucy murmured in his ear as she leaned close to nibble it.

He chuckled and put his arm around her. "I am that, lass," he said. "I'll just show ye how clever, too, now that we ha' a bit o' time tae ourselves."

Chapter 3

Sir Patrick MacRae watched Elspeth hurrying northward through the woods. Then, swiftly and silently, he followed her, wanting to make sure she reached her destination safely. As he went, he marked his trail, taking care not to let her see him and hoping that he had judged her motives accurately.

The thought that she might be laying a trap for him was not one he could afford to set aside in favor of a pair of beautiful eyes and an innocent air. For all he knew, she suspected him of even more dastardly deeds than those of which he was guilty and would betray him the moment she got home.

He had heard of Sir Hector Farnsworth but knew little about him. If the man served as clerk for Truce Day meetings, one could suppose he believed in the rule of law, but Patrick had heard the Earl of Angus speak Sir Hector's name.

If Sir Hector had allied himself with Angus, and if the English soldiers presently inflicting their presence on an undeserving Scottish countryside should demand that he turn his new falconer over to them for questioning, Patrick would be sped. And so, too, would the mission that had taken him into England and now brought him to the Scottish Borders.

On the other hand, if he could gather proof that Sir Hector was a traitor without being caught, the information might serve him well.

In any event, Elspeth was a bonny lass, and he certainly did not regret meeting her. Not only did he have a keen eye for beauty but she had also stirred a protective instinct in him that had lain dormant since the day he had left his laird and lady confined at Stirling Castle.

Having been helpless to prevent the King from taking Mackenzie of Kintail hostage and transporting him and other Highland chiefs and chieftains aboard the royal ship to Dunbarton and thence to Stirling, Patrick had thrown himself into making all safe at Eilean Donan. He had felt helpless again, however, in the face of Molly's continued determination to join her husband in confinement. Deciding to ride to Stirling himself to test Cardinal Beaton's scarcely veiled offer to help, he had agreed to take Molly with him, knowing she was fully capable of traveling by herself if he refused and that Fin would have his head if anything happened to her.

When Patrick took leave of them at the castle, he had said nothing about his intention to speak with Beaton. And, even now, should they learn that he was in the Borders, they would assume that he had traveled there from Eilean Donan to see to things at Dunsithe Castle, the property Molly had brought to the Kintail holdings upon her marriage. Located in the west march less than thirty miles from where he stood, Dunsithe was her inheritance from her father and thus now belonged to Fin.

As these thoughts passed through his mind, Patrick followed Elspeth unseen, then watched from the woods as she hurried toward a distant tower surrounded by a stone stockade. When she was safe inside, he returned to the cave, thinking hard.

What information he had gleaned during eight months of spying for the cardinal in England—his eminence's price for Kintail's freedom—would only reinforce Beaton's belief that Henry the Eighth sought to bring all Scotland under his greedy thumb. So, before Patrick left the Borders, he needed at least to confirm his suspicions about Sir Hector Farnsworth or prove them wrong.

In the meantime, he had to move with extreme caution, because the landscape teemed with potential enemies. Whether the bonny Elspeth was one of them remained to be seen.

Midgeholme Castle, Cumberland, England

The slap was unexpected, but Eleanor, Lady Percy, dared not complain. Clapping a hand to her stinging cheek, she gazed through welling tears at her half brother, the Scottish Earl of Angus. He had stormed into her bedchamber without a thought for her privacy, whereupon she had leaped up, thinking something horrid had happened. The result was that she had just made it easier for him to slap her.

"Well?" Angus's voice was harsh. Although he was fourteen years her senior, age and experience had done nothing to mitigate his volatile temper.

Drawing a deep breath and resisting an urge to wipe her damp eyes with her handkerchief, she said evenly, "Well, what, sir? As I do not know what precipitated your displeasure, I can scarcely—"

He raised his hand again, menacingly.

"Archie, I beg of you! What is amiss? I have done nothing to anger you so."

"Have you not? Have you not, Nell? Who was that man you nodded to earlier? What of him, eh?"

"What man?" Her heart was beating so wildly that she feared it might jump out through her mouth if she held it open too long. "I . . . I have nodded at several men since we arrived here at Midgeholme yestereve."

"I have noted that, and since I mean to arrange a marriage for you whilst we're here, I'll thank you to mind your manners more carefully."

"I do not want a new marriage," she said, hoping to divert him even if it meant another argument on that tired subject. He had been plotting and planning new marriages for a year and a half now, and although she had managed so far to disrupt each one, she knew her luck could not hold out much longer.

"You'll marry when I command you to marry, Nell, but presently I want to hear what you know about Sir William Smythewick."

He was watching her narrowly, and she hoped he could not detect her relief. "I know no one named Smythewick," she answered truthfully.

"And what of Sir Patrick MacRae?" he asked silkily.

Realizing that he had led her into a trap, she deftly turned the strength of her shock into equally strong annoyance, saying, "Godamercy, sir, if you mean to ask me about every man here at Midgeholme, I know not what to say to you. At present, the only ones I know by name are your men and our host."

He held her gaze for a long, tense moment, but she bore up under his fierce scrutiny until he gave a sharp nod and said, "We'll soon see, madam, for if it is MacRae, you certainly ought to have recognized him. I've sent men and dogs to track him down, and when they catch him, we'll get the truth out of him. Then may God help you if you have lied to me, for I will make you sorry you were born."

She believed him, for he was a violent man and had made

her sorry before. And all this, she thought, for a single un-guarded moment. She had been at Midgeholme less than twenty-four hours when, seeing a group enter the great hall for the midday meal, she had suddenly encountered the gaze of one of the last men she had expected to see at Midge-holme, or anywhere in England.

Something in his expression warned her, and she had let her gaze slide past him to another in his company. But ap-parently someone had noted that single unguarded instant of recognition and had reported it to Archie.

Perhaps the man in Lord Dacre's retinue who had waved to Patrick had been the one. Whether he had recognized Patrick as Patrick or as someone called Sir William Smythewick, Patrick had slipped away soon afterward. How he had managed it she did not know. One moment he had been there, the next he was not.

"Wherever you are," Nell murmured, "may God grant you safe haven."

Finding the cave again, Patrick examined the area near its opening to make sure that in departing he and the lass had left no sign of their presence. Knowing he might have cause to seek the cave's shelter again, he left signs that, while not noticeable to anyone else, would lead him back to it.

Then, deciding to give Elspeth time to settle into her normal routine before making his appearance, he explored the nearby woods in case he had to hide there again. As he moved about, he remained alert, knowing that as long as he could hear woodland wildlife going about its daily business, the nearby area was safe.

He listened particularly for altered notes in their chatter, for he knew that one could follow an enemy's progress by heeding the squirrels' warning scolds and the echoing cries of the raven, followed as both inevitably were by ominous silence. Most creatures fell silent at his approach, but they soon resumed their normal chatter after he passed, recognizing that he meant no harm.

The sun was much lower in the afternoon sky before he extended his rambles to include the area along the cheerfully babbling burn. Moving uphill from the water, he found a vantage point from which he could see some distance to the north. He perceived no sign of his seekers, which gave him cause to hope they had moved to the northeast in mistaken belief that he was making for Edinburgh or Stirling.

He was in no hurry, however, being more concerned with staying alive.

He was in Douglas country, and although none of that obstreperous, divided clan was in good odor with the King of Scots, Douglases still wielded strong influence throughout the Borders. Stubborn adherents to the defunct Black Douglas and those loyal to the Earl of Angus, the Red Douglas, rarely saw eye to eye, but when pressed, a Douglas of any ilk remembered first that he was a Douglas.

Fin's Molly was Angus's niece, but she had had scant time to cultivate her Red Douglas connections, for she scarcely knew her own mother. Angus had abducted both Molly and her little sister when they were children but had gone into exile soon afterward, taking their mother, Eleanor Douglas Gordon, with him. James, King of Scots, had controlled Molly's wardship and had sent her to the Highlands, where she had lived happily and eventually married the Laird of Kintail.

Her mother, now Lady Percy, had reunited with Molly nearly two years before, at which time, for reasons unknown to Patrick, the two had decided that Molly's sister, Bessie, long missing and presumed dead, was alive and being held prisoner somewhere. In hopes of persuading Angus to reveal Bessie's whereabouts, Nell Percy had returned to England, where Angus still lived in exile.

Kintail had sent searchers to scour the area around Tantallon, Angus's seat on the east coast of Scotland. But although they expanded the search to include the east and middle marches and Douglas holdings in the west, everyone who had heard of the child insisted she had died soon after Angus abducted her, and the searchers had long since given up. Molly had tried writing to Nell but without success, and no one at Kintail had heard from her since her return to England.

Patrick had seen her unexpectedly at Midgeholme, however—indeed, she had nearly unmasked him—and he knew that she was living as Angus's prisoner. Therefore, despite the slight connection, he could not count on help from any Douglas and would have to take great care until he was safely out of the Borders.

When he judged the time to be nearly five o'clock, he moved purposefully toward Farnsworth Tower, easily identifiable even had he not followed Elspeth, since it was the only tower standing near the burn. The place looked secure and was clearly the property of a man of worth.

Patrick wished he had thought to quiz Elspeth more carefully about Sir Hector. He had not done so for fear of revealing a stronger than normal interest, but applying to the man for a position when he knew little about his antecedents or politics was a risky business. On the other hand, nearly everything he had done for the past eight months had been risky business.

Straightening his shoulders and grinning in anticipation of yet one more battle of wits, Patrick strode confidently to the stone stockade's timber gate.

Farnsworth Tower was typical of its ilk, a robber baron's fortified tower overlooking a vast expanse of land in every direction. Even the woodland flanking its water source stood at a safe distance, near enough for general protection, far enough away that it would provide an enemy with no useful concealment. And doubtless Farnsworth boasted a well inside its wall. Five stories tall and wide enough to look comfortable, the square tower sat solidly on a knoll surrounded by its solid stockade, commanding a clear view of approaching visitors.

The gate was shut, but at Patrick's approach, someone shouted from the walkway atop the wall, demanding that he identify himself.

"They call me Patrick the Falconer," he shouted back. "I beg leave tae speak wi' Sir Hector Farnsworth."

"Be he expecting ye?"

"Nay, but I'm told he has need of a man tae tend his birds."

"Wait there, and ken fine that there be six armed lads up here a-watchin' ye."

"I'm peaceable," Patrick shouted.

He decided that he had little to fear from the interview ahead, for he was confident that he knew as much about birds of prey as any ordinary falconer did. During the childhood he had shared with Fin Mackenzie, and since their years at St. Andrews University, the Mackenzie falconer had taught them all he knew, and Patrick had learned even more than Fin had. For one thing, the crusty old falconer had been quicker to punish faults in the MacRae whose duty it was to look after the Mackenzie than to punish the Mackenzie himself. For another, Patrick had displayed more patience than Fin. Neither had had much to begin with, but Patrick had discovered a well of it within himself where raptors were concerned.

He had to exert more patience than he liked now, first waiting for the man-at-arms to return and then for the tall, heavy gates to open and admit him.

"I'll take ye tae the laird," his greeter said, looking him over with a frown. Since he was much smaller than Patrick and built on a wiry frame, the man's wary glances were not surprising. Patrick was accustomed to smaller men regarding him with both disapproval and awe, and it did not bother him except when he feared their suspicion might lead them to act without considering likely consequences.

He wondered as he often had what it must be like to look up at someone else all the time. The only man he knew who was taller than he was, was Fin Mackenzie, and the difference was slight. Moreover, since he knew that he was better with weapons than Fin, and since Fin knew he had nothing to fear from Patrick, the two had not really tested their mettle against each other since childhood. A near exception had occurred a year ago when Fin had lashed out angrily at a flippant remark of Patrick's, and had sent Patrick toppling into the swift-flowing tidal channel between Eilean Donan's islet and the nearby mainland.

Fin had thrown him a rope before the tide could sweep him away, and Patrick, feeling guilty about the remark, had apologized. Even so, whenever he remembered the incident, guilt nagged him. The remark, stupid and impulsive, had flown from his impertinent tongue before he had come to know and admire Molly Mackenzie. He had never apologized to her for it, although she had witnessed his unexpected swim. He had been ashamed to tell her what he had said, and he was as certain as one man could be about another that Fin had never told her.

It seemed odd that just thinking about relative sizes would bring that incident to plague him now when he was miles from both Fin and Molly, striding across Farnsworth Tower's inner court in the wake of his guide. Generally, it was easy to separate his mission from anything personal, but as he followed the man up steep wooden steps, his thoughts drifted to Molly again. Inside a shallow archway at the top, his guide unlatched and pushed open a tall timber door, whereupon Patrick ruthlessly dismissed everything from his mind except the confrontation ahead.

In the courtyard, he had automatically noted the layout of the tower, and he knew the steep wooden stairway had brought them to the second level. When the door opened onto a wheel stair, he deduced that they were above the great hall. The guide went up three steps to another door. Rapping sharply, he opened it and led Patrick into a private chamber that was clearly a sanctuary of the tower's master.

A colorful Turkey carpet covered the timber floor, instantly proclaiming the master of Farnsworth to be a man of wealth, for only people with money to spare walked on carpets. Most who could afford them draped cold walls with them rather than laying them underfoot. The primary piece of furniture in the room was a large, well-polished writing table upon which rested five or six thick, rolled documents, an inkwell, and an ironbound desk box. Sir Hector Farnsworth sat behind it in a carved armchair, a quill pen poised in his right hand as he looked steadily at Patrick.

Grizzled and blue-eyed, Sir Hector appeared to be somewhere in his fifties. His gray beard was neatly trimmed and his hair cut fashionably short, just touching the frilled lace at his collar band. Over his white shirt and plain green woolen doublet, he wore what appeared to be a short black gown faced with gray fur, its sleeves puffed and full from elbow to shoulder. He did not get up but dismissed Patrick's escort with a gesture.

As the man was leaving, Sir Hector said, "Stand just outside the door, Gray. I will require you shortly either to show this man out or to take him to the mews."

"Aye, laird," Gray said, shutting the door behind him.

Patrick realized that he was staring at Sir Hector like an equal and quickly lowered his gaze, aware that he would otherwise appear rude or impertinent.

"My man tells me that you claim to be a falconer."

"Aye, sir," Patrick said.

"Where did you hear that I might be looking for such a person?"

"At Graham's alehouse in Canonbie," Patrick said. "A chappie there said ye lost your man nobbut a sennight ago."

"Unfortunately, that is true. What references can you offer?"

"I ken the birds."

With an impatient gesture, Sir Hector said, "God's body, sir, I would hope you do, but I want to know where you have served before. If you are any good, I find it odd that you must seek work here."

"Aye, sure," Patrick said, nodding as if he only then realized what Sir Hector had meant. "I ha' never served as chief falconer, sir, only as second, and I'd liefer no say where, lest ye think ill o' me for nowt but havin' served there."

"I want to know, nonetheless."

"Aye, well, it were across the line, then, at Naworth Castle, wi' the laird there, but I dinna be English, sir, although I do ha' kin on both sides o' the line. Sithee, I thought it best tae learn wha' I could where I could learn it. It were that or the reiving, ye ken, and me mam wanted better for me. She lost me father, reiving, and I promised her I'd keep tae the birds and beasts so as no tae end on a rope."

He knew he was taking a grave risk by claiming connection to Naworth and Lord Dacre, but any tale he created would carry risk. An honest Sir Hector could not check this one as easily as some but might harbor suspicions about any man who came into Scotland from England. A traitorous Sir Hector would have contacts of his own across the line and be able to look into the story with greater ease, and since Angus had mentioned his name, Sir Hector most likely had at least one contact in England, which meant that at best his loyalties were divided.

"I know of Naworth Castle," Sir Hector said, nodding. "Indeed, I have met Lord Dacre, because he serves as warden of England's west march."

"Aye, sir," Patrick said, wincing inwardly at hearing that Dacre was a march warden. Still, the likelihood was small of a Truce Day being held under present conditions, with English Catholics fleeing the wrath of their king's new church in droves, and with luck, he would be away soon. "I learned me craft at Naworth," he said, "but I want tae be closer tae me kin, so I were making me way home when I chanced tae hear ye had need o' a new falconer."

Sir Hector grimaced. "I do, indeed," he said. "My chap knew his birds, as you say you do, but he overstepped his place. If I employ you, I hope you will show better sense than he did."

"I ken my place fine, sir. It be wi' the birds."

"See that you remember that."

"Aye, sir," Patrick said with a nod, but his thoughts flew to Elspeth's gray-green eyes, rosy lips, and soft skin, and he knew that it would be hard to keep her out of his mind for more than minutes at a time.

Sir Hector said, "I'll call Gray back in now unless you have aught you want to ask me about your duties."

"Nay, sir, I ken me duties fine. I'll need only tae learn where I'm tae sleep and where I'm tae eat, and who tae tell when I find what supplies I'll need."

"Apply to my steward for supplies, and Gray will show you the chamber where my falconer sleeps. I'll give you a fortnight's trial unless I find cause to turn you off before then. If you prove satisfactory, I will pay you forty merks a year."

"I thank ye, sir."

" 'Tis I who will thank you, I believe. Indeed, I would like you to do one particular thing for me if you are able. The King is to celebrate the birth of his second child soon,

God willing, and I would take him a young hawk or falcon
as a gift. Can you acquire and train one to the fist in short
order, do you think?"

"How long will ye give me?"

"We leave for Stirling in about ten days."

Patrick hesitated. For more than half that time, men would
be seeking him on the Scottish side of the line. When Sir Hector raised his eyebrows, he said hastily, "The time be short, but
if I can find the right bird straightaway, I can do it."

"Excellent. See that you do. Gray!"

The door opened, but instead of the sinewy man-at-arms,
Elspeth entered. Her smooth flaxen hair was tidily plaited,
and she wore a simple white cap tied under her chin. She
had also changed her apron for a fresh one, Patrick noted.
"What is it, lass?" Sir Hector said.

"Begging your pardon, sir," she said, bobbing a curtsy,
"but her ladyship desired me to inform you that she has ordered supper set back a half hour."

"What evil spirit possessed her to do that?" he demanded
querulously.

Shooting an oblique glance at Patrick, she said, "She did
not deign to inform me of her reason, sir. Is there aught I
may bring you to stave off starvation?"

Patrick felt his loins stir in response to her sidelong look
and quickly shifted his gaze to the floor, hoping he presented
the appearance of an obsequious retainer.

Sir Hector said with a sigh, "I require nothing yet. This is
Patrick, lass. He is to be my new falconer. I told Gray to
wait, but he seems to have disappeared. Pray, find him and
tell him to take this fellow to his birds."

"Gray stands outside the door, sir, but I warrant he must
be anxious to return to his post. If you like, I can show the
new man to the mews."

"Do you not have tasks to attend?" he asked with a slight

smile. "I know 'tis the Sabbath, but you have incurred her ladyship's displeasure already today. She will not like your going outside again so soon."

"She will not scold if you command me, sir," Elspeth said with a smile.

"Saucy lass. You deserve to suffer the rough edge of her tongue."

Patrick waited, but the girl did not reply.

After a moment's pause, Sir Hector said, "Very well, send Gray back to his post and take this fellow to the mews. Then you must return to your duties."

Elspeth curtsied and smiled at Patrick, but Sir Hector was not finished. "You, lad, heed me well. Your business is to tend my birds and to find and train a hawk for me to give to the King. Trifling with this maidservant or with any other here will result in your instant dismissal. Do you understand me?"

"Aye, sir," Patrick said, knowing that he failed to conceal his astonishment.

"Mayhap at Naworth your master was not so strict, but here we keep a close eye on our lasses, so beware."

"I will, sir," Patrick said with a bow. Grateful that Sir Hector had misread his amazement, he added with sincerity, "I thank ye."

The reply this time was no more than a grunt and a dismissive gesture, so he turned and followed Elspeth from the chamber, waiting with barely suppressed impatience until she had sent the man-at-arms back to his post. But although he would have spoken then, the lass put a finger to her lips and hurried toward the stairs. Not until they were outside did she speak.

"What is it?" she said then as they strode across the flagged courtyard.

He glanced at her. "What is what?"

"You were going to speak before. You must not speak to

me inside, though, because both Drusilla and Jelyan listen at doors and in the stairwell."

"Impudent brats! They should be soundly skelped."

"Did your mother beat you when you listened at doors?"

"My mother is a gentle soul. 'Twas my father who doled out punishment in our household, and I certainly never would have listened at a door anywhere that he might have learned about it. Why did you not tell me?"

"Tell you what?"

The very innocence in her tone betrayed her. "You know perfectly well that I mistook you for a daughter of this house," he snapped.

"You are angry with me."

"I could not remain so, even if that were true," he said with a sigh. "You saved my life today." He realized that he was not bothering to disguise his manner of speaking and mentally chided himself for his carelessness. What was it about the lass that caused him to forget his most basic rules of survival?

"Does it matter?"

The question disconcerted him, coming as it did just when he was asking himself about his unnatural reaction to her. He had to collect his wits, to realize that she had leaped back to his accusation that she had misled him. Then, without thinking, he said bluntly, "I do not like deception."

"Indeed."

The sarcasm in her tone struck his conscience like a whip. He could think of nothing to say that would not increase his guilt, so he said nothing.

The silence between them lengthened until she said quietly, "That building yonder in the corner of the wall serves as the tower mews."

Feeling much as he had long ago when caught in mischief and scolded for it, he had been looking at the ground, but he looked up at these words and followed the direction of her gesture.

The structure she indicated was a good-sized timber shed leaning against the stone wall, but when she led him inside, he found conditions worse than he had expected. Three hooded birds were tethered to arched perches, and despite its hood, one bated wildly at their entrance, falling from its too-high perch and hanging, frantic, in its jesses. Patrick leaped forward, snatching up a filthy towel to capture the bird and set it back on its perch. The floor was a morass of mutes, or droppings.

"I'll need a glove," he murmured as he stroked the breast of the nervous bird with his fingertips to calm it. "I brought practically nothing with me."

"I collect that you left your last place somewhat abruptly."

"Aye." He was gently examining the bird he had replaced on its perch, a small brown-and-white female sparrow hawk.

"I wonder if that is the one the lad said should be put down," Elspeth said.

"Nay, not her. She's just hungry. I'll soon find her something to eat, though, if one of your men will lend me a bow and some arrows. I'll wager 'tis the hen harrier yonder that your lad fretted over."

Cautiously, and cursing the dim light, he examined the harrier on the end perch without touching it, then gently stroked its soft gray throat as he studied its dark trailing primaries. The bird moved nervously on the perch but did not start.

"How will you train them to your fist?"

"These must already be manned to accept more than one fist. Otherwise, since Sir Hector does not train his birds, he would not be able to hunt with them."

"But did I not hear him say that you must also train a new one?"

"First I must catch it," Patrick said, his attention still on the harrier.

When she did not reply, he glanced at her and saw that she was reaching toward the sparhawk. Even as he opened his mouth to tell her to stand back, she stroked the bird, and to his astonishment, it accepted her touch without a twitch.

"Did you help the previous man with these birds?"

"Nay, I was here only once before today."

"But she behaves as if she knows you."

She shrugged, still stroking the hawk with her fingertips. "All animals trust me," she said. "Even as a small child, I was able to pick up wild birds or calm an injured fox kit by stroking it. I thought mayhap I could help by keeping this one calm whilst you tend the others. What is wrong with the harrier?"

"Hunger trace, for one thing," Patick said. "That means that at some point or other he did not get enough to eat. You can see the evidence here." He pointed to what looked like a semi-circular slash across the bird's white tail plumage. "That line shows where the feathers are weak. Two have broken."

"Can you mend them?"

"Aye, in time. Where is the lad who's been looking after them?"

"I do not know, but Small Neddy is a bit daft, so do not scold him if he did not do everything the way you think he should have."

"I will not scold him at all," Patick said. "I want him to continue to help if that will not stir coals with anyone."

"He helped the previous man sometimes, but mostly he helps in the stable."

"I'd like him to muck out the floor in here, and to do so regularly," Patick said. "Should I speak to Sir Hector before I give Small Neddy orders?"

"I'll ask him. Will you show me how to mend feathers?"

Her nearness made him conscious of how desirable she was. "Do you mean to barter with me whenever I want something?" he asked.

She licked her lips with her tongue, and a jolt of sexual desire shot through him. He wanted to shake her, but even more did he want to kiss her and tease her body until she writhed with matching desire for him. He had liked her well enough when he thought she was a daughter of the household. That she was a maidservant seemed to make her even more desirable, or perhaps it was just that he knew a maidservant would be more accessible.

Her gaze collided with his. "I did not mean to barter," she said. "I only asked because earlier, when we were in the woods, you said you would teach me to mend feathers, but men often change their minds after they promise things."

"I do not," he said. "If I make a promise, I keep it." He was facing her now, looking down into those wide gray-green eyes. He could almost taste her lips.

"When will you teach me?"

"You should not spend time here alone with me," he countered reluctantly, albeit pleased to discover that he still possessed a conscience.

"I am alone with you now."

His longing for her overcame both conscience and good sense. Without another thought, he caught her by both shoulders and kissed her hard.

She made no move to stop him, and when his lips touched hers and found them soft and willing, he wrapped his arms around her and held her close, cradling the back of her head with one hand.

Although she was small and slender, she fit against him perfectly.

Chapter 4

Elspeth could not breathe, and his beard tickled her cheeks and chin. Never had a man kissed her before—not since she was small, at all events, and then only if her father had done so. Since he had given her away to strangers when she was little more than a bairn, then left the country and stayed away for as long as she could remember, she did not know if he had ever kissed her or not. In her dreams he had, but in reality, it seemed unlikely.

In any case, she was certain that no fatherly kiss could be like this one. Patrick's lips were hot against hers, hard and demanding. His hand at the back of her head felt large and powerful, and warm. He smelled of woodland and smoke, and he tasted unlike anything she had ever tasted before. It was pleasant, that taste, and she wanted to savor more of it.

His other hand was at her waist, and he had spread his fingers so they spanned the small of her back. Fire radiated through her from every place he touched, but when his tongue pressed against her lips, then slipped between them, she gasped, knowing that she ought to stop him. Nice girls did not let men take such liberties. But what could she do, particularly when she did not want to stop him?

He was pressing hard against her in front, too. His body seemed to want to swallow hers, to possess her. Hearing a slight moan, she realized with a start that it had come from her throat. She was kissing him back, and she was doing it as easily as if she had done such things for years. What must he think of her?

At that thought, she stiffened and raised a hand to his hard chest, pressing her palm against him, reluctantly giving him a push. She assumed that it would do no good, and she was a little disappointed when he stopped kissing her and let her go.

"Sorry, lass," he said gruffly. "You're a tempting morsel, but I should ken better than to defy Sir Hector's orders when I've been less than a quarter hour out of his company. If you'd like to smack me, go ahead." His expression softened as he added, "Molly would."

"Why?" she asked. "Would you not smack me back if I smacked you?"

"Is that what men hereabouts do? They'd best not try it whilst I'm about," he said. "Who dares to strike you?"

"No man has since I was a child," she said, surprised at his reaction.

"Well, I had best not see any man lift a hand to you," he said.

Her heart seemed to swell within her. No man had ever spoken so to her, nor taken her part so firmly. Sir Hector was considerate, and when he noticed others being unkind to her, he often intervened, but his intervention had never felt like this. And Patrick had done nothing but speak a bit fiercely.

"Who is Molly?" she asked.

"What?" The question clearly disconcerted him.

"You said she would smack you if you kissed her."

"She is just a friend," he said brusquely. "No one to concern you."

She looked into his eyes, thinking she might judge better by what she saw there, but the gaze that met hers was too intense, and she looked quickly away again and stepped back. If she had hoped the extra distance would make a difference, she immediately learned her error, for it was as if there were no distance, as if she could still feel his hands and his lips on her.

"I . . . I must go," she said, turning away. She could almost feel him reaching for her, and the feeling lent wings to her feet. When he did not catch her and hold her, the odd sense of disappointment struck again, but she ignored it and ran outside, only to come up short when an irritated Drusilla stepped into her path.

"What are you doing out here, Elspeth?"

Her world righted itself, and gathering her wits, she replied glibly, "I was seeing to an errand for Sir Hector. Did you want me?"

"It is nearly time for supper," Drusilla snapped. "You should be helping in the kitchen. I'll wager my mother does not know you came outside."

Stifling a sigh, Elspeth said evenly, "You will tell her whatever suits you, of course. If she wants me, she will know where to find me."

Turning, she walked away, feeling small concern for what Drusilla might do. For once, she had more interesting things to occupy her mind.

She attended to her supper duties with speed and dispatch. Cook was a kindly soul and did not scold when a person was a few minutes late. She knew that Elspeth would make up for her tardiness by working swiftly and capably. Elspeth had learned young that whatever the other servants might think about a person's birth or antecedents, they appreciated a willing worker who did not complain or insist that certain duties were not hers to perform. Thus, they did not resent the affection Sir Hector showed her or the affection she felt for him in return.

There were times when someone would ask her to speak to Sir Hector about one thing or another. She would always try to help, and sometimes she would succeed in smoothing over a bit of trouble. Just as often, however, she could do nothing, as when the previous falconer had been dismissed.

When the meal was served, her kitchen duties were done, and she took her place in the lower hall with the other servants. Not until after Sir Hector had spoken the grace before meat did she allow herself to look for the new falconer. She realized she had left the man abruptly without showing him where he was to sleep, and she hoped that someone had shown him.

At first, she did not see him, and a new worry stirred. What if he did not think he should leave the birds? How would he eat? She had seen no sign that he had carried food, and it was too early for him to have found berries in the woods.

Just as she was thinking she would have to collect food for him and take it out to the mews, she saw him sitting with other menservants near the hall entrance. They were laughing, and he was clearly enjoying himself.

She watched him, waiting for him to laugh again, and so she was looking right at him when he turned his head. His gaze met hers, and he grinned.

Heat flooded her cheeks, and the tingling that stirred in the center of her body made her look swiftly away from him and hope that no one else had noticed him looking at her. It would be just like Drusilla to be watching, hoping for her to put a foot wrong, so that she could make more trouble.

Supper dragged on after that, because Elspeth dared not look toward the falconer again, and yet she remained strongly aware of his presence. The others at her table were chatting and laughing, but no one paid heed to her silence, and she was grateful. Again she recalled that she had promised to show the falconer his chamber, but the thought sent more heat to her cheeks. Someone else would show him, or he could sleep on the hall floor with the men-at-arms who slept there.

It would serve him right, she decided. The man was too full of himself. A night on the hard stone floor would do him good.

As Brown Claud paced the parlor floor, waiting for Maggie, he was feeling pleased with himself. Not only had he accomplished the mission she had assigned him and arranged things in a way he was sure she would approve, but in the doing he had improved his own life, as well. And Maggie would like Lucy Fittletrot.

Lucy was everything that the wicked Highlander, Catriona, was not. To be sure, Catriona had been splendidly beautiful and clever, so clever that Maggie had despised her and called her dreadful names. But Lucy was plain and sensible. Maggie had only to look at her to know that this time Claud was really in love.

He sighed, for the unhappy truth was that when he was with Lucy, he was sure Maggie would like her. But when he was alone, as now, doubt crept in. Maggie was difficult to please, and when she was not pleased . . .

A noise diverted him, and his waning confidence vanished like smoke.

"Mam, be that ye coming in?"

"Aye, and who else would it be?" Maggie demanded testily as she bustled into the parlor. She looked him up and down in disapproval. "Why do I find ye here, lad? Did I no tell ye tae keep searching for our lass?"

"But I've found her!"

"Aye, well, that be another matter," Maggie agreed. "Be ye sure?"

"Aye, for all that they call her Elspeth now and no Bessie anymore."

Maggie grimaced. "Who calls her so?"

"The folks wha' that bastard Angus left her wi'," Claud said. "She be happy enough, though tae my way o' thinking, they dinna be kind tae her."

Maggie frowned, disappointing him. He had expected praise for his success.

"Are ye no happy that I found her, Mam?"

"I'm wondering how ye managed it so quick this time," she said. "We ha' been looking a fierce long while without turning up so much as a hair o' the lass."

"I did ha' help," Claud admitted, adding quickly, "I met a lass, but she's no like ye'd think. She be a good lass, Lucy, and she guessed straightaway that the Elspeth living wi' her cousin's people had tae be our Bessie. Said the lass came in the night, that Angus brought her years ago and tellt the folks there that she were his, born out o' wedlock, and they was tae look after her."

"Then, likely that'll be the truth, and she's no our Bessie at all. She wouldna be the first misbegotten brat o' that fiend Angus. Ye've got yourself in a lather over another wench, is all. When will ye learn, Claud?"

"But Lucy be different, truly!"

"They all be different, ye dobby."

"I havena seen ye since the meeting o' the Circle, Mam," he said, hoping to divert her. "Were they horrid tae ye after they sent me away?"

She shrugged. "Some feared we had revealed more tae

them in the mortal world than they ought tae ken," she said. "Once I'd explained, though, most o' them seemed satisfied, but they set me a task as a penance."

"What task?"

"I'm tae keep out o' trouble by reconciling differences betwixt two obstreperous factions o' our clan, the Merry Folk and the Helping Hands."

Claud grimaced. "The Merry Folk be Catriona's tribe."

"Aye, but I'm tae deal only wi' their council. The problem be that the Merry Folk dislike having tae look after mortal clans that ha' roots in the Borders. They say they should look after only them what be Highland bred."

"Still they asked ye," Claud said. "They must ken ye can do it."

"Oh, aye, but it will take a deal o' time and talk," she said. "I'd no give the business wi' the Circle another thought did I no suspect Jonah Bonewits be meaning tae make trouble. 'Twere his notion, me dealing wi' the Merry Folk."

"Ye dinna like the man. I saw that straightaway."

"He's one as likes tae make game out o' others," Maggie said.

"If he be loyal tae Angus, why did ye no connect him tae Bessie afore now?"

"Because Jonah's loyalty tae Jonah be greater than Jonah's loyalty tae anyone else," Maggie said. "He may admit his duty tae serve Angus, but since he rarely spares a thought for anyone but Jonah Bonewits and his own amusement, it isna odd that I didna think o' him when I first came tae see that our Bessie must still be alive. Now that I think on her disappearance as a mischief though . . ."

Again she fell silent, lost in thought, and this time Claud had no desire to interrupt her. He kept his own counsel, hoping she would forget about Lucy.

Elspeth arose from the table, intending to go to the bed-chamber that Drusilla and Jelyan shared abovestairs, but she no sooner turned toward the stairway than a familiar voice spoke her name. Reluctantly, she turned to face the new falconer.

"Good evening," she said, trying to ignore the warning emotions that surged through her. "I am glad to see you were able to leave the birds long enough to eat."

"Oh, aye, I'm a handy lad at finding forage, lass. But, sithee, ye left afore showing me where I'm tae sleep, and I've nae notion where I'm tae lay me head."

Elspeth gave him a long look, then turned and gestured to one of the kitchen lads hurrying past. When he stopped, she said, "Show this man to the falconer's chamber, if you please. He has taken the previous man's place."

Turning abruptly, she walked away, but so conscious was she of his startled gaze that she paid no heed to where she was going and bumped into Drusilla before she realized that the older girl had stepped in front of her.

"Clumsy drudge," Drusilla snapped, slapping her. "Watch where you walk!"

Clapping a hand to her cheek, Elspeth struggled to remain calm, embarrassed and aware that Patrick had likely seen the incident. She remembered what he had said about men striking her and hoped fervently that he would not try to intervene with Drusilla. He could accomplish no good thereby.

Certain that he still watched even if the lad had tried to take him from the hall, she said hastily, "Forgive me, Drusilla. I did not see you. Did you want me to do something for you?"

"I saw that new man talking to you," Drusilla said, watching her narrowly. "Doubtless you think he is very handsome."

"Sir Hector asked me to show him to the mews this afternoon," Elspeth said. "Thus, he took the liberty just now of asking me where he is to sleep. As you saw, I told one of the lads to show him the way."

"That was wise," Drusilla said. "My mother would be displeased to hear that you had been flirting with him and would doubtless order harsh punishment for such sluttish behavior. Mayhap she would forbid you to accompany us to Stirling when we go to celebrate the birth of the King's new son."

"Are you so certain that the babe will be a boy?" Elspeth asked, hoping to divert her thoughts. Drusilla was entirely capable of reporting to Lady Farnsworth that she had been flirting even when she had not.

"Kings require sons," Drusilla said with a shrug. "I would not want anyone to think I had encouraged the fates to present him with a daughter."

The temptation was great to point out that God or any other power great enough to affect the royal birth was unlikely to heed Drusilla, but Elspeth resisted, knowing she would gain nothing and would likely suffer for her insolence. Instead, she asked patiently if Drusilla required anything of her.

"I mean to sit with my mother and Jelyan in the solar for an hour," Drusilla said casually, as if this were not her practice nearly every evening. "Go and prepare my bed, and mind that you do not burn the linen when you warm it if you do not want more of what I just gave you."

"I'll attend to it straightaway," Elspeth said, bobbing a curtsy.

"Perhaps you had better practice your curtsies if you are to attend us at Stirling," Drusilla said. "That one was too hasty. I shall ask my mother to see that you do not disgrace us with your slipshod ways. You may go now, Elspeth."

Her voice had risen, and Elspeth felt her cheeks flush when she saw that others were watching them. Nevertheless, she knew she could not win a debate with Drusilla, so she nodded and walked away, taking comfort in the fact that Drusilla had neither forced her to repeat her curtsy nor to lose her temper. It was a small victory, but since she never won large ones, she savored the small ones.

Crossing the hall, she entered the spiral stairway. As she turned to go up, a strong hand shot out and grabbed her arm, turning her sharply.

Patrick's eyes glittered with anger. "I collect from that wench's attire that she is a daughter of the house," he said. "From her manner and voice, I collect also that she is the screecher who disturbed the peace of the woods before the searchers came. What I do not know is why she slapped you. Did you give her cause?"

"Apparently, I did," Elspeth said evenly, trying to ignore her pounding heart. "You startled me half to death. I thought you had gone to your bedchamber."

"I apologize if I frightened you, but I want to know why she slapped you."

"I cannot imagine how that concerns you," she retorted.

His gaze held hers, and she knew the anger she saw in his eyes was aimed as much at her as at Drusilla. He was too close, still holding her arm in a firm grip. As the silence between them lengthened, she became aware of the noises in the hall.

"Someone will come," she muttered. "Release me."

"What did you do to deserve slapping?"

"I did nothing," she said more sharply than she had intended.

"Then why—"

"Because you spoke to me! Now, let me go before someone comes. Recall what Sir Hector said. You cannot afford to lose your position the very first day."

With chagrin, he said, "I did not know she would . . . She should not have—"

"Are you daft? She can do as she likes. She is Sir Hector's elder daughter. I am just a maidservant, dependent on her goodwill and his. Now, go!"

She had intended to pull away from him, but he released her just as she did, with the result that she lost her balance on the stone step and slipped. He caught her quickly, so that she stumbled against him, and she pulled hastily away.

To her surprise, he chuckled. "Lassie, you are going to be the death of us both. I apologize for my part in what happened. I'll not put you in such a position again, but mind that you don't stir that termagant to violence again."

Indignant that he would give her such a command, she opened her mouth to read him a description of his character that would astonish him, but a burst of laughter from the hall reminded her of where she was and what peril she risked if she lingered. Therefore, without another word, she turned and hurried up the steps, knowing that he watched until she went around the first turn and out of his sight.

Patrick watched her go, still fighting the rage that had swept through him when the screecher slapped her. His opinion of Sir Hector had altered considerably in the past few minutes, for what manner of gentleman permitted his daughters and doubtless his wife, as well, to mistreat the maidservants in his household? Certainly Patrick would not allow such goings-on in his. If he saw his sister slap a servant, she would earn at least a sharp scolding. Bab would never behave so, however. Flighty and impulsive as she could be, she would never be unkind.

Turning, he headed downstairs and found the lad he had

left below standing just beyond the first turn. With a stern look, Patrick said, "Were ye listening?"

"Nay, master, I come up tae see what were a-keeping ye."

"It be just as well if ye didna hear, for if ye did and I should come tae learn that ye'd been speaking out o' turn, I'd ha' summat tae say tae ye."

"I heard nowt! Did ye want tae see where ye're tae sleep or no? 'Cause if ye dinna ha' need o' a bedchamber, I've me chores tae do."

"Lead on, lad. I'll no get much sleep, though, for I've a hawk tae catch tomorrow and preparations tae make afore then." As he followed his small guide, he decided that Elspeth was right and that he had better keep his mind on his duties. To risk his life for a kiss and a cuddle would be stupid. Still, sweet Elspeth would make quite an armful. Just thinking about her stirred his body to express its regret.

Cumberland, England

Midgeholme Castle's great hall was impressive, particularly at suppertime, with its myriad candles and both great fireplaces burning merrily. Their magnificent carved chimneypieces were the talk of Cumberland, but Nell felt only gratitude for their heat. At this time of year, the hall would be icy without it.

She ate her supper quietly at the high table, eyes fixed on her food, hoping that the men there would assume she was paying them no heed when in fact she was listening intently to all she could hear. The company was smaller than it had been the previous night, but the hall still contained noisy retainers, and every seat at the high table was occupied. Nell and her tirewoman, Jane Geddes, were the only females, however, because their hostess, Lady Renwick, had begged off at the last moment, saying she had had her fill of male company for the day. It was sadly unhostesslike behavior, but Nell did not mind. Lady Renwick was too high in the instep to count as a friend and flaunted her disapproval with snide barbs and irritating discourtesies.

To Nell's right, Angus talked with their host, Sir Ralph Renwick, and Lord Dacre, who had ridden the five miles from Naworth Castle that morning to discuss important matters. Their early discussion having been interrupted by the search for the spy they had nearly trapped in their midst, they had apparently decided to continue their conversation through supper.

Their murmuring was hard to hear above the cacophony of conversation from the lower hall, but Nell had already heard enough to know they discussed Henry of England's threatened invasion of Scotland. Not that Henry intended to lead the invasion, of course. With fifty hard-drinking and carousing years behind him, far too many pounds on his flabby body, and a fifth wife in his bed, the King of England had no desire to ride into battle. He had agreed to travel as far as York to meet with his nephew James, High King of Scots, but thus far Jamie had shown the good sense to refuse to meet so many miles inside his wily uncle's country.

"You should go up to bed, Nell."

Startled from her thoughts, she forced herself to wait a beat before turning to her brother and saying calmly, "I have not finished my meal, sir."

"With so few women present, Lady Renwick showed proper discretion by deciding to sup in her solar. You should have joined her there."

"Lady Renwick did not invite me to join her, Archie, nor did I know she had decided to sup elsewhere until I had been at table for some time. I will retire to my chamber when Jane and I have finished eating."

To her relief, he merely grunted and turned back to his

conversation. She did not want to anger him, because to do so always cost her dearly, but neither would she simply bow to his capricious commands. In any case, she did not want to leave, because the men were discussing matters that might prove useful to her.

Lord Dacre, a man in his thirties whom Archie had called a dolthead not worthy to fill the previous Lord Dacre's shoes, said disapprovingly, "Far too many people in the north of England remain true to the Popish church, resisting the wishes of his majesty the King."

Hearing fat Harry called "majesty" never failed to amuse Nell, and she suppressed a smile now. In her opinion, Scotland's form of addressing its ruler was more tasteful, for the Scots called their king "his grace," a term in keeping with the behavior they expected of him, for they looked upon the High King of Scots as merely the chief of all clan chiefs.

Henry, however, seemed to regard himself as some sort of god. Had he not already put himself in place of the Pope, insisting that he, not the Holy Father, was head of the Church in England? Perhaps he was mad. Many had suggested as much, even Angus, yet still they called him "majesty."

It occurred to Nell then that it was just as well the Scots did not expect majestic behavior from Jamie, for he was barely capable of grace. Nonetheless, he was a much better man than his unpredictable uncle.

Although her thoughts had drifted, she continued to listen as the men discussed the local troubles, and she winced at hearing Renwick say testily, "People will learn. At least ten thousand have already paid for their treachery."

Nell hated the savagery of so many dying for the simple crime of disagreeing with their king's decision to shrug off a church that did not approve of his relentless search for a wife who could give him numerous, healthy sons. And Jamie's wife was expecting again, for that was his latest excuse for delaying his meeting with Henry. If Marie of Scotland produced a second son, Henry would not rejoice.

Dacre said, "Many who refuse to give up the old faith for Henry Tudor's new one are seeking refuge in Scotland, where Davy Beaton insists on keeping faith with Rome and punishes reformers as severely as Henry punishes the papists."

"Aye," Angus growled. "Whole families are leaving England in droves, so the roads to Longtown, Canonbie, and Kershopefoot are littered with papists."

Kershopefoot. Nell knew the town. Indeed, she had heard that it was the easiest place to enter Scotland and had crossed the line there once herself.

She cared little about politics, but over time she had learned to pay heed to them, and occasionally bits of information she gathered proved useful, as now, discovering that Midgeholme lay only twenty miles from the line. She had not been this close to home in months, because Angus had kept her confined in the house Henry provided for him near York. Her brother hoped to use her again to further his aims, but perhaps she could put an end to those plans for good.

At one time, Angus had been the most powerful lord in Scotland. Married to Jamie's mother, who was Henry's sister, Margaret Tudor, Angus had served as both stepfather and regent to Jamie before the lad had come of age and seized control of Scotland's Crown for himself. Angus had fled the country then to seek sanctuary in England. Those events, thirteen years ago, had strongly affected Nell, not least because he had forced her to accompany him into exile.

Widowed before Angus's downfall and subsequent exile, she had found herself at his mercy late one night at Dunsithe, her first husband's castle in the Scottish Borders. Angus, still at the height of his power, abducted her two tiny daughters that night, determined to control both, but particularly the elder, Molly, Maid of Dunsithe, who was Scotland's greatest heiress.

Although Angus had not then known that his star would soon fall, he, like Henry, dealt his cards to protect himself, and he had arranged another marriage for Nell with an elderly knight in the powerful English Percy family. Sir Barnabas Percy had not cared that she had been born on the wrong side of the blanket. That she was daughter to one Earl of Angus and sister to another had been enough. As for Archie, he had cared only about establishing powerful allies in England.

Nell had suffered the loveless marriage for years before the baron died and left her a comfortable fortune, despite the fact that she had given him no children.

Only thirty-four and still beautiful, she had wanted so badly to return to Scotland that she agreed to carry messages there for Angus when he demanded her aid, because she could travel in relative safety and he could not. Unfortunately, she had failed to achieve his objective, and as punishment, he clapped her up again, hoping to arrange yet another marriage for her that would benefit him.

She knew that he had dragged her to Midgeholme because he hoped to arrange a marriage for her with Dacre's son, but his lordship was plainly not interested. And since the son had barely entered puberty, Nell was glad, because that little detail would not deter Angus.

Now that she had found one daughter, she yearned to find the other. Angus still insisted that Bessie had died soon after leaving Dunsithe, but Nell was sure he lied. When she had returned to confront him and he said again that Bessie was dead, she had seen the lie in his eyes.

Kershopefoot was just twenty miles away, so all she had to do was slip away from Angus. The problem was more daunting than mere words made it sound, but she was determined, and thanks to that evening's conversation, an idea began to stir.

Chapter 5

Awaking hours before dawn, Patrick dressed, broke his fast with some bread and ale, and went outside. Having made most of his arrangements the previous day, he had only to collect the bow net he had found and mended, a decrepit falconer's bag and glove that Small Neddy had unearthed for him, a live pigeon he acquired from the bakehouse, and sundry other items. Carrying his pigeon in one of the twig cages, he persuaded the guard captain to open the gate and let him out.

A low mist covered the ground, giving the landscape an eerie appearance and veiling the moon so that it cast but a pale glow. During his rambles the previous afternoon, he had noted several places that he thought might prove fruitful.

One in particular was a tall, dead, bare-branched tree of the sort that stood at the edge of the woods, overlooking a grassy meadow. Since hawks liked a good view in all directions, he decided that under that tree would be the best place to set his trap. At least, it would if he could find it again in the dark, misty moon-glow.

Working in the dark, in territory with which he was

barely familiar, would not be easy, but if he waited until daylight, he would lose at least a day's time, because it would take that long for the creatures to get used to alterations he made in their habitat and return. Moreover, at night he could work without disturbing any hawks, which would be asleep on their high perches elsewhere.

The woodland slept. No owl hooted. No shadowy fox stole across his path, and only once did he hear a wakeful cow lowing in the distance.

By following the sound of the burn and keeping to the edge of the woods, he made his way swiftly and found the tree he sought without difficulty.

He worked efficiently, using his sharp dagger to cut long, heavily leafed branches for his hide, then pegging half of the bow net to the ground fifteen yards away, beneath the tree he had chosen. Stringing fishing line from the top half of the trap to his hide, so when his quarry entered the trap he could yank it shut and catch the hawk inside the netting without harming it, he hid the trap by strewing moss, leaves, dust, and dried twigs over it. Then he staked his pigeon so it could move about within the circumference of the trap, scattered enough grain to keep it occupied through the day, and withdrew to his place of concealment to wait.

This was the part of the process he enjoyed least, because the hide was only a bit longer than he was and not much wider, and he knew from experience that he might have to lie there all day without much movement. Indeed, catching a hawk could easily take a number of such inactive days unless he was lucky.

He slithered inside and discovered that with care he could turn over without shaking or undoing the entire structure, but that was all the movement it allowed. Setting the rolled end of the fishing line where he could reach it again, he shut his eyes, knowing that with at least an hour still to go before dawn, he could sleep.

This time, however, sleep eluded him. Instead, he found himself thinking about Elspeth. Dreamily, he wondered what she would look like unclothed, but to his surprise, the moment the thought entered his head, instead of seeing a gloriously nude Elspeth in his mind's eye, he saw the prim-looking one he had seen the day before when she had informed him that felonious activity was not a matter for humor. It was much easier to imagine her with her hands on her hips, glaring at him like an angry great-aunt, than to imagine her lying in his bed, sensuous and eager.

He smiled. He had five days left before it would be safe for him to leave Farnsworth Tower. Surely, in that time, he could make enough of an impression on the lass so she would smile when she saw him.

Elspeth was enduring a normal Monday morning. Having risen at five and eaten a hasty meal of barley porridge, she had opened the curtains and shutters in the hall to air it out. The men who had slept there collected their own oatcakes and porridge, and two of them swept the chamber while another two dealt with raking the coals and building new fires in the two great fireplaces.

Her primary duty was to make herself useful to the two young ladies of the household, but until it was time to waken them, she helped with other tasks. Since Farnsworth Tower boasted only a kitchen maid, a scullery maid, a laundry maid, and a maid of all work, she spent as much time helping them with their chores as doing her own. Lady Farnsworth had her own tirewoman, of course, but Martha

Elliot kept herself to herself and resented any task that she did not think fell within her purview. Thus, she looked upon Elspeth as her assistant, and when she issued commands, Elspeth had little choice but to obey them.

When it was time, she took hot water upstairs and woke her charges, opening their curtains and shutters and then leaving them to get themselves out of bed while she carried hot water to Lady Farnsworth's chamber. Sir Hector's man had wakened him already, and Sir Hector had gone to his sanctuary to break his fast amidst his documents, but Lady Farnsworth's woman informed Elspeth that her ladyship would take her breakfast in her chamber.

Hurrying back down to the kitchen, Elspeth put a manchet loaf, a plate of grilled fresh haddock, and a jug of ale on a tray. Carrying it back upstairs, she handed it to Martha Elliot at the door of her ladyship's chamber.

Then she hurried back to the chamber shared by Drusilla and Jelyan.

"Where have you been, and why has it taken you so long to return?" Drusilla demanded shrilly. She stood barefoot in the center of the room, still in her nightdress, arms akimbo, her long dark hair hanging untidily down her back. "You should have built up the fire before you left," she snapped. "It is cold in here."

Jelyan smiled and said nothing. Shorter and slimmer than her elder sister, she had put on her shift, skirt, and petticoat. She had also put her arms through the sleeves of her square-necked bodice, but because she could not reach the fastenings, she was holding it tight against her waist, still open at the back, waiting for help.

Elspeth moved to do up the back of Jelyan's bodice. Shifting the younger girl's long chestnut plait over one shoulder, out of the way, she said, "Drusilla, you told me yesterday that it annoyed you to hear me fussing about in your room after I wake you, and you wanted me to find other things to do until it was time to help you dress. I cannot stir the fire to life from outside the room."

"Don't be impertinent," Drusilla said. "It is getting warmer, and I did not think we would need a fire, but we do and you should have attended to it directly after you wakened us."

"But Elspeth is right, Drusilla," Jelyan said. "You were very sharp with her yesterday, complaining that she had disturbed your slumber before it was time and need not bother with a fire. Also, Mother said that we should not waste firewood. Can you do my hair the way you did yesterday, Elspeth?" she asked.

"Yes, of course," Elspeth said. "Sit on that stool."

"She has no time to do fancy things to your hair," Drusilla said. "Wear your French hood. I have changed my mind about what I'll wear, Elspeth. I want my crimson mock velvet instead of the one you got out last night, so fetch it quickly."

"The crimson is ready to pack," Elspeth reminded her, knowing she was probably wasting her breath.

"Then you will have to freshen it later, but I want to wear it today. Moreover, I want you to press all my other clothing, so that I can see everything at its best in order to choose exactly what to take. You had a nice holiday yesterday, so I warrant you can accomplish much more than usual today."

"Have you finished my mending yet?" Jelyan asked.

"Most of it," Elspeth said. "Everything will be done in time."

Although it was a morning like any other, with the ladies of the household planning to depart in a matter of days for a month's visit to Stirling, Elspeth had many extra tasks to do. When she had seen her charges on their way downstairs to break their fast, she made the bed they shared, then raked the hearth and laid a new fire ready to light when needed. She was washing her hands with leftover water when Martha Elliot entered with an armful of her ladyship's linen.

"Here are more things for you to launder," the woman said curtly.

"I'll attend to them straightaway, Martha."

"See that you do."

Elspeth dealt with the last assignment first by delegating it to the laundrymaid with the caveat that the lass should bring the finished items to Elspeth to return. Next, she asked the stable master to send one of his lads to help in the kitchen. Then she dealt with Drusilla's clothing, carrying an armload to her own chamber where she laid the items on her pallet.

She had no fireplace in her bedchamber, but the kitchen fire was close by to heat the iron and she could use the side table in her chamber for her ironing. She would have to carry the garments back and forth, but the iron had to reheat frequently, and she was accustomed to the process.

As she dealt with the ironing, she wondered what the new falconer was doing. She had been careful to avoid him the previous day, not wanting to give Drusilla cause to suspect any undue interest in the man. Doubtless, he was at least going through the motions of preparing to look for a bird that Sir Hector could give to the King, but since he hardly had time to train a hawk before he would leave for Stirling himself, she did not think he would spend much time on the effort.

Thus, it was with surprise that when she found a few moments to step outside, assuring herself that she did so merely to get a breath of fresh air after working with a hot iron for two hours, she learned that Patrick was nowhere to be found. According to Small Neddy, he had departed hours before dawn.

"He ha' gone tae fetch a new bird," Neddy said. "He did

take Old Lachlan's bow net. He knotted fresh netting round it hisself, too, he did."

Elspeth was reassured. Telling herself that she had just wanted to be sure he was not shirking his duties, she returned to her own. But when he did not appear for dinner, she told herself that she was being foolish to feel disappointed at not having seen him and reminded herself that even if she dared leave during the afternoon and risk a worse scolding than she had endured the previous day, he would not thank her if she interfered with his preparations to trap his hawk.

At that moment, Patrick was lying on his back wondering if the wild pigeon that had lighted on a branch inches above his face was about to commit a nuisance. Unwilling to find out, he poked its belly with a twig, grinning when it flew off with an indignant clatter of wings. The mist had cleared, but with the thick canopy of trees, he could not see the sky or any hawks that might have been soaring overhead.

Wakened after an hour's slumber by a symphony of birdcalls, he had lain on his belly, watching his trap, letting his thoughts drift to his time in England and then to events that had led to his mad dash for the Scottish line. From there they drifted naturally to Elspeth. Whatever he thought about, his thoughts kept returning to her, and he realized that his interest in the lass was greater than he had thought.

He felt as if he had known her for years instead of a day, but the comfort he felt in her company had already led him to make errors he did not normally make, and he would have to take care. He tended to forget that he was playing a part with her and talked to her much the way he talked to his sister or to friends he had known all his life. He liked her, but why he should think of her as a friend merely because she had been handy with a hiding place when he needed one, he did not know. He owed her gratitude, but he felt more of an obligation than that. When Drusilla had slapped her, he had wanted to throttle the shrew.

He speculated for some time in this fashion, but he had reached no reliable conclusion by the time his stomach began to rumble. Turning over he found his skin of water and the bread and meat he had packed for his dinner. As he did, he heard the distant kittenlike mewing that was the hawks' hunting call. At that distance, they might have been kestrels, kites, sparrow hawks, or even peregrine falcons. He munched slowly, listening, wondering if the pigeon in the trap was too large, if a blackbird might have made better bait, since it would tempt smaller hawks as well. Although Sir Hector had said nothing to him about the laws governing ownership of hawks and falcons, Patrick suspected that, as a man of law, he would know that a landed knight was not entitled to own a peregrine.

In the Highlands, few men heeded such laws, and more than one clan chief boasted at least a golden eagle or gyrfalcon in his mews despite the fact that only emperors or kings could legally own such splendid birds. Since this one was for the King, Patrick decided he would take what came and worry about any consequences later. He was bored, restless, rapidly growing stiff, and the day was far from over.

Two hours later, as he lay watching the trap, his mind numb with boredom, something flashed across the line of his vision, flying an inch or two above the grass. Knowing that if he saw the bird, the bird had seen him, he was careful not to move. The bird turned and flashed past again, soaring upward, turning, then losing height and seeming to float down toward the trap. Soundless now, almost hovering, and unseen by the pigeon, the hawk drifted in at an angle, talons ready.

The pigeon squealed twice and was silent.

Swiftly, Patrick pulled his line, and the net snapped over and down.

Elspeth saw the falconer in the first group of men that entered that evening to eat their supper, and seeing how pleased he looked, she decided his hunt must have met with success. She allowed him to catch her gaze only once, though, and ate her meal as swiftly as good manners allowed. Then she left before he could speak to her. She did not want to incur Drusilla's ire, or anyone else's, not two days in a row.

Upstairs, she attended to her duties efficiently, taking water to the young ladies' chamber and laying out their nightclothes and the clothing they would want in the morning. Then she hurried to her own chamber, where she waited patiently for half an hour, in case someone should think to send for her.

Knowing that the hawk would be calmer after nightfall, Patrick had left it hooded and jessed, leashed to its low perch in the shed to settle, while he ate his supper. He allowed himself only a few casual glances at Elspeth, noting that wisps of her hair had escaped from her coif and from the plait coiled at the nape of her neck. His fingers itched to smooth the stray wisps back into place.

She looked tired, and he wished he had the authority to tell her to go to bed. When she left after finishing her meal, he hoped she was retiring for the night.

He returned to the mews shortly thereafter to find the hooded hawk still on its perch. Pausing in the doorway, he watched it for a few moments, then entered quietly, drawing on his glove and taking a bit of fresh rabbit liver from the bucket of parts the lad had prepared before supper. The bird twitched nervously.

Slowly, he approached the perch and released the leash, twisting it around his gloved hand. Then, gently, he stroked the bird's talons, holding the liver in the open leather palm. Each step took time. Stroking its chest, he felt it quiver, but it tolerated him. He stroked it gently and murmured softly to it for nearly an hour before he reached with his free hand to loosen the hood and remove it.

The bird pecked the gloved hand, which he had closed over the bait, but it did not seem frightened, letting him stroke its chest and talons. It was young but nearing adulthood and amazingly calm for a fresh-caught bird. From time to time as he stroked it, he whistled the warbling tune he would use in future to call it, and thirty minutes later, it stepped onto his gloved fist, bent its head, and took the rabbit liver from between his fingers. From now on, it would take food only on the fist.

The hawk's talons felt like sword points stabbing into his hand through the aged leather, its grip convulsing almost rhythmically as it shifted its weight. Its head was lowered but thrust forward, and one mad yellow eye glared at him for an instant before the hawk bated, taking a headlong dive in a wild, twisting bid for freedom.

In a flurry of feathers, like a chicken about to be decapitated, the bird hung upside down by its jesses, struggling, flapping, in imminent danger of damaging its primaries. Patrick reached with his free hand, intending to lift it back to his fist.

"Faith, do you mean to wring the poor thing's neck?"

Starting nearly as violently as the hawk had, Patrick

whipped his head around to see Elspeth in the doorway, hands on her hips, glaring at him. Her expression was exactly as he had imagined it while lying on his back in the hide.

"Don't chatter," he said, keeping his voice even as he gently set the bird back on his fist. "I have begun the watch, but if you keep still, you may stay." He spoke in the same soft tone as before, but his tone made no difference to the hawk. It bated as wildly as before, flinging itself off his fist again.

Patiently and just as gently as before, he lifted it back.

"Won't she hurt herself?"

"He's a male," Patrick said. He nearly reminded her to be silent, but the hawk had remained still, not reacting to her voice as it had to his.

"Very well, then," she said. "Won't *he* hurt *him*self?"

"He might," he said, hesitating to say more than a couple of words at a time. Although the bird seemed to have calmed, that calm would not last.

"Why does he fling himself about so fiercely?"

"Are you supposed to be out here? I thought you had gone to bed."

"Not yet. I finished my evening chores, so I came out to see how you were faring. Why *does* he fling himself about like that?"

"He is angry and frightened," Patrick said. "He is only doing what is natural for him, and I cannot stop him, but he will soon learn. The easiest way to train him is to wear him out, so I must keep him awake now until he accepts food from me."

"What kind is he? Have you given him a name?"

He smiled. "He is a goshawk, and I think I'll call him Zeus."

"Ruler of the gods," she said thoughtfully. "The name suits his fierce and haughty look, to be sure."

"Aye." He enjoyed watching her, and apparently Zeus did, too. "I thought you were angry with me," he said.

Color flooded her cheeks, but her tone was even when she said, "Why?"

"You would not even look my way in the hall, and you ran away before I had finished my dinner. I wanted to tell you that I'd caught him."

Without replying, she glanced around. "Where is Small Neddy?"

"Listening to the men tell stories in the hall, I expect. About all he's suited for is trapping rabbits, preparing food, and feeding the other birds. He's useless for training them, so he'd just be in the way here now."

"How long will it be before Zeus takes food?"

"He took some from me earlier, but if you mean how long before he is manned, before he looks to me for his food and to the gloved fist as his natural perch, it usually takes me two or three days."

"Two or three days!"

Goaded, he said, "It takes most falconers and austringers longer than that. Only a good one can manage the trick so quickly. Even then, it is an ongoing process, for the bird will soon return to its wild ways if left alone."

"But how will you stay awake so long?"

"The lad will have to help. All he has to do is feed the other birds and carry this one about for a few hours at a time whilst I sleep. I can manage the rest."

"I could help."

"I do not think that is a good idea," Patrick said gently, having no wish to offend her. "Recall that Sir Hector warned me to stay away from the maidservants, and I warrant Lady Farnsworth would not like your being out here in the mews."

She was silent.

"Well?"

"It is true; she would not," Elspeth admitted.

"You had better go in then. Neddy may return any moment, and his mouth rattles like a beggar's clap-dish."

"I do not think he would say anything purposely to get me into trouble," she said, "but he might speak without giving thought to any consequence. Do you really think Zeus can be ready when we leave for Stirling?"

"Sir Hector asked only that he be manned to the fist by then, and ten days should be plenty of time for that," Patrick said with a smile.

"Aye, it is ten days," she said with a sigh. "The way Drusilla and Jelyan behave, one would think they were departing tomorrow, but I think he means for the family to leave on Thursday, to give us three days for the journey. Her ladyship will not travel on the Sabbath, you see, and certainly not on Palm Sunday."

He had hoped she would return his smile, but she did not, and the intensity of the disappointment he felt surprised him. He reached for her, but the bird bated the instant he moved, and for the next few seconds his concentration was fixed on returning Zeus to his fist. When he looked again, Elspeth was gone.

With a sigh, he told himself it was just as well. He liked women, and he had enjoyed more than one liaison with a willing lass, but a dalliance now would complicate matters considerably.

The hawk was glaring at him again, and he glared right back, only to regret it when Zeus took another dive. Predatory birds, as he knew, did not appreciate a direct look. One did better to look beyond them. Perhaps, like humans, they saw it as a mark of submission when an inferior did not dare meet their fierce gaze.

The following day passed much the same way as its predecessor for Elspeth. She had only to think she could take five minutes to herself for someone to give her another task to do. Jelyan's mending and other plain sewing had taken most of the afternoon, and although she had finished ironing Drusilla's garments the previous day, she had to endure an hour with that young lady while Drusilla decided yet again what she would take to Stirling and what she would leave behind. From experience, Elspeth knew Drusilla would change her mind many times and would probably end up taking everything she could stuff into her sumpter baskets, but that did not alter the present circumstance one whit.

The falconer did not appear at either the midday meal or at supper.

Spying Small Neddy at the latter meal, Elspeth took him aside and told him to take food out to Patrick.

"Aye, he did say I should bring him summat tae eat," the lad said, nodding.

"Well, do not dawdle. He must be hungry."

Shooing him on his way, she went upstairs to turn down the bed that Drusilla and Jelyan shared and lay out their nightdresses. Intending to slip out to the mews again as she had done the previous night, she hurried down the service stairway, only to encounter Lady Farnsworth at the bottom.

"Elspeth, I am glad I found you. I stepped downstairs to speak to Cook, and she said you would be coming down any minute, so I waited for you."

Elspeth suppressed a sigh. "Yes, my lady?"

"I have some small tasks I want you to see to before you go to bed."

"Yes, madam."

How nice it would be, she thought, just to do as she pleased for once without having constantly to be at someone else's beck and bay.

Chapter 6

It was late by the time Elspeth finished the myriad tasks Lady Farnsworth had assigned to her. Knowing that, nonetheless, her ladyship would expect her to rise at her usual time the next morning, she hurried downstairs to her bedchamber as soon as she was free. Fortunately, she carried a candle, for someone had already snuffed the torches in the kitchen and in the corridor that led to her chamber and the postern door beyond it. Entering her room, she set the candle in its stand on the side table and was preparing for bed when she heard a male voice in the corridor.

Curious, she moved to stand with her ear to the door. Then, certain the voice was Patrick's, she snuffed her candle, eased the door open, and peeked through the crack. Light spilled into the narrow corridor from somewhere to her right. Knowing that the falconer's chamber and the one allotted to the cook and kitchen maid stood between hers and the kitchen, she deduced that he had lighted candles or a torch in his chamber and that the door stood open.

He was walking toward her with the glow behind him, reciting something, holding the hawk on his gloved left fist. His eyes were shut, and so were the hawk's. Despite

Patrick's recitation and the fact that he was walking, both man and bird looked sound asleep.

She watched silently as he walked to the postern door and turned. Then, half afraid she would startle the hawk, even more afraid that she might anger Patrick, but unable simply to shut her door and go to bed, she stepped into the corridor.

She saw that he swayed on his feet. Zeus opened one eye and shut it again.

"Patrick," she said softly.

The hawk made a sound like a robin's cheep, and Patrick opened his eyes.

He smiled wearily. "Is that your chamber, lass?"

"Aye."

"I did not know. I'm sorry if I wakened you with my muttering." His voice was low and vibrant. It seemed to touch her deep within.

"You didn't wake me," she said. "I came down only a short while ago and was getting ready for bed."

He frowned. "What are they thinking, putting you so close to the falconer's chamber? Or does another maidservant share your room?"

"Nay, but the previous falconer was in his forties, and despite Drusilla's claims, he was not a flirtatious man. I warrant no one has thought about the unsuitability of letting you sleep so near to me. Or perhaps Drusilla has thought of it and is biding her time, waiting for a chance to make trouble."

"Who sleeps in that chamber between us?"

"Cook and the kitchen maid. I did share my chamber with our last scullery maid, but the present one lives with her parents in the village up the burn."

"Doubtless Sir Hector thinks the cook keeps an eye on you."

"Perhaps, but I do not think anything would waken her or the kitchen maid. They both sleep like the dead."

"You should not be out here talking to me like this. It is unseemly."

This from the man who had kissed her in the mews, she thought. With a smile, she said, "I doubt that you could manage any unseemliness at the moment. You were asleep on your feet only moments ago, and Zeus looked as if he were asleep, too. Indeed, he still looks that way."

Glancing at the bird, Patrick nudged it with his free hand, and for a moment Elspeth feared that the hawk would fling itself off the fist again, but it did not.

"He's not quite asleep yet," Patrick said. "It would not do for both of us to fall asleep, though. He must stay awake, and to that end, so must I."

"I could walk with him for an hour, so you could sleep."

Patrick's eyes twinkled, and she felt her heart begin to pound. She had been foolish to make the offer, because she needed sleep to get through the day ahead, but that twinkle was irritating. Clearly, he thought she could not do it.

In a teasing voice, he said, "Put your hand to his chest as you did to the hawk that first night in the mews, but take care. My fingers smart from his pecking."

"He won't peck me," Elspeth said confidently.

"Don't be too sure," he warned.

Gently, she stroked the bird, and Zeus allowed it, his manner tolerant almost to the point of disinterest.

"You have no glove," Patrick said.

"You can lend me yours," she said.

"It is too large for you."

"I'll manage," she said. "It will not matter if my fingers don't fill it. It need only protect my hand and wrist."

"His talons sometimes poke through."

"Try it," she said.

As if he were still humoring her, Patrick said, "I expect he'll accept the stool in my chamber as a perch long enough to make the trade. I brought him in because Neddy is afraid of him, and I can be more comfortable here, but I'm exhausted, and if he and I both go to sleep, the time is wasted."

"Then let me help," she said.

"If he will let you carry him, I'll gladly agree, although I don't doubt I'm mad to let you put yourself at risk."

She followed him into his bedchamber, knowing that if anyone caught her there, her punishment would be severe. No one would come now, though, and somehow she knew she could trust Patrick not to harm her.

In moments she had pulled on the large gauntlet, and to her delight when she placed her forearm and fist before the bird as Patrick directed, Zeus stepped onto her arm as if it were perfectly natural for him to do so. He was large but not nearly as heavy as he looked.

"Don't look directly at him," Patrick said quietly. "He'll soon grow used to you. And don't worry if he squirts mutes all over the floor. It's only dirt, and I'll clean up any mess he makes. Do you really think you can manage him?"

"I think he is too tired to make trouble," she said, feeling inexpressible delight at the hawk's acquiescence.

"Very well then, walk him up and down the corridor, or take him into your chamber if you fear that someone might come. Have you any light in there?"

"I put out my candle before I opened the door."

"I'll light it for you," he said, going to her room on the words and returning with her candle. "This one will burn out soon, so I'll mark another one to show you when to wake me. Be sure that you do. You must not oversleep in the morning."

She nodded. "What do I do if he flings himself off like he did before?"

"Just put him back again if you can, or open my door," Patrick said. "I'll waken at once and help you." He looked at the hawk, sitting quietly on her arm, and shook his head with a smile. "I think he likes you."

"Sleep then," she said. "We will do very well without you."

Nodding, he followed her to the door and shut it behind her.

Calculating that with the time he had spent trapping the hawk and watching it he had been awake nearly forty-five hours, she was determined to let him sleep as long as possible. Remembering that he had talked to the bird, and unable to think of anything she knew well enough to recite, she began counting aloud.

Zeus kept his eyes open, watching her, but by the time she reached one thousand, he had shut them again. Remembering Patrick's instructions, she touched the hawk's breast, and its eyes opened again.

She had meant to count to five thousand, sure that to do so would take her more than an hour, but when she lost count and feared that she had dozed off for a moment or two, she stopped counting and tried talking to the bird instead.

"What do you think of this, Zeus? Do you like us, or do you wish Patrick had just left you flying free? How wondrous that must be!"

Unfortunately, she could think of little to talk about, particularly since the bird seemed uninterested and all she really could think about was the man sleeping just the other side of the closed door.

Zeus tried to sleep but woke each time she touched him. Patrick had told her that the hawk would not have "given in" until it stayed asleep even when touched. At that point, he said, Zeus would truly have accepted the fist as his normal perch.

When the candle in her chamber began to gutter, she lit the second one and set it in the pool of wax, holding it until the wax cooled and it stuck. Zeus watched the process with interest, so afterward she paced the confines of her room, hoping that his interest in the flame would keep him awake for a while. It had been a long day, though, and her determination to stay awake ebbed as the time crept past. She watched the flame inch closer to the mark Patrick had made on the candle, and when it touched that mark, her resolve weakened. She counted to one hundred, then to one hundred again, knowing that little more than three minutes had passed.

When she stumbled, she realized she might hurt the hawk if she tripped over her own feet. Accepting defeat, she went into the corridor and turned toward Patrick's room. She was passing the cook's chamber when he emerged from his.

"Good lass," he said, reaching gently to take the hawk from her. "I'll stay awake easily now, and the way he's behaving, I don't doubt he'll give in before the coming day is done."

She nodded, glad that she had not had to waken him and unnaturally aware of his presence. She stared at him, finding it hard to breathe normally.

He smiled. "Go to bed, Elspeth."

She nodded again. Gently, he gave her a push with his free hand, whereupon she collected her wits and went to bed.

The castle stood atop a hill in the distance, its crenellated walls and turrets creating a crown that glittered like gold in the last rays of a blazing sunset. The sky beyond it was a peachy pink and purple, making a spectacular backdrop, but the castle seemed no nearer than it had seemed the last time she had seen it.

She walked and walked. It seemed as if she had been walking forever, and the castle just seemed to hover in that same unreachable distance.

The sky overhead darkened, and nervously she fingered the heavy key dangling from its ring on her kirtle. She did *not want to be caught in a storm, but neither could she stop to take shelter. She had to go on, and quickly.*

A hand shook her shoulder, and candlelight flickered near her face.

"Elspeth! Elspeth, lass, wake up!"

Startled, Elspeth shot upright on her pallet of sheepskins, nearly banging heads with the kitchen maid, who jumped back, jerking her candle out of the way.

"Cook says Mistress Drusilla will soon be a-shoutin' for ye, d'ye no get up and get about your work," the maid said.

Wiping sleep from her eyes with the back of her hand, Elspeth muttered, "What time is it?"

"Time tae be taking up the ladies' water," the maid said. "When ye didna come tae fetch it, she sent me tae see were ye still sleeping. Be ye sick, Elspeth?"

"I'll probably wish I were before the morning is done," Elspeth said. "Jenny, help me do up my dress and then hand me my comb and cap."

"How came ye tae oversleep then? Ye never do."

"Never mind that. Just hurry."

The day deteriorated from there. Everyone seemed to be in a bad humor, despite the fact that a messenger had arrived in the night from Stirling with news that the Queen had gone into labor and that the grand fête was still set for the evening following the King's birthday. Although clearly his grace had no qualms about enjoying such a splendid celebration during Lent, he had apparently drawn the line at celebrating on Palm Sunday.

One might expect that with a sennight yet to go, preparations would simply go on as before, but the news sent the household into a tizzy instead, and Elspeth endured even more scolds than her oversleeping might otherwise have incurred.

She missed her dinner because her morning chores were not done, and although she had expected to catch up by suppertime, Lady Farnsworth's tirewoman gave her a new gown for her ladyship and told her she was to hem it before their departure. The skirt contained yards of material.

"I'll do it as soon as I can, Martha," Elspeth said quietly.

"See that you do. We depart for Stirling on Thursday next."

"Yes, I know."

She had hoped to get outside, but it was as if a conspiracy existed to prevent it. She did not see Patrick all day, nor did she see Small Neddy, so she went to bed that night without knowing if the hawk had given in or not. As she passed Patrick's door on the way to hers, she listened but heard nothing to indicate that he was there. Nor would she have had the nerve to knock if he were.

Less than a quarter hour later, as she lay in bed waiting for sleep, she heard him in the corridor, pacing again. For a few minutes she resisted the temptation to get up, then pulled on her bodice and skirt in the dark and opened the door.

He was looking right at her when she did, and the relief she saw in his weary face gave her a sense of deep satisfaction that vanished abruptly when he said, "You look like someone dragged you through a bush backwards, lass. Did it not occur to you to comb your hair today?"

Stiffening, she said, "I got out of a warm bed to see if you needed help again tonight, Patrick Falconer. A man with any manners would show some gratitude."

He had the grace to look ashamed but said defensively, "I was afraid you might suffer a scolding if anyone else saw you looking so untidy."

"If anyone sees me, you may be sure I'll be punished," she retorted. "My appearance will not enter into it, however, only the fact that I am here alone with you. I have already endured a dreadful day, so I hope you mean to take yourself off to bed at once and leave me to Zeus's more civil company."

He grimaced. "You are right to call me uncivil, lass.

What a villain I am to carp when you are doing me a kindness. I will be greatly in your debt, more greatly in your debt, if you will walk with him for an hour."

"I will, and gladly," she said.

"You say you had a dreadful day," he said as they turned toward his chamber. "Is it possible that you overslept this morning?"

"Aye, and Drusilla found fault with everything I did," she said, following him into his room. "Lady Farnsworth scolded me, too, and even Sir Hector spoke sharply. It was my own fault, though," she added when he frowned.

"Nay, that it was not," he said, turning away but not to set the hawk on the stool as she expected. "You were up late on my account," he went on as he sorted through things on his table, "and I knew well that you must be overtired."

"You were tired, too, and you went on walking all night after I went to bed."

"That was my duty," he said with a glance over his shoulder. "The least I could have done was see that you wakened at your usual time."

"Well, the hour is much earlier tonight," she said.

"It is," he agreed, turning back to her, "and I've a gift for you. Small Neddy found this glove, and I think it will fit you. He said he outgrew it and the previous man, Lachlan, gave him a larger one. This one was a bit stiff, but Neddy oiled it and worked it a bit, so it shouldn't chafe you much. Try it on."

The thought of having her own glove was strangely exciting, as if Zeus were now partly her charge as well as Patrick's. Her gaze met his. "It's really mine?"

"Aye, if it fits."

She pulled it on. "It does," she said, delighted. She held her fist under the hawk's belly and felt a thrill when Zeus stepped onto it without hesitation.

"Let me light a candle for you," Patrick said, taking one

of his and lighting it at his fire. "I've marked the hour, so mind you don't let me oversleep my time."

She nodded but did not speak. Although she had been tired when she lay down, she was not tired now.

Patrick touched her shoulder, urging her through the door ahead of him. The warmth of his hand spread through her, and the thought that she and he were alone, with the kitchen empty and Cook and the kitchen maid fast asleep in their beds, made her unduly conscious of his touch. She could hear him breathing, could feel the vitality of his body and sense its power.

His accent was like hers now. He had stopped using the rougher speech with her, and he spoke with unusual familiarity, as if he had known her for years.

"Sleep well, Patrick Falconer," she said.

"Aye, and fast," he said with a teasing grin. The grin faded as he reached his doorway, and he gave her a long, unreadable look before he closed the door.

The time passed more quickly than the previous night. She talked to Zeus, and although he was sleepy and kept nodding off, he would wake when she touched him. And once, when she moved too quickly, he flapped his wings and opened his fierce-looking beak, making her hold her breath, terrified that he would fling himself into a frenzy and hurt himself before she could waken Patrick.

Patrick did not awaken by himself, so she rapped on his door when it grew hard to keep her eyes open. The candle was past its mark but only a little. He glanced at it and glanced at her, but although he looked as if he were going to say that she should not have let him sleep so long, he did not. He merely thanked her, took the hawk, and told her to go to bed.

He woke her the same way she had wakened him, by rapping on her door before he took Zeus out to the mews.

She got up at once, slipped on her flannel petticoat and skirt, and quickly laced her bodice over her shift before she went to fetch water for herself. Only when she did not see Patrick outside did she realize how much she had hoped she would.

All day, as she went about her chores, her thoughts stayed with the man and the hawk. Zeus seemed unusually tame, but he still wakened when touched, which meant that he still did not altogether trust them.

The conquest was visible. Patrick had seen it before, but it always astonished him when it happened. Zeus sat on his fist, head drooping. His wings drooped, too, and when Patrick touched him, Zeus ignored him, so sleepy he would trust the fist not to betray him, would trust the falconer not to harm him.

The next step was the manning. Patrick would continue to carry Zeus nearly everywhere he went, getting the hawk accustomed to horses, sudden noises, other people, the everyday life of a human hunter. The quickest way was to carry the bird at least twelve hours a day. It would live on his fist, so that when the day arrived to let it fly free, it would return to the glove automatically. But before they began, both man and hawk needed some sleep.

Warning Small Neddy not to disturb the hawk or try to feed it but to look after the other birds, Patrick went to his room to sleep until suppertime.

He saw Elspeth at supper, but the lass took only enough time to swallow a few morsels before leaving, and he caught her eye only once. She looked almost as tired as he had felt before his rest, and he wanted to follow her, to speak to her, to tell her that Zeus had given in, but also to tell her to go to bed early.

Since he had no authority for the latter and knew that even catching her eye might land them both in trouble, he finished his supper and returned to the mews. He was rested now, and a few hours spent introducing the hawk to such unfamiliar sights as men-at-arms and the torchlit courtyard would do them both good.

When Patrick did not appear in the corridor outside her bedchamber that evening, Elspeth was disappointed, but she was tired and grateful to get to bed early. The following day, however, when he did not appear for the midday meal, she sought out Small Neddy when she finished eating.

"Does the falconer no longer take his meals in the hall?" she asked.

The lad shrugged. "He be wi' the hawk. Carries him everywhere, he does, but he says Zeus be nae fit company at table yet, so I'll take some bread and meat tae the mews when I go."

"Is the hawk still resisting him?"

"Nay, Zeus give in yesterday. Patrick did eat his supper here yestereve. Did ye no see him then?"

"Aye, but if he left you to look after the hawk then, why did he not now?"

Neddy shuddered. "Zeus were sleepin' then, and I didna ha' tae feed him. He's a fierce-looking bird, is Zeus, and mean besides. Pecks me fingers."

Elspeth kept him no longer but went upstairs to attend to her afternoon duties. Having finished all but the large pile of mending, she hurried out to the mews, where she found Patrick alone, carving twigs with a small knife at a table.

He grinned when she entered and rose to greet her.

"Did ye miss me, lass? Small Neddy did say ye were asking for me."

His accent was thick, and she frowned, looking around, expecting to see Neddy tending the other birds.

"He's no here just now," Patrick said, taking his seat again. "I sent him tae tell Cook I'll be walking out wi' the bird all day tomorrow, tae get him used tae being in the wild wi' me. But he should be back any minute now."

Understanding, she nodded. "He said Zeus had given in," she said, looking at the hawk, which was on its perch near Patrick, ignoring her presence.

"Aye, he did," Patrick said. "I walked him all morning, even outside the wall, but he bated at a horseman, so I brought him in tae let him calm down a bit."

"May I watch you work with him?"

"Aye, if ye like. He doesna seem tae mind ye. First, though, mayhap ye'd like tae see how I'm tae mend the harrier's feathers."

"Oh, yes, please."

She saw that he had neatly trimmed the stubs of the two broken primaries, and now he picked up a piece of black feather and what looked like a two-inch bit of white twig from the table. Indicating the twig, he said, "'Tis called an imping pin. I've shaped each pin to fit into an extra bit of feather, so," he said, suiting action to words. "Now, you can help me with the next step."

"How?"

"I'll hold the harrier," he said, "whilst you slip a feathered pin into the end of each broken primary just as you saw me slip the feather onto each pin."

Surprised, she said, "Would you really trust me to do

that? I should think it would be better if I were to hold the bird. I'm sure it would let me."

"Aye, but I did promise to teach you to mend feathers," he said, grinning.

They were so close that their arms touched, and her body reacted at once to his, but she was determined to prove worthy of his trust. Focusing her attention on the wing as Patrick held it steady, she guided the first pin into place.

"Good lass," he said approvingly.

"Will that really hold the feather pieces together?" she asked as she repeated the process with the second tip. "Won't the wood rot in time?"

"Not before the harrier loses the feathers naturally in its next molt," he said. "Now I'll show you what else I've been doing."

He slipped his glove on now and moved back to Zeus. "Watch," he said, holding his gloved fist about eighteen inches in front of the hawk and then, with a musical, warbling whistle, moved it nearer. When his fist was a foot away, Zeus spread his wings and hopped onto it. Patrick hooded the hawk, then detached the leash from the perch, saying, "I want to try something new now."

Reaching for a coil of thinly plaited leather, he said, "This is about fifty feet long. I want to see if he will fly to me from a distance, and this leash, or creance, as we call it, will keep him from flying away."

She watched as he detached the short leash, exchanging the longer one for it. "Will you take him outside the wall?" she asked.

"Aye, I canna try it amidst all Sir Hector's louts," he said, glancing toward the yard and apparently remembering his accent. "Would ye like tae come along?"

The pile of mending loomed large in her mind, but the thought was fleeting.

"Aye," she said happily. "I would."

Chapter 7

As they walked out through the main gate, Elspeth half expected someone to stop her, to demand to know where she was going with the falconer, but no one did.

The air outside the wall always seemed fresher and gave her a sense of freedom that she never felt inside Farnsworth Tower. Today the stolen pleasure of Patrick's company increased that sense considerably. Guilt stirred when she thought about the mending she had left undone. She had never shirked her chores so openly or so defiantly before.

"I wonder if God will punish me for this," she muttered.

Patrick chuckled.

She looked at him in astonishment. "Do you dare to laugh at God?"

"Nay, sweetheart, only at you for thinking that He has so little to do that He would chide you for taking a walk in the woods on a fine day."

"He might not approve of my walking in the woods with you, though," she said bluntly. "Lady Farnsworth and Sir Hector certainly would not approve."

"Then why did you come?"

"I don't know," she said. "No, that is not true. I came because I wanted to come. That is the plain and short of it."

He chuckled again, and his humor warmed her to the bone, but then his brow furrowed, and he said, "Are Sir Hector or her ladyship likely to punish you?"

"*Very* likely." She sighed. "I have been thinking about how free you are and how confined I am by my position here and all the tasks I must do each day. In truth, I am jealous of your freedom. After all, the worst that could happen to you would be if someone accused you of enticing me to leave the Tower today and Sir Hector dismissed you from your post."

Patrick shrugged, apparently unconcerned about such a fate now that he was nearing the end of the six days. "If you do not like it here," he said mildly, "you should look for a post elsewhere."

"Even if I knew where to seek such a post, how ungrateful I should look!"

"Ungrateful?"

"Aye, because Sir Hector and his lady have given me a home here since I was small, long before I was worth anything to them as a servant, and with no recompense. Moreover, Sir Hector has always been kind and willing to teach me. I owe them both my duty and my loyalty."

"If you've lived here since you were small, you've long since repaid them."

"But leaving suddenly would undo that," she said. "It may not seem so to you, but they depend on me, and finding competent help is not easy. Surely, it is wicked of me to feel so restless after all they have done for me. I should simply be grateful and obey them willingly and gracefully."

"Is that what they tell you?"

"Aye, but it is true and the least they should be able to expect from me."

"Have you no people of your own?"

"None whom I know," she said.

He looked at her, clearly expecting her to say more, but despite their growing intimacy, she felt strangely reluctant to reveal more to him about herself. Instead and rather abruptly, she said, "Zeus seems quite content on your fist."

"Aye, for the moment," he said with a narrow look that told her he knew she was purposely changing the subject.

She feared he meant to quiz her more, but he said only, "We'd best pray that the men searching for me have gone back to England. This would not be a good time for them to reappear." He chuckled again. "They'd scare Zeus."

She glanced at him, thinking it was more likely that they would scare him, but Patrick did not look scared. He looked happy and handsome and . . .

Feeling heat flood her cheeks, she looked quickly away, but her mind's eye retained the picture of him, striding along with the hawk on his fist and his falconer's bag and the loosely coiled creance slung over one shoulder. She had never known anyone like him, and given a real choice, she thought she would rather stride along with him forever than return to her dreary life in the Tower.

"Will you enjoy going to Stirling with the family?" he asked.

"Aye, I like Stirling Castle," she said. "I'll have naught to do with the King, of course, nor would I want to. He seems cruel."

"Jamie?" Patrick chuckled again. "'Tis said he respects all his people."

"But not so long ago he ordered Lady Janet Douglas burned at the stake for a witch!" She shivered, still horrified that anyone could suffer such a dreadful fate.

"Aye, well, she was Angus's sister, and he hates all Angus's lot, that's sure."

Elspeth was silent. Patrick sounded as if he, too, hated

the "Angus lot." Would he hate her if he learned that Angus was her father? She did not think much of Angus either, but would Patrick believe her? Surely her disaffection was not odd, since Angus had given her away, clearly having no more use for her.

Thinking of Angus reminded her of times in her childhood when Drusilla and Jelyan had taunted her. "Since you are an earl's daughter," Drusilla would say, "doubtless you think we should curtsy to you, *Lady* Elspeth." Sometimes they would do so, and once Lady Farnsworth had whipped her bare legs with a willow switch because Drusilla had said Elspeth *insisted* that they curtsy. When Elspeth denied it, Lady Farnsworth had whipped her even harder for lying.

When she was young, they had easily stirred her to tears, but she had learned that her tears only made them tease her more. It had been a long time since either Lady Farnsworth or her daughters had made her cry.

She was taking a chance today, she knew, but surely Patrick would not stay out long. In an hour or so it would be time for supper.

"Here, this is good," he said, snapping her from her reverie.

They had reached a grassy clearing in the woods.

"This meadow is a good place to try Zeus," he said. "You can help again if you will put on your glove and hold him for me."

Obediently she held her gloved fist under Zeus's belly until, with a flap of his wings, he hopped onto it.

"Now then," Patrick said, "hold the free end of the creance so, as I move away and whistle for him. It may take some time, but I think he will fly to me."

Striding to a point about ten feet away, Patrick held out his fist, gave the warbling whistle he used when he fed Zeus, and the hawk flew straight to him.

Visibly astonished, Patick fed Zeus a bit of rabbit liver from his bag.

Delighted, Elspeth exclaimed, "Do you think he would fly to me?"

"Can you whistle?"

"I think so," she said, determined to learn how if it killed her.

"Then I'll teach you his call and we'll try another day," he said. "He should get used to me first, and doubtless for a time he'll be contrary as often as he obeys."

They tried it again several times, and although Zeus did not allow Patrick to call the tune every time, Elspeth could tell that Patick was pleased with him.

As they walked back, she felt a sense of deep contentment. When Patrick slipped his free hand under her elbow as they crossed the burn, steadying her from one stone to the next, she felt as if the warmth of his hand penetrated to her soul.

He did not speak, and she felt no desire to break the silence between them. The only sounds were the bubbling water and woodland birdcalls. Occasionally, Zeus cheeped, but his comments were brief and required no answer.

The contentment lasted until they entered the courtyard.

"Her ladyship be looking for ye, Elspeth," the guard at the gate told her with a sympathetic look.

Her spirits sank, but when the guard was out of earshot, she said calmly to Patrick, "Thank you for letting me help."

"She can't murder you," he said. "Just bow your head and let the flood of her words flow over you. And don't, for mercy's sake, be impertinent to her."

"I am never—" Encountering his direct, knowing gaze, she broke off with a rueful smile. "Well, hardly ever," she amended.

"Tidy your hair before you go to her and put on a fresh apron," he said. "And don't look at me as if you'd like to slap me. 'Tis good advice I give you. I know, for I've faced such confrontations more than once myself."

Lingering annoyance with him blunted her fear of what lay ahead, and the knowledge that he was right sent her in search of her comb and a fresh apron. Then, feeling as if she were armed for battle, she went to Lady Farnsworth's solar, where she found not only her ladyship but also Drusilla and Jelyan.

The scene that followed might well have elicited impertinence had Patrick not warned her to avoid it, because Lady Farnsworth had learned not only that she had slipped outside the wall but also that she had not finished hemming the gown that Martha had told her to hem. Her ladyship, never at a loss for words, hurled past and present transgressions at her like darts at a target.

Elspeth bowed her head and tried to imagine the words as no more than harmless water, albeit the flood that Patrick had described. She tried to imagine him standing passive before such a tirade but could not. She had seen his eyes flash at much less and doubted that he would be so submissive.

"Have you naught to say for yourself, girl?"

Her attention thus sharply recalled, she said, "No, madam. I beg your pardon and will certainly finish hemming your gown straightaway."

"Where did you go?" Drusilla demanded.

Elspeth glanced at her, surprised that she did not know. It occurred to her then that in all Lady Farnsworth had said, she had not mentioned the falconer. Was it possible that they did not know she had been with him?

"I walked in the woods," she said.

"You should not do that," Drusilla snapped. "Tell her she must not, mother."

"She'll have no time for such," Lady Farnsworth said. "She'll have time only for her chores. You will forgo supper to finish hemming that gown, Elspeth."

"Aye, madam," Elspeth said quietly.

Drusilla was not satisfied. "She should be punished more severely!"

"Hush," Lady Farnsworth said. "Your voice is giving me a headache."

Suppressing satisfaction that certainly bordered on the impertinence Patrick had warned her against, Elspeth bobbed a curtsy and made her escape.

Nell Percy's mind was on escape, too, and she was taking care to keep out of her brother's way while trying to learn all she could about what was happening. Thus, she was quietly sewing in a corner of the great hall while the men talked.

It was the sixth day, and not only had Angus's men failed in the previous five to lay hands on the runaway spy, but Angus had received a message from King Henry, a complaint that Scotland's James continued to defy him. Angus was to drop everything, his majesty said, and get word to loyal Douglas followers to meet the English army south of Berwick. Henry would grant the Scots safe passage.

Angus being Angus and having small regard for laws of any sort, he dismissed the King's messenger with a curt reply and when his own men reported failure in the west march, gave it as his opinion that a six-day limit for catching spies was utterly unacceptable.

"Go back and tell them to search until they unearth that damned scoundrel," he ordered the rider who had brought him the report.

Both his host and Lord Dacre objected at once.

"Don't even contemplate such a thing," Dacre begged. "If we overstep the bounds, those dreadful Scots will do the same and insist that they have every right to create riot and ruction wherever they choose."

"They do as they choose anyway," Angus snapped.

"Aye, perhaps, but if we break the laws by which we agree to abide, we sound like hypocrites when we insist that they abide by them," Dacre pointed out.

Angus would have ignored Dacre, for whom he had small respect and who showed no interest in marrying his heir to Angus's half sister, but when Renwick made the same argument, Angus subsided into smoldering, silent anger.

Nell observed these familiar symptoms warily. His mood would not improve when his men returned the next day empty-handed, as she was sure they would, because if they had not found Patrick yet, they would not find him. He was free, and freedom was a wonderful, albeit fragile condition. She had enjoyed a brief period of it herself two years ago, and she wanted to enjoy it again. To do so, she would have to escape as Patrick had, and before Angus could arrange a new marriage for her.

To that end, she went in search of Jane and found her in her own room, mending one of Nell's smocks. She continued with the task even when Nell said briskly, "We must pack my things at once, Jane."

"Indeed, mistress," Jane said placidly. "I had not heard that his lordship meant to depart, but I know that a messenger came from York, so it is not . . ."

"He does not mean to leave," Nell interjected, "although Henry did order him to do so. Still, he will go any day now, and we may not get another chance."

Jane pursed her lips but did not speak.

"Freedom, Jane, just think of it! After Percy's death, I learned that a widow has much more freedom than a female in any other position. I have money of my own and my jewelry, and although the Percys control my money, they will disburse it to me even if I reside in Scotland. There are laws, Jane, for widows."

"Truly?"

"Aye, truly," Nell said. "But only if I can prevent my horrid brother from marrying me off again. If he does, my new husband will control even my allowance from the Percy family."

"Then I think we shall do better without a new husband," Jane said.

Nell grinned. "Just so," she said.

Elspeth finished the hemming and her evening chores and went to bed. She was fast asleep, dreaming she was rapidly approaching the castle on the mist-shrouded hill, when she was startled awake by a hand gripping her shoulder.

"Lass, wake up! Searchers have entered the castle."

The room was pitch dark but the quiet voice was unmistakable.

"Patrick!"

"Aye," he said. "One man stands outside the postern door at the end of the corridor, and several more are crawling around inside. I dare not go upstairs, I dare not go outside, and they'll search every chamber. Can you hide me in here?"

Fear for him swept through her. "Where? I've only that small table and the chest I keep my clothes in, and you are too big to fit under the one or in the other."

Male voices sounded in the corridor.

"Your bed," he said tersely.

"There is no room! 'Tis just a straw pallet under a few sheepskins."

"They won't know what it usually looks like," he said.

"If I climb under the sheepskins and you lie atop me with your quilt over all, they will not see me."

The thought of him in bed with her was disconcerting enough to silence her, but even as she began to get up, the voices stopped.

"Where is Zeus?" she asked.

"Cursing loudly on a makeshift perch in my chamber. I warrant they are with him now. They'll not harm him, but if someone thinks to tell them I never leave him alone, they'll grow more suspicious than ever when they cannot find me."

She could hear the voices again.

"They're coming, lass. Quickly now, get up!"

She was wearing only her smock, but she stilled her nerves, got up quickly, and helped him pull the heavy fleeces off the straw pallet beneath them. As he was drawing the first fleece over himself, she heard voices in the corridor.

"Hurry," he said. "Throw the other ones on me and then lie down so it looks as if you are curled atop your pallet as usual. Spread the quilt over yourself."

She did as he told her, lying on her side as she normally did. She felt him shift beneath her, either trying to make himself more comfortable under her weight or because she had poked him with an elbow or a foot. It occurred to her that his booted feet might be hanging out at the end, but there was not enough light to see, and she dared not get up again to look anyway.

The voices were louder now, and the accompanying feminine shrieks told her that the searchers were in the cook's chamber next door. She could hardly breathe, and she could feel herself trembling.

"Easy, lass," he murmured. "Ha' fortitude."

"Quiet, they'll hear you!"

The door flew open, banging back on its hinges, and the orange glow of torchlight touched her eyelids.

She stiffened, keeping her eyes shut.

"Faith, lads, look wha' I ha' found!" The voice was gravelly, its English accent that of a common henchman.

Hoping she looked as if they had wakened her from a deep sleep, she opened her eyes to find a man standing over her with a torch. As she took in his rough, soldierly appearance, two others crowded in behind him, filling her tiny chamber.

She swallowed, but even so, her voice sounded unnaturally high and tremulous as she said, "Wh-what do you want?"

"A good question, that," the spokesman said, leering at her. He wore some sort of livery and carried a sheathed sword at his left side.

The thought of what that sword could do to Patrick made her shudder.

"You should not be here," she said.

"Get up, lass. Let's ha' a look at ye."

"She looks tae be right bonny," one of the others said. "Better than them other two besoms. Pull off that coverlet, Forster, and let's see does the rest o' her look as bonny as the wee bit we can see."

Realizing that if they pulled off the quilt, they might find Patrick, she gathered her dignity and said, "You need not snatch me from my bed like horrid ruffians. I will get up if I must. But who are you, and why are you here?"

"We be men o' Midgeholme wi' permission from Sir Hector Farnsworth tae search this tower from ramparts tae kitchens," the one called Forster said.

"But what do you seek?" she said as she carefully sat up and swung her feet to the floor.

"I seek a damned treacherous villain," Forster growled.

"Mercy! Who?"

On the pallet, even sitting on Patrick, she was low to the ground, but standing made her feel awkward and even more vulnerable. All three intruders stared openly at her breasts, barely concealed beneath her thin smock, but she could not stop them and it would at least divert their attention from the pallet.

Forster had not bothered to answer her last question. His gaze remained fixed on her breasts, and apparently the sight had enthralled his powers of articulation.

"Ye dinna speak like a serving wench, lass," one of the others said.

Warily, she ignored him and continued to watch Forster.

He reached out an ungloved hand to touch her.

She stepped back, turning as she did so that her back would be to the rear wall and not the pallet.

"There is no one in here, as you can see," she said, striving to sound calm.

"Dinna run from me, lass," Forster said. "I willna harm ye. Ha' ye heard aught o' one Sir William Smythewick, a traitorous spy?"

"I know of no such person. Surely Sir Hector would be more likely than I to know such a man, although I do not think he would befriend a spy."

"He claims no tae ken the wicked rogue."

She heard more voices. Dear God, she thought, were there more of them?

Certain that Patrick would not remain hidden if the men truly threatened to harm her, and fearing for his safety more than for her own, she allowed her temper to show as she said, "Sir Hector has powerful friends, even in England, and he will take strong exception if you bully his maidservants."

"Aye, he does ha' friends," Forster said. "Our master be one o' them."

"Then you should know that if you touch me, Sir Hector will be displeased."

"Be ye his familiar, then—his particular wench?"

"I am not," she snapped.

One of the other men grabbed her arm and turned her to face him. "Ye're insolent, lass. Dinna speak so tae your betters unless ye want tae feel a hand sharp across your mouth."

Patrick had had to exert himself to that point to remain where he was, but hearing the threat he nearly threw the fleeces aside and leaped to his feet. Only the fact that the lass said nothing to further inflame the man's temper stopped him—that and the fact that he, too, could hear voices approaching in the corridor.

He knew there must be more than three louts hunting for him, and although he would confidently pit his skills against three, he knew he could not hold out long against more. Such a brawl would only make matters worse. Had they simply walked into his chamber and arrested him, it would be different, but he would not allow the lass to suffer for protecting him, and the plain fact was that if they discovered that she had done so, her life would be worth no more than his.

"Easy," he heard the one called Forster say, and he relaxed as the man added, "Doubtless she learned tae talk so pretty because she serves the ladies o' the house. We dinna want trouble wi' Farnsworth."

"Aye, sure," the other said, "but if ye dinna want a kiss, Forster, I'll ha' one afore we finish here, for I've no tasted a bonny lass in months."

Hearing the lass squeal as if someone had hurt her, Patrick tensed.

"By God's body, *what* goes on here?"

Hearing Sir Hector's voice, Patrick grinned with relief. The lass was safe. Whether he was or not remained to be seen, but his sense of humor—never predictable—stirred at the thought of the scholarly Sir Hector facing down the surly, well-armed searchers who had invaded his home.

Forster said quickly, "We told ye, sir, we'd be a-searching o' this whole place. The lass might well know summat about our missing man."

"This lass knows naught that could help you," Sir Hector said testily. "I allowed this search because of my respect for your master, Sir Ralph Renwick, but I have known this lass from her infancy, and she can have no knowledge of the knight you seek. Your behavior here tells me you lack ordinary decency, for even Border reivers rarely manhandle innocent women or children. Therefore, you and your men are no longer welcome at Farnsworth Tower. Begone at once!"

"My master willna be pleased tae hear that ye sent us away," Forster declared belligerently. "Ye may claim his friendship now, but—"

"I have many friends on both sides of the line, as do most Border gentlemen," Sir Hector snapped. "As to Sir Ralph, I know him through my close friendship with Lord Dacre. You may trust me when I say that one word to Dacre will undo any power you possess through Renwick. Do you understand me?"

"Aye, sir, but—"

"I'll hear no 'buts,'" Sir Hector said. "Consider, please, that you brought only twenty men with you and that all of them are inside my wall. My captain has roused more men-at-arms to support the ones you saw when I allowed you to enter. I am willing to let you go now in peace, but only if you go at once."

"But I thought—"

"This conversation is over," Sir Hector said. "Don't be foolish, man," he added warningly. "Keep your sword in its sheath unless you want me to introduce you to my gibbet."

"Ye're nae baron, man. Ye dinna ha' the power o' the pit and gallows."

"I do have a gibbet, however. Mayhap you would like to see it?"

More footsteps, followed by sounds of a brief scuffle, told Patrick that Sir Hector had not come alone. But Forster made one last attempt.

"Me master were told ye would help," the man snarled.

"I am a Borderer like you," Sir Hector said gently. "First, I protect my own."

Chapter 8

Elspeth stood silently, watching Sir Hector's men take the searchers away.

"I apologize, lass," Sir Hector said gently. "Had I known they meant to disturb you, I'd have sent some of my men with them."

"They did not harm me," she said quietly. "But thank you for intervening."

"Aye," he said. "I did swear to protect you, lassie. I always will, but you'd best get back to bed now." Turning, he left the room, shutting the door behind him.

Reminded that she was barefoot and scantily clad, she was grateful for the solid darkness as she turned toward her pallet.

"It is safe now," she said. "They did not even ask about you."

She heard rustling and then he stood in front of her. She could feel his presence, his size, and his strength. Her body tingled in response to the energy she felt from his, and when he touched her arm, she nearly jumped out of her skin.

Instead of the gratitude she expected, however, his first words were harsh. "What were you thinking, to stand before them clad only in your smock?"

"It was all I had on," she said. "Would you have had me take the quilt to wrap around me?"

"Aye, you should at least have taken that. Seeing you so lightly clad might well have stirred them to take even more liberties than they did."

"Had I taken the quilt, 'tis most likely they would have discovered you," she pointed out. "I should think you might forgo your incessant criticism for once and thank me for hiding you."

It was not the first time she had made him feel like a scoundrel, but her rebuke bit deep this time. After a brief silence, he said, "You are right, *mo chridhe*. I should be flogged for putting you in such danger."

The Gaelic endearment slipped out again, as it had more than once since he had met her. She never seemed to notice, however, and he was just as glad. Bad enough that he kept forgetting the damned accent. Trying to explain how a Border lad had come to speak the Gaelic would try even his fertile imagination.

Feeling her tremble, he said, "They are truly gone, lass. Art still afraid?"

"Only of you," she said.

He chuckled and impulsively clasped his hands to her waist and pulled her close. Relishing the feeling of her body pressed against his, he said, "Once again you have saved my life, lassie. I owe you much for your courage."

"They weren't searching for you," she said. "They wanted someone called Sir William Smythewick."

"No matter what name they gave, they were seeking me," he said, slipping his arms around her and holding her tight.

She leaned into his body, savoring its strength and warmth. He was so big, and she felt amazingly safe and content while he held her so. For all she knew, Farnsworth Tower still teemed with Englishmen hunting for him, but he was here and safe, and so was she. She sighed, happy to let him hold her, not caring that it was wrong for him to be in her room, wishing they could remain so forever.

She was not aware that one of his hands had moved until she felt his fingertips beneath her chin, tipping it upward. As she opened her mouth to ask him what he was doing, his lips found hers.

His were warm and soft, and when she tried to close her mouth, his tongue prevented her, thrusting inside, tasting her, exploring the interior of her mouth and sending thrills through her body unlike anything she had felt before.

She moaned, thinking that what they were doing was wicked. It was probably—no, centainly—a sin, and God would punish her, but since she was going to be punished anyway, it could not hurt to savor the moment. She moved her lips against his, and daringly, touched her tongue to his. She had never done such a thing before, had never even thought about putting her tongue in another person's mouth, and yet the sensation that shot through her as she did was pure delight.

One of Patrick's hands was at her waist now, pulling her tight against him. The other was stroking her right arm, and stirred by its touch, she put both arms around him, hugging him back. God would definitely punish her, but maybe in such black darkness, even God could not see what they did. The sacrilegious thought almost made her let go of Patrick to cross herself, but he moved his free hand to the side of her right breast, and the breath stopped in her throat. She could no more have stopped him then than she could have flown up to heaven on a prayer.

He moved his other hand to her back, feeling, exploring. When it slid around her waist to the front, she knew he was looking for her smock laces. He found them, and his fingers tugged before she came to her senses.

"No," she said, putting her hand on his. "You mustn't."

"Ah, lassie, don't stop me now. I've a hunger on me that will not go away."

"Then you should eat something," she said practically.

He chuckled again. "I want to eat you up, sweetheart. I want to taste every inch of your smooth skin, to explore every curve. Would you deny me?"

It occurred to her again how large he was, how strong. If he decided to bed her, she doubted she would be able to stop him. Worse, she was not certain that she wanted to stop him. Although the thought of God's vengeance kept intruding, she was not a particularly religious person. Most Borderers weren't. They changed religions like others changed clothes, donning the expedient, and shedding any beliefs that might stir trouble for them.

These thoughts flitted through her mind while her body responded eagerly to Patrick's caresses. He was kissing her again as if he took her submission for granted. How like a man, she thought as she kissed him back.

When his fingers undid her smock laces, and his bare hand touched her breast, she stiffened, coming to her senses again in a rush of discomfiture. Catching hold of his hand, she said, "Please, no."

Even as she said the words, she assumed they would prove useless. In her world men did as they pleased, and although Patrick was different from most, he was still a man. She did not fear that he would hurt her or force her, just that he would continue because he wanted to and she would find it impossible to resist him. To her astonishment, he took his hand away from her breast at once.

His other hand rested lightly at her waist, and for a moment she had an urge to apologize, to tell him she had not meant it.

Before she could speak, he said gently, "I should have stopped before, sweetheart. Clearly, you are not experienced in such matters, so this is hardly proper payment for your kindness to me this night. I would not knowingly harm you."

"I know," she said softly. Again, the urge swept over her to apologize, at least to explain to him that she had not disliked his touch or his kisses.

Again, before she could speak, he said, "I should go before my desire for you overcomes my good sense. Thank you again, lass. I won't forget this."

Drawing a deep breath, she bit her tongue before she could ask him to stay, but when his hand left her waist, she felt a longing unlike anything she had known before. She did not want him to go.

She heard his footsteps, light thuds on the dirt floor. Then the darkness lightened when he opened the door. Briefly, she saw his dark form outlined against the dim orange glow of a candle or torch in the corridor, and then he began to shut the door, to plunge her room into blackness again.

Just before the door shut, she heard a familiar feminine voice say sharply, "Well, well, and just what mischief have you been up to now, falconer?"

The voice was Drusilla's.

"Mam, Mam, be ye here?" Claud hurried into their little parlor and skidded to a halt when he saw his mother sitting by the fire with her eyes shut. "Mam, wake up, I need ye!"

"Only a dead mortal would sleep through the racket ye're making, ye witless dobby," Maggie said without opening her eyes. "What be amiss now?"

"Everything! Och, I dunno, mayhap nowt's amiss, but I dinna ken what be what anymore, and Lucy said she were bored and left, and I dunno wha' tae do."

"Then calm yourself and tell me what has disturbed ye."

"Well, our Bessie and Sir Patrick ha' feelings for each other, but that screecher Drusilla ha' caught them out together, and the English be still a-looking for him, and likely summat dreadful will happen, and I dinna ken wha' tae do."

"That's all verra clear," she said sarcastically, opening her eyes at last.

"Well, I dinna ken how I can be clear when I dinna ken what's going tae happen. I must do summat. Can ye tell me how tae make yon vixen Drusilla forget what she saw? They were getting on verra well wi'out her."

Maggie stood up, glowering at him in the way that made his knees quake. "I'll no tell ye any such thing. How many times must I tell ye, lad, we do what we can tae make life pleasant for our mortals, but the rules o' the Circle forbid any action significant enough tae alter the course o' their lives."

"But—"

" 'Tis one thing tae guide an arrow on its course, or tidy up a kitchen in the dead o' night, or guide a man's hand when it hovers over his pawn on a chessboard. It even be acceptable tae alter the weather a wee bit if a black storm can be hurried on its way wi'out causing destruction."

"But—"

"Ye canna mend emotions, Claud—not love nor hate nor spite—and ye mustna interfere wi' the doings o' mortals gin ye can avoid it."

"But ye turned back history, ye did, in the Highlands, and

Sir Hector said he would dismiss Patrick if he trifled wi' any maidservant, and our Bessie—"

Maggie raised her chin, saying firmly, "The turning back o' history were different, Claud, as I told ye afore, and we'll no discuss that again."

"But doesna Sir Patrick ken about our Bessie? Could ye no tell her tae tell him who she is so he can—?"

"Sir Patrick kens that his Lady Mackenzie believes her younger sister yet lives, but he kens as well that his master sent searchers throughout the Borders without finding her. He kens nowt o' the treasure or us, and if the lass were tae tell him what she willna believe herself, what d'ye suppose he would say tae her?"

Claud sighed. His imagination did not expand to such visions.

More gently, Maggie said, "Will that Drusilla go straight tae her father?"

"I dinna ken what the leprous witch will do. She hurried off wi'out saying."

"And Sir Patrick?"

"He just looked long at our Bessie's door, then went tae his room, tae bed."

"Then he, at least, does not think anything more will happen before morning," Maggie said. "You would do well, my lad, to get some sleep."

"But—"

"Claud," she said warningly, "recall that I ha' problems o' me own. Nae sooner do I think them wretched Merry Folk will agree tae summat than they fly into a fury again. It be as if some'un be stirring them tae mak' trouble, and if I could find that fell-lurking cur, Jonah Bonewits, I'd ask him do that mischief be his."

"Ye canna find him?"

"Nay, but that be nowt tae shake a leg about. That wretched

quicksand o' deceit oozes from one mischief tae the next wi'out letting anyone share his plot, so I canna just shout his name tae the skies and expect him tae float down tae me."

Claud sighed.

"Nae matter," she said. "I warrant Jonah Bonewits could answer me questions, but 'tis likely I'll no see him again till the next meeting o' the Circle. In the meantime, ye'll keep an eye on our lass, and if I must, I'll take a hand in that."

The sun's rays had not yet touched the eastern horizon when Nell Percy woke Jane Geddes and bade her make haste to dress.

"Angus and the other men have gone to meet the men who were searching the Scottish Borders for that spy," Nell said. "This may be our only chance."

"Mayhap 'tis no such a good notion, m'lady. His lordship . . ." She let the words hang in the air, either unwilling or unable to speak her fears aloud.

"We are going to Scotland, Jane, just as we decided," Nell said firmly. "Now, hurry, for we must take all we can. I've the jewelry Angus let me wear here at Midgeholme, and whilst it will not help to pay our way, for I know not how to sell it, it will add to our consequence once we are safe. I have some money as well." She did not think it necessary to mention that she had taken a sack of coins from Angus's chest as soon as he and his man had left his chamber. The money was as much hers as his, after all, since he kept nearly every penny the Percys sent her.

"But Scotland is far from here, madam."

"Only twenty miles. 'Tis nothing."

"On horseback, perhaps, but if we must walk, carrying—"

"We won't walk," Nell said impatiently. "We have our own horses and we'll take a sumpter pony for our bundles. We'll just say we are riding out. Renwick's people will not stop us, and Angus's men rode out with him, so hurry!"

They were soon ready, and for once all went smoothly. Lady Renwick never rose until long after sunrise, and no one else paid them any heed. The lad who looked after Nell's horse and Jane's, as well, made no objection to saddling them or his own, or to loading the sumpter, and in less time than even Nell had hoped the three riders were passing through the castle gates toward freedom.

When they had gone beyond sight of the ramparts, Nell said matter-of-factly to the lad, "We mean to cross the line, Seth. I want you to come with us, but if you are afraid of Angus, you may ride back and tell them that we rode off and left you."

"His lordship be like tae hang me were I so daft as tae show me face just when he's learned what ye've done," the lad said sagely. "I've kin on the other side I can bide wi' till it be safe tae return. But will they let us cross the line, mistress?"

"They say the road is littered with refugees seeking sanctuay in Scotland from King Henry's obliteration of papists," Nell explained. "If we meet any such, we'll join them. If we don't, we'll simply tell anyone who tries to stop us that we seek sanctuary. It is true enough, God knows," she added under her breath.

She had no illusions. If her brother caught her, he would kill her or sell her into a punitive marriage. Nor could she be certain what awaited her on the other side of the line, for that matter. She had family in Scotland, too, but the only ones who cared about her lived in the distant Highlands, and she dared not seek them out until she had spoken to Jamie and made sure he would welcome her. It occurred to her that she could ride for Dunsithe—she even had clothing there, albeit outdated. But Dunsithe was well to the west of Midgeholme, and she was not sure of the route. Getting to Jamie was safer—she hoped.

The King of Scots was unpredictable. Once he had stood her friend, but his own nobles could not trust him, and Nell certainly knew better than to do so. Indeed, it was a risk that she was returning to Scotland without first seeking his permission to do so, a risk for which she could pay with her life if Jamie chose to be difficult. Baseborn or no, a Douglas was safer outside Scotland than within. Still, she would go to the King. According to Angus, James had told Henry he expected to welcome a second heir any day. With luck, he would be in a generous mood.

The mood in Sir Hector's sanctuary an hour later was tense.

"You must dismiss the falconer," Lady Farnsworth said shrilly. "Indeed, he should be hanged, and Elspeth should be whipped before the entire household for her wanton behavior!"

A shiver of fear sliced through Elspeth's body. She avoided Patrick's gaze as Lady Farnsworth went on and on, furiously shredding their characters.

She had expected to be hailed before Sir Hector soon after hearing Drusilla's voice in the corridor, but if Drusilla had reported her encounter with Patrick right after it happened, her father had not acted then. Elspeth had remained on tenterhooks in her bedchamber, sleeping little and restlessly.

Arising at her usual time, she had seen to her early morning chores, but the summons had come before she went to the ladies' bedchambers, and she knew that they had not yet broken their fast. She stood apart from the others, between Sir Hector's writing table and the open window, through which slanting early-morning sunlight spilled across the polished oak floor.

Not wanting to meet anyone's eye until she had some idea of what would happen to her and to Patrick, she gazed at the familiar, cluttered writing table, wishing she could hide beneath it as she had when she was small. She was aware of everyone else, nonetheless, and could see each one, albeit obliquely.

Jelyan and Drusilla flanked their mother, who stood directly in front of Sir Hector's writing table, her massive red wig quivering with her rage. As she declared her notion of what Elspeth's punishment should be, she pounded the table with a fist to emphasize her feelings, and she pounded again and again as she gave vent to them. Not that they needed emphasizing. Her fury was plain for everyone to hear.

Patrick stood near the closed door. Having been summoned from the mews, he held Zeus on his gloved fist, and although the hawk was hooded, it looked edgy and unhappy. Indeed, Elspeth thought, it looked as if it felt exactly as she did.

Apparently, Lady Farnsworth had said much of what she was saying now before they had gathered in the sanctuary, because Sir Hector remained quiet, letting her spew words at him until she had said all she wanted to say.

When at last she fell silent, he waited a beat, as if to let her speak again if she had not quite finished. The silence spurred Drusilla to say, "Father, my lady mother is right. Elspeth must be punished for her wickedness, and the falconer, too."

"Be silent, Drusilla," her father said sternly.

Drusilla looked shocked, but Jelyan, standing beside her with eyes downcast, appeared to repress a smile.

Just as sternly, Sir Hector said, "Elspeth, what have you to say about this?"

"Nothing, sir."

"Do you understand what they accuse you of doing?"

"Not exactly, sir, no."

"Drusilla declares that she saw the falconer come out of your bedchamber last night after I left you. Is that so?"

"Yes, sir, it is."

Drusilla exclaimed, "You see how shameless and insolent she is, Father! She does not even try to deny it!"

"This," Lady Farnsworth said with a dagger look at Elspeth, "is how the wicked girl repays us for sheltering her all these years."

Ignoring her, Sir Hector said evenly, "Drusilla, before you accuse others, you might consider how you will answer me when I ask you to explain what you were doing in the kitchen corridor at such a late hour. I mean to do so directly after you have broken your fast. You will return here to me then."

Flushing deeply, Drusilla bit her lower lip.

"It is not our daughter who is at fault, husband," Lady Farnsworth snapped. "Must I remind you—?"

"You need remind me of nothing, madam. I would ask you, however, how it is that a daughter of yours deems it proper to be walking unattended after midnight in a corridor generally peopled only by servants."

Silenced at last, Lady Farnsworth folded her lips tightly together.

Beside her, Jelyan clasped her hands at her waist, smiled sweetly, and said in a gently curious tone, "Then it was all right, Father, what Elspeth did? I thought—"

"It was not all right, Jelyan," Sir Hector interjected. "It is never all right for an innocent girl to entertain a man in her bedchamber."

His words ended on a note of exasperation, and the note was still there when he said, "If you choose not to explain, Elspeth, you leave me no choice but to—"

"The lass but did me a kindness, Sir Hector."

Gasping, Lady Farnsworth turned toward Patrick, and

everyone else looked as shocked as she did to hear him speak. Clearly, they had assumed he was there only to accept his dismissal.

Gruffly, Sir Hector said, "I do not doubt that you think it a kindness, but I warned you about making free with the lasses here."

"I didna mean that the way ye think," Patrick said, affecting his heavy Borderer's accent.

"How so, then?" Sir Hector demanded.

"I were on the stairs by the hall when them chaps demanded tae search the place, and I recognized two o' them from me time in England. They be nae friends o' mine, sir, and I ken fine they'd do me a mischief an they could. I dinna like fratching, so I asked the lass tae hide me. She did, and that be all there be about it."

"But how absurd," Drusilla protested. "There is no place in Elspeth's bedchamber for a grown man to hide."

"Clearly, there must be," Sir Hector said, "since I did not see him there and you say he emerged after I left her."

Elspeth felt heat in her cheeks as she waited for the obvious question, but it did not come. Instead, Sir Hector said to Patrick, "How is that bird coming along?"

"He's a splendid lad," Patrick said, stroking Zeus.

"Do you think he is fit to give the King?"

"I do, and all," Patrick said.

"Then you have done as I bade you, and as I have no cause to doubt your version of what happened last night—"

"Husband!"

"Father!"

"—I shall not dismiss you until you have delivered the hawk to Stirling," Sir Hector went on as if his wife and daughter had not spoken. "However, it will be better for all, I believe, if you leave at once. You may take Small Neddy to help you tend the bird along the way."

"Zeus will need more training afore he'll be fit for his grace," Patrick said.

"Yes, I know, and since you are starting out a few days ahead of us, you will still have time to work with him. Even half trained, I warrant James will like him."

"Am I tae deliver him tae the royal mews then, sir?"

"Nay, you'll await our coming, for I want to present him to James myself. We'll leave on Thursday and should be in Stirling by Saturday."

"Where do I go then?" Patrick asked.

"To the house of my cousin Oscar Farnsworth in St. Mary's Wynd. Come to me before you depart, and I will give you a letter for him and sufficient funds to get you there. You'll have your wages after I give the bird to the King. Now you may leave us." Patrick went, and Elspeth braced herself, bereft now of any support.

Before Sir Hector could speak, Lady Farnsworth said angrily, "He should be flogged, and I certainly hope you do not mean to let Elspeth off so lightly, sir. What she did is unconscionable. I do not care if the devil himself was after the falconer. She had no business to be hiding him in her chamber. Indeed, she must have hidden him in her bed, since there is nowhere else she can have concealed him."

Sir Hector grimaced, but whether his distaste was for his wife's demands or because he had already deduced as much, Elspeth did not know.

He said quietly, "You are right, madam, although I do Elspeth the courtesy of believing that she acted out of innocence. Although you may have thought you were doing a kindness, lass, what you did was wrong. He should not have asked so much of you, but the doing was yours as much as his."

"She must be punished," Lady Farnsworth snapped. "Severely."

"What would you suggest, madam?"

"Well, she certainly cannot go with us to Stirling, not with that man there, too, just waiting for her. Whether you choose to believe him or not, husband—"

"I agree, madam. If the gossips learn of this, and babble, we would all dislike it. Very well, you will remain here, Elspeth. Martha Elliot can serve my ladies, and if she does not suffice, I will hire a town maidservant to assist her. You may go."

"Is she not to be whipped then?" Jelyan asked in her usual sweet voice.

Elspeth did not know which she disliked more, Drusilla's shrillness or Jelyan's false virtue. Both were usually aimed at her undoing.

To her relief, Sir Hector said, "To miss going to court is punishment enough. If you disagree, madam, she can go without her dinner today. She will have to work hard, in any case, to see you all ready to leave by Thursday's dawn light."

Elspeth knew from the look Lady Farnsworth gave her that she would not get dinner, and she doubted that she would get her supper either. None of that mattered, however. What mattered was that she was unlikely ever to see Patrick or Zeus again. That thought brought tears to her eyes.

"Save your weeping until you have something to weep for," Drusilla said as she followed Elspeth from the room. "And take care to mind your manners until we depart, because my mother will not be as lenient with you as she usually is. Your wicked behavior has shocked us all, you ungrateful slut."

Elspeth did not know if they were shocked or not, but she did not doubt that it would behoove her to tread lightly until they left for Stirling.

*Chapter 9*_____

Patrick began his preparations, certain that Sir Hector would expect him to go as soon as he had eaten his midday meal. He had made some preparations already in case his departure occurred more spontaneously than anticipated. Those preparations had not included Zeus, however, so as soon as he reached the mews, he spurred Small Neddy to furious activity, collecting necessities.

"Do I ha' tae go wi' ye, then?"

"Sir Hector said ye should," Patrick said, wondering if the lad would be much use to him. Neddy had taken Zeus in dislike from the first, but they would need rabbits. He realized then that he would need other things, too, and Sir Hector had said the ladies had not broken their fast before the meeting. Doubtless they were all in the hall doing so now, leaving their chambers empty.

On the thought, he leashed Zeus to his perch. Then, emptying the falconer's bag and slinging it over his shoulder, he strode across the yard to the postern door and up the stairs to the floor where he knew Lady Farnsworth's chamber lay. Barely pausing at her door, he opened it quickly and stepped inside, his gaze already fixed on the wardrobe against the opposite wall between the two open windows.

He was halfway across the floor before he realized he was not alone.

"Whatever are you doing here?" Elspeth demanded.

As she spoke, she stepped out from the far side of the tall, curtained bed that occupied much of the wall to his left, and he realized that the half-closed bed curtains had concealed her when he entered. She held an armful of feather bed, and the rest of the bedding was turned down. Clearly, she had been making the bed.

Grinning and shrugging the falconer's bag from his shoulder, he said, "I've come for a bit of thievery. Will you betray me, *mo chridhe*?"

She shook her head, but a smile touched her lips. "Have you no shame, sir? You should not call me your sweetheart. What if someone were to hear you?"

"D'ye speak the Gaelic then, lass?"

She frowned. "The Gaelic? Is that not the language of the Highlands?"

"It is," he said, watching her narrowly. "How is it that you understand me?"

" 'Sweetheart' is broad Scot or English," she said, clearly confused.

"I said *mo chridhe,* though, 'my heart.' "

"Did you? I suppose someone must have told me the meaning sometime or other, and I simply translated it in my mind when I heard it. I do not recall hearing you say it before, though, only 'sweetheart.' "

Impulsively, he dropped the bag and went to her, pulling the bedding away and dropping it to the floor so he could gather her into his arms. "I could say that I came here in search of you, *mo chridhe*. Would you believe me?"

Her lashes fluttered adorably as she put her arms around

him and looked up into his eyes, searching them as if she would find answers to her questions in their depths. "Aye," she said. "I might believe you. *If* you were to say it."

"Well, I won't say it because it would be a lie," he said, still grinning. "I did mean to search for you before I left, to bid you farewell, but the fact is I told you the truth before. In a perfect world, those Englishmen would believe I'd disappeared and cease to look for me. But as you pointed out, I'm too large to travel hereabouts unnoticed. Therefore, if I'm to reach Stirling safely, I may at some point or other need a disguise, so I had it in mind to borrow one of her ladyship's frightful wigs."

She laughed, quickly smothering the sound with a hand clapped over her mouth. "You wouldn't!"

"But it's an excellent notion," he said, gently stroking her arms, delighting in the way just touching her sent waves of heat through his body. It took effort to keep his voice light as he said, "If I see anyone coming who seems threatening, I shall pop the wig on my head and peer down my nose at them until they go away again."

"But you are too big, and even if you shaved off your beard, no one would mistake you for a woman!"

"Nonsense." He kissed the tip of her nose. "Even if someone should think me a particularly ugly lady, no one would insult me by saying so."

"A lady would wear a dress!"

"Aye, sure," he said, " 'tis another wee thing I shall need, and mayhap a handsome bodice and scarf as well. Ha' ye any tae spare?"

She pushed him away and put her hands on her hips. "Art daft, sir?"

"Nay, I swear. Don't run away, lass. I like holding you. You should come with me, I think, for you would be safer

with me than here at Farnsworth without Sir Hector to protect you."

"You *are* daft."

"Nay." He reached for her again, enjoying the way her
face revealed her warring emotions. "You want to come, do
you not, *mo chridhe?*"

"Aye," she said softly. "I'm that wicked, I fear, but I dare
not."

"Why not? I swear I'll protect you."

Her gaze searched his again, and for one wondrous moment he believed she would agree to flee with him. The
thought delighted him even more than he had suspected it
would when the impulse struck him to ask her.

Then, bluntly, she said, "I told you before how it is. I cannot run away when they have sheltered me since I was a
bairn. I owe them my loyalty."

"You owe those bad-mannered shrews naught but the
rough edge of your tongue," he said flatly. "When I think
how monstrously they treat you—"

"I think one of her ladyship's petticoats or skirts might fit
round you," she interjected firmly, "but I do not think she
has a bodice that will. Even she is smaller than you are
around the chest. She is also a good deal shorter than you
are."

"I borrowed a long cloak that one of the men-at-arms left
lying about."

Her eyebrows arched. "Borrowed?"

"Aye, well, he'll not miss it soon enough to reclaim it,
and although it is short for me, no one will notice that if I
wear it over a skirt. Find me that petticoat now, *mo chridhe,*
and the wig and a scarf, so we may continue our conversation."

"We have no conversation to continue," she said. "You

have not thought, sir, and in your situation, not to think things out carefully is foolhardy."

"Fortitude will see us through," he said. "I think well on my feet, and I promise that if you come with me, I'll keep you safe."

"By pretending that I am your daughter, I expect."

"My daughter!" He stared at her, wondering how she could say such a thing.

"Aye, or perhaps when you wear her ladyship's wig you can pretend to be my tirewoman. With a hawk on your fist, no doubt, a very odd creature indeed."

"Lass—"

"No," she said more firmly than before. Her hands were no longer on her hips, but when he reached for her, she eluded his grasp. "I'll fetch those clothes," she said, "and the wig. Then you must be off before anyone comes."

She hurried to the wardrobe, flinging it open and reaching for a basket on the high shelf inside. As he moved to help her, he heard the sound of approaching steps.

"Someone's coming up the stairs," he muttered.

"Quick!" She pushed the basket back where it belonged. "Get onto the bed and lie across the very top of it."

Without question, he flung himself onto the straw matting that covered the bed ropes and rolled to lie across the top with the falconer's bag tucked under him.

Swiftly she scooped up the featherbed and flung it atop him, flipping the rest of the bedding up over it and pummeling it into place over and around him as if he were some sort of long bolster.

When the latch clicked, she was smoothing the coverlet, and he knew his feet were sticking out on the side nearest the door. He dared not move though, and could only hope the bed hangings concealed his boots from the person entering the room.

As the door opened, Elspeth grabbed the nearest bed curtain and yanked it closed, startling a spider from its web and sending it scurrying. The curtains at the foot were open, of course, but at least now sunlight could not shine from the nearest window across the head of the bed.

"Mercy, are ye still here?" Martha Elliot demanded as she bustled in.

"I was delayed this morning, as you must know, Martha, and when I shook the hangings just now, I disturbed a spider. I must be sure that there are no more. Mayhap you will say that with her ladyship leaving so soon for Stirling, I need not waste my time with such—"

"I'll say no such thing," Martha Elliot declared. "Ye're in enough trouble without her ladyship being wakened in the middle of the night by a spider strolling across her face. See that ye shake all the bed curtains, and shake them well!"

"I'd be quicker if you would help me," Elspeth said, grabbing an end curtain and pulling it shut, then reaching for its mate.

"Ye ha' no need for my assistance with such a menial task," Martha said, moving to the wardrobe without another glance at the bed. "Just see that ye dinna dawdle. There's much yet to be done. I came only to collect two more of her ladyship's skirts. She thought she didna want them, but she has changed her mind."

Elspeth moved to the other side of the bed and reached to shake the curtain there before she saw that it barely concealed Patrick's feet. Her throat tightened at the thought of what could have happened had Martha had a more generous nature.

Watching obliquely as the woman took one skirt from the

wardrobe and reached for a second one, Elspeth shook the curtain wildly, surprised at how much dust had accumulated in the two days since she had last done so. At the end of the bed, she repeated the action, sending another cloud of dust into the air.

Coughing, Martha exclaimed, "Mercy on us! I hope ye take time after everyone has gone to give these rooms a thorough cleaning!"

"I will," Elspeth said as Martha bustled out and shut the door.

The minute it was shut, she flew to pull back the bedding. "Oh, please, sir, hurry. I do not think she'll come back, but I've never been so frightened in my life!"

"You!" Patrick exclaimed, sitting up and scrambling to his feet. "How do you think I felt when you asked if she would help you?"

"I knew she would not. Indeed, I hoped it would make her leave at once, because even Martha Elliot is bound to feel a stab of guilt if she stands by scolding whilst I struggle to shake these dusty hangings."

"Well, I had no way to know that," he said. "I was shaking enough to set the whole bed atremble, expecting that woman to grab hold of the bed hangings and set up a screech when she saw my boots sticking out of her precious mistress's bed."

Elspeth chuckled as she hurried to the wardrobe. Snatching the wig basket from the shelf, she pulled out an older red one that she hoped her ladyship would not want to take with her to Stirling. Thrusting it into his hands, she pulled a black skirt, a pattern scarf, and a red flannel petticoat from the wardrobe.

Handing these items to him as well, she said, "Take these, but truly, sir, you must get out of here. As it is, I do not know how you imagine you can just walk downstairs and outside without anyone stopping you to ask your business."

His impudent grin flashed as he stuffed the items into the bag, which bulged at the seams when he strapped it shut. "I need go down only one flight of stairs, for I mean to go to Sir Hector and ask for that letter and the money he promised me."

She stared at him. "You dare to do that whilst you carry his wife's wig and clothing in your falconer's bag! What if he demands to see what you have in there?"

"He will not," Patrick said, catching hold of her and pulling her close. "Now, lassie, kiss me before I go. I want to savor the taste of your lips on mine as I speak to Sir Hector."

She kissed him willingly, trying not to think about how much she would miss him. His lips were warm and demanding, and his arms wrapped tightly around her. Her body responded to his, wantonly pressing against him, and she would have let him kiss her forever had she not feared that someone else would come in. At last, she pushed him away, saying more fiercely than she had intended, "Take care!"

"Aye, I will, and you, too, sweetheart. I'll not leave until I have finished my dinner, so if you should change your mind—"

"I won't. I can't!" Feeling tears pricking her eyelids, she said, "Go!"

He did, and she stood staring at the door, letting the tears trickle down her cheeks. She knew little more about him than she had known when he surprised her in the woods, but what she had learned told her he was no common falconer. Not only did he frequently forget to speak like a Borderer but there was too much confidence in the way he carried himself and the way he had spoken to Sir Hector that morning, and for that matter, the way he spoke to her. Had he not been fleeing the English like any common felon, she might mistake him for a gentleman.

"Aye, and what if he is? Would ye go wi' him then, lass?"

Startled nearly out of her wits at hearing an unfamiliar female voice in a room she had believed empty, Elspeth spun around but saw nothing out of the ordinary. Puzzled and not a little frightened, she peered more carefully around the room as she said, "Who spoke to me? Show yourself at once!"

"Aye, sure, and ye'll see me if ye'll only look this way."

Realizing that the voice came from the bed, she whisked open the hangings at the foot and gave a cry of astonishment at the sight of a large, golden wildcat curled in the middle of the coverlet. As she jumped back in fright, she saw a plump little woman take form, two-thirds the size of the cat, nestling against its furry side. She wore a green cloak over a gray and black dress, and she sat with her legs stretched in front of her, her black-booted feet crossed neatly at the ankles.

The hairs on the back of Elspeth's neck tingled, and she could not seem to move or speak. Where had the odd creatures come from? She shut her eyes tight, and then opened them again. Both creatures were still there.

The little woman's eyes twinkled.

"Mercy," Elspeth said, finding her voice at last, "who are you?"

"I be Maggie Malloch, nobbut that'll mean much tae ye."

"It does not. How did that dreadful cat get in here?"

"I brought it wi' me, o' course."

"But how did *you* get in?"

"I just popped in, as ye saw. The cat willna harm ye, but we shouldna waste time talking about that, for it takes a deal o' energy for me tae stay visible."

"Visible!" The tingling sensation increased. Her fingers felt numb.

The little woman nodded. "If ye'll be kind enough tae listen, I'll tell ye why I've come, and then I'll pop off again."

"Do you mean to say you can disappear?"

"Aye, but now if ye dinna mind—"

"Will the wildcat disappear with you?"

"Aye, o' course it will. Didna I just say it takes a deal o' energy tae remain visible? D'ye think it takes less tae show ye the wee cat?"

"He does not seem so wee to me," Elspeth said. "Moreover, if it takes such a deal of effort to make the cat visible, why do you bother?"

"Aye, well, at least ye understand. Most mortals dinna see that."

"Mortals?" The tingling at the back of Elspeth's neck turned icy. Her stomach clenched, and she wished Patrick would return.

"Aye, mortals." Maggie Malloch grinned at her. "I let ye see the cat, because if I first appear wi'out him, folks tend tae fear me. Since they fear wildcats more, when they see me control it, they fear me less. Ye're no scared o' me, are ye, lass?"

"No," Elspeth said, realizing that her fears had vanished. "Are you . . . ? That is, I have heard of wee people, but I have never met one before, so . . . ." She paused.

"Aye, well, now ye have," Maggie said cheerfully.

"Elspeth! Elspeth, are you still in here?"

Startled and recognizing Drusilla's voice, Elspeth turned warily toward the bedchamber door as it opened, then glanced back at the bed.

Maggie and the wildcat had vanished.

"Martha said you might still be in here, but I did not believe it," Drusilla said in her customary shrill, accusing tone. "I should think you had had enough trouble for one day. Why is that wardrobe door standing open?"

"Because I have not shut it," Elspeth said. "What do you want, Drusilla?"

"My mother and Martha want you in the solar. Mother has decided she needs two more of her bodices let out before we leave."

"Very well, I'll come straightaway," Elspeth said with a sigh.

"Did ye see the lass, Mam?" Brown Claud asked when he found Maggie pacing angrily back and forth in their tiny parlor. "What did she say?"

"Aye, I saw her," Maggie said, "but I dinna ken what be the right thing tae do. She has enemies, as we ken, but some be more powerful than others, mayhap more powerful than we be."

"Nae one be more powerful than ye, Mam," Claud said confidently.

"Lad, ye'd best ken the truth of it," Maggie said grimly. "Nae matter how strong a body or spirit be, there be always another more powerful. Never forget that, lest ye rue the day or cause harm tae them ye're meant tae protect."

"But the most powerful in our world all serve the Circle," Claud said. Then, remembering, he exclaimed, "That Jonah Bonewits! Be he the one, Mam?"

"Aye, he has great power," Maggie said. "Jonah be a great shape-shifter, so he could be in this room wi' us now, and we'd never feel his presence."

"But ye can change shape, too, Mam. I ha' seen ye do it."

"Aye, I can," she agreed, "but I've no had as much practice as Jonah. I've other powers greater than his, but his shape-shifting makes him a fierce adversary."

"Then ye'd better practice more," Claud declared.

"Aye, well, I mean tae find out what mischief he be planning, but for a time I'll keep me eye on our lass," Maggie said grimly. "As for ye, Claud, I want ye tae learn more about that lass ye met, the one that told ye where tae find her."

Astonished and delighted, Claud said, "Aye, Mam, I'll do that verra thing!"

Patrick was nearly ready to leave. He had hoped the lass would come to the mews to bid him farewell but was not surprised that she had not. Her duties were many and filled her time, and the screecher would doubtless be watching her.

He gazed around the shed, making sure he had forgotten nothing he would need. Sir Hector had given him sufficient funds and had written a letter that he was to give to his cousin, Oscar Farnsworth of St. Mary's Wynd. Patrick would need the letter, because regardless of what his own plans required, he was committed now to delivering Zeus safely.

His gaze came to rest on the figure of Small Neddy slumped on a stool near the perches, and easily reading the lad's emotions, he said, "Ye dinna want tae go wi' me, do ye, lad?"

Neddy looked up. "I ha' nae choice. The master said I were tae go."

"Aye, but he'll need someone here tae look after his other birds," Patrick said. "Ye'll do that better than anyone else, will ye no?"

"Aye, for ye showed me all I must do, but Sir Hector did say—"

"If I say ye're tae stay, ye'll stay," Patrick said firmly.

Neddy straightened. "Aye," he said. "Even Sir Hector

wouldna think I could make ye take me. Nae one could make ye do summat ye didna want tae do."

With a rueful chuckle, Patrick kept his thoughts about that to himself, saying only, "Come now, and help me finish lashing the pony's pack."

"Aye, I will, that!" The boy leaped up as if he had cast a heavy burden aside. In the yard, he yanked on the ropes that held the sumpter pony's pack in place, checking each knot and pulling to be sure the load would not shift.

When the job was done to the boy's satisfaction, Patrick clapped him fondly on the shoulder. "Perhaps someday ye'll want tae see more o' the world, lad."

"Aye, but for now, I'm content."

Patrick went in to fetch Zeus, checking to see that the hawk had not loosened his hood, a trick Zeus had deftly managed the day before. Outside again, with the hawk on his fist, he mounted and let Neddy hand him the pony's lead rein.

"Go wi' God, Patrick Falconer," the lad said, waving as he rode away.

Ten minutes later, as he rode over the first hill with Zeus quiet on his fist and the pony clip-clopping behind, it struck him forcibly that he might never see the lass again. He had come to like her, even to depend on her help with Zeus, but he knew that was not the primary reason he would miss her. The deep sense of emptiness inside him had evolved from much more than that.

He felt as if he had known her for years instead of just a few days, and the realization struck him that the time he had spent in her company amounted to only a few hours. He could not count the nights she had walked with the bird, because he had slept while they walked.

It was his own fault, too, that he would not see her at Stirling. Not that he would have had much time for her there. His master awaited him. Indeed, both masters, because for the past eight months he had served two, with Sir Hector making a third if anyone were keeping an accurate count.

She probably blamed him—and rightly, too—for Sir Hector's ordering her to stay at Farnsworth while the rest of the family enjoyed the delights of Jamie's court. Patrick had not found the King's court particularly delightful, but he knew that his opinion was tainted by the circumstances that had last taken him there.

Doubtless she was vexed, but at least she did not hate him. She had made it plain that she wanted to leave with him. Only her foolish loyalty had stopped her.

That thought stuck uncomfortably in his mind. Loyalty was not foolish, and not only did a child owe loyalty to the family that raised her but a maidservant owed loyalty to her master. Had he not risked his life out of loyalty to the Mackenzies of Kintail? He had no business condemning her for her loyalty to the Farnsworths.

When Zeus cheeped, making a pathetic sound like a kitten's mewing, Patrick shook himself from his reverie and began to talk to the hawk instead.

"Doubtless you think I'm a fool, but I feel as if I've known her forever." Zeus made no comment, but his silence did not trouble Patrick.

"My sister Bab would think me a fool for letting my thoughts dwell at such length on a maidservant," he went on, "but I've an odd, protective nature where lasses are concerned. That's all this is, I'm sure. It is not as if there could be any grand future in the relationship. She is a maidservant, and I am a MacRae, sworn to serve the Mackenzies of Kintail. She owes her duty to Farnsworth and I owe mine to Kintail and my family, and I am expected to marry well. Moreover, I am dutybound to carry out this mission of mine before I give thought to aught else."

Zeus mewed again, clearly agreeing with him.

Elspeth was counting the hours, certain that if the family did not leave soon, she would commit murder.

She was not certain which of them she would kill first, but the thought of her ladyship stretched lifeless on the solar floor was a vision that made her cross herself quickly. Surely, it was a sin even to think such a thing, but that made the thought no less delicious. Even more delicious was the thought of Drusilla disappearing into thin air just as Maggie Malloch had. Indeed, she would much rather it had been Drusilla who disappeared. She wanted to talk more with Maggie.

All her life she had heard tales of the wee folk. One could not attend a Truce Day, a wedding, a market day, or any other gathering without hearing stories about them. The fairies and the brownies who tended kitchens through the night and took offense if someone offered them clothing—such characters filled song and story throughout the Borders, but she had not known before now that they were real.

She would not offer Maggie anything, because she did not want the little woman to take offense. Maggie was the most interesting thing that had happened to her at Farnsworth Tower except, of course, for Patrick.

As she toiled through chores that seemed unending and ten times more onerous than usual, she thought often of him and wished she had had the courage to leave with him. Although she told herself that it had taken greater courage to stay, she had begun to think that loyalty and obedience were highly overrated qualities.

Indeed, she doubted that Patrick's loyalty to her, if he felt any, would last beyond his arrival in the busy royal burgh of Stirling. That thought was depressing.

"Elspeth, pay attention to what you are doing," Drusilla snapped.

Recalled to her senses, she realized that she had carried a pile of laundered and ironed shifts and petticoats up to the young ladies' chamber without giving a thought to what she was doing or where she was going. Drusilla sat on the bench in the window embrasure, sorting threads on a white cloth in her lap, and Elspeth had plopped the pile of folded laundry down right beside her.

"I beg your pardon, Drusilla," she said. "I was air-dreaming."

Drusilla folded the cloth with the threads inside and stood, saying, "I have decided that you should address me as Mistress Drusilla."

"Why? I have never done so before."

"Because it is the proper way for a maidservant to address her betters, that's why. We are Mistress Drusilla and Mistress Jelyan. See that you remember."

"I have called you Drusilla since I first came here," Elspeth said, her voice rising as some hitherto unknown demon took possession of her tongue. In a tone nearly as sharp as Drusilla's she said, "I will call you Drusilla until you marry, because you are *not* my mistress. If you desire any greater degree of respect from me, you should treat me more courteously."

Drusilla's angry slap nearly knocked her off her feet.

Clapping a hand to her stinging cheek, she felt a strong temptation to strike back, but even as her free hand flew up, Lady Farnsworth said harshly from the doorway, "Do not dare to strike her, Elspeth! Whatever is the meaning of this?"

As she spun to face her ladyship, the enormity of what she had said and nearly done silenced her and sent a chill of fear through her body.

Chapter 10 _____

Her ladyship said, "I have no time to punish you now, Elspeth, but I shall certainly speak of this incident to Sir Hector, and I promise you, he will not be as lenient as he was over the business with that dreadful falconer."

"No, madam," Elspeth said. "I . . . I am dreadfully sorry."

"Indeed, and so you should be. I have told Cook you are to be at her beck and bay whilst we are gone, but see that you do not shirk your own duties. Since you will not have to wait on Drusilla or Jelyan, it will be a nice holiday for you. Now, go and see if Martha has any additional tasks for you to attend to."

"Yes, madam," Elspeth said, thankful to escape immediate punishment. Nevertheless, she scarcely had a moment to herself for the rest of the afternoon or evening. Martha Elliot had numerous tasks for her, and Drusilla and Jelyan changed their minds almost hourly, demanding that things already packed be unpacked and that things they had been certain only an hour before they would not take, they would take, until Elspeth could cheerfully have throttled them all.

In addition to these annoyances, she had to endure their discussions of the entertainments the ladies expected to enjoy during their sojourn at Stirling, for all three were excited about returning to the King's court. They had visited the court each spring for several years and enjoyed themselves enormously. Elspeth had also enjoyed those trips, and she was disappointed that she would miss Stirling this year. She would miss Sir Hector, too, but she would not miss Drusilla or Jelyan.

"I warrant even the King himself will take note of your red court dress," Jelyan said to her sister as Elspeth repacked their sumpter baskets for what seemed like the hundredth time.

"Aye, and mayhap we shall find knights of our own at the celebration ball," Drusilla said, laughing. "It is high time for Father to choose husbands for us."

"It is well past time," Jelyan said sweetly. "You are nearly twenty, Drusilla. You should have married years ago."

Drusilla shrugged. "You are but a year younger, Jelyan. Moreover, I have yet to meet any gentleman who interests me, and our father will not force me to wed just any man who asks for my hand. In truth, I am content here for the present."

"Aye, because you know that no husband will be as kind as our father or as willing to let you do as you please," Jelyan said shrewdly. "I do want to marry, however, and until now, the only such eligible men I have met are those we have met at Stirling, but Mother will not allow us to be alone with any of them."

Elspeth knew that Jelyan had set her cap at more than one young man the previous year, but Lady Farnsworth had high notions of what her daughters required in the way of husbands, and her ideal suitor had not yet presented himself.

The rest of the day passed quickly despite the extra work, or perhaps because of it, and if she had little time to think, she spent nearly all of it thinking of Patrick and wondering where he was now and what he was doing. When at last she made her way to her bedchamber, she paused to look into his empty one. The hearth was cold, the straw pallet bare.

Doubtless Cook or the kitchen maid had taken his blankets as extras for themselves.

With a sigh, she carried her taper into her room and shut the door.

"At last, lass, we can talk a bit!"

Although she had been hoping that Maggie Malloch would appear again, the voice startled her. Holding the candle high, she said, "Where are you?"

"Here," Maggie said, and peering into the shadows, Elspeth saw her nestled in a fold of the quilt on her pallet. The little woman appeared to grow then, right before her eyes, until she was the same size she had been earlier. This time she held an odd implement in one plump hand. It looked like a tiny white bowl on the end of a slender, round, white stick. White smoke curled upward from the bowl.

"What is that thing?" Elspeth asked curiously.

"'Tis called a pipe, and it comes from a distant land, but one day they will be as common as dirt hereabouts, 'cause puffin' on one gives a body pleasure."

Eyeing the implement warily, Elspeth said, "You did not bring the wildcat."

"Nay, I dinna need him now. Set your candle in the dish and sit ye down." Maggie patted the quilt with her free hand. "Ye must be nigh asleep as ye stand."

"Aye, I am." Dripping wax into the dish, Elspeth stood the candle in it and held it until the wax set. Still wary, she moved to stand by the pallet, looking down at the little woman. "You won't disappear if I sit by you?"

Maggie put the pipe into her mouth, drew on it, took it out, and blew a stream of smoke into the air. "Ye said ye ha' nae fear o' me, lass."

Elspeth nodded. "I said that."

"Then sit." As she spoke, Maggie seemed to float to the

head of the little bed, where she leaned comfortably against the wall, looking slightly smaller.

"How did you do that?"

"Do what?"

Wondering if her odd visitor would ever answer a simple question, she sat down on the pallet and leaned against the other wall, gazing at her in wonder.

"Are ye fond o' the name Elspeth?"

Blinking, Elspeth said, "What an odd question."

"Will ye answer it?"

"Elspeth is my name."

"Be it the only name ye ken?"

"What other name *should* I know?" It occurred to her that Maggie might be trying to learn her surname, but in that same moment a memory stirred.

"Tell me," Maggie said, as if she could see right into her mind.

"I often dream about a castle on a hill," Elspeth said. "It is always the same castle, but it used to be a happy place where people laughed and where the sun was always shining. In those dreams, people used to call me Beth or Bethie, but now I'm always alone and the castle is always distant and mist-shrouded. It still feels right to think of myself as Bethie, though, even in the gloomy dreams."

"Aye, it would," Maggie said.

"Why?"

"I canna tell ye that, lass. We ha' rules in my world, and I shouldna break them, but I can say that we lost ye for a time. We ha' only just found ye again."

"How did you lose me?"

"Ah, now, that would be telling. But ye'll be safer now."

"Was I not safe before?"

Maggie shrugged.

"How did you find me?"

"Claud found ye. He's me son. Brown Claud they call him. I sent him here tae the west march in search o' ye, and he met wi' a lass. Claud always meets lasses, but this one showed him where tae find ye. Now, o' course, he ha' fallen in lust wi' her, but at least this one be an improvement on the last. Mayhap this time he'll no come tae grief."

"Well, if he has fallen in love with her—"

"Nay, nay, Claud doesna fall in love. He falls in lust, which means that any pretty lass can lead him around by his . . . by his nose, as ye say."

Elspeth nodded. She had known serving maids capable of leading strong men-at-arms in just such a fashion. Usually, however, it was the maid who came to grief, not the man. A vision of Patrick flitted through her mind's eye.

"Why did ye no leave wi' yon falconer when he asked ye?"

Elspeth stared. "You know about that?"

"Aye, I ken much about much, lass. Why did ye no go wi' him?"

"Because it would be wicked, and this is my home," Elspeth said.

"They're no your people, though."

"Are they not? They are all I know, all I remember."

"What o' your dreams then?"

"They are but dreams. This is real, and I am obliged to Sir Hector and his family, because my father never paid them for my keep."

"Indeed? And what d'ye ken o' your father?"

"If you know all about me, you must already know that I was baseborn, that my father is the Earl of Angus, and that he abandoned me here when I was small."

Maggie puffed a cloud of white smoke. "Earls' daughters, even them born wrong side o' the blanket, dinna end as serving maids—no as a rule, any road."

"Mayhap if my mother had been a gentlewoman . . . but she was not."

Maggie's lips pursed, and her eyes flashed. She seemed to struggle with herself, but when she spoke, her voice was calm. "Mortals admire loyalty but generally offer it only because they want security. D'ye fear risk, lass?"

Remembering that in many of the stories she had heard about wee folk, they led mortals into mischief or even deadly peril, she said carefully, "Surely you do not suggest that I should follow the falconer. Even if I were so lost to propriety as to fling myself after such a man—one, I might add, who seems, despite his inconsistent attempts to appear otherwise, to be higher born than I, and is most likely in mortal danger himself—"

"I dinna think he be higher born than ye," Maggie said thoughtfully.

"I do not even know what route he will take, and he's been gone half a day."

"Then ye shouldna tarry."

"There are Englishmen looking for him, dangerous men who wish him ill."

"Nae one follows him at present," Maggie said.

"Are you saying that I should?" The thought stirred tremors in her midsection, but whether they represented anxiety or anticipation, she did not know.

Maggie said firmly, "Your future be for ye tae find, lass. I can do nobbut help ye now and again, but ye'd do a sight better if ye'd stop clinging tae false loyalty and follow your heart. Some'un o' my world seems tae ha' given ye certain gifts tae protect ye even whilst he hid ye from us, and I can grant ye others, but ye'll ha' tae make your own decisions and discover your own truths."

"God's mercy, what truths?"

But Maggie was gone.

"I think your Catriona were a Glaistig," Lucy Fittletrot said as she and Claud lay entwined on a grassy hill, staring up at scudding white clouds in the azure sky.

"I dinna ken any Glaistigs," Claud said. At her request, he had told her about the splendid lass he had left in the Highlands, but it occurred to him that since he had met Lucy thoughts of Catriona no longer stirred his body instantly to mourning her loss. "Catriona were one o' the Merry Folk, and a lovely lass she was, too."

"A Glaistig," Lucy said firmly. "'Tis certain from what ye ha' said about her. Did she no insist that ye meet wi' her in a glade wi' a burn running through it?"

"Aye, she did, but we met other places, too."

"Still, the water be important. Glaistigs be water spirits. I warrant she were hiding her goat's feet under that long green gown ye say she always wore."

"Nay," Claud said. But as he protested, he realized he could not recall ever seeing Catriona's feet, which was odd, because he had certainly seen the rest of her.

"Did she do domestic chores?" Lucy demanded.

"Nay, she didna even like looking after the man she were supposed tae look after. She were always after me tae be doing things for him."

"Then she's a feckless wench, or mayhap she gave her loyalty tae someone else in his family, his father perhaps."

"Aye, the man did ha' a father."

Lucy laughed. "O' course he had a father, Claud. We all ha' fathers."

"I dinna ha' one."

"Ye must!"

"Nay, I've a mother but nae father."

"Well, that's very odd."

"Aye, I suppose it is," Claud agreed, wondering why it had never struck him as odd before. At all events, he did not want to think about Catriona anymore. He pulled Lucy into his arms, determined to make her forget Catriona, too.

He had barely begun, however, before he was rudely interrupted.

"Claud, cease your daffy tail-toddling for once," his mother commanded, grabbing his shoulder and flinging him upright.

He never knew how she did that so easily, because he could not do such things himself, but he was in no position now to demand explanations.

"Who is *this* person?" Maggie demanded, glaring at Lucy, who was casually rearranging her clothing.

"Why, that be Lucy Fittlettrot, o' course. What's amiss now, Mam?"

"Our lass will be on the move by morning, or I ken nowt about mortals," Maggie said. "Ye must be ready tae follow her, because I must attend a council wi' the Helping Hands tae discuss our negotiations wi' the Merry Folk. Dinna lose sight o' our lass for an instant, Claud. We dinna ken what lies ahead."

"Aye, I'll look after her," he promised.

"See that ye do," Maggie said, and was gone.

Claud reached for Lucy. "Our lass hasna gone yet, me dearling, but when she does, will ye go wi' me tae keep watch o'er her? Ye did find her for us, and all."

"Aye, Claud, I'd hoped ye ask me," Lucy said, snuggling into his arms. "What were we a-doing when your mother interrupted us? D'ye recall?"

"Aye, I do," Claud said, showing her.

After a nearly sleepless night, Elspeth got up at her usual time Sunday morning, having made her decision, and with less difficulty than she had expected.

Tidying her chamber and hurrying to the kitchen to break her fast with a few bites of coarse bread, she put the rest of it, along with a slice of cold beef and an apple, in her pocket. Then she went upstairs to open the windows in the hall and make sure the men who slept there had wakened and gone about their duties.

Next, she returned to the kitchen to fetch the two ewers she usually filled at the well outside for the ladies of the house. With ewers in hand, she left the kitchen and turned toward the door at the end of the corridor but stopped at her bedchamber on the way. Setting the ewers down, she prepared a bundle to take with her.

She possessed nothing of value except a tiny gold leaf on a thin gold chain, a baby's necklace that had been around her neck when Angus left her at Farnsworth Tower. She had worn it until the day they told her she would have to work to earn her keep. Then she had taken it off and put it in a slim wooden box that Sir Hector had given her for the purpose. The chain was too short to wear around her neck, so she doubled it around her wrist as a bracelet.

The only things in her bundle were a clean smock, a comb, the glove she had worn to help Patrick with Zeus, and the food she had taken from the kitchen. She would take nothing else with her. Except for the necklace, Sir Hector or his lady had given her everything she owned. It was bad enough that she was taking the clothes on her back and the warm, hooded cloak.

Although she had tossed and turned most of the night, she had dozed from time to time, and she had dreamed of the castle on the hill. There had been a path at last, leading to a tall, arched door. And someone was with her. Usually, when she dreamed of the castle in the distance, she was alone, but this time, she had sensed a presence beside her. She had begun to turn her head but wakened, tangled in her quilt, before she could see who walked with her. Since she had told Maggie Malloch about her dreams, she wondered if the little woman had cast a spell to alter them. It did not matter if she had, because after their talk, little doubt had lingered about what she meant to do. Clearly, she had needed only a nudge to do what she had longed to do from the moment Patrick had asked her to go with him.

Picking up the ewers, she returned to the kitchen, holding her head as if it ached, and said to the kitchen maid, "My head is pounding, Jenny. Would you be so kind as to tend the young ladies for me this morning?"

"Aye, I'll do it," Jenny said, taking the ewers. "Will ye no be going tae kirk wi' the family then?"

"No, I think I'll just lie down on my bed and try to sleep."

"Aye, well I'll tell them, but like as not Mistress Drusilla will be down in a trice, insisting ye be hardy enough, and worrying ye tae go tae kirk."

Well aware of that possibility, Elspeth went to her room and lay on her bed. Realizing then that if Drusilla did not come to see if she was really sick, she had no way to judge passing time, she counted to a hundred for each finger of both hands, then did it again. At last, judging that at least half an hour had passed, she was about to get up when the door opened. To her relief, it was only Jenny.

"We're just going, so I peeped in tae see were there aught I could get ye."

"No, thank you," Elspeth said. "I feel better, but I do not think it would be wise to walk into the village until I can be sure it is nothing contagious."

"Aye, sure. Then I'll look in again when we return."

"You need not, Jenny. You have your work to do, and I will just sleep."

Nodding and smiling, Jenny shut the door.

Elspeth counted to one hundred again. Then, getting up, she opened the door and listened for voices. All was silent. The servants attended kirk in a nearby village with the family, but there would still be men in the yard and guarding the gate.

Swiftly, lest her courage fail her, she donned her cloak, tied her bundle under it, then hurried out the postern door and across the yard to the gate.

"I am going out now," she said to the guard, certain no one would have bothered to inform him that she was ailing.

"Aye, lass," he said, his attitude making it plain that he took no interest in her comings or goings. He swung open the heavy gate and shut it when she had passed through, and the sound of it thudding into place lifted her spirits. She might suffer later for her impulsiveness, but for the moment she was free.

Walking briskly, she made for the forest, and within the shelter of the trees, her confidence increased. She had walked these woods many times in her lifetime and had done so without incident. A niggling voice at the back of her mind suggested that while she had wandered unmolested in the vicinity of Farnsworth Tower, where nearly everyone knew her and knew, too, that she lived under Sir Hector's protection, the same would not be true as she traveled farther north. She ignored the unnerving voice, quickening her step.

Although she had told Maggie she did not know what route Patrick would take, most folks traveled only one road north to Glasgow, and from this part of the west march one typically passed through Glasgow to reach Stirling. But what if Patrick had gone another way? He had taken horses, so he could travel swiftly, and he had revealed more than once that he was unpredictable.

Suppressing second thoughts that told her she was being

foolhardy to follow such a man, that fleeing Farnsworth Tower was more likely to end in disaster than in finding her future, as Maggie had described it, she hurried onward.

Nell's little party had made slow progress. She had realized that Angus would quickly hunt them down if they headed directly for Kershopefoot, so when they met a group of some twenty refugees—men, women, and children—seeking a route through Kielder Forest to Carter Bar, she and Jane had decided to join them, although the distance was considerably greater.

Nell wore her drabbest gown and a simple, black hooded cloak, but she knew that she stood out from the others nonetheless. The group was comfortably large and varied, though, and many of its members were walking, so she and Jane dismounted, making friends by offering to let the women and children take turns riding their horses. Seth, the lad from Midgeholme, led their sumpter pony.

Nell grew nervous every time a stranger approached the group, for she knew that no matter who was riding her chestnut gelding—a particularly fine one—Angus would recognize it in a flash. They encountered no trouble, however, until Sunday morning when some in their group insisted upon finding a church. Nell had no objection to attending a Sunday service, but she would infinitely have preferred to seek one on the Scottish side of the line, and they were still miles from Carter Bar.

Accordingly, she ordered Jane and Seth to fall to the rear with their horses, and noted that one other family did the same. When they reached the crest of a hill, heard bells, and saw a spire not far away, the majority of their group surged ahead.

Nell hesitated, reluctant to enter a hamlet still dangerously near Midgeholme. "Archie's men will be searching everywhere for us by now," she murmured to Jane.

"Aye, madam. 'Tis best we keep going."

Just then, the man who had stayed behind with his wife and two children pointed and exclaimed, "Riders! Yonder to the south!"

Horrified, Nell followed his gesture and saw sunlight glinting on steel. "Quickly," she said. "Ride along the other side of the hill and head north. Whether 'tis Archie or the King's soldiers, we do not want to meet them!"

They were soon deep in the forest, and she plunged ahead, seeking a place of concealment. The little family had followed, so they were too many to hide easily.

Jane said, "Those soldiers looked more like King Henry's men than the earl's, my lady. If they are harassing papist refugees, would they not let us go in peace?"

"Archie will be riding the line," Nell said. "So will those soldiers, if they are indeed hunting refugees. We'll be safer, I think, if we lie low for a time."

"Aye," said the man who had followed them. "The mistress be right. We'll bide here in these woods today and see how the landscape looks tomorrow. 'Tis safer at present tae keep clear o' both priests and men-at-arms, I'm thinking."

Chafing at the delay but certain that an encounter with soldiers would prove as deadly as one with Angus, Nell bowed to good sense.

Several miles from Farnsworth, keeping to woodland, Elspeth unwrapped the cold beef she had saved from her breakfast and took a bite, chewing hungrily. Just then, a boy, a chestnut pony with a pack strapped to its back, and a large ash-gray dog stepped out of the woodland ahead of her.

The boy looked a year or two younger than Small Neddy. His curly red hair looked as if it had never seen a comb, but his tattered brown breeks and jerkin looked cleaner than one might expect, and his boots looked stout, albeit large for his feet. He led the pony on a length of rope, but it was the dog that drew her eye and stopped her in her tracks, for it was huge, nearly as tall at the shoulder as the lad was.

The boy grinned, showing that he was missing his two front teeth. "Dinna be afraid o' Thunder," he said. "He willna bite ye."

"I am not afraid of him," she said, "but he is the largest dog I've ever seen."

"Aye, sure, he's a big 'un. I be Wee Jock o' the Wall," he added, still grinning and eyeing her expectantly.

She hesitated. She was still too close to Farnsworth Tower to offer her name to just anyone. The lad might tell those who would soon be looking for her which way she had gone. Impulsively she said, "I am Beth."

"We can walk along together if ye like, Beth," Wee Jock said.

"But you do not even know where I am going."

He shrugged. "We dinna care. We'll go where ye go. Sithee, it be gey better for us tae travel in a group. The reivers be less likely tae set on us, so."

"Do you know a great many reivers?" she asked, teasing him, because he seemed so serious and much too sure of himself for one of such tender years.

"Oh, aye," he said, surprising her. "There be mortal many o' them hereabouts, and Jackie here be a fine pony. Ye can see that yourself."

"I can," she said. "He's a handsome fellow."

"Aye, sure, and they'll be wanting tae take him from me,

but Thunder looks fierce enough tae scare any reiver, dinna ye think?"

"He does," she said. "But I don't think even a reiver would steal your pony."

"Aye, they would."

"Why, what makes you so sure?"

"'Cause I lifted 'im from the reivers," the boy answered with a cheeky grin.

Taken aback by this blunt statement, but well aware that most folks in the west march saw nothing amiss with "lifting" items, including livestock, that legally belonged to someone else, she said diplomatically, "Then I expect you are right, and they will be looking for you."

"Aye, doubtless."

"You say you are called Wee Jock of the Wall," she went on. "Does that mean that your father is Big Jock of the Wall?"

"He were afore the English killed him," Wee Jock said. "Now he's dead."

"And your mother?"

"She died when me brother were born. Him, too." He grinned again. "So there be nae reason I shouldna walk wi' ye. Moreover, the pony be stout enough tae carry us both if ye like, or we can take turns."

"Did you steal the dog, too?"

"Nay, he found us yestereve. He looks fierce, though. Belike he'll scare off them reivers if they try tae take back me pony. So where be we headed?"

Accepting his assurances both because she would enjoy his company and because he did not seem as if he would accept dismissal, she said, "I want to go to Glasgow by way of Moffat, but the only way I know is through Lockerbie, and I do not want to pass through that village if I need not."

"Nay, village folk be too curious about a man's business," Jock said, shaking his head. "I ken a wee track up Annandale. It be shorter and less roundabout than the highroad. Steeper, though."

It took only a moment's thought to realize that Patrick would also avoid the highroad and that it would not be long before people began to look for her.

"Are you sure you know the way?"

"Oh, aye," he said blithely. "Tae Moffat, I do, but tae miss Moffat and travel past it without losing ourselves, we'll ha' tae stir our brains a bit."

"I am looking for a friend who is also traveling north," she said. "He is big and can help protect us if we find him, but I do not know which way he will go."

"We could ask folks we meet if they ha' seen him," Jock said doubtfully."Likely they'll have seen more than a few big men, though."

"He is carrying a hawk," she said.

"Folks will remember the hawk." He gazed at her speculatively, the question clear in his eyes, although he did not ask it.

She said, "He . . . he is a friend. I know it is not safe for a woman traveling alone, so I was hoping to catch up with him."

"Aye, well, I'll look after ye now," Jock said, "but we'll keep a sharp eye out for this man o' yours." He gave her another look. "He won't be the sort as wants tae tell Jackie and Thunder and me wha' tae do, will he? Or that we should ha' grown-ups tae look after us, 'cause we dinna need any o' that."

"How old are you?"

He shrugged. "Old enough. I were born the year after the King came tae the west march wi' his army and hanged Johnny Armstrong."

She had heard of Johnny Armstrong, a notorious reiver, but she had no idea when his hanging had occurred, so that information was no help. He was small and slight, so she judged him to be about nine or ten years old.

"Do you not live with anyone?"

"Nay, I dinna need nae one."

When she looked sternly at him, disbelieving that a boy his age could fend entirely for himself, he added, "I did live wi' me uncle, but he clouted me head too many times, so I left. I wanted tae live wi' the reivers, but they dinna want me."

"Mercy!"

"Aye, I did think they'd take me on, 'cause I'm no afraid o' hard work."

"But surely boys do not go a-reiving!"

"I'm old for me age," he said firmly. "Still, I did think they slept days and spent nights riding about the country looking for beasts tae lift, and that seemed a fine life, but I learned that they dinna go reiving all the time but ha' tae go home tae their wives in between. I dinna ha' a wife or a cot," he added with a sigh, "so I lifted the pony tae carry what I do ha', and I left them reivers tae seek me fortune."

"I'm glad you did," she said, smiling. "I shall be glad of your company."

It occurred to her then that since Maggie Malloch had said she would help when she could, perhaps the little woman had conjured up the odd trio to escort her. In any event, she had spoken the truth when she told Jock she welcomed their company, and by the end of the day, she knew she had judged right.

She had traveled farther by then than she had ever gone on her own before, but her new companions made her feel safe and Jock proved skillful at building a fire and spearing a large trout for their dinner from the burn they had followed for much of the day. She had not thought about how she would stay warm that night or where she would sleep. But Jock speedily made soft beds of sweet-smelling grass, and when she had wrapped herself in her cloak and the boy had done the same with the blanket that had cushioned the pony's back, and with Thunder stretched warmly between them, the night passed comfortably enough.

Chapter 11

Nell and her little party crossed the line at last late Monday morning. Feeling safer on the other side and not trusting Angus to stay in England if he learned she was in Scotland, she urged her companions to greater speed, soon outdistancing the family of refugees who had crossed with them.

"Where be we headed, mistress," Jane asked when Nell finally eased the pace enough to allow them to converse without shouting.

"I must go to James," Nell said. "We know he has not left Scotland, so he will be either in Edinburgh or Stirling, and the easiest road to both is the main one through Hawick and Selkirk to Galashiels."

"I've a cousin in Stirling," Jane said, "but ye've kinfolk aplenty in the Borders, madam."

"I do," Nell agreed, "but we'll not seek their aid. I go to James as the widow of Adam Gordon, Jane, to ask his permission to stay in Scotland. I'll fare better if no one can say that I consorted with Douglases along the way."

Jane sighed. "Then we'll sleep on the ground again tonight, I expect."

"Oh, no, we won't," Nell declared. "We'll find a nice, tidy convent and request hospitality."

She hoped Patrick had found comfortable lodgings, wherever he was.

Patrick had taken care to avoid towns and villages, not wanting to leave a trail the English could follow. Having made camp Sunday night in a narrow dale some distance from the fast-flowing Annan but with a tumbling burn of its own, he decided to spend Monday morning working with Zeus.

Tying the free end of the long creance to a tree limb, he set the hawk on a makeshift perch nearby, and then walked a short distance up the grassy hillside. Giving his tuneful whistle, he waited patiently while Zeus preened himself. He was about to whistle again when suddenly, with a mighty flapping of wings, Zeus swooped toward him. Patrick raised his gloved fist, but although he was quick, Zeus flew with such speed as to astound him, ignoring the fist and landing on his shoulder, forcing him to turn his head away in self-defense.

He had trained many birds of prey, but the awesome thrill that exploded in him then was the same as when his first hawk had answered his whistle. Zeus was learning with amazing speed for a goshawk, making him wonder if someone had captured him before and he had escaped before becoming fully trained.

He waited patiently while Zeus paced down his arm, talons spasmodically gripping the leather sleeve of his jerkin until the hawk reached the gloved fist and pounced on the bit of liver it held. Then, suddenly, Zeus paused, body aquiver, head cocked, to gaze intently downhill. Several seconds passed before Patrick heard the distant, deep-throated bark of a dog.

Instantly, his senses sharpened, and as the barking continued, he recognized the sound as that of a sleuthhound on a scent. As far north as he was, the likelihood of English searchers was remote, so it was more likely that the animal lived nearby in one of the myriad cottages he had seen along the way.

The barking drew nearer, and sooner than he had expected, he saw the dog, a giant gray deerhound. It seemed to be alone, bounding up the hill toward him. Having no way to know if it was friendly, Patrick drew his sword.

"Easy, Zeus," he murmured to the nervous hawk on his left fist.

To his relief, the dog stopped yards away, cocked its head with its tongue lolling, and wagged its long tail.

"Good lad," Patrick said. It was one of the largest dogs he had ever seen, deep-chested and long-legged, its tapered head nearly as high as his waist. He recognized the breed easily, because Mackinnon of Dunakin, a neighbor on the Isle of Skye, owned four and hunted with them regularly. They were valuable animals, he knew, so valuable that by law, only earls, clan chiefs, and men of greater estate could own them. Thus, he wondered what this one was doing running loose.

As he waited, letting the hawk grow accustomed to its presence, and to see if it would come nearer, he became aware of movement below. Two people emerged from the thicket of trees flanking the burn, the smaller one leading a sumpter pony.

Deciding they were travelers like himself, he watched them warily until he recognized the lass. His body's strong sensual awareness made him certain that it was Elspeth, and when he realized that the boy was not anyone he had seen before, his temper stirred much the same way it would have had Elspeth been his sister.

No, he decided, drawing breath, he was angrier than he would be with Bab.

Zeus flapped his wings, and Patrick gave a slight flick of his wrist to induce him to grip the glove again instead of bating. Realizing that the hawk was reacting to his temper, he drew another, deeper breath and sheathed his sword.

She was smiling! Had she no sense of the risk she had taken or the danger she stood in now? She should be grateful that he had to consider the hawk and could not grab her by her shoulders and shake her until she saw the error of her ways.

He strode to meet her, depending on his quick strides and the bird's need to grip tightly to keep it on his fist, only to come up short when he realized that the creance would reach no farther. Frustrated, he stood and waited for her.

"You shaved off your beard," she said when she was near enough to hear.

"What the devil are you doing alone so far from home?"

The expression on her face changed from delight to wariness, and she glanced at her young companion.

The lad rolled his eyes and muttered something to her.

She shook her head, frowning, and although Patrick had not heard what the lad said, he did hear her. "You stay here," she said. "I'll talk to him."

"Nay, ye will not!" the boy protested. "He looks fierce enough tae eat ye, and he's no even looked at our Thunder, so the great dog'll be nae use tae ye."

"I am not any more afraid of him than I am of Thunder, Jock. Stay here."

"Do as she says, lad," Patrick commanded.

The boy looked at him, seemed to weigh the risk of disobeying, and made his choice. "I said I'd protect her, mister," he said. "D'ye lay a hand on her, I'll set the dog on ye. He'll rip your arms off, both of 'em, and he'll eat 'em for 'is supper!"

Patrick snapped his fingers. "Come," he said.

The dog loped to him, wagging its tail.

"Lie down, sir!"

The dog flopped to the ground, its tongue lolling from the side of its mouth, its bright dark eyes fixed on Patrick's face, waiting for the next command.

"Now, then," Patrick said, looking sternly at the lad, "I've some things to say to this lass, and they are not for you to hear."

"Aye, sir," the lad said, finally accepting superior authority. With a rueful glance at the lass, he stayed where he was.

The chestnut pony dropped its head to graze.

"Come here to me and explain this madness," Patrick said to Elspeth.

When she hesitated, looking thoughtful, he wondered if he had frightened her. He hadn't meant to, but just as he thought that perhaps he ought to gentle his tone, she said, "It is unfair to scold me when it was your idea that I leave."

"Don't be daft," he said, his temper leaping again as much out of his awareness that he had suggested it as from his knowledge of the dangers she might have met. "It was never my intention that you should travel alone, unprotected."

"Here now," the lad said indignantly. "She ain't unprotected. She's had me and Thunder tae look after her!"

"You are not supposed to be listening," Patrick reminded him.

"Aye, well, but I canna help it when ye bellow like a boar in rut."

"Like a—! Now, see here, my lad—"

"Oh, please don't scold him anymore," she said, shaking her head and clearly suppressing amusement. "If only you could see your face!"

"Do you dare to laugh at me?"

"I am trying very hard *not* to laugh," she said. "Jock is only a boy, but he has looked after me very well."

"But what madness sent you after me on your own?" he

demanded, horrified at the thought of her traveling so far without proper protection. A thought occurred to him. "Did those harpies do something horrid to you?"

"No, sir, not really, and you may well call this madness," she said. "I am not going to try to explain it to you when I am not sure I understand it myself. I expect the sad truth is that I'd had my fill of Drusilla and Jelyan even before you found me that day in the woods. Ever since, however, my envy of your freedom to do as you please has nearly eaten me alive. Though it pains me to admit it, every chore has seemed more onerous, every command more arbitrary and unfair. Therefore, when Drusilla slapped me—"

"Slapped you! Again? She did not dare!"

"Aye, of course she did, and not for the first time, as you know. But this time it angered me so much that I actually raised my hand. I do not know that I would have had the nerve to strike back, but it is just as well that Lady Farnsworth entered the room just then."

"Somehow I do not think you ran away to avoid punishment."

"No, of course not. I'm afraid I had already given more thought than I should to the notion of going away with you, but until then it had felt wicked and wanton. Indeed, it feels so again now," she added in a small voice.

"Pay those feelings no heed," he said firmly. "You are safe with me."

She eyed him with wary amusement. "Am I?" she asked. "Forgive me if I seem cautious, but I do recall what happened in the darkness the other night."

"I did not press you when you refused," he reminded her, shooting an oblique look at the boy, who was still listening with undisguised curiosity.

"I know you did not," she said, "but you seem to think I am experienced in the ways of men. Many young women in my position do know about such matters, I believe, more than they should, but I have never done such a thing as this before. Still, I did it, so I expect my good character is lost forever."

He had suggested that she accompany him because she attracted him and because he had hoped she would provide amusement along the way. Aware that his reasons were boorish and that he had known she was naive, he was surprised to realize that the emotion uppermost in his awareness just then was guilt.

He was delighted to see her, but he was dismayed that she had run away, and he realized that he bore much of the responsibility for her decision. Recognizing that such responsibility placed a burden on him to protect her, he was willing to do so, but he wondered what on earth he would do with her and her three odd companions when they reached Stirling. Clearly, she had not thought that far ahead.

"I hope you do not mean to scold anymore," she said.

"No," he said. "I was just wondering what I will do with you."

"You need not concern yourself about that," she said airily. "Henceforth I am going to make my own decisions. Although I shall be very glad to have your company and protection until we reach Stirling—"

"You will have more than that, my lass," he interjected as anger stirred again. "You are going to stay with me until I can think what to do with you, and you will obey me—you and your fierce companion both," he added, looking at the boy.

She pressed her lips together, telling him as surely as if she had said so that she wanted to argue with him. When she glanced at the lad, he knew she hesitated to do so in front of the boy, and he was glad. He did not want to fight with her.

"Are you going to introduce your companion?" he asked gently.

"He is called Wee Jock of the Wall."

"What wall?"

Her eyes began to twinkle. "I don't know."

They both looked at the boy.

Jock shrugged. "I dunno neither," he said. "It be me name is all, and the pony be Jackie and the dog be Thunder."

"What position does your father hold?" Patrick asked, wondering how the lad had come by a dog that only a man of high estate should own.

"Me father's dead. The damned English killed him."

"I'm sorry to hear that. Is it possible that he was a gentleman?"

"Nay, he were a reiver."

"I have learned that such an enterprise does not necessarily preclude his having been a gentleman," Patrick said with a chuckle.

"Huh?"

"Never mind. How did you come by that dog?"

"I didna come by him. He came by me."

"I see." That was disturbing news, because someone of power and resource would undoubtedly be looking for such a valuable animal.

"In truth, the pony is what ought to concern you," the lass said with an undercurrent of amusement in her voice that made him look at her sharply.

"Why?"

"Because Jock 'lifted' it from a gang of reivers, and he thinks that perhaps they will want it back."

Patrick chuckled, then threw back his head and laughed. "I've been told I need never seek trouble because it always finds me, and today that is certainly true."

"Who said that trouble always finds you?"

He could hear Fin's mocking voice in his head, but he said only, "A friend."

"Do you want us to leave you in peace?"

"Nay, lass, you are not leaving. I already told you that."

"Well, I won't stay if you mean to go on scolding. I had a surfeit of *that* at Farns— That is to say, I have heard enough harsh words to last me a lifetime."

He held her gaze for a long moment, realizing only then that her young companion did not know where she lived.

Jock said with his odd grown-up dignity, "I think we should leave him be, Beth. He doesna ha' much pluck, and we dinna need a hindrance."

"See here," Patrick said, "how old are you?"

Jock shrugged, but the lass said, "He does not know exactly, but he was born the year after the King hanged Johnny Armstrong."

Patrick did the calculation. "He'll be ten or eleven then, which is quite old enough to accept the consequences of an insolent tongue. Come here to me, lad."

She put a restraining hand on his arm. "You should know," she said, "that Jock ran away from his uncle because the man hit him rather too often."

"Aye, he did," Jock said. "Made me lugs swell up like mutchkins. The man were so peevish ye'd think he pissed nettles."

She raised her eyebrows. "Lugs like mutchkins?"

"Ears like ale mugs," Patrick said, adding, "Lad, if you talked to your uncle the way you talk to me, you deserved what you got."

"Aye, sure," Jock said, nodding, "but when a chap can look after hisself, he doesna stand still and let folks bang 'im about."

"Can you trap rabbits?" Patrick asked abruptly.

"Aye, or shoot 'em. I've me own bow and arrows."

"Do you see this hawk?"

"Aye, he looks right fierce."

"He likes fresh rabbit pluck, so if you can trap a brace of them, we'll give him the innards, and we can roast the rest and carry it with us."

"I seen rabbits aplenty in yon woods by the burn," he

said. Eyeing Patrick askance, he added, "Ye'll no be taking our Beth and leaving me here, will ye?"

"He will not," she said, giving Patrick a look. "In any event, I'd not go with him unless you were along to protect me."

"Good enough then," he said, turning to open the pony's pack. "Ye'd best keep Thunder wi' ye, sir. He'd scare off them rabbits."

"He'll stay," Patrick said, "and so will our Beth. Oh, no, you don't," he added, catching hold of her arm when she turned as if to go with Jock. "I still have much to say to you."

When Jock had run off down the hill, Beth pulled her arm from Patrick's grasp, grateful when he did not try to hold her but a little disappointed, too.

"Now, sir, you may say what you like to me," she said, "but you did promise that you would not scold anymore."

"Am I to call you Beth now?" he asked bluntly.

She knew she was blushing, but she said steadily enough, "I did not want to tell him my name when we met, because we were too close to Farnsworth Tower. I am sure that I could have trusted him even then not to give me away, but in truth I have rather liked his calling me Beth."

"Why?"

She hesitated, but something about Patrick made it easy for her to talk to him, and she decided to tell him the truth. "In certain dreams I have over and over again, I think of myself as Beth rather than Elspeth. I don't know why."

"Both Elspeth and Beth are nicknames for Elizabeth, which is a common name everywhere. Perhaps someone called you Beth when you were small. Do others call you Beth in the dreams?"

"Not anymore," she said. "I think they did once, but I am usually alone in them now, just wandering. Still, it is like being in another world, and I like visiting it occasionally to escape from Farnsworth Tower."

He frowned thoughtfully, but before he could put his thoughts into words, Zeus bated, and he had his hands full until he got a hand under the hawk's belly to lift it back to his fist.

"Where are your horses?" she asked. "Have you made camp nearby?"

"I have, but if you think that discussing my camp will keep you from hearing what I think of this impulsive journey of yours, you will soon learn your mistake."

"If we are to talk of mistakes, sir, you must realize that Jock does not think of you as a common falconer. You have been speaking to me as you usually do, you know. Did you not observe that he called you 'sir' just now?"

He frowned again, and that told her that he had not noticed. A man who was unaccustomed to being treated with that measure of respect would have.

With a sigh, he said, "I do not know what it is about you, lass, that makes me forget myself as I do." He looked as if he would say more on the same topic, but he did not. Instead, he gave himself a shake as if to resettle his thoughts and added, "I do not suppose it would help now for me to begin to speak as Jock does."

"He would notice the change in an instant," she said.

Patrick nodded. "I'm surprised that you do not quiz me more yourself."

"It is not for me to question your behavior," she said.

"You have not hesitated to do so before," he said, grinning.

She nibbled her lower lip, knowing he spoke the truth, but before it had been easy to pretend that they were equals. Now, that was harder to do, and worse, where Patrick was concerned she did not trust her emotions or her own body.

Even now it was singing to her, stirring in response to his proximity. When he had grabbed her arm, she had not felt fear although she had known he was angry with her. And, too, there had been that brief disappointment when he let go. Her usual sensible nature had deserted her, because the man disturbed her senses whenever he was near her. Here she was, miles from home, courting disaster, all because of him. Remembering Maggie Malloch, she decided that she could not lay all the blame at Patrick's door. Maggie had encouraged her, and she had acted on that encouragement. Her own impulses had had much to do with it, too.

She wanted to tell him how she felt, but she knew that to do so would make her more vulnerable, because she doubted that he had similar feelings for her.

To him, she was merely a handy maidservant, someone with whom he could amuse himself. Although she was naive, she was not stupid, and she understood that men took advantage of unprotected females, and that many men regarded maidservants as accessible toys for their entertainment.

Nevertheless, when Patrick set the hawk on a dead branch, tied the free end of the creance to another, and put his hands on her shoulders, she did not resist.

Drawing her closer, he looked into her eyes, and she knew that he was not going to scold her. His intent was plain.

He hesitated, as if to give her time to protest, but when she kept silent, he drew her closer yet and bent to kiss her. When his lips touched hers, she knew she had been waiting for him to do so from the moment she had seen him above her on the hillside. She had recognized him instantly, and knew that she would have, beard or no beard, hawk or no hawk. She was glad he had shaved the beard, though. She did not miss its soft prickling at all.

The hawk cheeped, and clearly taking the sound as encouragement, Patrick touched her lips gently with the tip of his tongue. Then one hand slipped to the small of her back, pulling her closer so that their bodies seemed to melt together.

Daringly, she let the tip of her tongue touch his, and his slipped inside her mouth. Her breasts, her whole body, pressed hard against him, and she could feel him move against her. She tasted his lips, savoring them, and for several moments, it was as if the rest of the world vanished, leaving them alone with each other.

"I've got two good 'uns!"

The voice floated to them from the bottom of the hill, and turning, they saw Jock running toward them with a rabbit in each hand.

Patrick caught one of Beth's hands and lifted it to his mouth, kissing it gently as he looked into her eyes. "We'll continue this later, lass. I look forward to it."

A surge of heat swept through her, and she could not look away.

Patrick unwrapped the hawk's creance from the branch, muttering, "I wish you had simply come with me from the outset. We have too much company now."

Smiling, she nearly agreed, but sensibly, she kept her mouth shut, telling herself she should be grateful for her protectors.

Back at his camp, Patrick set Jock to skinning the rabbits. "We'll have a hot midday meal," he said, "but I'd like to be out of the west march before sundown."

He smiled at Beth, delighting in her blushes. He had no trouble thinking of her as Beth instead of Elspeth. Beth suited her better, he thought.

Jock watched them both critically. He had said nothing

about seeing them kiss, but Patrick knew he had, and he knew that Beth knew it, too. The knowledge seemed to make her self-conscious, for she kept glancing at the lad, but she did not bring up the subject herself.

He felt relaxed and comfortable with her, as if he had known her forever.

After their meal, they set out, and Patrick let Jock set the pace while he and Beth took turns riding and carrying the hawk. Thunder had found his own dinner and amused himself along the way by dashing after birds and other wildlife, and then trotting back to his companions with his head high, obviously enjoying the illusion that he was protecting them from harm.

They followed Annan Water but stayed high on the ridge above it, seeing only a few other travelers. No one disturbed them, and at Patrick's suggestion, they made camp before sundown, eating the rest of their roasted rabbit except for the liver and lights, which he saved for Zeus.

He did not build a fire, having no wish to draw attention, and although the evening was chilly, it was not uncomfortable. When Beth said that she had spent her first night out with only her cloak to cover her, he pulled a blanket from his pony's pack and promised that she would not be chilly tonight.

He hoped to share his bed with her, knowing the heat of their bodies would keep them warm. But when he laid the blankets out, Thunder plopped down in the center, and she laughed, saying she was not about to share Patrick's bed and that the dog would not allow it even if she were the sort who would do such a thing.

Jock glared at him, too, so Patrick gave up, rolling himself in one blanket and giving the second to Beth. She lay down on her cloak with the warm blanket over her, and no sooner had she done so than Thunder stretched out beside her with his back against hers. His eyes were open, and they remained unblinking, watching Patrick, until Patrick gave up. Clearly, both dog and boy meant to guard the lass.

Jock chuckled as if at some private joke, then rolled himself up in the pony blanket and fell asleep.

The next morning, Patrick said he wanted to work with the hawk. "Fetch your glove, Beth," he said. "We'll see if he'll fly to me again. You carry him."

She laughed with delight, and his heart leaped at the sound. Her eyes were bright, and she looked happier than he had seen her before. Freedom suited her.

Turning his attention to Jock, who had been folding blankets and readying the packs, he told him to see if he could trap another brace of rabbits.

"Aye, sir," Jock called. Without further comment, he gathered what he needed and ran off down the hill.

Their little glen was quiet, and they had seen no other travelers nearby, so Patrick moved toward the river. There were dips in the landscape along the way, some boggy still from winter, and even a few ponds of water.

The hawk flew to him on command twice more, the second time landing awkwardly on his shoulder, one sharp talon scratching the side of his neck where the jerkin did not cover it. He let Zeus ride on his shoulder back to camp, and when they were ready to leave, he lifted Beth onto his horse and told Jock to ride his pony. Patrick still had Zeus on his shoulder, and as he watched Beth settle herself, he felt Zeus's beak nudging his neck.

Beth laughed. "I think he's sorry he hurt you," she said. "He's kissing you."

"He's tasting my blood," Patrick said, awed by the bird's behavior. Then it began to tickle, and he chuckled. "Let's hope he doesn't develop a fondness for it."

Chapter 12———————————

The three companions quickly settled into a routine, spending part of each morning working with Zeus and the rest of the day traveling north, continuing to skirt villages and towns. On Wednesday, they camped on a ridge above Douglas Water a few miles from its confluence with the River Clyde. The next morning, as they prepared to work with the hawk, Patrick said, "Leave Thunder here, lad, and tie a string to one of the rabbits. I want to see if Zeus is ready for his first kill."

Beth held the hooded Zeus on her glove. "The rabbit might like to have a say in that," she said as they walked down the hill to find a good place to fly the hawk.

Patrick said, "Zeus has to learn what we expect of him. A bird of prey will attack nearly anything that moves when it's young. One of my father's peregrines tried to carry off a red deer. Zeus must learn to hunt game that is suitable for him."

Beth nodded, knowing that people and animals eat what they must. That the rabbit might have other plans stirred her sympathy, but such was Nature's way.

Not far from their camp they found a grassy meadow

with a spring-fed pond in the center. Following Patrick's orders, Jock ran ahead to tie the rabbit to a stake near the pond.

Zeus lifted a talon and snatched off his hood, dropping it to the ground and stepping off Beth's glove, sinking his sharp talons painfully into her forearm.

Suppressing a cry and realizing that she should have been watching him instead of Jock, she moved him back to the glove with a hand under his belly as she had seen Patrick do. A bead of blood showed through a rip in her sleeve, and she glanced at him, but he was watching Jock, and she was glad he had not noted her carelessness. He turned then and, smiling, took Zeus from her.

"You took off his hood," he said.

"*He* took it off and flung it to the ground," she said, bending to pick it up.

Patrick chuckled. "He has done that before. We must remember to be sure the ties are snug."

"There they be, Lucy," Claud exclaimed.

"I see them," she said.

"Thank the fates!" Claud felt as if he could breathe again for the first time since they had discovered their charge had gone. "I canna think how we missed her leaving Farnsworth, but even so, we should have found her long afore now."

"The west march be large," Lucy pointed out.

"Aye, but still, it be a good thing me mam dinna ken we lost the lass," Claud said, flitting to sit on the leaf of a thistle so he could see what the mortals were up to. He patted the leaf beside him invitingly.

Grinning, Lucy joined him, saying, "Claud, ha' ye ever flown wi' a hawk?"

Waiting until the hawk had fixed its attention on the rabbit, Patrick launched it into the air with a flick of his wrist.

Zeus flew low and fast, and for a moment, it looked as if he would fly straight to the rabbit, but he passed over it, heading for the pond. Only then did Patrick see the large green turtle plodding toward the water.

Talons out, the hawk gripped the turtle's shell, but the turtle kept moving forward, ignoring its extra burden. As Patrick, Jock, and Beth watched, it trudged into the water, its pace slow and sure. The hawk, still gripping the turtle's shell, looked over its shoulder at Patrick as if to say, "Is this right?"

Stifling laughter, Patrick watched, wondering as the turtle moved deeper if the hawk would have the sense to let go. The turtle was under now, and the water reached Zeus's belly. Just as Patrick decided he would have to save the hawk, it flapped its wings and awkwardly half swam, half flew to the shore. There, clearly annoyed, the soggy Zeus stood glowering at him.

Hearing Beth and Jock burst into laughter, Patrick gave up trying to hold his in, and laughed so hard his sides began to ache. Tears ran down his cheeks, and he could not see, so he did not know Beth was beside him until she touched his arm.

"He's pouting," she said, her voice still bubbling with merriment.

Rubbing his eyes, Patrick saw that Zeus had turned away and hunched a shoulder. He would not look at them even when Patrick whistled.

"Poor baby," Beth said.

It seemed perfectly natural to put his arm around her, and

when she leaned against him, he looked down to find her smiling at him. Her eyes were bright, and her lips were inviting. He kissed her.

She turned toward him, responding at once, and a jolt of desire shot through him. "Ah, lassie," he murmured against her soft lips, "were it not for Jock's presence, I'd make you mine right here on this soft grass."

"I'll yield to no man without a proper marriage, sir," she said.

"Marriage?"

"Aye, so if you had one in mind, which I doubt, we'd need a priest, and I doubt, too, that we'd find one near enough to suit your unseemly desire for haste."

"Scotland has ways of marrying that do not require priests," he said, smiling, wanting to see if he could disconcert her.

She stiffened, looking at him more narrowly. "Would you have me believe that you do want to marry me, Patrick Falconer?"

He sighed. "I'll not lie to you, *mo chridhe*. You must know enough about me by now to know I'm in no position to promise marriage."

"I guessed long since that you were no common falconer."

He chuckled. "Nay, I'm an uncommon one, to be sure." He glanced at the hawk, still flapping its wings, trying to dry itself.

"Can you not ever be serious?" she demanded.

He grimaced. "I am perfectly serious, lass. The plain fact is that I'm a spy."

"A spy!"

"Aye," he said, glancing to be sure that Jock could not hear them. "Jamie holds my master hostage at Stirling, and because Jamie and Cardinal Beaton disagree about a number of things, the cardinal offered to help me win my master's freedom if I would spy for him in England."

"You know Cardinal Beaton?"

"Aye, I do."

"But he is very powerful. Even Sir Hector holds him in awe."

"I don't doubt it. I swear the man has agents throughout Scotland and England—in Europe, too, even at the Vatican. I am but one amongst hundreds, and I nearly met disaster following someone for him from London to Cumberland."

"Who?"

"That I am not going to tell you, *mo chridhe.* You are safer not knowing."

"That's why you were running from those men the day we met."

"Aye, their master and his friends would like to see me hanged."

"How did they unmask you?"

"A man I knew years ago recognized me. Fortunately, he thought I had good reason to be there, and I managed to slip away before he could learn his error."

"It seems to me, if you were deceiving people, you should have expected that to happen," she said. "Spying is a crime, is it not?"

"I can see we need to discuss this at length," Patrick said. "It was not, however, the conversation I had in mind a few minutes ago."

She did not smile, and her voice was tight when she said, "I know it is not. Clearly, you are a man of consequence, so I suppose I should not think less of you for expecting a woman in my position—particularly one so brazen as to follow you across the west march—to fall into your arms at the first hint that you'd welcome her. But I do think less of you. Men in your position should take more care."

"You are right," he said quietly, feeling small.

"I know I am," she said. "A man in your position wields power over lesser persons and should, therefore, treat them with careful respect."

"*Mo chridhe,* I—"

"I asked you before not to call me 'sweetheart,' " she said, stepping away from him. "I would prefer that you just call me Beth."

"Master!" Jock shrieked. "Mind Zeus!"

Startled, they turned as one to see the hawk rising into the air, jesses dangling. The creance had come loose, and Zeus was flying free.

"How did ye do that, Claud?" Lucy asked.

"Me! I thought ye did it. Should we bring it back?"

"Nay, I'm no so clever as that," Lucy said innocently, "And I dinna think we should interfere, Claud. D'ye no want tae ride the hawk?"

He regarded her suspiciously. Was it possible that his current love was playing tricks on him? "I dinna want tae ride the hawk," he said firmly, still watching her. "We'll just keep our eye on the lass, as we should."

Beth stared in horror as Zeus soared up and away. She had heard tales of hawks and falcons escaping only to be entangled on branches by their jesses and left to hang upside down until they died.

"Keep watching," Patrick ordered. "He'll be seeking prey. He has not eaten."

Hearing Thunder bark, Beth glanced away from the hawk long enough to see that the deerhound had abandoned their campsite and was loping after him.

"What if Thunder catches him?" she cried.

"He won't, but mayhap he can keep pace with him. Zeus will take to the trees. Jock," he shouted, "run up to the ridge and shout if he heads toward our camp or over into Annandale. We must catch him."

The boy dashed up the hillside.

Beth saw Zeus circling lower over woodland below them.

Patrick saw him, too. "Those woods lie along Douglas Water," he said. "I'll head toward the north end of them. You go south."

Their mission seemed doomed to failure, but Beth obeyed without question. Entering the woods, she listened for any sign that the hawk was near but heard only rushing water nearby, and Patrick's whistling. It was the hawk's special tune, and she knew that as long as she continued to hear it, Zeus had refused to obey its call.

She tried to whistle the tune herself, but she could not get it right.

Slanting golden sunbeams pierced the canopy overhead. It was too thick to let her see the sky, and thus her chances of finding the hawk seemed dim. She kept walking and watching, but her thoughts drifted back to when Patrick had kissed her.

They had been so happy, so filled with laughter, and yet the mood, her mood, had changed abruptly. She knew that she cared for him. Indeed, she cared too much for her own good, but no matter what Maggie Malloch had said about following her heart, following it now could bring her nothing good.

Things had been bad enough when she had thought Patrick was just a man of somewhat higher stature than a falconer. To learn that he had actually spoken to Cardinal Beaton, the man many called the most powerful in Scotland, meant the falconer was far grander than she would ever have imagined.

He had said, too, that he had a master who was hostage to the King. Ordinary gentry did not have masters who drew royal attention, nor did they give orders as casually as Patrick did. Plainly, Patrick was a man of rank, and men of rank did not marry maidservants—not even ones to whom wee people appeared, and just, one middle-aged, rather plump wee person at that.

She saw movement ahead, and for a moment thought fearfully of wild boars and the like. Then she recognized Thunder running through the trees like a fleet but silent gray shadow. He did not bark, but when he stopped a few yards from her and turned, she knew as clearly as if he had spoken that he wanted her to follow.

Catching up her skirts, she ran, following him easily, leaping over fallen logs and darting around bushes as if her feet had taken wing. When he stopped again by a tree and looked up, she knew what she would see, and even before she reached it, she heard Zeus mewing overhead like a lost kitten.

The tree had been lightning struck, for its top was charred, and Zeus glared at her from a high, stubby black limb, his fierce look at odds with his pathetic mewing.

"Good lad, Thunder," she said quietly, patting the dog's rough fur. "Fetch Patrick now." She pointed. "Go."

She was accustomed to feeling as if animals understood her, but those animals were, for the most part, ones she had grown up with. So it was with particular satisfaction that she saw Thunder lope off toward where she had last seen Patrick. She did not want to shout for him, lest Zeus take fright and fly away.

He cheeped again, and she said, "Foolish Zeus. Not many goshawks would reject a home in the royal mews." She held out her gloved fist. "Come down, Zeus."

Again she tried to imitate Patrick's whistle, but Zeus turned, flicked his tail at her, and disdained further acknowledgment of her invitation.

"Zeus, please."

The hawk turned and glowered at her, hunching a shoulder.

Did he realize that she had no food for him? It had been foolish to come after him without a bit of rabbit liver. Were his jesses tangled on the limb? They did not seem to be, but perhaps—

With a single flap of its great wings, the hawk lifted off the branch and swooped down to her glove.

Startled, she nearly ducked away but managed to hold herself steady.

"Good lad," she said, just as she had to the dog. Then, realizing that Zeus was still free, she caught his jesses and wrapped them securely around her gloved fist, saying, "Patrick will be pleased with us both, I think."

She walked slowly and steadily, but apparently Zeus had had enough adventure for one day, because he sat quietly, giving a soft mew or cheep from time to time, as if he were chatting with her.

As she emerged from the woods, she heard a distant feminine shriek and saw Thunder nearing the crest of the hill, racing in the direction of their camp.

More shrieks followed.

She saw no sign of Jock, and since she was sure Thunder

would have stayed with Patrick had he found him, she hurried after the dog. As she crested the hill, still some distance from where they had made camp, she saw several armed men. One reached out and grabbed Thunder by the scruff of his neck.

As he did, the dog's speed and weight pulled him to one side, revealing the astonishing sight of a large, redheaded figure sitting on a flat boulder near the little burn where they had camped, wrapped in a voluminous cloak and petticoats with its head submissively bowed.

Claud and Lucy Fittletrot suddenly found themselves sitting in a ring of bright flowers on a sunny hillside, staring at each other in amazement.

"What happened?" Claud demanded. "What did ye do?"

"I? I did nowt! What did ye do?"

"Ye ken fine that I did nowt," he snapped. "One minute I were watching our lass seeking the bird, and the next I were here a-staring at ye. What place is this?"

Lucy shrugged. "We are near the dancing place, I think, where me people play music and dance every night. Will ye dance wi' me, Claud?"

Exasperation stirred. "Lucy, we canna dance till we find the lass."

"We'll find her, Claud. They be going tae Stirling, they said. We'll find them there, ye'll see. They willna get there for a day or two, but I can amuse ye betimes." Giggling, she leaned over and pulled off his shoe.

"Here! What be ye doing?"

Lucy lay on her stomach and caught hold of his toes. "I'll show ye summat ye'll like, Claud. Pay heed now."

Her hands were warm on his foot, and her fingers pressed firmly into the pad below his toes. The feelings that shot through his body were unlike any he had felt before, and when she began to suck his toes, he nearly swooned with delight. All thought of his charge slid into oblivion.

After sending Beth to the south end of the woods, Patrick had headed north toward the confluence of Douglas Water with the River Clyde. They had been following Douglas Water since late the previous day, and they would follow the Clyde when they met it until they reached Bothwell Castle, where he knew a track that headed north, skirting Glasgow.

They were deep in Douglas country, and he had taken care to avoid meeting travelers, keeping to ridges, away from the main tracks, which followed the water routes. But with Zeus free, he had no choice. If the hawk looked for a perch, it would seek barren top branches such as those he could see amongst the trees near Douglas Water. So intent was he on watching the sky that he nearly missed the movement of horsemen through the woods near the bottom of the hill.

The riders wended their way south, clearly following Douglas Water, and they would soon encounter Beth if she did not have enough warning to elude them. From where he stood, he could see sunlight glinting on steel weapons or jacks-of-plate, but he could not make out any banner that would tell him who they were.

Trepidation stirred, not for himself but for the lass. Not only were they in territory where doubtless many were loyal to Angus but the riders could be English, searching for him. Or, they could as easily be armed henchmen of some local baron, or—even this far from the Border—they might be Jock's reivers looking to reclaim Jackie the pony. In any event, Patrick dared not trust them to leave the unguarded Beth alone. At best, they would enjoy teasing her. At worst—

On the thought, he turned and ran up the hill, away from the trees, knowing that at least one horseman would be alert enough to spy such movement. If he could get over the ridge to the other side, he might reach their camp in time.

When he heard a shout, he knew the riders would follow, but even so, until he reached the ridge top, he affected a limp, hoping that if they believed him injured, they would also believe it unnecessary to push their horses up the hill. Once over the crest, he increased his speed, running full out until he reached the shelter of the woods where they had camped.

Unsheathing his sword as he ran, he flung the sheath, belt, and his jerkin into thick shrubbery, yanked the borrowed cloak, wig, scarf, and petticoats free of the pack where he had stowed them, jammed the wig on his head, and scrambled into the clothing. He was not concerned about how it fit, only about concealment.

As he tied the cloak strings and straightened the petticoats and wig, he realized that his rawhide boots might give him away and that if he moved about, the cloak would not cover him sufficiently. So he sat on a flat boulder near the trickling burn and yanked and arranged the petticoats to cover all but the tips of his boots. Sliding his sword under a pile of leaves at the base of the boulder where it would be handy if he needed it, he straightened his wig, wrapped the scarf around his neck, and tucked his chin down into it, hoping the arrangement and the quick shave Jock had given him that morning would suffice to conceal his gender.

It was shady, so he could avoid strong sunlight, but as he watched the horsemen bearing down upon him, his heart seemed to pound in time to the thundering hooves. He still could not make out the banner, but when he judged that the time was right, he let out a falsetto shriek, paused, and then screeched again. The first rider wrenched his mount to a plunging halt and slid from the saddle, drawing his sword. "Why the devil be ye screeching, ye auld besom?"

"An enormous man! Limping!" Patrick made a gesture toward the tumbling burn, careful not to disarrange his cloak. "Yonder!"

The first man waved three others on, but two stayed with him.

Patrick now recognized their banner, but it was too late to take advantage of it had he dared to do so. Silently, he cursed the first man for not leading all five of his cohorts off after the mythical limping man.

"What be yer name, mistress?" the leader demanded.

"Pray, do not leave me," Patrick said, clutching his hands together under his chin and hoping the weak falsetto voice he affected sounded feminine enough to keep them from snatching off his wig. "That horrid man gave me such a fright!"

"Ye say ye saw a man wha' limped pass this way?"

"Did I not just say so, sir?"

"But what be ye doing here all alone like ye are?"

"I . . . I'm waiting for my mistress and . . . and her page." Perhaps if they thought their search had disturbed persons of quality, they would move on.

"Who be your mistress then?"

"I do not think her identity need concern you," Patrick said haughtily.

"Now, see here—"

A shout from one of the others diverted his attention, and Patrick, following the shouter's gesture, saw Thunder dashing toward them.

"Christ Jesus," the first man exclaimed. "Seize that fiend, one o' you lot."

Seeing one of the others reach for the bow stretched across his back, Patrick said quickly, "The dog is friendly and quite valuable. Do not harm him!"

"That be a deerhound," the leader said.

"Aye," Patrick said.

The man looked at him more narrowly. "Stay your hand," he said to the man with the bow. "Deerhounds belong tae clan chiefs and the like. Catch it instead."

The erstwhile archer slipped from his saddle and faced Thunder, arms wide.

"Look yonder," the third man shouted. "A lass comes!"

The leader looked at Patrick. "Your mistress?"

"Aye, and if you value your life, my man, you will speak respectfully to her. Her father does not tolerate disrespect to his daughters."

The man trying to catch Thunder did so then, and although he stumbled a bit trying to hold him, the great dog stopped readily enough. Then it turned and stood calmly, watching Beth's approach.

"What manner o' bird be she carrying?" the leader asked.

"A peregrine falcon," Patrick said instantly, hoping the man knew as little about birds of prey as it seemed he did. It was all he could do to suppress his delight at seeing Zeus again, and he wondered how the lass had managed to capture him. He added tartly, "If you know aught of peregrines and the laws that govern them—"

"Aye, I ken well that a peregrine be reserved for them o' high estate, just as a deerhound be," the leader said.

"Earls, in fact, and men of even higher rank. Take care how you speak."

Beth strode toward them, her skirts swirling about her feet, her fist held high. Her flaxen hair was loose and flowing free, her stride was long and swift, and the hawk lifted its wings wide from time to time, steadying itself. They made a magnificent picture, Patrick thought, but his hands itched to wring her neck for walking so swiftly into danger. He barely dared to breathe.

She stopped some yards away, looking uncertain and wonderfully beautiful.

Before anyone spoke, Jock stepped out from behind a tree and bowed low, saying cheerfully, "Welcome back, me lady. How did ye fare wi' your hunting?"

Accepting her cue, Beth said, "We fared well, thank you, lad." Pretending to ignore the men-at-arms, she looked at Patrick, saying, "Who are these men, Sadie? I do not recognize their banner, but I trust they've not dared to molest you."

Zeus bent his head to examine the tear in her sleeve.

"Nay, my lady," Patrick said in the grating, falsetto voice he had affected, his eyes narrowing. "As to who they be, I cannot say."

"What be your name, mistress?" one of the men demanded.

Recalling Jock's words and what Patrick had said about deerhounds, she gathered Lady Farnsworth's persona to herself, ignored Zeus's interest in the scratch he had put on her arm, and said haughtily, "I am Lady Elizabeth Douglas."

She felt safe enough, because although Patrick had said they were in Douglas country, she knew that the banner the men carried was not a Douglas banner. To the leader, she said, "Who are you, sirrah, that you dare to question me?"

"Ye shouldna be wandering about on your own, m'lady," the leader said.

"Insolence! Do you dare give me orders, as well as to question me?" Now *that,* she thought, was pure Drusilla.

"Nay, mistress," the man said, "but since we dinna ken the man who ran this way, and since we ha' no captured him, I'd advise ye tae go home straightaway."

"Very well," she said, abandoning her haughty attitude in favor of a more conciliatory one. "We are going to my uncle. He will look after me."

"Aye, sure, and who would your uncle be then?"

Since she had not the slightest idea whom to name, she was grateful when Patrick said, "We go to Bothwell. Her ladyship stopped only to let the hawk hunt for its dinner. I told her we should not tarry, but she does as she pleases."

"Doubtless you would like an escort," the leader said. "I could perhaps spare two o' my lads here tae see ye safe tae Bothwell."

"Aye," Patrick said feebly. "That is kind of you."

Beth knew he did not want them, so she drew herself to her full height and said testily, "You would better serve us, I believe, by catching the man who ran through our campsite. You say you do not know who he is. Is he dangerous?"

"In truth, my lady, we dinna ken that either. It be clear enough he were running, but why he ran be a puzzle. Still, ye ha' the right o' it. We should track him down afore he does any mischief. Be ye sure ye ha' nae need o' us?"

"I am sure," Beth said. "As you see, we are not grandly dressed, so I doubt that any ruffian would think us worthy of attack. If one does, my dog will protect us, and we have only a short distance to go."

He gave her a long look but did not argue. Signing to the others to follow, he mounted his pony, and soon the last lingering hoofbeats faded into the distance.

"Jock," Patrick said, "follow them, and be sure that they have truly all gone."

Chapter 13 _____

Patrick said no more, and his expression was such that Beth, too, held her peace for the few minutes it took Jock to run to the top of the hill and back.

"Only the six," he said. "They be a-riding on tae the next dale. I counted."

"Good lad," Patrick said. "Where did you pop from so handily, anyway?"

"I were on the ridge, like ye said, and I saw them riders, so I ran tae the woods tae hide, lest they be reivers after Jackie. Ye near clouted me wi' your sword belt when ye flung it."

"Why did you not come out then?"

"Ye started heaving things about like ye were having a fit, and them men was coming, too, so I laid low till I saw the mistress and heard ye say that about Thunder and Zeus. I ken fine that an earl's daughter be a lady, and since ye couldna warn her, I showed m'self. Sithee, she's got a brain and all, so I kent she wouldna say I were daft if I said 'your ladyship' tae her."

"You were splendid, Jock," Beth said. "Quick-witted, too."

"You played the lady of the manor as if you'd been born to it, lass," Patrick said, tugging off the red wig.

Beth detected an edge to his voice that made her look at him more carefully. "I just pretended to be Lady Farnsworth with a bit of Drusilla thrown in," she said. "What if they go to Bothwell Castle and find that no one there knows us?"

"We're not going anywhere near Bothwell now," he said. "We'll take the north road out of Lanark instead. They'll not seek us there."

"I do not even know who they were," she reminded him. "They never said."

"They carried Cardinal Beaton's banner," he said.

"Cardinal Beaton! But I thought you said—"

"Not now, lass." He cast a glance at Jock. "We can trust no one until we reach Stirling."

"Aye, he ha' the right o' that, mistress," Jock said wisely. "Ye canna trust anyone on the road. Likely, they'll only want tae lift what's yours for theirselves."

"Ready the ponies, Jock," Patrick said. "Stow your things in my pack, so you and Mistress Beth can ride Jackie. I don't think those men will return, but if I am wrong, I want to be away as soon as possible."

When Jock had gone to do his bidding, Patrick gave Beth a look that sent a shiver to her toes and made her glad that Thunder stood beside her and that she still carried the hawk on her fist. Not that it paid any heed to Patrick. It was more interested in the bit of blood showing through the rip in her sleeve.

"What were you thinking, to come striding into that nest of vipers as you did?" Patrick demanded as he cast the cloak aside and stepped out of the petticoats.

She was sure no other man could look dangerous while ridding himself of women's clothing, but Patrick's gaze never left hers, and his expression was stern.

Swallowing carefully and striving to sound calmer than she felt, she said, "You should be grateful that I did. They would soon have discovered that you are a man. It is a miracle you fooled them at all, because you do not look very ladylike."

"We'll leave my appearance out of this discussion. What were you thinking when you walked bang up to them like that?"

"That you were in danger and that I could help," she retorted.

"And what of yourself? Do you not know what men like those are capable of doing to young women like you?"

"They seemed very much like you!"

"You know they are not."

She did know that. "You said they were Cardinal Beaton's men," she said. "Surely, men of the Holy Kirk would not harm me."

"Cardinal Beaton does not hire his men-at-arms because they are men of the cloth," Patrick said scornfully. "In sooth, he did not win his vast power by being gentle, so you would do better not to trust him, either, lass."

"Clearly, then, you are the only man I should trust," she snapped.

"Exactly so," he said.

She had had enough of his scolding, and his advice. "I have listened to you, sir," she said, giving rein to her temper, "and now you will listen to me. I heeded your advice, perhaps more than I should have, because for years it has been easier for me to heed the advice of others than to thwart them. But you ask me to trust you and you tell me that you obey Cardinal Beaton. Then you say—"

"What happened to your arm?"

Startled by the non sequitur, Beth said, "Zeus scratched me when he pulled his hood off, but as you see, he feels just as he did when he scratched your neck."

"Why did you not tell me about it when it happened?"

"I did not want you to scold me for my carelessness," she

said, eyeing him warily. "I was not paying attention to him as I should have been."

He sighed. "I only want you to be safe, lass. If I scold, 'tis because I know I've set a bad example. 'Fortitude' is my watchword, and thus I dare much, but a male can defend himself more easily than a too-impulsive lass can. You should wash that scratch carefully in the burn before we leave."

"Aye, sir, I know," she said, resisting the temptation to point out that trying to defend himself in skirts might have proven beyond even his skill.

"The ponies be ready, master," Jock said, startling them both.

Patrick held Beth's gaze for another beat. "We'll talk more anon, lass."

Nell and Jane reached Edinburgh that afternoon, after a blessedly uneventful journey from the Borders. As they wended their way toward the castle, Nell felt a charge of energy. She was nearing her goal at last. As soon as Jamie granted her permission to stay in Scotland—and she trusted that she had enough information about Henry and Angus to exchange for safe haven—she would go to Molly, and together they would find Bessie if Molly and Kintail had not done so already.

At the castle gate, she inquired as to the King's whereabouts, just in case James had recently come to Edinburgh.

"His grace be at Stirling, celebrating the birth of the new young duke," the guardsman told her. "There's tae be a grand fête on Monday. They say Davy Beaton doesna approve o' such goings-on during Lent, but his grace did say 'twas his ain birthday and he'll celebrate the bairn's, too, Lent or no Lent."

Amused, Nell was tempted to ask the man if he had heard that conversation for himself. Resisting, she said instead, "A grand celebration, you say?"

"Aye, mistress. They do say all the nobility and gentry will be present."

"Your captain has gone to Stirling then."

"Nay, mistress. Sir David and Lady Gordon willna leave Edinburgh till Saturday afternoon. He'd leave it longer, likely, but he doesna travel on the Sabbath and there are to be goings-on all day on Monday."

"Then will you be so good as to show us to his quarters?" Nell asked. "Tell him that his cousin Adam's widow begs hospitality if he will kindly welcome her."

"At once, my lady," the man said, hastily summoning a minion and giving him orders to escort her to the inner bailey.

As Nell and Jane rode after the man, Jane said, "Praise be, we'll have two whole nights in a good bed."

"One night," Nell said. "I mean to visit the shops in the morning, but then we're for Stirling, and I do not want a chaperon, certainly not one as stiff-rumped as Sir David Gordon."

Patrick and Beth moved swiftly to Lanark, keeping watch for Beaton's men along the way, and skirted Glasgow without incident. When they stopped for the night, Patrick was satisfied that they had left Beaton's men behind and that the clearing he found for their campsite would be safe. Nevertheless, they did not build a fire but ate cold rabbit and apples that Jock had begged from a cottager.

When the lad began to lay out their beds, Patrick said,

"Take the dog and make your bed yonder at the edge of the clearing. I want to talk privately with Mistress Beth. If anyone comes, Thunder will warn us."

"Aye," Jock said, giving Patrick a look that said he understood more than Patrick was telling him. Patrick did not attempt to dissuade him, knowing it would be useless and knowing, too, that such a conversation would disturb Beth.

"It is not right that I sleep here alone with you," she said.

"You want to talk, do you not?"

"Aye, but could we not talk just as easily whilst we travel?"

"Not without the lad overhearing and doubtless adding his mite," he said. "Moreover, this may be our last chance to talk, since we should reach Stirling late tomorrow afternoon. I judge we're about fifteen miles away, so there will likely be considerable traffic on the main road. No one will heed three more travelers."

"I did not know we were so close." She stayed where she was, hugging herself, avoiding his gaze.

He looked steadily at her. "*Mo chridhe,* if you have learned aught of me, you know that you can trust me not to harm you. Come here."

"But others will think—"

"It is too late to worry about what others will think," he said bluntly. "Have you thought about what will happen when we reach Stirling?"

Her wary expression told him that she had not.

"Well, I have," he said, "and I believe I know how to protect you, but you will have to trust me. In return, it is only fair that I tell you exactly who I am and a bit more about what I've been doing."

Despite the dim light, he saw her eyes widen.

"You will tell me everything?"

"As much as I can, but it is my hope that the more you

understand, the more you will trust me, because now that you have claimed to be Lady Elizabeth Douglas, the sooner I get you into safe hands, the better it will be for both of us. An avowed Douglas is unsafe anywhere near the King."

"It seemed the right thing to say, since you had said we were deep in Douglas country and the 'lady' part came naturally, since I am—"

"You are what?" he asked when she broke off and looked guilty.

"I had supposed you knew all about me by now," she said. "You were certainly at Farnsworth Tower long enough to learn my entire history."

"I did not mingle much with the Tower people," he said. "I was busy, for one thing, and it is better not to gossip with folks if you cannot add to their knowledge. What did you suppose I had learned?"

"That although my mother was a common maidservant like me, they claim that my father was an earl."

He grinned. "I don't believe you. You played the lady well enough, but it would take more than that to persuade me that you had even met an earl."

"I don't remember doing so, but I expect I must have," she said. "I do not think highly of him, however. A man worthy of such high estate would not abandon his child to be raised by others."

"Is that what Farnsworth said your father did?"

When she nodded, an angry knot twisted inside him at the thought of anyone abandoning her. Then she shrugged and said, "But our purpose is not to talk of me, sir. You must keep your promise to explain yourself."

The way she spoke reminded him of how she had made him feel earlier, and he stifled an impulse to apologize again. A vision of his mother flashed in his mind. That Beth did not use his father as a threat to make him behave made no difference. She had the same knack for revealing his faults and making him feel small.

"I'll explain, but you'll get cold if we don't make our beds first," he said.

She did not argue, and he made them while she saw to her ablutions. When she returned, he left her alone and went to tend his own needs and Zeus's. When he returned, he saw that she had shifted her bed a little away from his.

He made no comment but punched his jerkin into a pillow, then lay on his back with his sword near at hand, his hands clasped behind his head, wondering how to begin.

She did not speak.

At last, he said, "What would you like to know first?"

"I suppose I should first know your true name."

"It's Patrick. I am Patrick MacRae, from a place in the Highlands called Kintail. My master is Mackenzie of Kintail. For as long as anyone can remember, the MacRaes have served the Mackenzies as I serve him."

"Then do others in your family serve him and others of his clan?"

"Aye, although my father is dead. I've only my mother and sister left of our lot, but I've cousins and such who do. My master and I have known each other since childhood and were schooled together, so when the King took many of the Highland leaders hostage, I swore to do what I had to, to win Kintail's freedom."

"Who is Molly?" she asked.

He barely recalled speaking of Molly to her, but he remembered he had mentioned her when he had said she would slap him if he dared to steal a kiss from her. "Molly is Lady Kintail." His voice softened as it always did when he spoke of her, and he smiled to think that he would soon see her again. "My first task after Jamie took Kintail hostage was to escort Molly to Stirling to be at his side."

"You like her," Beth said quietly.

"Aye, I do," he said. "She is not only beautiful and spirited but also kind."

"Do you love her?"

"In truth I suppose she is the only woman I have ever loved, in my fashion—which I promise you is wholly chivalrous." He chuckled, thinking of what Fin would do to anyone who dared to love Molly in any other fashion.

"Why do you laugh?"

"They call her husband Wild Fin Mackenzie," he said.

"He cannot be so wild if you dare to laugh at him."

"Faith, lass, I'm not laughing at *him,* just at the notion that my love for his wife could be anything but chivalrous in nature."

"Oh."

"I took her to Stirling because it was my duty and Beaton had suggested— Did I mention that the cardinal was present when Jamie took Kintail hostage?"

"No, was he?"

"Aye, and he made his disapproval of Kintail's seizure plain, because Kintail has ever been loyal to the Crown. Beaton suggested he might help arrange Kintail's release, so when we reached Stirling, I went to Cambuskenneth Abbey to see him."

"And then?"

"He said he'd do what he could, but he never acts directly. Since Jamie's present favorite, a slimy worm called Oliver Sinclair, seems to fear all Highlanders and is determined to hold on to the hostages, Beaton said he would help only if I proved my loyalty to him and to the Holy Kirk."

"So he sent you to England to spy on Henry. Did you like spying?"

"I did not," he said indignantly. "A gentleman does not spy on others, but I learned that Beaton has spies everywhere. He arranged for someone to introduce me at Henry's court, but just so I could watch a Scotsman, the Earl of Angus—the most powerful of your supposed Douglas kinsmen, my lady," he added on a teasing note.

Beth's breath stopped in her throat, and she was glad darkness had fallen so he could not see her face.

Choosing her words, she said, "Angus cannot be so powerful anymore. He has been in exile for years, has he not, and his lands given over to others?"

"Aye, but he's a treacherous fiend all the same, and having thrown in his lot with Henry of England, he is more dangerous than ever. After Henry's court moved to York, I followed Angus north, where he met with men who say that if James refuses to meet Henry at York, they will invade."

"But James has been awaiting the birth of his child, and Henry is his uncle," Beth protested. "A peace between them would make the Borders safe for everyone."

"Henry Tudor demands that the two realms grow closer to each other, by which he means that the greater shall swallow the smaller."

"That England will swallow Scotland?"

"Aye, and he wants Scotland to reform her Kirk as England has done, and to throw off the Vatican, thus eliminating all cause, he says, for disharmony."

She was silent, uncertain what to say.

"Would you trust Henry, lass?"

"In truth, sir, I know not what to think about the Kirk. Folks here in the Borders carry their religion lightly, I fear. Doubtless, you will think less of us for that, but Borderers tend to give religious loyalty where they think it will serve them best. Sir Hector and Lady Farnsworth lean toward the reformers, but if the Pope—or Cardinal Beaton, for that matter—were to show his face at Farnsworth, they would instantly express their total allegiance to the Vatican. I warrant they will find it expedient to behave as fiercely devout papists whilst they are at Stirling."

He chuckled. "Folks are no different in the Highlands, although if you tell Davy Beaton I said that, I shall deny it. The fact is, both your people and mine are far from Stirling and even farther from London or Rome. We heed our own laws and ignore those of the King or the Pope."

"But if you serve Cardinal Beaton—"

"I serve Mackenzie of Kintail," he said. "Kintail is loyal to Jamie, so I likewise serve him. Since I must serve Beaton to free Kintail, I serve him, too, but if Jamie meets his uncle Henry, the rules may swiftly change."

"How long will Henry wait at York?"

"No one knows. He's in a foul mood, but I think he will wait some time, because he believes he has only to speak to Jamie to persuade him."

"Will you go with James if he goes?"

"He is not such a fool as to ride a hundred miles into England to meet Henry, but I'll do what Kintail commands. In truth, I hope he commands our return home."

Beth shivered, wrapping her cloak more securely around her. "It is colder tonight than it has been, is it not?"

"No, but you have shared your bed with that blasted hound these past nights," he said. She heard rustling, and then his arm slipped under her shoulders and he drew her close. "You'll be warmer now," he said.

"Will I?"

"Aye."

He was on his side, and she could see him outlined against the starry sky as he leaned over her. His lips gently touched hers, and when she did not draw back, he kissed her again.

She moaned a little but did not try to push him away. She did not want to, and if that made her wanton, she thought, so be it.

His body radiated warmth, so she was certainly no longer cold. He was gentle, his kisses soft, as if he were tasting her lips and then her cheeks and eyelids. Her head rested on his arm. As his lips trailed a path from her eyelids to her earlobes, newly grown whiskers lightly prickled her cheek.

"It is as well that you are no longer posing as a woman," she murmured. "Your beard has grown since our visitors were here."

"Has it?" His lips moved to her neck, and she felt her pulse beat against them. The touch of whiskers on her neck and cheek shot tingles through her body. She drew a breath as his free hand moved to her shoulder and pulled her closer.

"Don't fear me, sweetheart," he whispered. "I want to taste you everywhere, but I'll not harm you, I swear."

She could not speak, even to tell him she had no fear of him, only of herself. Her body pressed against his, wanting him, and without a qualm, she cast all thought of consequences to the wind sighing through branches overhead.

He was not holding her so tightly now, for his free hand moved to caress her breasts, and his lips moved back to her mouth, kissing her more fiercely now, his tongue demanding entrance. The sensations he stirred were new and delightful, and she began to experiment, teasing his tongue with hers and moving her hands on his body, exploring him as he explored her.

When his fingers moved to the laces of her bodice, she turned to make it easier for him, and for a brief moment, her breasts felt the kiss of the cool breeze. His hand cupped first one and then the other, stroking lightly at first, then gently kneading the right one, using a fingertip to brush the nipple.

She gasped at the jolt of desire that swept through her, and she heard him moan softly as his kisses became fiercer, more demanding. Then his lips left hers and he bent his head lower. Before she realized his intent, his lips closed around the nipple he had teased and his hand moved lower, stroking her bare belly.

He continued in this manner for some time, and when he paused at last, she gasped in disappointment.

"Don't stop!"

He chuckled low in his throat. "I must, lass. If I don't, we'll both be sorry."

"I won't!"

"You will, and what's more, if I continue, you'll likely soon hate me."

"I won't, I swear! I've never felt such feelings before. Please don't stop."

He kissed the tip of her nose. "I shall barely retain a clear conscience as it is. You tempt a man sorely, sweetheart, but I promised I'd protect you on the road and when we reach Stirling, and I know of only one way I can do both."

His tone had changed, and she knew she did not want to hear what he had decided. "I'll be with you," she said. "You can protect me easily."

"Nay, sweetheart, that would be the worst thing you could do, for I cannot protect you and serve Kintail as I must. As it is, your reputation will suffer, do what I may to prevent it, but we've had the lad and the dog with us, and Jock is no prattler. If anyone asks him, he'll swear you remain chaste, as indeed you do."

"But who would dare ask, if I were under your protection?"

He gave her a little shake. "I'll not willingly cause your ruin, Beth. Don't think that of me. Sir Hector will ask, certainly. It is his right and his duty."

"Sir Hector?" She could scarcely breathe.

"Aye, I can entrust you to him. He has always been kind to you, has he not?"

"Others have not, though," she said, fighting her emotions, not wanting him to know how close she was to tears.

"I don't want to go back, Patrick, and you are cruel if you make me. They will beat me for running away."

"They will not," he said firmly. "You will apologize to Sir Hector for running away, and I will see to it that no one harms you."

"I won't do it!"

"Oh, yes, you will."

She argued with him until the following afternoon when the royal burgh of Stirling loomed ahead on its craggy hilltop, creating a stark contrast with the low, rolling, green hills to its east and west.

She called him every evil name she could summon to her tongue, vowed that nothing he could say or do would make her return to the Farnsworths. She ignored him when he tried to talk of other things, even when he pointed out the field at Bannockburn as they passed, and tried to tell her its history.

She was riding his pony while he strolled beside her, the hooded Zeus on his shoulder. Jock rode Jackie and led the sumpter pony, and Thunder loped ahead, exploring the countryside first on one side of the road, then the other, sniffing every bush and marking every tree.

There were several horsemen on the road some distance ahead of them, but no one besides Jock was near enough to hear when she snapped, "I know all about Bannockburn and Robert the Bruce. The battle took place in 1314, and years later it was a Douglas who carried the Bruce's heart back from the Holy Land. Douglases of that ilk still display the heart on their crest."

Patrick remained silent long enough to make her wish she had not spoken so sharply or mentioned Douglases of any ilk. In general, she felt so comfortable with him that she tended to forget that he had small opinion of Douglases and did not yet know that she was one, but she did not feel comfortable now. The silence lasted too long, and it was heavy with his displeasure.

When at last he spoke, he said quietly to Jock, "Ride on ahead for a bit, lad. Wait, though. Leave the sumpter pony, and take Zeus. Lend him your glove, Beth."

She had tucked it into her belt, because she and Patrick had been taking turns carrying the hawk. She pulled it free, and he took it from her, giving it to the boy when he rode near enough and taking the lead rein from him.

Jock slipped on the glove without comment, and then held his gloved fist against the hawk's belly until Zeus stepped onto it. No one spoke as the lad rode on ahead. Thunder joined him, trotting alongside.

Beth was sorry to see them go. The air was charged with Patrick's irritation as he stood silently, watching them.

She could think of nothing to say, nothing that would soothe his temper, and she realized that she wanted to soothe it. In general, she found it exciting to argue with him, to say things she had never said to anyone else, to relish the freedom of saying whatever came into her head without stopping to consider how it would be received. But now, she wished she could unsay the last few things she had said.

He turned toward her at last, dropping the lead reins. The two horses would not wander off, but he clearly gave them no thought.

Beth braced herself, but she was not prepared for him to clasp her around the waist and lift her from the horse. He held her dangling in front of him for a moment, glaring at her, eye to eye, and then set her on her feet with a bone jarring thud. His hands moved from her waist to her shoulders, holding her firmly where she stood.

Her temper flared despite her fears. "What—?"

"Be silent," he snapped, giving her a shake. "You have said enough, and I have listened as patiently as I know how, hoping you would say all you wanted to say and be done with it. Apparently you can spit words indefinitely though, and I have heard enough. I do not want to hear any more."

"But I—"

He gave her another shake, saying, "You will return to Sir Hector and his lady, and that is that. You would not be safe anywhere else. Innocent, respectable young women do not look after themselves in Stirling or anywhere else, and you cannot stay with me. Nor can I take you to Kintail or Molly. Even if Jamie would permit that—and we would have to ask his permission—they have enough on their plates without having to worry about you."

"But I *told* you, I mean to make my own decisions now."

"And I am telling *you* that you will not," he said, his fingers gripping her so tightly that she was sure he was bruising her. "At this moment," he added, "I'm not even sure I want to prevent Sir Hector or his lady from punishing you. Consider yourself fortunate that I *generally* draw the line at putting females across my knee on the highroad, but don't tempt me further. My palms are fairly itching."

A thrill of fear shot through her. "You wouldn't!"

"I would."

They stood glaring at each other, his hands still gripping her shoulders.

The tingling in her body increased as her awareness of his size and power, and his pulsing anger with her, altered into something altogether different.

The day seemed warmer, and she felt as if she had been running. Her breathing came quicker, and her heart pounded. Even her cheeks tingled. Her lips felt dry. She licked them.

"Damn you," he muttered, yanking her against him and kissing her hard.

Chapter 14

Beth's body stirred in response to Patrick's kiss as it always did, and without thinking about the folly of her reaction, she kissed him back, meeting his tongue with hers, pressing against him as if she could melt right into him and become a part of him always. If only she could, she thought, if only she need not go back to them.

She felt his body move against hers, and his kisses became more possessive, hard and demanding. His hands moved urgently over her, caressing her arms and her breasts, the curves of her sides and her hips, and then they slipped around to cup her bottom. He pulled her tight against him.

She held on to him just as tightly, savoring every sensation.

"Oh, sweet Beth," he murmured. "How you torment me!"

His lips moved from her mouth to the side of her neck beneath her right ear. His teeth nibbled her earlobe, sending flashes of heat through her body.

She gasped, and he stopped nibbling. She could feel his warm breath against her neck, and she could still taste his kisses on her lips and feel the impression of his teeth on her earlobe. His scent enveloped her, musky with an herbal hint of woodland and a tangy, lingering touch of wood smoke.

Neither of them moved.

A lapwing's high-pitched *weet-weet* sounded in the distance, accompanied by the fading drumbeat of Jackie's hooves on the road ahead.

Patrick straightened, saying gruffly, "If we don't stop this madness, you'll have more to worry about on the highroad than just being put across my knee."

She did not reply. She understood him and could hardly say that she did not care if he did take her right there. The thought startled her. Clearly, she had grown even more wanton than she had feared. Could even a merciful God forgive such behavior? Neither the punishing God of Cardinal Beaton nor Henry of England's more compliant one would do so. Their versions of Him would order her straight off to hell for even thinking such shameless things.

She caught her lower lip between her teeth, remembering the horrid things she had said to Patrick. Looking up into his eyes, she said, "I'm sorry I spoke to you as I did. I do not really think you are a milk-livered dolthead. Indeed, I am not certain I know what 'milk-livered' means."

His lips twitched. "I liked 'knavish, plume-plucked gudgeon' best."

"Did I say that?" She wrinkled her nose. "I do not remember, but Sir Hector sometimes says that, so I suppose I did. Must I really go back to them, sir?"

"You must, sweetheart, and I want you to promise you will stay with them, too, no matter what they do to you."

She hesitated.

His lips tightened. "If you run away, Beth, I will find you and make you wish you had never been born," he said, his tone stern enough to send shivers through her again. "It terrifies me to think of what could happen to you, all alone in Stirling."

She sighed. "Very well then, I will do as you say, but I hope you will not be so cruel as to encourage Sir Hector to punish me or to allow Lady Farnsworth to do so. It will be hard enough to face them without enduring that."

"I can make no promises where they are concerned, sweetheart, but I do promise to try. Whatever they do, they cannot murder you."

With that, she had to be satisfied. Indeed, she thought, as he lifted her to his horse's back again, it was more than she deserved after all the things she had said. It was strange, though, to think how easily she had given rein to her temper when she rarely had done so before. She believed she had become adept at controlling it, but with Patrick she seemed to have no control over any part of her body.

The rest of their journey was without incident, and soon they were wending their way up the steep, narrow confines of Spittal Street and Bow Street to the tall, narrow house of Sir Hector's cousin, Oscar Farnsworth, in St. Mary's Wynd.

Leaving Jock to mind the horses, Patrick lifted Beth down and stood for a moment with his hands at her waist, gazing into her eyes.

"I know you don't want to do this," he said, "and I wish it weren't necessary. But I do believe it's the best course for now. I'll stay until I can arrange proper care for Zeus, or until Sir Hector arrives and takes him to the King, but I must visit the cardinal and Kintail soon to let them know I am here." He paused, and when she did not speak, he added gently, "I meant what I said earlier about running away."

She sighed heavily. "I know."

He was silent, still gazing at her. Then he said, "If you cannot bear it after I've gone, or if they do something dreadful, seek me at the castle."

She tried to smile then and failed. "Is that where you'll be?"

"Aye, for I must join Kintail and his lady as soon as I can, and even if they get permission to leave at once, it will be a sennight at least before they can go."

"I doubt anyone at the castle would let me in," she said. "Last year, Lady Farnsworth let me accompany them all when they went to court—to care for their gowns and such and dress them, not to attend court, of course. But they always held cards of entrée, and whatever else she may do, I doubt she will let me go this year."

"Send a messenger, or if you need to find me there yourself, you need only apply to the royal porter. Tell him you are a servant in Sir Hector's household and that you have brought a message that you must give to me personally."

"Won't he wonder why Sir Hector would send a female on such an errand?"

"If he is so impertinent as to question Sir Hector's orders, just tell him you can give him no information other than that you were so commanded," he said.

At the door, they learned as expected that Sir Hector and his family had not yet arrived, whereupon Patrick asked the gillie to take them to Oscar Farnsworth.

The next half hour passed far too swiftly for Beth.

Oscar Farnsworth greeted them as heartily as if they had been friends of Sir Hector and Lady Farnsworth rather than their servants. He was a much larger man than his cousin, with a round, pink face framed by a bushy gray beard and side-whiskers. The little hair remaining on top of his head was fashionably short. He recognized Beth at once, greeting her as Elspeth, and if he thought it odd to see her in company with the falconer, he did not say so.

Patrick gave him Sir Hector's letter of introduction.

"Yes, yes, I've been expecting you," Farnsworth said. "A

running gillie arrived from Hector yesterday to tell me they will be here by noon tomorrow and warning me to expect you. Is that hawk of his ready to give to the King?"

"Aye," Patrick said. "He asked only that I man 'im tae the fist, but he ha' responded gey quick, sir. He'll need more training yet afore he'll be fit tae take part in a royal hunt, but I warrant his abilities will astonish his grace. I ha' brought a lad tae help wi' the bird, and two ponies, as well. Where would ye like us tae stay, sir?"

Hearing him affect the strong Border accent again, Beth suppressed a smile, although she had little cause for humor. She knew that Oscar Farnsworth must wonder why she had traveled with him. Farnsworth kept glancing at her, but he had not said a word to her since his greeting.

"Hector said most likely you would not be staying," Farnsworth told him. "I have my own mews, you see, and an experienced falconer, so you need not. But Hector did ask that you present yourself here at two o'clock tomorrow, since he means to give the bird to his grace at once and wants you to be present, in the event that his grace has any questions about the hawk's training."

"Aye, I'll be here," Patrick agreed, glancing at Beth.

Farnsworth smiled. "If you cannot find a room in town— which is likely with so many here to celebrate the young duke's birth, you are welcome to return. I can also pay whatever Hector may still owe for your services, so you will have money."

"Thank ye, sir, but he owes me naught," Patrick said.

"And what of this young woman with you?" Farnsworth asked abruptly.

"She be a servant in Sir Hector's household," Patrick said.

"Aye, I ken the lass," Farnsworth said, eyeing him narrowly. "Indeed, my wife and I have hitherto had a great fondness for her. Hector did not mention her, though, and what stirs my curiosity . . ." With a sweeping gesture, he coupled the two of them, clearly assuming that Patrick would take his meaning.

"There be nowt o' that, sir. The lad and me just brought her here safe."

"I see," Farnsworth said, frowning.

"Ha' ye some'un wha' can show the lass where she is tae sleep?" Patrick went on, avoiding Beth's eye. "I would ha' further speech wi' ye in private."

"Aye, surely." Farnsworth shouted for a servant and gave the order.

Thus, Beth heard no more, and she tried to imagine what Patrick might say to him that could ease the reception she would endure when Lady Farnsworth arrived.

"Ye were right, Lucy," Claud said with satisfaction. "Our lass be safe in Stirling just as ye said, but I canna think why we couldna find her again afore now."

Lucy shrugged. "What does it matter since we have found her?"

She reclined on a cushioned chest in the chamber to which they had followed Bessie, and Claud liked being near her, just looking at her. She was so comfortable, his Lucy, more comfortable than Catriona had ever been. But she had secrets, he was sure, and had Maggie not warned him that someone was up to mischief? Could it be Lucy? He did not want to think such a thing, but the plain fact was that one moment he was watching Bessie on the hillside with Lucy, and in the next, he and Lucy were in another place entirely. And she had been at his side ever since.

Not that he minded that part, he told himself as she gently altered her position to lay her head in his lap. Her fingers became busy, too, and his thoughts shifted abruptly. He gave no more thought just then to Bessie.

Having done what he could to protect Beth, Patrick delivered the two horses and Zeus to Oscar Farnsworth's people. He was reluctant to part with the hawk because he had developed a fondness for it, but he was even more reluctant to find himself afterward still saddled with young Jock and his two faithful companions.

"You can stay with Zeus, you know," Patrick said, for he had asked the Farnsworth falconer if he could use Jock's help, and the man had agreed to try him.

"Ye'll no be leaving me wi' that lot," Jock said scornfully. "I've nae use for townsfolk. Sakes, man, ye'll ha' much more need o' me than them. I doubt they'd let me within ten feet o' our Zeus. Most likely they'd set me tae all the chores and muck they dinna want tae do theirselves, and sithee, I'm for a better life than that. I'll go along wi' ye for now, and mind yer boots and such for ye."

"Will you indeed?" Patrick said grimly.

"Aye," Jock declared. "I'll let ye use Jackie anytime ye want, too, and Thunder will guard your things better than ye could yourself."

"An offer like that is hard to resist."

"Aye, that's wha' I thought, so where be we going now?"

Tempted though he was to go first to the castle and make sure that Fin and Molly were safe, Patrick knew his first task was to report to Beaton. He was not eager to take his small entourage along, but seeing no other course that would not require a heavy hand, he said, "We're bound for Cambuskenneth Abbey."

Jock nodded. "Right, then. How far?"

"Two miles and a bit," Patrick said. "We'll cross the River Forth."

"Good," the boy said. Leading Jackie, he chattered until they were halfway across Stirling Bridge, when they came within sight of the tall abbey tower. Then he stopped in the road and said in an awestruck voice, "Be that where we're a-going?"

"It is," Patrick said. "You can hear its bells ringing from Stirling town. The man I must see keeps his apartments behind those double windows there, and under the altar of the church by the tower, our third King James and his wife are buried."

"Aye, well, if they dinna trouble us, we'll no trouble them," Jock said, tugging on the pony's reins to urge it forward again.

"You will stay outside to look after Thunder and Jackie," Patrick said. "If anyone speaks to you, say naught of my business or of our journey to Stirling."

Jock nodded and made no objection to being left outside, which was good, since Patrick's disposition had deteriorated considerably since leaving Beth. He was in no mood for more of the lad's impudence.

Leaving him in the cobblestone yard between church and tower, he strode to the tower entrance, where he asked the black-cassocked porter to inform Beaton that he had returned from his journey and would like to have speech with him. An hour's delay would not have surprised him, for he knew that Beaton enjoyed pomp and circumstance. On his first visit, the porter had taken him to the prior's chamber first. This time, however, the man said brusquely, "Come with me, sir."

Patrick's satisfaction lasted only until the porter showed him into a bleak chamber on the second floor.

"What's this?" he demanded. "I want to see the cardinal."

"Aye, sir, so ye said," the porter replied, "and his eminence will want to see you, too, but he is away until late tonight. He gave orders that if you arrived in his absence, you were to bide here and speak to no one else until he speaks with you."

Patrick opened his mouth to argue, realized the futility of it, and said only, "I've a lad with me who tends my beasts and boots. Ask someone to send him here when he's stabled the pony."

The porter nodded. "He can fetch your supper to you."

"I must be elsewhere tomorrow at two o'clock," Patrick said.

"His eminence will doubtless see you first thing in the morning, sir."

Left alone, Patrick wondered briefly what Beaton was up to. It didn't much matter though. He cared more about Beth's fate than about Beaton's or his own.

Nell and Jane arrived in Stirling that evening and rode directly to the cottage of Jane's cousin, Agnes Geddes. There was little rest for them, however, for Nell meant to attend court the next morning, and she did not mean to look dowdy when she did. James had an eye for a beautiful woman, and although she showed her age more now than the last time they met, she still meant to catch that eye.

"I depend on you to furbish me up, the pair of you," she said when Agnes sent her grown son to fetch a bathtub into the little kitchen.

"Tae my mind, ye'll no need much furbishing, m'lady," Agnes said, looking her over critically. "Ye've kept yourself well, and nae mistake."

"Nonetheless, I must win the attention of his grace," Nell said bluntly. "I have no man to speak for me, nor do I want one, so Jamie will have to notice me. And unless custom has altered since my last visit to court, a woman cannot simply march up to the King and say 'how do you fare, sire?' "

Jane sniffed, but Agnes chuckled, assuring Nell that times had not changed.

"Then do your best for me," Nell said, "both of you!"

It was by no means "first thing in the morning" when the abbey porter came to fetch Patrick, but it was before noon. Leaving Jock to return their breakfast things to the kitchen and ready himself to leave when Patrick returned, he followed the porter to the cardinal's chambers.

Davy Beaton looked just as he had the two previous times they had met. His elegant red garments might have been the same as he had worn on those occasions, and his smile was the same quick, confident smile. He sat in an elaborately carved chair on a raised, carpeted dais, and as he invited Patrick to enter, he dismissed the two clerics sitting with him, first asking one to pour wine for them.

"So, Patrick MacRae, you return safely," he said, holding out his hand with its cardinal's ruby winking in a ray of sunlight from a nearby window.

Obediently, Patrick knelt and kissed the ring. "As you see, eminence." Standing, he added, "I've come to appreciate the size and facility of your network of informers, so I do not know how much of what I've learned will be news to you. Still, I've done as you asked and I trust that you will now see to Kintail's release."

"I have already set matters in train," Beaton said. "Oliver Sinclair continues to insist that the chiefs are dangerous, but I am confident I can now persuade his grace they are not, and awaited only your return. Now, tell me what you know about Henry's plan. I learned some time ago, of course, that he'd arrived safely in York."

"Aye, and awaits his grace's arrival there with impatience."

"His mood does not interest me, and he will continue to wait," Beaton said. "When did you see him last?"

"I traveled with him to York, and then followed Angus to Midgeholme."

"Ah, yes." Beaton nodded. "That nest of Cumberland vipers has been busy for some time. Dacre was there, I expect."

"He was, but Angus is more dangerous. He boasts that he retains loyal followers thoughout the Scottish Borders, and he means to help Henry bring Scotland under his rule. The prize for Angus, of course, is Henry's promise to restore all the Douglas lands to him."

"Angus believes Henry, does he?"

Patrick nodded.

"You have not been at Midgeholme all this time, I warrant."

"I nearly came to grief when I arrived there," Patrick admitted. "I was careless after having strutted around the English court with apparent impunity. I even had dinner with young Donald of Sleat, for he, too, enjoys Henry's court. You will recall that Donald took ship for England rather than welcome his king."

"I remember," Beaton said dryly. "You have done well, and now that God has blessed Jamie with a second son, I be-

lieve I can stir him to release at least Kintail, who has remained loyal. Do you mean to attend the festivities Monday?"

"I heard there was to be a celebration, but I had not given
it much thought."

"Have you aught to wear other than that commoner's rig
you stand in?"

Patrick smiled. "If you recall, my lord, you recommended that I purchase court attire from an English tailor, so
I left my things with Kintail. I was forced by circumstance
to leave all my English-made courtly attire at Midgeholme,
but fortunately, fashions do not change as quickly here as
they do in London."

Beaton's eyes twinkled, and since he was known for his
sartorial sensitivity, Patrick was not surprised when he said,
"You will be sadly out-of-date, but so are most of Jamie's
courtiers. You should attend the ball, I think, and pay your
respects to his grace."

"As to that," Patrick said, "I should tell you that Sir Hector Farnsworth desires me to accompany him to court this
afternoon."

"Does he? Why?"

When Patrick explained, Beaton's eyes twinkled merrily.
"Making your bow to Jamie as a falconer should be highly
amusing. I wonder if he will recognize you."

"It matters not if he does," Patrick said. "I have done with
falsehoods, sir. I accompany Farnsworth because he has
been kind to me and I do not want to upset him, but he will
see me as myself soon enough, especially if I am to attend
the ball. Will Kintail and the other hostages do so?"

"No, and that is why I think you should go. Once Jamie
recognizes you, he will remember the courtesy that Kintail
and his lady showed us at Eilean Donan."

They talked more about Patrick's time in England, and

his escape, and it seemed to him yet again that Beaton was singularly well informed.

"What have you learned from all this?" Beaton asked at last.

"That the threat of invasion looms large. If his grace continues to defy Henry and refuses to meet with him, I believe the threat will become a reality."

Beaton nodded. "How came you to stay so long at Farnsworth Tower?"

Having come to like Sir Hector, Patrick was reluctant to explain his initial motive. He said, "Has Farnsworth ever figured in your intelligence, eminence?"

"Not yet," Beaton said. "Should it?"

"Angus mentioned him at Midgeholme. Seems Farnsworth is one of his tenants, although he lives in the west march. That area teems with Douglases of one ilk or another, but most are loyal to the Crown, I believe."

"In my experience, Borderers reserve their loyalty for their clan chiefs, and no Douglas loves the King," Beaton said. "Indeed, I know of no Borderer that I'd trust completely. What more do you know of this Farnsworth?"

"Naught against his credit, for he showed me only kindness," Patrick said.

"A clever ploy, playing the falconer to learn more of him," Beaton said.

"I did not set out to do so," Patrick said. "Chance took me there, and he seems a gentle, scholarly sort, unlikely to be a conspirator. He arrives in Stirling today at the house of Oscar Farnsworth in St. Mary's Wynd. Angus did not connect him to their plot, and instinct tells me that he is no party to it."

"But he was kind to you. That may have weakened your instincts."

"Aye," Patrick admitted.

"You've kept your word, and I'll demand no more of you," Beaton said, "but I'd be grateful if you could keep an eye on him until we can be sure of his loyalty."

"I'll do what I can," Patrick said. It was an excuse to maintain contact with the house in St. Mary's Wynd, and he was certainly willing to do that. He already missed Beth so much that his body ached for her.

Beth was peeling vegetables for Saturday's dinner when the family arrived shortly before noon. Her summons arrived twenty minutes later.

Wiping quaking hands on her apron, she smoothed her hair and retied her coif despite knowing that such details would make no difference. Following the gillie to the chamber where she and Patrick had met Oscar Farnsworth, she found Sir Hector alone with his cousin.

"Come in, lass," Sir Hector said, nodding encouragement when she hesitated on the threshold. "I am not going to eat you, but you did give me a dreadful fright."

"I beg your pardon, sir," she said, curtsying deeply. "I . . . I behaved impulsively, and . . . and foolishly."

"Jelyan told me that she and Drusilla were unkind to you," he said gently. "I have spoken to them, and they will apologize. I hope you will not find it necessary to run away again, lassie. I missed you sorely."

She was stunned. "I thought you would be angry."

"I am certainly not pleased," he said. "Running away like that was foolhardy. It is fortunate that Patrick Falconer found you, and fortunate, too, that apparently he is a man who can be trusted with an innocent young girl."

Since she did not know what Patrick had told Oscar

Farnsworth, and could not tell Sir Hector that Patrick was only barely that trustworthy, she said, "He was kind, sir. He scolded me fiercely for leaving, but I am grateful for his protection."

"So you should be," Sir Hector said. He hesitated, then added, "I wonder, did he speak to you of anything unusual that he might have learned at Farnsworth?"

Suprised by the question but glad she could answer honestly, she said, "Why no, sir. Indeed, he told me that he knew little about the household because he was always busy with the hawk and kept to himself."

Sir Hector frowned but did not pursue the topic. "I shall not scold you, my dear," he said. "I wager Lady Farnsworth will say enough for both of us, but do not fear her. She may scold, but I promise she will do no more than that."

Beth suppressed a sigh, hoping she could believe him.

An hour earlier, Nell had ridden up the hill to the castle with Jane and young Seth in attendance. Encountering no trouble at the gate, she gave her name to the Lord Chamberlain, who greeted her cheerfully, clearly remembering her from her previous visit to Stirling.

"I shall require a chamber where my maid and my page can await my pleasure," Nell told him.

He agreed at once, and thanking him, she made her way to the great hall, where she found acquaintances and even a few friends, but she was not interested in gossip. Instead, she kept her eyes on the royal dais, where James sat surrounded by chattering courtiers. He had aged more than she had, she decided. His once-slender body had thickened, and his complexion was not as fine and smooth as it had been, but his red hair was still thick and healthy-looking, and his blue eyes still lit with laughter. He was a handsome man. She waited until he rose and, flanked by two gentlemen, stepped off the dais and into the crowd. Then, timing her movements carefully, she managed to bump into one of his escorts.

"Godamercy, sir," she exclaimed, sweeping a low curtsy and adding with a chuckle, "one of us seems to have been a trifle clumsy!" Then, as her gaze met the King's, she bowed her head submissively, drawing a deep breath as she did and adding as if she had just recollected her manners, "Pray, forgive me, sire."

"You may rise, madam," James said, amusement clear in his tone. "Or you may remain as you are and afford us all that splendid view a wee bit longer."

"You flatter me, your grace," she said, looking up and smiling.

He held out a hand, and she put hers in it, allowing him to assist her. He did not let go, tucking her hand in the crook of his arm instead, and putting his head near hers to say, "I want to do more than flatter you, Nell. Are you conveniently alone, or have you come encumbered with yet another new husband?"

"I am entirely alone, sire," she murmured, fluttering her lashes.

"Then I know exactly what you can give me for my birthday," James said.

"Your wish is my command, sire, as ever," Nell said demurely, satisfied that the first move in her game had gone just as she had planned.

Chapter 15

When Cardinal Beaton dismissed him, Patrick collected his companions and went back into town, arriving in St. Mary's Wynd at the appointed time. He saw no sign of Beth, but Sir Hector was ready and eager to present Zeus to the King.

They walked up to the castle, where the Lord Chamberlain led them directly to James in the new palace audience chamber. Patrick felt the jolt of excitement that always accompanied risk, the same jolt he had experienced facing the cardinal's men in Lady Farnsworth's red wig and petticoat.

Following Sir Hector and keeping his eyes lowered, he made an awkward bow when they stopped in front of the dais and the Lord Chamberlain announced Sir Hector's name. The hooded Zeus sat quietly on Patrick's glove and seemed perfectly calm to be meeting the King.

"Welcome, Sir Hector," James said. His voice held a note of boredom, doubtless from the strain of spending the whole day receiving nobility and gentry and accepting their gifts.

Sir Hector said, "Thank you, your grace. It is my humble wish that you will accept this splendid hawk both as a small token of my devotion and to celebrate your birthday and the birth of your new little son. It is my hope that Zeus will give you great pleasure on the hunting field. I have brought with me the falconer who trained him, so if you have any questions about the hawk, he can answer them."

"Good day, falconer," James said, sitting straighter in his chair. "Let us see this hawk of yours."

"Aye, sire," Patrick muttered, keeping his head down.

James, who prided himself on taking interest in even the least of his subjects, even to the extent of dressing as a beggar and walking amongst them to hear their views, said encouragingly, "Come forward, man. You've no cause to fear me. Here, chamberlain," he added, "fetch me a glove."

The chamberlain having already anticipated the need, the glove was quickly produced, and James slipped it on. "Will it come to a stranger?" he demanded.

"Aye, your grace," Patrick said, hoping Zeus would not disgrace them both by shooting a stream of mutes across the audience chamber's highly polished floor.

As he stepped toward James, the hawk moved uneasily on his fist.

In a different tone, James said, "Here now, have we met before, falconer?"

Careful to maintain his submissive posture, Patrick equivocated, muttering, "I warrant I'd recall it if we had, your grace."

"I see," James said, amused. "Well, give us a look at this handsome chap."

Nodding, praying the hawk would behave, Patrick held it out on the glove.

As James's fist neared, Zeus raised a talon and yanked the hood half off.

James chuckled. "This lad wants a look at his new master."

"Aye, sire," Patrick said. "Ye mun pull the ties tight, for he has the knack."

James touched his fist to the hawk's belly, and Zeus stepped onto it. "Now, lad," James said, "let's have that hood off the rest of the way, shall we?" Twisting the leash around his gloved fist, he gently removed the hood with his free hand.

Patrick held his breath, but Zeus did not bate. He gazed about in fierce disapproval at his surroundings, but when James stroked him, Zeus allowed it.

"He seems amazingly tame," James said. "Is he a good hunter?"

"As tae that, he be young yet, your grace," Patrick said. "He lacks experience, but he has the talent and bids fair tae be a splendid hunter."

The hawk's behavior astonished him, for it continued to remain at peace while James stoked its wings and back, and when the King paused to express his delight to Sir Hector, Zeus nudged the royal hand with his head as if to demand that his grace get back to what he had been doing. The gesture was one Patrick had often seen from cats or dogs, but never from a hawk.

James, too, was astonished. "Did you see that?" he demanded.

Sir Hector said, " 'Tis plain he admires his new master."

James turned to Patrick. "Is there aught else about him I should ken?"

"Only that he be accustomed tae riding on me fist or shoulder most o' the day," Patrick said. "Likely, your lads will soon teach him his place, though."

"He's a fine fellow," James said. "I thank you, both of you."

He was clearly delighted with his gift, but Patrick was dumbfounded. Hard as it was to imagine, given Zeus's youth, he was certain now that before he had captured the hawk, a master falconer or austringer must have begun its training.

Perched above them, atop one of two great chandeliers in the chamber, Maggie Malloch watched the scene with satisfaction, certain that it could not hurt to give the King of Scotland reason to admire the trainer of such a splendid hawk. Making the bird behave like an affectionate kitten had been easy, a spell that would keep it behaving so was more difficult, but she was not one of the most powerful members of the Secret Clan for naught.

King and hawk would form a special bond that would last at least a sennight. After that, James would blame any failure on factors other than the bird's initial training. Overall, she decided, it was a good day's work, and it was good to oil the workings of any plan from time to time, especially since it could not be long now before the King discovered Sir Patrick's true identity.

※

Dismissed from the royal presence, Patrick excused himself to Sir Hector and went in search of Kintail, finding him by means of directions from the Lord Chamberlain in an elegant suite of rooms on the second floor of the new palace.

Kintail greeted him with a handshake, a bear hug, and a demand for a report of his activities since their parting. Patrick complied, telling him everything about his time in England. He ended by saying that he had taken shelter at Farnsworth and trained a hawk there, but he left out nearly everything about Beth. He was nearing the end of his account when the door to the chamber flew open with a bang.

"Patrick! You're back!"

Leaping to his feet, he opened his arms, and Molly ran into them, hugging him tightly. Her long, thick red-gold curls were loose and flying, much the way they had been the first time Kintail and he had seen her.

"You look like an untidy bairn," he said fondly. "I'm very glad to see you."

"Here is someone else I hope you will be glad to see," she said, stepping back and gesturing toward the doorway, where his beautiful, dark-haired sister stood watching them, her blue eyes sparkling with mischievous delight.

"What the devil!" he exclaimed.

"Hello, Patrick," Barbara MacRae said, grinning impishly at him.

Still stunned, he said only, "How did you get here, Bab?"

"Mother became as bored as I was at Ardintoul, so she brought me."

"Our *mother* is here?" Their mother detested court life.

Bab looked guilty, but she said, "She wanted to see Molly and Fin, and when she grew tired of court, she agreed that I should bear Molly company until his grace allows Fin to go home."

Her eyes were wide and innocent, but Patrick had known her all her life.

He glanced at Kintail. "How long did my mother stay, Fin?"

He grinned. "Less than a sennight."

"Patrick, you won't send me home. I won't go!"

Fin said, "Silence, brat, or I'll tell him all the mischief you've been up to."

Patrick turned a stern eye on his sister, but she ignored it, rushing up and hugging him hard. "I'm so happy to see you," she said. "Oh, Patrick, don't be cross! Indeed, you must escort me later when Molly and I attend the court. There . . . there is someone I particularly want you to meet."

He raised his eyebrows and glanced at Fin. "Molly attends the court?"

"Aye," he said. "Jamie permits it, and some of us have indulged the hope that our wives may persuade him that at least a few of us are harmless."

"Do you also attend?"

Fin chuckled. "Nay, we men are too dangerous, and even the women will not attend the fête or the ball Monday night. We are comfortably housed, Patrick, but we are prisoners nonetheless."

Barbara tugged on Patrick's sleeve. "You *will* escort me later, won't you? At least . . ." She eyed him disapprovingly. "You do have more presentable clothes to wear than those dreadful things you're wearing now, I trust."

"If I don't, I'll borrow some from Fin," he promised her. "I want to meet this particular someone so I can tell him what I think of his impudence."

"Impudence!"

"Aye, what else can it be if he is singling out my sister for his attentions without first applying to me for permission to address her?"

"You were not here!"

"Fin is here. Did your particular someone apply to him?"

She evaded his gaze.

"Just so."

"But, Patrick—"

He scowled. "You'd better be on your best behavior for a while, I think."

Unimpressed, she said, "You can be ready by four, can you not?"

"Aye, lass, I can and I will," he said, smiling and hugging her tightly.

He kept his word, but after tedious hours negotiating the social maze of the court, dancing attendance on Molly, and dealing with a steady stream of his sister's panting swains, he longed for open countryside again. He met Bab's "particular someone," one Francis Dalcross, and thought little of him. He also encountered a friend, Sir Alex Chisholm, whose land abutted Kintail to the east, but Bab had known Alex from childhood and had no interest in chatting with him, so Patrick was drawn away willy-nilly to meet more of her friends.

To Patrick's relief, he did not have to face the King, for although Jamie was present when they entered the great hall, courtiers and their ladies crowded the room, and he was on the royal dais surrounded by his favorites. No presentations were made during the afternoon, and by suppertime, his grace had disappeared.

The truth was that Patrick was bored. The Scottish court was no worse than its counterpart in London, but by the end of the long evening, all he wanted was to breathe fresh air and talk with Beth.

By the end of her second day in St. Mary's Wynd, Beth had decided that she would have preferred a beating to the tense, disapproving atmosphere that she had had to endure instead. At least, by now, the beating would be over.

After Sir Hector left for the castle, Lady Farnsworth had scolded her harshly and at length, but when a vision of Patrick flashed into Beth's mind, strong and reassuring, the scolding became no more than a sea of words that left her unscathed.

Dealing with Drusilla was worse.

"I do not know how my father allows you to be in our presence," she said tartly. "After spending days with that falconer, doing heaven knows what with him, you should not even be allowed in this house."

Beth could not quite bring herself to insist that she and Patrick had never been alone together, to assure Drusilla that Jock had been with them the entire time. It was true enough, but she knew that Jock would not have interfered if they had decided to ignore his presence. Indeed, they nearly had done just that.

Jelyan was kinder than Drusilla. "I'm glad you came," she said. "A town maidservant would not know how we like things done. We'd have to show her."

Both young ladies meant to accompany their mother to the Chapel Royal for Palm Sunday service the next day and to the grand ball on Monday evening. They were excited and not easily pleased, for they wanted their appearance to be perfect.

Each time one of them snapped at her, Beth felt her temper stir, for she found it harder now, after her brief taste of freedom, to return to service. Several times that afternoon she had been tempted to rip up at Drusilla just as she had at Patrick.

Nell had spent most of the afternoon with the court. For a time, James was busy chatting with favorites and friends, and kept her at his side, but when he retired to receive gifts in his audience chamber, she had taken the opportunity to find Jane Geddes, to tidy her hair and brush her skirts.

James returned to the hall briefly about four o'clock, and once again invited her to join the group on the dais, but less than half an hour passed before he whispered, "Do you recall where to find my private chamber, Nell?"

"Aye, your grace, I do."

"Meet me there in ten minutes then. I've something to show you."

She grinned, certain she knew what he meant, but when he let her into his private chamber, he did not take her in his arms. Instead, with schoolboy delight, he said, "Look at my new lad there! Is he not splendid?"

To her astonishment, a sleek, brown hawk wearing a red and black Dutch hood with a white plume occupied a low perch in a corner of the room.

"Godamercy, sire, have you set up a mews in here?"

He chuckled. "Is he not magnificent? Watch this!"

He moved to the perch, taking up a glove from a nearby chest and slipping it on, murmuring to the bird as he did. "This fine gentleman is Zeus," he said as the hawk stepped onto his fist, and he stroked its wings. "Look how tame he is!"

When she had admired the bird to his satisfaction, James set it back on its perch and turned to her. "Come here," he commanded, his voice husky with desire. "I like that gown but I'll like it more when you are out of it."

Smiling, she untied her bodice lacing. "Do you mean to let Zeus witness our activities, sire?"

"Zeus is hooded and cannot see you. I reserve that delight to myself." He reached for her, and she soon stood naked before him. "Ah, Nell," he said, "you are as bonny as ever. You do not even seem to age."

Nell stifled a sigh of relief. She worked hard to maintain her looks, but she was nearly seven years his senior and had feared he might not still admire her. Giving thanks that such was not the case, she dampened her lips invitingly.

James kissed her passionately, letting his hands make free with her body for some minutes before he stood back, murmuring, "Now you may undress me."

Their first coupling was swift, and after a burst of furious activity, James collapsed atop her, burying his face in her neck and breathing deeply.

"You still wear the same French perfume," he said. "I like it."

Drawing a deep breath and easing herself away from an encroaching elbow, she noted movement in the corner.

Zeus had removed his hood and was glowering at her in fierce disapproval.

Beth's prediction that Lady Farnsworth would not let her attend them at court proved accurate. Her ladyship did not even allow her to go with them to kirk on Sunday. Instead, she left orders that Elspeth was to help in the kitchen when she had attended to her own duties.

Beth liked Oscar Farnsworth's cook and kitchen maid, who were kind and cheerful, so she was happy to help prepare dinner, although, according to the cook, it was doubtful that anyone would return from the castle to partake of it.

"No wi' the court in such a stir over the birth o' our wee royal duke!" Cook said comfortably. "If ye've finished wi' them beans, lass, tak' a measure o' grain and scatter it for me chickens in the hen yard back o' the garden. Ye can gather any new eggs, too, whilst ye're there."

The kitchen maid, pouring a measure of grain into Beth's outstretched apron, said, "Mind the rooster now. He's a mean 'un, and he pecks!"

Slipping out the side door, through the kitchen garden, Beth found a fenced yard crowded with clucking chickens. The rooster eyed her suspiciously as she entered, but when she began scattering grain, his attention shifted to his dinner. So engrossed was she in her task that when a large, firm hand grasped her shoulder, she started violently and only managed to suppress a scream when she saw that it was Patrick, albeit a Patrick dressed more splendidly than she had ever seen him.

"Easy, lass," he said with amusement.

"Mercy," she said, taking in his blue velvet doublet and puffed hose, both embroidered and slashed with snowy white silk. His blue velvet cap boasted a silver brooch set with amber and a white plume.

"I did not mean to startle you," he said, glancing warily

around the yard. "But I've been watching the house for what feels like hours and this is the first chance I've had to speak to you."

She wanted to throw her arms around him, but she managed to say matter-of-factly, "I thought I'd never see you again."

"Don't be daft. When I saw Sir Hector, his lady, and those two viragos she gave birth to entering the Chapel Royal, I decided it was an excellent time to leave."

"I hope you left before they recognized you!" Only days ago, it would have seemed absurd to think of him anywhere near the Chapel Royal, but now, dressed as he was, she could easily imagine it.

"I do not think they'd recognize me in this rig unless I walked bang up to them," he said, looking down at himself. "I look very dapper, don't you think?"

"Aye," she said, chuckling. "Too dapper for a hen yard, sir. You should go before someone demands to know your business here."

"Do you think I cannot deal with such impertinence, sweetheart?"

"I know you can," she said, "but I might not fare so well afterward."

With a near growl in his voice, he said, "Has it been dreadful?"

"Only Drusilla. The rest have not been so bad. They say my reputation is ruined, of course, but I expected worse. Whatever did you tell Oscar Farnsworth?"

"Just that I'm close to Cardinal Beaton," he said glibly. "I said I was grateful to Sir Hector for his kindness and knew he would extend the same kindness to you as he always has. Thus, he could have no cause to fear my telling Beaton about anything I might have learned whilst in residence at Farnsworth Tower."

"Merciful heavens! That explains why he asked if you

had spoken of anything unusual you might have learned there. What does he think you know?"

"I suspect he may have had traitorous contact with the English," Patrick said. "But it does not matter what he thinks I know, only that he treats you well."

"He is no traitor! He couldn't be. He's the only one who's been kind to me."

"So your judgment may be tainted," Patrick said gently. "In any event, whilst he thinks you are under his eminence's protection, he will be prudent."

"But the cardinal does not know me. He would not protect me."

"No, and I hope he does not learn how I depicted my relationship with him."

"How did you dare?"

"Fortitude," he said, grinning. "One does what may work. I see that you do not approve, but be kind to me, sweetheart, for I have spent nearly a day in my sister's company. She chatters incessantly, and she has a host of drooling suitors, but I think constantly of you, and I'm burning to kiss you. You won't deny me, will you?" He put two fingers under her chin and lifted it gently.

Releasing her apron without a thought for the grain in it, she put her arms around him and stood on tiptoe, ignoring the chickens clucking around their feet.

"Ah, lassie," he said after kissing her thoroughly, "I wish I could keep you with me at Stirling."

She wished it, too, but not, she was certain, the same way that he did. "You said your sister is here, did you not?"

"Aye, but she stays with Molly. Moreover, it is not just female company I want, and you know it," he added with mock sternness. "I'd rather dance with you tomorrow night than with her, I promise you."

"You mean to attend the King's grand ball, then?"

"Aye, I must." He frowned thoughtfully. "I wonder if there might be a way for you to slip in for at least one dance. Doubtless, anyone could get lost in such a crowd as there will be."

Knowing he was capable of taking any risk that suited him, she said hastily, "I cannot. You know I cannot. Only think what would happen if Lady Farnsworth found out! Or the King! Invoking your cardinal would not protect me then."

"I suppose not," he said, giving her a squeeze. "But soon Kintail will be free again, and when he is, we'll talk more. You can be sure of that."

He was gone a moment later, leaving her amidst the chickens. She could still taste him, and she savored that taste, but her mood was sorrowful.

She had no doubt that he wanted her. She held a place in his heart, but not the place she wanted. He would have to marry a woman better suited to his estate, and she would not take second place in the life of the man she loved.

She stood lost in thought, until the rooster recalled her to her sense—and to the fact that all the grain was gone—by sharply pecking her ankle.

Not until she retired to her bedchamber that night after the ladies finally returned, bubbling with gossip from their day at court, did she have another moment to herself to think, and to curse her foolishness in following Patrick.

"Art sorry then that ye came tae Stirling?"

The voice startled her, but she was glad to hear it.

"Maggie Malloch!"

"Aye, 'tis m'self, and sorry I am tae hear ye weeping and wailing in your head over yon Patrick," Maggie said, taking form at the head of the little cot. "Did ye no enjoy your time wi' him?"

"I did, but now I will have to return to Farnsworth, and they are all so angry and so certain that my virtue has been compromised, and he—"

"Pish tush," Maggie said. "We needna concern ourselves wi' small-minded sorts. Were I such a despiteful giglet as that Drusilla, I'd throw m'self away."

Beth smiled, thinking that if she could disappear at will as Maggie did, she might discount Drusilla, too. With a sigh, she said, "I just hope my temper does not stir me to say something to her that I'll be sorry for."

With a fluttering gesture, Maggie conjured up the little white pipe with a spiral of smoke already curling up from its bowl, then leaned against the wall and crossed her feet at the ankles. She wore clothing that any common woman of her age and appearance might wear, not the flowing, shimmering garments one might expect someone with her gifts to wear.

"We must ha' a think about this," she said. "Clothing, now," she added, as if she had been listening to Beth's thoughts, which Beth suspected was as easy for her as it was for most folks to listen to spoken conversation. "What color suits ye best?"

"Why?"

"Because ye wouldna want tae wear summat that doesna become ye."

"But I do not choose my own clothing," Beth said. "Lady Farnsworth gives me things for which she and her daughters have no more use."

"Aye, sure, but this time it matters," Maggie said, puffing away.

"Why?"

"Because the man ha' asked ye tae go tae the ball. D'ye no want tae go?"

Excitement leaped, but Beth suppressed it. "Even if I did want to go, Lady Farnsworth would never permit it, and the King did not send me an invitation."

Maggie frowned. "I didna think o' the invitation," she admitted. "It will be better then for her ladyship tae take ye there."

"Oh, aye," Beth said, unable to prevent a note of sarcasm from entering her voice. "That would be *much* better."

"Aye, then, we agree," Maggie said. "I think a certain shade o' pale blue silk would suit ye best, or do ye prefer summat else?"

"See, Claud," Lucy Fittletrot said cheerfully, "we needna worry about your Bessie anymore. Your mother's taken her in hand, so we can ha' fun."

"Aye, perhaps," Claud said, "but Mam willna like it an I disappear even an she's taken it into her head tae meddle. I'd best ask her first."

"Dinna be a daffy," Lucy begged. "We ha' scarce had a minute tae ourselves, and I want ye tae meet my father. Surely, your Bessie or whatever she calls herself now will be safe whilst your mam watches her."

"Ye want me tae meet your father?"

"Aye, and ye'll like him, Claud, I promise ye. Ye ha' never heard music like he can play, and I'll dance wi' ye when he plays his pipes for us."

Flattered, Claud felt strong temptation to agree. Instantly, though, he was struck by a mental vision of his mother in a temper. "I canna go now, Lucy, but if the lass does go tae the ball, we can dance there whilst we watch over her."

Lucy grimaced, but she said, "Ye promise, Claud? Ye'll dance wi' me then?"

"If she goes tae the ball, or else I canna leave her till me mam says I may."

"Then tomorrow we'll dance, Brown Claud. Until then, mayhap we can amuse ourselves and still keep an eye on her." She put her hand on his thigh.

Claud groaned, but when he saw that Bessie had drifted off to sleep, he quickly submitted to Lucy's encouragement.

Nell missed Palm Sunday services at the Chapel Royal by sleeping until noon, but when she wakened, she gave orders to Seth and Jane to prepare to remove to the castle. James had objected to her living in town, saying it was unsafe for her and inconvenient for him.

When they reached the castle, the Lord Chamberlain gave her a message from the King, asking her to meet him, as before, at two o'clock; and since it was nearing that hour, she went at once to his private chamber to wait for him. Then, willingly, she let him take her to his bed.

It had been a long time since she had indulged herself in sins of the flesh, but Jamie was an able and enthusiastic partner. She was well aware that many—the Queen and Oliver Sinclair to name but two—would consider their interludes immoral, but it was hard for Nell to view the marriage bed as sacred. As a prize offered to men of power to advance her brother's position, she had been a pawn in political games all her life. To her, the only difference now was that she was using her considerable experience to gain position for herself and those she loved.

"Ah, Nell," James murmured as he nuzzled her plump breasts, "I've missed you grievously. No one understands my needs as you do."

Nell chuckled, stroking his thick, red hair. "'Tis a kind lie, sire, but I ken fine that you've been too busy to miss me. Moreover, your queen is said to be a bonny woman, and canny besides."

"Aye, she is both," James said. "Sometimes I think Marie is more politically astute than I am, but I have never been a man one woman could satisfy. I'm glad you came to Stirling. 'Twas a splendid birthday gift."

"Then you will permit me to stay in Scotland, sire?"

He hesitated. "Do you wish to remain at court?"

"Only if that is your grace's will. I want to visit my daughter, Lady Kintail, and with her help and that of her husband, to find my younger daughter, Elizabeth."

Visibly surprised, he said, "I thought the second one died a bairn."

"So Angus told us, sire, but I believe she lives. Indeed, I met a woman last time I was here, with a maidservant she claimed was Angus's natural child. The woman was encroaching, and I paid her scant heed, but I wonder now if that maidservant might not be my Bessie. Perhaps you know the woman," she added hopefully. "Her husband is a knight with maternal connections to Angus. They might even be here now, taking part in the celebration."

James shrugged. "Many are kin to Angus, but few now claim to be. You may question my Lord Chamberlain if you like." His eyes twinkled. "Have you moved your things to the castle yet?"

"I have," she said, "but with your permission, sire, I shall remain only for the festivities tomorrow and then travel on to the Highlands."

"Why?"

"I told you. I'm eager to see Molly."

"Oh, aye, I remember now," James said, fixing his attention on her breasts. "We'll see if I've had a surfeit of your company by then."

————————————

Chapter 16

Monday morning Patrick awoke to a cold, wet nose pressed against his cheek. Warily opening an eye, he found himself face-to-face with Thunder.

"What the devil!" Sitting bolt upright, he saw that not only had the huge dog invaded his bedchamber but Jock had, too. "Who let you in here?" he demanded.

"I let m'self in," Jock said. "I dinna like them louts in the stables. They think I'm their slave or summat like, so I left me pony, and we came tae see should I do yer boots. Ye ha' nae one else tae look after your trappings yet, do ye?"

Patrick winced at the thought of the lad dealing with his clothes, but the fact was that although Molly and Bab had seen to collecting a semblance of a wardrobe for him, he had no one to help him dress or see to his everyday needs. "Just what do you know about looking after a gentleman and his trappings?" he demanded.

"Two days since, I'd ha' said as much as ye ken about being a gent," Jock said, "but I've eyes in me head. I think ye was just pretending tae be a falconer."

"How the devil did you get that dog in here?"

Jock's eyes twinkled. "I just said his lordship wanted tae see the lad."

"His lordship?"

"Aye, 'cause ye said he'd belong tae an earl, right?"

"Did no one ask you which earl wanted to keep such an ill-kempt beast?"

"Aye, but I looked down me nose the way ye do when ye're miffed, and said it were none o' his business," Jock said. "Now, what will I do first here?"

"Take that ewer and find some hot water," Patrick said, resigned to the fact that he had apparently hired an eleven-year-old manservant. "After that, you can take this beast to the stable yard, give him a bath, and brush him thoroughly. And if we're going to keep him, we'd best decide what to tell people about him."

"They say your master be a Highland chieftain," Jock said suggestively.

"He is," Patrick admitted. "I suppose we can say the dog is his."

"That's what we'll do then," Jock said. He grabbed the ewer and soon returned with Patrick's hot water. "Shall I shave ye afore I tend tae Thunder?"

"You will not," Patrick said firmly, having learned through painful experience on the road that it was safer to shave himself. "Take him and go."

Although he had misgivings about Jock as a manservant, he had no doubt the boy would deal easily with Thunder. Thus, it was with surprise fifteen minutes later that he learned that the dog had objected strenuously to its bath.

"Thunder run off," Jock informed him, looking bereft. "When he saw the tub, he scarpered, and them fool men at the gate didna even try tae stop him."

Tears welled in the boy's eyes, and Patrick put an arm

around his shoulders. "He'll come back," he said, hoping he was right.

"Aye, perhaps." Jock gave a sniff, then said, "What'll ye wear then? I hope I dinna ha' tae iron anything or use one o' them poking sticks I hear tell of."

Patrick was able to reassure him but decided it was not yet time to dispense entirely with Molly and Bab's able assistance.

An hour later, he entered the hall with his sister on his arm, and knowing he could no longer put off paying his respects to the King, he gave his name to the Lord Chamberlain. Fifteen minutes later, while Patrick was fending off the most persistent of Bab's would-be suitors, the Lord Chamberlain approached them.

"His grace will receive you if you will but follow me to the dais, sir."

As they turned to follow, Barbara said sotto voce, "I wish you would be kinder to Francis Dalcross, sir. He is handsome and charming, and has several times sought to have speech with you."

"I do not like his manner," Patrick said. "Now, hush, lass. His grace should not see us muttering."

She had already turned her attention to the King, smiling brilliantly and making a deep curtsy as the Lord Chamberlain announced them.

James Stewart appreciated beautiful women, so Patrick was not surprised to see him return Bab's smile. As he made his bow, however, he was surprised to hear him greet her with casual familiarity.

"I like that gown, lass," James said. "'Tis a yellow that becomes you well. But can this be your hitherto mythical brother who escorts you? Arise, Sir Patrick. We are pleased to welcome you to our court. Was your journey a pleasant one, sir?"

"Aye, your grace," Patrick said, wondering how much

James knew about his adventures. "May I congratulate you on your birthday, sire?"

The King's eyes narrowed, and Patrick knew the moment was at hand.

"Here now," James said, frowning. "You look devilish familiar, sir. I am certain we have met before."

"Aye, your grace, on Saturday," Patrick said, hoping James possessed a sense of humor. He waited a beat, but when James continued to frown, he said ruefully, "I had the honor to be present when you received the goshawk, sire."

"Ah, yes, my fine Zeus!" James peered more narrowly at Patrick. "God's feet," he exclaimed, "the falconer!"

"Aye, sir."

Barbara looked from one to the other but had the good sense to keep still.

James clapped Patrick on the shoulder. "You did an excellent job, sir. We must discuss falconry at length one day, for I would know more of your ways."

"Gladly, your grace."

Another courtier claimed James's attention, and as Patrick and Barbara stepped away, she said, "You did not tell me about the hawk."

"No," Patrick said, adding quietly, "I hope his grace does not number himself amongst the many you have tempted, lass."

"No, sir," she said. "Fin warned me to behave like a witless virgin in his presence. He said Jamie—that is, his grace—prefers more experienced women."

He nearly rebuked her for speaking so familiarly of the King but realized from her blushes that she quoted Fin, so he said only, "Take care nonetheless, lass. Jamie is not always so choosy. His illegitimate offspring could populate a village."

"I'll be careful. But, Patrick, could you please just speak to Francis Dalcross? He knows Oliver Sinclair and says he can persuade him to let Fin go home."

"I doubt the truth of that. Dalcross merely boasts to impress you."

"But—"

"No, Bab. I'll not dismiss him out of hand if you care for him, but neither will I encourage his suit. And you are not to wear your feelings on your sleeve."

"I would never do that," she said, raising her chin.

"Good lass," he said, believing her.

She linked her arm with his and looked up into his eyes. "You will not forbid me to dance with him tonight, will you?"

He grinned at her. "Saucy wench. Torment him all you like."

She chuckled, clearly satisfied.

Beth spent the morning helping Drusilla and Jelyan prepare to spend the day and much of the night at court. They would dine at two, and then the court would retire for a few hours to prepare for the grand ball. The previous year, when they had spent an entire day at court, Beth had packed any other gowns they needed, and Sir Hector had hired porters to carry them to the castle. Beth assumed, however, that today the family would return to St. Mary's Wynd to dress for the ball, and she had laid out the young ladies' clothing accordingly.

She was brushing Drusilla's hair when Lady Farnsworth bustled in and exclaimed, "Mercy, are you not ready to depart yet? Why are those things still lying about? Martha has had my boxes packed for an hour or more."

Drusilla said snidely, "I cannot imagine why our gowns are not ready."

Looking from one to the other, Beth said, "No one told

me that I was to pack them, and since you *did* say that I am not to accompany you—"

"We do not need you when we have Martha and my aunt's woman to attend us," Drusilla snapped. "You should have known we would not be traipsing up and down the hill merely to avail ourselves of your services."

"You should indeed have known that," Lady Farnsworth said, "but Mistress Farnsworth's woman is ailing, and Martha will not have time to attend properly to all four of us before the ball, so you will have to come, because we want to look our best. You are not to leave our rooms for any reason, however. Now, stir yourself about. Sir Hector wants to leave within the hour."

A rap at the door announced the arrival of the kitchen maid.

"What do *you* want?" Lady Farnsworth demanded.

"Beg pardon, my lady, but that big dog be back."

"Dog? What dog?"

"The large one what came wi' Mistress Douglas and the falconer."

Beth, hoping Thunder's presence meant Patrick was nearby, said, "I'll deal with him, madam."

"Nonsense," Lady Farnsworth said sharply. To the kitchen maid, she said, "Shoo the creature away, girl. I do not know why you have bothered me with this."

"He willna go, your ladyship. We ha' been shooing forever."

"I'll go," Beth said. "It will take only a moment, and he should not be running loose, for he is quite a valuable dog, you know." Taking a leaf from Patrick's book, she added, "I believe he may belong to the falconer's master."

Lady Farnsworth opened her mouth and shut it again. "Very well," she said, "but hurry. You've little enough time without wasting it on that wretched creature."

Downstairs, Beth discovered that Thunder was alone, which presented her with a dilemma. When she called, he wagged his tail but kept his distance as if he suspected that, given any opportunity, she might lock him up somewhere.

"Come, Thunder," she coaxed again.

He did not stir a step.

Knowing she had no more time, she gave up. "Please don't get hurt or lost," she said. "I do *not* want to have to tell Jock that something bad happened to you."

She hurried back upstairs, packed the young ladies' gowns in haste, and managed to be ready only a few minutes after the time Sir Hector had set to leave. Since they had to wait while Lady Farnsworth finished one or two more small things, no one scolded, and the company was soon ready to depart.

Lady Farnsworth, her daughters, Oscar Farnsworth's wife, and Martha Elliot all rode palfreys. Beth walked with the men and the porter who transported the ladies' other gowns in a two-wheeled cart. She did not mind the walk.

The way was crowded, the atmosphere that of a holiday. Many people wended their way to the castle besides those who would attend the grand ball, for there would be public tournaments, jousting, and wrestling contests, as well as feasting in the courtyards, and later the ball for those of the gentry and nobility who had received the gilt-edged royal invitation cards.

Beth found the journey through the crowded streets highly entertaining, because they met jugglers and minstrels, showing off their skills. The air was filled with shouting, laughter, and music. At one point, she found herself walking beside Sir Hector, who smiled and said, "It is a merry day, is it not, lass?"

"Aye, sir." She hesitated, and then, because he seemed to expect her to say more, she said, "Was his grace pleased with Zeus?"

"Aye, I've never seen the like. Our erstwhile falconer did a splendid job. Indeed, he said you helped him train Zeus."

"Aye, sir. One day I must tell you about his first capture."

"Tell me now," he said.

She did, and he laughed heartily at hearing of the hawk's turtle ride.

Just then, a cold, damp nose pressed into Beth's hand, and she turned to find Thunder beside her. She stroked his head, and since no one objected to his presence, he accompanied them to the castle.

Passing through the gate, they entered the crowded outer close where pipes skirled merrily, then slowly passed on to the inner close. Acrobats, jugglers, and minstrels performed there, but soon Beth and the family were inside the King's building, making their way up the wide stairs to the elegant third-floor suite of rooms that they would occupy for the day and evening ahead.

The ladies refreshed themselves and then set out to enjoy the entertainments. Beth was tempted to explore, but she knew that if she did, Drusilla or Jelyan would be sure to tear a hem or suffer a headache and would certainly report that she had slipped out. Wondering what had possessed her, so casually to consider disobeying Lady Farnsworth's command, she began to unpack.

When she had no more to do, time passed slowly, and knowing that Patrick was nearby increased the temptation to explore. She might have cast her fears to the wind, had she known how to find him, but she did not.

Stirling sprawled across the top of its crag like a sleeping lion, providing a splendid view of Stirling Carse to the east and west. She could not see the River Forth, but she knew that one could see it from the battlement walk. And although she did not know where Patrick's apartment might be, she knew that the building she was in, the King's House, did not house the King. The royal chambers were in the New Palace, at a right angle to the King's House and forming the second side of the inner close. The great hall, opposite the King's House, formed the third side and the Chapel Royal formed the fourth.

She occupied some time by shaking out Drusilla and Jelyan's dresses again and tidying the room, but with little else to do and Martha in the other room with the door firmly shut, time crawled.

Patrick spent the afternoon dancing attendance on his sister. He had quickly realized that despite Molly's careful guardianship, Bab had enjoyed too much unaccustomed freedom since their mother's return to the Highlands. Moreover, her great popularity had gone to her head.

When he caught her fluttering her eyelashes at one young swain over her gold-lace fan, he intervened swiftly, saying, "Faith, lass, cease your flirting, else you'll be giving him unsuitable notions."

"Oh, Patrick, don't spoil my fun," she said, tossing her head. "You sound just like Alex Chisholm!"

"I am glad to know that someone has been keeping a rein on you."

"He has no business doing so, however, and I can assure you, I do not heed him. Moreover, sir, any man who sees *you* at my side, glowering so fiercely, would have to have the courage of a lion to approach me, no matter what invitation he thought I had sent him. Surely such courage should impress you."

"Nevertheless, you will oblige me by behaving yourself," he said. "Casual flirting is unbecoming to one who bears the name MacRae, and I doubt that you want me to take you back up to Molly just yet."

The scarcely veiled threat was enough, and although she rolled her eyes and sighed like a martyr, her sunny temperament soon reasserted itself.

Claud and Lucy perched atop a wardrobe in the room allotted to Drusilla and Jelyan, trying to stay awake as they watched Beth make work to occupy her time.

"I want tae see these mortals disport themselves at their grand ball," Lucy said anxiously. "Has your mother said nowt yet about her plan for your Bessie?"

"Nay, lass, and I dinna mean tae ask her, neither."

"But I—"

"Hold your whisst now! I warrant ye can think o' a way tae entertain ourselves an we dinna get tae dance."

"Oh, aye," she said, wriggling closer.

"That's my lass! I'll show ye summat I learned in the Highlands."

No longer bored, they proceeded to amuse themselves.

Lady Farnsworth and her sister-in-law returned after dinner, and both ladies napped for an hour. Martha arranged to have food served in the anteroom for herself and Beth, for which Beth was grateful, but they saw no sign of Drusilla or Jelyan until it was time to dress for the ball.

The two hurried in, delighted with their afternoon's entertainment but full of demands and complaints. Even so, Beth was glad to have something to do and easily quelled any stirring of her increasingly volatile temper.

The rooms vibrated with noise and activity, but at last all four ladies were ready, and when Sir Hector and his cousin came to take them to the great hall, the oppressive silence descended again.

Beth tidied up, trying to imagine what it would be like to

dance at a royal ball. Although Maggie Malloch's hint that she might attend the ball had crossed her mind many times that day, she had not seen even a wisp of white smoke to indicate the little woman's presence, so she had forced the enticing visions aside.

"Will it be the pale blue then, or would ye fancy a white, lacy one?"

"Maggie!" Beth looked around but saw no sign of her.

"Aye, lass, I'm here," the disembodied voice said. "Ha' ye washed your face? We ha' nae time tae dawdle, and ye'll be needin' a mirror so ye can see yourself and decide what tae wear."

As the words floated to Beth's ears, a mirror appeared in the air before her, higher than she was tall and without visible means of support.

"At last," Lucy murmured, pushing Claud away and arranging her clothing.

"Wait, lass, I'm no finished yet!"

"Aye, well I am," she whispered, putting a finger to her lips as she leaned to peer over the rim of the wardrobe. "Now, whisst, for I want tae be sure your mam doesna fail us."

Tugging her skirt, he hissed, "Are ye daft? She'll see ye!"

"Nay, she won't," Lucy said, tugging back.

Putting his mouth to her ear, he muttered, "Ye dinna ken her powers, lass." When she ignored him, he slumped, unhappily resigning himself to yet another confrontation with his temperamental mother.

At four o'clock, Patrick and Barbara retired to dress for the evening ahead, and at six they met again to rejoin the company. By the time the orchestra began to play for the dancing, Bab had accepted invitations to dance from so many partners that Patrick had lost track of them.

At her imperious command, however, he escorted her into one of the first sets that formed after the King and members of the nobility began to dance. The company was merry, the music lively, and Patrick was pleased to see that his sister acquitted herself well. The hall teemed with brightly dressed ladies and their equally splendid escorts, and even when Bab had perforce to stop accepting invitations, she continued to draw more than her share of admirers.

Patrick did not dance again, because he was in no mood to partake of social banter with flirtatious ladies. Moreover, he did not want to take his eyes off Bab. With no one else there who could call her to order, the lass was perfectly capable of finding some way or another to fling herself into the suds.

He watched folks pay their respects to the King, who sat at his ease with Oliver Sinclair at his side. The Queen had not arrived, but the Lord Lyon had announced that her grace would take supper with the company at eleven. Patrick also saw Cardinal Beaton, recognizable as always in his splendid scarlet attire.

Shortly after Beaton left the royal dais, Patrick saw James frown at something Sinclair said. Then, with an impatient gesture, the King turned his attention to one of several beautiful ladies standing nearby. Sinclair turned away peevishly and engaged another gentleman in conversation. The gentleman's back stirred a sense of familiarity, but it was not until he turned that Patrick recognized his sister's most persistent suitor, Francis Dalcross.

When the mirror appeared, Beth saw Maggie at last, for she perched atop the long glass, leaning forward, elbows on her knees, peering down at Beth with one hand cupping her chin, the other hand holding the slender white pipe.

"Tell me now," she said. "Which color d'ye think suits ye best?"

Beth scarcely heard her, for she was gazing in rapt amazement at a reflection so clear that it was as if another Beth stood facing her. Then the serviceable gray gown she wore turned to snow-white silk and then to shimmering blue.

As she stared, mouth agape, Maggie said, "The blue, I think, but we'll alter the color tae match your eyes." The hand holding the pipe twitched slightly.

Beth gasped at the change that occurred in the mirror.

The new gown was of iridescent blue-green silk and was the most splendid dress she had ever seen. Its lace-edged, square-cut bodice plunged low, revealing the creamy softness of her breasts, and its long sleeves were the same blue-green material, their upper parts puffed and slashed with cream-colored silk. The skirt, festooned in scallops, revealed a creamy lace underdress over a snow-white silk petticoat. The bodice fit snugly to her waist, the skirt flaring out from a belt of linked gold squares, each one elaborately etched. From the long end, a round golden pomander hung. Her shoes were white silk with little gold heels, and her short gloves were of fine, soft, white kid.

As she stood speechless, Maggie made another gesture, and the fine, flaxen hair that Beth had twisted into its usual untidy knot came undone and spilled down her back in a soft, silken sheet. As she opened her mouth to protest that she could not appear at a royal ball with her hair down, her image blurred. When it cleared again, her hair was parted in the middle and smoothed away from her face, then caught at the back of her head in a soft, intricately woven knot held in place by a neat, narrow braid that wrapped around it.

The image blurred again, and this time when it cleared, she wore a French hood of the shimmering blue-green material over a fashionable, soft white velvet cap. Gold lace edged the border of the hood, which covered her hair, showing less than an inch of her part. The style emphasized her peaches-and-cream complexion and rosy lips, as well as her large, black-fringed, gray-green eyes.

Maggie cocked her head. "Turn about," she said, gesturing with her pipe.

Beth obeyed, hardly daring to believe that the wondrous creature reflected in the glass was herself.

"Aye, but she's gey beautiful," Lucy whispered.

Claud was beside her on his stomach, peering over the edge, his curiosity having overcome his good sense. He saw Maggie stiffen as if she had heard, and he put a finger to his lips.

Lucy smiled mischievously.

She had done something, he decided, and whatever it was kept Maggie from knowing they were there. Claud had no idea what sort of spell could affect his powerful mother, but he was glad it seemed to be working.

"Jewelry," Maggie muttered, frowning as she made another gesture with the pipe. "Now, what d'ye think o' that?"

Beth gasped again, for now the border of her hood, the golden belt, its pomander, and the gold heels of her shoes all glittered with sparkling, inset jewels. A gold knife with a jeweled hilt, a gilded feather fan, and a pair of jeweled scissors dangled from rings on the belt, and around her neck, a gold chain set with diamonds held a pendant shaped like a gold leaf with veins of tiny diamonds. A larger diamond marked their intersection at the stem. But for the diamonds and gold, the leaf looked real. It also looked familiar.

"This is a larger version of the leaf on my baby bracelet," Beth said.

"Aye, sure, for it be that same one," Maggie told her. "I ha' made it bigger and put it on a finer chain. I do think ye be ready now tae go downstairs."

"Yes!" Lucy hissed. "Come on, Claud; now we can dance!"

"Wait," he muttered when his mother stiffened again.

"What?" Lucy demanded impatiently.

"We'll bide a wee yet," he murmured, nervously watching Maggie.

"I am to go to the ball by myself?" Beth felt her delight and her courage slipping away. "I do not even know where to go!"

As she spoke, a knock sounded at the door.

"I ken fine that ye'll need a page," Maggie said, and the door opened to reveal Wee Jock o' the Wall, wearing fine silver livery.

"Jock!"

He bowed with exquisite grace, his eyes twinkling, but he spoke not a word.

Beth looked at Maggie in astonishment. "Can he see you?"

Maggie grinned. "Dinna fash yourself. He canna see or hear me, and when his part in this be done, he'll remember nowt. But he'll act like himself wi' a few extra manners and graces, and he'll be about when ye ha' need o' him. But afore ye go, I ha' some few things I'm bound tae tell ye."

"But—"

"Dinna interrupt. Ye'll go tae the ball, as I promised ye, but ye must promise summat tae me in return."

"Anything."

"Aye, sure, but sithee, ye shouldna make boundless promises. I ask only that ye say nowt o' the source o' your finery, and nowt o' the wee folk or me. An ye do, your fine garments and jewelry will vanish, and ye'll be standing in your smock, wherever ye be. D'ye mark me words?"

"I do," Beth said. "You may be sure I will not speak about this."

"There may be them who will press ye and press ye hard."

Thinking of Patrick and what his likely reaction would be, Beth hid a smile. He would press for information, but she would enjoy keeping her secret, and if he grew angry . . . She smiled then, looking forward to another match with him, one where for the first time since she had realized he was not a commoner she would feel properly dressed for the part.

"I'll say nothing," she said firmly.

"Good," Maggie said. "There be but one more thing. Ye must return afore your two young ladies do, so ye'll be where they expect tae find ye. If ye fail, I canna answer for the consequences, and they may be dire."

"I'll remember," Beth said.

"Then awa' wi' ye now, and ha' a pleasant evening!"

"Now, Claud?" Lucy demanded eagerly.

"Now," he said.

"One moment, ye two," Maggie snapped.

Claud sighed. He had known it was too good to be true.

"Come out where I can see ye," Maggie ordered sternly.

Claud looked at Lucy. Was it possible his mother could not see them?

Lucy gestured toward a draped table, and he followed her as she floated down to it and scooted under the drapery. She pushed him out again.

"H-here we b-be, Mam," he stammered.

Maggie glanced at the top of the wardrobe and back at them. Then, giving herself a shake, she said, "Dinna stand gaping, lad. Follow the lass and try tae keep her safe, but wi' out interfering overmuch. I ha' done enough."

"Where will ye be, Mam?"

"Jonah Bonewits be missing, and nae one kens where tae find him. I've a notion he's taken a hand in this game, so I mean tae track him down."

Chapter 17

Nell entered the great hall, now turned into a magnificent ballroom, and hesitated before approaching the royal dais. James had said he wanted to enjoy at least one dance with her and had promised that the Queen would not put in an appearance until suppertime. Even so, Nell could not draw too much attention, because the Queen could make a deadly enemy. A woman alone was overstepping the mark as it was just by being there, and James knew it. Nevertheless, his wish was as binding as his command, so here she was.

Keeping her eyes straight ahead to avoid diversion, she eased her way through the crowd until she knew she was in plain view from the dais. She had already seen James, surrounded as always by powerful men.

A hand gently touched her arm, and a masculine voice said quietly, "Forgive me, my lady, but his grace asked me to escort you to the dais."

"How kind of him," Nell murmured, laying a hand on the proffered arm.

As they approached, James looked up, his twinkling gaze meeting Nell's. How he delighted in such petty intrigues, she thought as she made her curtsy.

"I would dance, madam," he said, rising and offering his hand to her. Lines were forming for a reel, and as they moved to join the nearest set, he murmured, "It is unseemly for a female to attend a ball without a proper escort."

"Indeed, sire? Even if she does so at her king's command?"

"Even so," he replied. "I shall have to scold you severely for this."

"Will you?"

"Aye, so after we dance, you will go to my private chamber and await me there. I think I shall demand a forfeit as punishment for your impropriety."

She chuckled appreciatively as the music began.

James loved to dance, and the reel was a fast one, requiring Nell's concentration. At one point, however, as they paused to watch a couple skip up the line, she caught sight of a familiar-looking figure standing against the far wall, nodding in time to the music as he watched another set.

He turned his head, and her sense of familiarity was confirmed.

It was Patrick MacRae.

Beth swiftly recovered her confidence, and with Jock leading the way, she crossed the busy inner close to the main entrance of the great hall. She could hear lively music within, and the closer they got, the more excited she felt.

The double doors stood wide, but the entrance, with its screened, low-ceilinged vestibule did not prepare her for the lofty chamber beyond. The great hall boasted a spectacular hammer-beam ceiling, five splendid chandeliers, and an equal number of fireplaces. Red-velvet curtains draped the high windows as well as the bay flanking the royal dais with its elegantly accoutered high table. Musicians played from a gallery above the vestibule through which she had entered, and a veritable din of music, laughter, and conversation greeted her. The vast room was warm, too, thanks to fires roaring in all five fireplaces.

She had all she could do not to stop and gaze about in awe. She saw the King at once, for he sat in a magnificently carved, high-backed chair on the royal dais. A handsome man in scarlet and a younger man dressed with equal splendor occupied chairs on either side of him. Had she not recognized James from previous visits to Stirling, she might have mistaken one of the others for him, because his dress, although handsome, lacked their splendor.

She moved easily through the crowd, for no one challenged her. Indeed, except for an occasional curious glance, no one seemed to notice her.

Claud followed Beth, determined to obey his mother's orders to the letter despite his companion's displeasure.

"These mortals dinna ken wha' they be about when they dance," Lucy said grumpily. "Their fiddlers barely ken their instruments. I want tae dance proper, Claud, and ye promised we would if the lass came tae the ball. Well, there she be!"

"Aye, sure, but we dinna ken yet what will become o' her here," Claud said. "We certainly canna leave her until that Patrick lad takes note o' her."

"Well, where be the daffish man hidin' himself then?"

"Yonder." Claud gestured to where Sir Patrick stood watching the dancers.

"Can ye no winkle them together, Claud? Me toes be a-twitchin'!"

"Nay," Claud said, feeling wretched. "Ye ken fine that me mam were wroth wi' me when I winkled the lass into his path that day in the woods."

"And coaxed him along that path in the first place," Lucy reminded him.

"Aye, sure, but me mam doesna ken that bit, and I hope she never does."

Lucy was not listening. Her toes were tapping, and she said wistfully, "D'ye no hear the true music, Claud?"

He did hear it then. The screeching of fiddles and pipes faded away, and he heard a tinkling, distant melody that called hauntingly to him. His body responded to it, and responded, too, to Lucy's fingers sensuously tickling his neck. The old Claud, he knew, would have gone with her to follow the enticing music.

The new, resolute Claud said, "Nay, lass, we'll wait, I think."

Lucy huffed and stepped back, grimacing, but to his surprise, she did not argue or walk away. She stared grimly at Sir Patrick instead.

The music stopped, and Patrick waited for Barbara, who was approaching on her most recent partner's arm, as other gentlemen strode purposefully toward her from different directions. He noted that the man pressing ahead of the others was Francis Dalcross, and had opened his mouth to suggest that Bab accompany him to find liquid refreshment, when he saw a familiar figure moving through the crowd some distance away.

"Bab, is that not Molly yonder?" he asked, trying to see where she had gone.

"She did not receive an invitation," Barbara said, turning to smile at Dalcross. "And she would certainly not show herself without one."

"But I am quite—"

Realizing that his sister was already walking off on Dalcross's arm, he saw at the same time that the lady in shimmering blue-green silk had vanished in the crowd. Deciding that he had been mistaken and knowing it behooved him to keep an eye on his sister and Dalcross, he turned to see where they had gone.

He was still watching them when he caught sight of the blue-green silk gown again. The lady, walking with a page in silver livery, turned slightly toward him.

Surely, it *was* Molly, although she wore much more jewelry than he had ever seen her wear before, more than most Border wives wore.

Her gown was of surpassing elegance, too, and the jewel-decked French hood she wore covered her red-gold curls, emphasizing her creamy complexion and magnificent eyes.

Forgetting Barbara for the moment, Patrick strode toward the familiar-looking lady, but although she looked at him with a slight smile, she did not take a single step in his direction. Her expression looked strangely wary, and something about her was not right.

Oddly, the page at her side looked like Jock, but that certainly could not be the case. Even as the thought whisked through his mind, the page stepped into the crowd and vanished as if he had been a figment of his imagination. The young woman's expression challenged him now. Her chin lifted defiantly.

Patrick's world tilted, and he wondered if his unpredictable imagination had conjured up her presence, too, for he saw at last that she was not Molly but Beth.

"There, now," Lucy said with satisfaction. "Come and dance wi' me, Claud."

When he hesitated, she pouted.

"Ye promised!"

"Aye, lass, I did, and—"

Again, the nearby sounds faded, and he heard the fascinating melody. His feet began moving, the music grew louder, and before he realized he had made a decision, he was dancing with Lucy to the strangely beguiling tune.

In no time, he was laughing and twirling her, hopping and skipping as he had never known he could. She teased him with a smile, and the music stirred the same feelings in his body that she could stir with a touch. The more he danced, the stronger those feelings grew.

At last, the music stopped, and as Claud tried to catch his breath and his wits, Lucy said, "Now, come along and meet me dad, love. 'Tis him wha' were playin', and he wants tae meet ye 'cause I told him ye want tae marry me, and so he . . ."

Claud's knees threatened to give way, and he could not speak.

Beth had forgotten her fears in her enjoyment of the splendor of the hall, and with Jock moving silently at her side, she had wandered unmolested, watching the dancers until her gaze met Patrick's.

She watched the play of expressions on his face as he strode toward her. First, he looked delighted, then puzzled, and then astonished. Then he fixed a stern gaze upon her and kept it there until he nearly walked into a woman who crossed between them. He stopped in time to avoid a collision but then continued toward Beth. Now, almost upon her, he looked furious.

He glanced around as he occasionally had when they had traveled together, as if he feared encountering enemies, then caught hold of her arm and pulled her out of the way of passersby. "Are you mad?" he demanded in an undertone.

"Good evening, sir," she said calmly. "You invited me to attend the ball, but now that I am here, you do not seem pleased to see me."

"Where did you get that gown? Do you not realize you could be hanged for stealing it, not to mention for stealing all that jewelry?"

"I did not steal anything," she declared. "Everything I am wearing was provided out of kindness."

"By whom?"

"I am not at liberty to say," she replied, striving to remain calm. "Pray, sir, do not press me to tell you, for I cannot. Will you not dance with me instead?"

"What if someone recognizes you? What will you say?"

"Who else would recognize me in such finery?"

"Just who the devil are you?"

"Do not be absurd. You know perfectly well who I am."

He hesitated, frowning, staring at her as if he had never seen her before. She wanted to smooth the frown from his face, but although she felt like a different person in her finery—almost as if Elspeth Douglas of Farnsworth Tower had never existed—she knew that a gesture of such familiarity might draw unwanted attention.

Patrick said, "What happened to Jock?"

"Jock?"

He gave her a shake, apparently not caring if he drew attention. "Do not try to deceive me. I saw him, dressed as finely as you are, pretending to be your page."

"I don't know where he went," she said honestly.

"So you are here alone now." He continued to frown.

She understood his dilemma. He was not a man who could leave a woman to look after herself in such a crowd. He would believe her defenseless, and she could say nothing to contradict that notion without betraying Maggie Malloch, who surely must be watching. If she did betray Maggie, Beth had no doubt that she would instantly find herself standing right where she was, wearing only her smock.

Claud faced a huge dilemma. He felt the distinct tug of duty calling him to keep his eye on Beth, but he had to deal with Lucy first.

"What d'ye mean ye told your father we'd marry? I never asked ye."

Lucy giggled. "Claud, ye canna bed a lass without ye marry her afterward."

"O' course I can. I ha' done it afore, many times!"

"Well, ye canna bed me without marrying me," she said calmly. "I did tell him that ye wanted a wedding, though, so he willna be wroth wi' ye. If ye dinna want tae do it, ye'll ha' tae tell him. That be him yonder, a-waiting for us."

Claud stared at the man she indicated. He was tall and

muscular-looking, with a shock of green hair. His face was long and thin, and his beard was white with green flecks in it. He carried a fiddle in one hand and a set of pipes in the other.

"Well, come on, ye dobby," Lucy said impatiently. "He's a-waiting!"

Suddenly, sweet Lucy put him forcibly in mind of his mother. What in the name of the wicked Host, he wondered, had he gotten himself into?

Seeing Sir Patrick had stirred a tumble of thoughts in Nell's head. When the music stopped, they were at opposite ends of the hall, and her first thought was to wonder if he was there as himself or as Sir William Smythewick.

She quickly realized that too many people here would know him to allow for pretense. Thus, as James led her toward the royal dais, she said, "I thought I saw Sir Patrick MacRae amongst the company, sire."

"Aye, very likely," James said. "It was he who trained Zeus so thoroughly."

"I know he is a fine falconer, but why is he at Stirling without Kintail?"

"We'll discuss that anon," James said. "You owe me a forfeit first."

"I could claim Sir Patrick as my escort," Nell said. She glanced back at the crowd but no longer could see him.

"Nay, madam, it is too late. You will leave now, and you will await me in my chamber." Leaning near to murmur in her ear, he added, "I will come to you in an hour, and I want to find you waiting naked in my bed. Do I find you so, sweet

Nell, I will answer all your questions about Sir Patrick or anything else. Now, go."

"Please, sir," Beth said. "This was your idea. Won't you dance with me?"

She was so beautiful, so alluring, and Patrick's body had reacted instantly. He wanted nothing more than to dance with her, unless it was to take her instantly to bed with him, but his senses and thoughts were spinning. He could think of only one reason that he might have mistaken her for Molly, and if he was right . . .

He could not think straight. The possibility that she could be Molly's long missing little sister stirred his emotions in so many directions that he could not focus. He was furious with her one moment, crazy about her the next, and whenever he tried to bring order to his reeling thoughts, her perfume would waft to his nose and his thoughts would whirl into chaos again. Only one part of him knew exactly what it wanted, and that part was stirring hungrily, sending heat through his body that made it impossible to think about anything but the way her soft, creamy breasts rose above the lacy edging of her low-cut bodice. His fingers itched to caress them.

Her rosy lips pouted, and her lovely eyes twinkled, as if she sensed his dilemma. The twinkle stirred his temper and briefly cleared his thoughts.

He still held one arm, and he pulled her close, saying curtly, "I will dance with you, mistress, but only until I can see you safely back to your room. My sister is here, and I must see that someone with sense is looking after her, but then I will return you from whence you came. It is too dangerous for you to stay."

"But I do not want to go, and there is no reason to do so yet," she said. "The night has barely begun, Drusilla and Jelyan will not leave until after supper at least, and I doubt Lady Farnsworth will let Sir Hector to take them away even then if there is a chance that one or the other might meet someone wishful to marry her."

"It is not her ladyship or her shrewish daughters who concern me now," he retorted. "You are too finely dressed to escape notice, and since you will not tell me where you came by that finery, I must suppose that you dare not tell anyone."

He waited, but when she only nibbled her lower lip and avoided his gaze, he knew he was right, and the thought terrified him. Her jewelry was too valuable. He had seen Lady Farnsworth and her daughters earlier, and none of them wore anything half as fine as the gems the lass displayed, so it was unlikely she had borrowed theirs. The King might own such jewelry, but even Molly did not, and she had been Scotland's greatest heiress when Fin married her.

"I do wish you would stop frowning, sir," she said. "People will think I am saying rude things to you."

He looked into her face and was conscious of a strong desire to kiss her and to hold her close. Whoever she was, he wanted more than anything to protect her from the consequences of her actions.

The music stopped, and automatically he glanced toward where he had seen Bab. She was looking at them, and she grinned and rolled her eyes as she took the hand of yet another partner. With relief, Patrick saw that it was Alex Chisholm and understood why she had rolled her eyes, but he could trust Alex to look after her.

He turned back to Beth.

She smiled, and the musicians began to play music for a galliard.

"Do you truly want to dance, lass?"

"Aye," she said.

He had a sudden urge to teach her a lesson. Taking her hand, he drew her into the nearest set. The dancers had lined up as they would for a reel, ladies facing the gentlemen. But unlike a reel, couples would move from set to set, dancing all around the huge room. The musicians began to play in double time, which was fast enough, but Patrick knew the pace would quicken as the dance progressed. The galliard was for experienced dancers.

As the first notes sounded, he saw Beth frown, but when the ladies all sprang to their left, she sprang with them, crossing her right foot in front like the others as if she had danced the galliard for years. When her left foot was supposed to point to the ground, it did, and when it was supposed to point up, it did. She was easily the best dancer in the female line, and when it was her turn to dance to the other end of the room, Patrick had to exert himself to show his usual skill as he followed her.

Her feet fairly twinkled, and she seemed to have no concern for her skirts, as they swirled and billowed without once entangling her legs. Even her madly swinging pomander caused her no trouble.

As they faced each other again, she kicked high and he kicked higher. She grinned, catching up her skirt and executing an intricate step, daring him to match it. Other couples also competed with each other, and men competed against men, each trying to leap higher or execute more difficult patterns than the one next to him. In time, as the energy level and the pace of the music increased, couples paid less heed to other dancers and more to each other, teasing and flirting.

The musicians took turns, playing solo pieces, showing off their skills, and as they did, the dancers vied with them. And when the pipes began again, individual dancers began to display their own virtuosity.

"Papa, this is Claud," Lucy said happily. "This is me dad, Tom Tit Tot."

In a growl that sent a chill through Claud, the big man said, "So ye're wishful tae marry wi' Lucy, are ye, lad? What manner o' life d'ye offer her?"

Claud stammered, "J-just an ordinary life, sir. I be nae one special, and I ha' nae fortune tae boast about."

"Ye dinna sound verra enthusiastic about this wedding, lad. Dinna ye love her wi' all your heart?"

"Aye, sure," Claud said. "That is, I do an' all, but I'm no so sure I'm ready for marriage, sir, or that me mam will let me."

"Ye bedded the lass, did ye no?"

An ominous note in the man's voice stirred icy fingers between Claud's shoulder blades. Terrified, he nodded.

Tom Tit Tot clapped him on the shoulder so hard he nearly knocked him off his feet. "I applaud ye for testing the lass's value first," he said, "but she's a right tae see she's no got herself a loony, so we'll ha' a wee test o' your wits, we will."

"I dinna mind," Claud said, feeling a glimmer of hope. Had his mother and others not assured him since birth that he was nowt but a witless dobby? "What will I ha' tae do?" he asked.

"Nobbut tell me my true name, lad. That be all there be about it."

Bewildered, Claud said, "Lucy said your name be Tom Tit Tot."

The man laughed. "Aye, sure, many do call me that, but me true name be summat different, and I'll wager a sharp lad like yourself will soon sort it out."

"What if I canna do it?" Claud asked, clinging to hope.

"Why, if ye dinna win my Lucy, I'll report ye tae the Circle for your dissolute ways and ha' ye given over tae the Host for them tae mind."

Terror ripped through Claud. He feared the wicked Host more than anything.

"Ye wouldna do such a terrible thing!"

"Aye, but I would, and ye'd spend the rest o' your days flying wi' other lost souls through endless night, in endless pain, till ye atone for your sins. Or ye can exert yourself tae solve the wee puzzle I've set ye. Which will it be?"

"Ye ken fine which it'll be," Claud muttered wretchedly.

"Then back ye go tae the dancing wi' Lucy. Enjoy yourself, laddie!"

Beth watched Patrick as he executed a series of caprioles and entrechats. He was the handsomest man in the line and one of the most skilled. His sister danced well, too. She knew which one she was, because she had seen them together and had decided from the way Patrick frowned and spoke that either the girl was his sister or the wretched man scolded every woman with whom he had acquaintance.

Beth was glad she need only stand and sway in time to the music, and watch individual dancers display their skill. It was odd that she had seemed to know all the steps and patterns, because she had never danced before—not like this, at all events. It occurred to her that when she attended village reels and festivals she had always seemed to know what to do, too, but no one had danced the galliard at those events.

Barbara's partner was dancing now, grinning lazily at Patrick, daring him to match his high back- and side-kicks. Beth expected him to let Patrick take his place, but instead the gentleman stopped in front of her and bowed, holding out his hand.

Taking hold of it, she threw a saucy grin at Patrick and allowed the man, clearly his friend, to skip her down to the end of the room and back. They stopped halfway back and she easily matched her new partner's flurry of intricate steps, laughing at the astonishment on his face and Patrick's when she did. As her partner guided her back to her place, she suddenly met Drusilla's incredulous gaze.

Beth stared back, her mouth agape. Although she had known all along that the Farnsworths were all at the ball, she had been enjoying the dancing so much that she had forgotten the risk she took merely by attending.

She glanced at Patrick and saw that he, too, had seen Drusilla. Although his expression revealed less dismay than she knew her own must show, she could tell he was furious, and not for a moment did she think his fury was aimed at Drusilla.

The dancing continued, the pace fast and furious, but the music stopped at last, and thanks to the great energy required by the galliard, most dancers stayed where they were for a few minutes to catch their breath. A blast on a ceremonial horn brought quiet, whereupon the Lord Lyon King of Arms announced the Queen's arrival, and the company turned and bowed to her as she entered and took her place beside the King. Then one of the Lord Lyon's minions declared that entertainers would amuse the company while supper tables were set up in the hall.

"We're leaving," Patrick muttered to Beth. One hand grasped her upper arm, leaving her no choice but to go with him unless she wanted to scream and take whatever assistance came her way. Since that course was unacceptable, she allowed him to take her away from the dancers before she dug in her heels.

"Do you not need to look after your sister?"

"Don't tempt me with that innocent look," he growled. "If I were to give way to temptation, I'd put you over my knee right here and beat you soundly."

The look in his eyes told her he meant it. Nevertheless, she said, "I came here of my own accord, sir. I will leave when I am ready, and certainly not before I enjoy my supper. If you do not want to sup with me, I shall find another partner."

"I should let you have your way," he said. "Do you think Drusilla did not recognize you? I saw her expression, just as you did."

"She will not challenge me here," Beth said. "And when she returns to her room and finds me there, she will decide she was mistaken to think she saw me."

Expecting him to argue, she was surprised when he did not and instead let his glance slide past her. A prickling between her shoulder blades warned her just before Lady Farnsworth said, "I thought Drusilla must be mad to think she had seen you two dancing, but I see she still has her wits about her. How dare you, the pair of you, sneak in here to dance with your betters?"

Gasping, Beth turned. Finding herself face-to-face with both Lady Farnsworth and Drusilla, she knew her pleasant evening was over.

Chapter 18

"Just one moment, Lady Farnsworth," Patrick said curtly, striving to control his flaring temper.

"Do not fling your insolence at me, falconer," she snapped. "You may have fooled others with your idiot's tale of being highborn, but you do not fool me. You deserve flogging, sirrah! As for you, my girl," she added, grabbing Beth by an arm, "just see what you will get!"

Smirking at Beth, Drusilla said, "You will be very sorry, I think."

"Release her, madam," Patrick said in a voice that drew notice from bystanders. "You forget yourself."

"I forget *my*self?" Lady Farnsworth glared at him, but when he glared right back, she lost some of her haughty assurance.

"You'd be wise to listen," he said, "before you do something you'll regret."

Lady Farnsworth swallowed visibly. "Very well," she said, releasing Beth.

Drusilla protested. "Mother, you cannot mean to overlook this!"

Ignoring her, Patrick said to Lady Farnsworth, "You have

been acting under a misapprehension, madam. I am a Highland knight, my ranking senior to your husband's. When you and he gave me shelter, I was serving Cardinal Beaton and my own laird, Mackenzie of Kintail. My name is Patrick MacRae of Ardintoul."

"Beaton's knight!" Her eyes narrowed. "Then one should more properly call you Sir Patrick, I expect."

"One should. Now unhand that lady."

"*Lady!* Knight or no, sir, you overstep the mark, for Elspeth Douglas is my servant, and I promise you, I mean to deal with her as she deserves."

Douglas! Patrick wondered why Beth had not told him, but her white face and the scared look she shot him reminded him that she had once claimed to be an earl's daughter, and more pieces of the puzzle fell into place.

Putting his arm around her and drawing her close, he said, "If you believe she is Elspeth Douglas, daughter of a servant woman and the Earl of Angus, I can assure you that she is no more his daughter than your Drusilla is."

Rendered speechless for once, Drusilla managed only an indignant squeak, but Lady Farnsworth said, "You are mad, sir. Doubtless the truth is that you and this slut have *both* stolen your finery and deserve to be punished for your thievery and for your wanton ways, as well. Even if all you say is true, you have helped her run away from home and have doubtless lain with her every night since. I do recall, after all, why my husband dismissed you."

Struggling to control his fury, Patrick snapped, "I have never lain with her."

"Doubtless, you have paid others handsomely to swear to that, but I shall soon have the truth out of Elspeth. See if I do not."

"You will not lay a hand on her!"

"Indeed, and who will stop me? She is mine to treat as I please."

"No, she is not!" Patrick clenched his hands, wanting to throttle the woman.

"You *are* mad," Lady Farnsworth said flatly. "If she is not the same Elspeth Douglas whom we have sheltered all these years, then who is she?"

She would not believe him if he told her what he believed, and if she did not, he might be unable to stop her from taking Beth away and doing heaven-knew-what to her before he could rescue her. He knew only one way to do that now.

"She is Lady MacRae," he said curtly. "In short, she is my wife."

"Don't be absurd." Lady Farnsworth sneered. "If you have never lain with her, *that* cannot be true!"

"It is perfectly true," he said. Raising his voice, he added, "I do hereby swear and declare to you and to all else who hear my words that I am her husband."

"By heaven, then," she declared, "the heathenish slut has bewitched you!"

Stunned by Patrick's declaration, Beth gaped at him, but neither he nor Lady Farnsworth paid her any heed. Both furious, they glowered at each other.

Drusilla was watching Beth, however, and when Beth glanced at her, the older girl said, "I believe Mother is right. You *have* bewitched him. How else could you have come by such clothing and jewels? And what of that huge dog that came to my uncle's house? I have never seen his like, and yet he lets you pet him and even followed us to the castle today. Who . . . or more to the point, *what* are you?"

"Pray, Drusilla, do not talk wicked nonsense," Beth begged. "Someone lent me these clothes, and the dog is just a stray that followed us to Stirling."

She saw Patrick glance her way, but Lady Farnsworth reclaimed his attention by demanding to know when they had married.

"That is no longer your affair, madam," Patrick said. "We are leaving now."

He still had his arm around Beth's shoulders, and without a murmur, she let him take her away. Stunned by his declaration, she would not have known what to say even if she could summon breath to speak. Only when she saw that they had reached the vestibule did she offer a demur.

"Where are you taking me?"

Instead of replying to her question, he said, "What nonsense was that fool girl prating about Thunder? He ran from Jock and we've not seen him since."

"He came to St. Mary's Wynd," Beth said. "But it was nonsense all the same. She is more curious to know where I got these clothes and jewels."

"I own, lass, I want to know the answer to that, myself."

"I cannot tell you," she said. "I know you must be angry that I never told you Angus is my father, and I do apologize for deceiving you, but I promised I would tell no one how I got these things."

"You will, though, before we are much older," he said with a stern look that sent a shiver up her spine. Although he did not press her then to answer him, she knew he soon would, and she was not looking forward to it. He would doubtless have unpleasant things to say about her Douglas heritage as well.

They reached the exit, and a guard courteously opened the doors for them. Outside on the step, she stopped and faced Patrick.

"You should not have lied to them, sir. Lady Farnsworth will flay me."

"You are not returning to that tigress's den."

"But I must. I must at least be there to help Drusilla and Jelyan undress," she added, remembering that Maggie had said she would not otherwise answer for the consequences, and fearing to find herself suddenly wearing nothing but her smock.

"I know you want to protect me," she said as they crossed the torchlit inner close, "but despite what you said to her, you can do naught to shield me. At least I can now say I have attended a royal ball."

"You are not going back to them, lass," he said. "You are staying with me. There are things you do not know, and we must talk."

She hesitated, resisting, but saw by his expression that he would not change his mind. Reminding herself that Maggie had said only that her clothing would disappear if she revealed its source, and recalling that supper had just begun, she decided she could risk more time with Patrick before facing any Farnsworths.

"Lucy, we ha' tae go back," Claud said desperately.

"Dinna fash yourself," she said, grinning. "Ye'll sort it all out." She kissed him hard, moving her hands over his body in a way that normally would have distracted him from anything else. Now, it merely frustrated him.

"Summat's amiss," he said. "I can feel it! We must go back straightaway."

With an exasperated sigh, she said, "Very well."

The next thing he knew they were sitting side by side on

the royal dais, gazing upon a host of merrymakers, who were enjoying a splendid supper.

"Where is she?" Claud demanded.

"Oh, come along then, and we'll find her," Lucy snapped.

Having allowed Patrick to take her into the King's House and upstairs to the second-floor landing, Beth turned toward the next flight.

"Here, lass," he said with a touch on her arm. "My chamber lies this way." Moving his hand to the small of her back, he hurried her along the corridor.

At his door, she balked. "I cannot go in there with you! 'Tis unseemly."

"You can, and it is perfectly proper," he said. "Did I not, moments ago, declare you to be my wife?"

"Aye," she said, managing a smile despite her roiling emotions. "But that was not real, sir, and much as I enjoyed playing the grand lady, I must now return to my place. You are far above my touch, Sir Patrick, farther even than I believed."

He shrugged. "Even if we did spring from different stations in life, it would not matter now," he said. "By Scottish law, when a man makes a declaration of marriage before witnesses and the woman does not deny it, they are as married as any couple united by a priest. And as my legal wife, it is entirely proper—nay, it is your wifely duty," he added with a smile, "to enter my bedchamber."

Beth stared at him, astonished at the heat surging through her and the ache of yearning that accompanied it. She wanted to believe him more than she had ever wanted anything, but everything that had happened in the past few hours seemed unreal. Surely, it was all a result of Maggie Malloch's contriving, or that of others of her ilk, and when it ended, Beth would still have to face Lady Farnsworth's fury.

"I . . . I can't do it," she said, forcing the words past an ache that threatened to close her throat. "I want to, but it would not be right."

Much more than an hour had passed since Nell had entered the King's chamber, removed her clothing, and climbed naked into the royal bed, but James had not come to her. Still, she knew he would expect her to stay unless he sent someone with orders to the contrary, so she curled up at last and slept.

"Look yonder, Lucy," Claud said when they had searched nearly the entire great hall without seeing Beth or Sir Patrick. "See that old besom yonder, talking wi' the chap in scarlet livery? Isna that the woman my lass were livin' wi'?"

"Aye, and she looks agitated. We'd best hear wha' they be saying, I think."

With that, the two of them whisked close enough to hear Lady Farnsworth say haughtily, "The villain claims she is his wife, but I believe the slut has bewitched him. Something *must* be done."

"Come with me, madam," the man said. "My captain will want to hear this."

"By my troth, what a calumnious virago!" Claud snarled.

Lucy blinked. "Calumnious?"

"Aye, and that's our lass she be defaming. Hurry, Lucy!"
"D'ye no want tae hear what she says tae that captain?"
"Nay, 'cause by then we may be too late!"

Patrick did not want to stand arguing at the threshold of his
room. His first inclination had been to take Beth to Molly, but
the hour was late, and he wanted to talk to them before they
met. He was nearly certain now that Beth was Molly's missing
sister, but he knew he needed proof before anyone else would
believe it, and he had no idea what that proof might be unless
Angus could be made to speak, and that was unlikely. It was
therefore essential that he question Beth more thoroughly
about her past before he did anything else.

Lady Farnsworth's charge that Beth had bewitched him had
stirred a prickling of danger, the sort of instinctive warning he
had learned never to ignore, and wanting to get her away from
the great hall quickly, he had not thought much beyond that
point. In fact, not until after he had made his declaration did he
recognize the enormous consequences of that impulse.

What Kintail would think of it he did not want to consider. Fin was a good friend, but he was Laird of Kintail first
and Molly's husband second, and he would put both factors
ahead of anything Patrick might want. By tradition, he
should have gained Fin's permission before offering marriage to anyone, and he had not even considered it. If Beth
was indeed Molly's sister, all would be well. If not . . .

His declared marriage was legal, but he knew that anyone
with enough power could undo it until the marriage was
consummated. That meant there was only one way to protect
Beth, but the chance that she would agree seemed slim. The
thought of bedding her stirred his loins. What he really

wanted to do was to hold her close and promise her all would be well, but the likelihood of that seemed slim, too.

Hearing voices from the other end of the corridor, he grabbed her arm, pushed open his door, and urged her inside.

"They are here," Claud said with relief as he and Lucy flitted into the corridor. "I just saw him whisk her into his chamber."

"Aye, but who be coming up the stairs? Be it them men we saw below?"

"Nay, 'tis only a pair o' lovers, going tae the next floor, but them others will be along. I must hear what Sir Patrick says tae her afore then."

"Aye, sure," Lucy said, flitting ahead of him and swooping under the door.

The only light in the room came from glowing embers in the fireplace and from the pale light of a quarter moon high outside the uncurtained window.

"Unhand me," Beth said furiously, jerking away from Patrick's grasp. "You may think you can do as you like with me, but this is too—"

"Hush, lass," he said gently, shutting the door and standing in her way when she tried to reach the latch. "We must talk."

He put his hands on her shoulders, but released her instantly, knowing from his body's powerful reaction that it was a mistake even to stand too close. Alone with her, he recognized yet again how strongly she affected him.

When his loins stirred again, he knew he could not trust himself. Patience was hard to come by at the best of times, and with his body and soul aching for her, he had no patience. Only distance might serve and that for a short time. The room was too small. He stepped away from her and knelt to put another log on the fire.

She moved toward the door.

"Don't," he said sharply. "You are safe here for now, but—"

"Am I?"

He grinned despite himself as he got to his feet again. "As long as I can keep my hands off you, you are, *mo chridhe,* but do not trust me farther than that."

"I should go. No good can come of this." She reached toward the door latch.

Lunging, he smacked a hand hard against the door so she could not open it. With his other hand, he threw the bolt into place.

Hands on her hips, she said indignantly, "Stand aside, sir."

"By heaven, you will listen to me first, and you will answer my questions, too, so that I can see where we stand."

"Why should I?"

"Because unless I am mistaken, you are as wellborn as I am. Your father—"

"We will leave my father out of this," she snapped, raising her chin. "He may be an earl, but since my mother was only—"

"I believe your mother is a lady, Beth, and she still lives."

"What?" Her eyes widened, and even in the dim light, he could see the color draining from her face.

"Easy, *mo chridhe,*" he said. "If I am right, I saw her the day I met you, and without meaning harm, she was nearly my undoing. I believe you are the younger daughter of Lord Gordon of Dunsithe. Thus, Angus is your uncle, not your father."

She stared at him. "Her ladyship is right. You are mad."

"Not mad, but a blind fool not to have seen the resemblance between you before tonight."

"I bear no resemblance whatsoever to Lady Farnsworth!"

"Nay, but you do look like Lady Mackenzie. I see now that your eyes are very like Molly's, and your countenance is similar, too."

"Doubtless you imagine such a resemblance because, having so impulsively declared marriage to me, you want to see one," she said quietly. "If such a resemblance truly existed, surely you would have noted it before now."

"I did," he said. "I just did not realize I had. From the beginning of our acquaintance, I have experienced a strange sense of familiarity for which I could not account. Tonight is the first time I have seen you with your hair covered."

"What has that to do with anything?"

"Molly's hair is red-gold and very thick—a vast, unmanageable mass of curls. She covers it only when formality demands it, and when I met you, I had not seen her at all for some time, let alone formally dressed. You are younger, your eyebrows are lighter and less strongly arched, and your voice is much lower-pitched and more melodic to the ear." That he had never reacted physically to Molly the way he reacted to her he not think it necessary to mention.

She was blushing now, but she said, "My father is certainly the Earl of Angus. Sir Hector and his lady could not be wrong about that, for he said as much to them when he gave me to them. Indeed, he provided funds for my care."

"If he truly were your father, all that would be utterly out of character for him. Angus is not a man of compassion, lass. If his coupling with a servant were to produce a child, he would take no interest in it but would simply leave it with its mother or her family to rear. I can think of only one reason he would seek fostering for any child, let alone contribute so much as a penny to her upkeep."

"He promised he would continue to provide for me," she said thoughtfully, "but he did not keep his promise, so I had to earn my keep."

"I hope to meet the earl again, just once," Patrick said grimly, reaching out to hold her but remembering the danger and pulling back his hand. "I'll warrant when he reached England and could no longer get to you easily, he decided you'd be better hidden if he let them turn you into a servant. How much do you recall of your childhood before Farnsworth Tower?"

"Nothing," she said. "I remember little of it after I arrived there, for that matter, until I was about five or six and overheard Lady Farnsworth berating Sir Hector because Angus had not sent payment for my keep. I only remember that because I listened at the door and Drusilla caught me." She grimaced. "My legs stung for days from the switching Lady Farnsworth gave me."

Anger stirred at the mistreatment she had suffered, but he forced himself to say calmly, "Are you certain you remember nothing before then? What about keepsakes? Were there no personal treasures you kept from your early days?"

She fingered the chain around her neck, as she said, "Nothing of any value."

"And you recall nothing about where you lived before?"

"Only in my dreams," she said wistfully. "But I told you about them."

"Tell me more."

"I thought of them tonight when I entered the great hall. It seemed familiar."

"What else?" he asked.

"Only that I am always Beth or Bethie in them, never Elspeth."

"Aye. Wait, though! Bethie, not Bessie?"

"I think Bethie, but there is small difference," she said.

"A difference nonetheless," he said. "Molly's sister was called Bessie."

"Do you really think I am she?"

He grimaced. "Aye, but we'll have the devil's own time proving it. Elizabeth is one of the most common names in Scotland—England, too—and women bearing its nicknames are legion. Neither the name nor your dreams will suffice to prove you are Molly's sister. For one thing, no one expected to find her in the west march, and although I have learned that Sir Hector has ties to Angus, I cannot prove that."

She frowned. "His mother was connected to Angus, but I know him better than you do, sir, and I promise you, Sir Hector is a loyal Scottish subject."

"I believe you, *mo chridhe.*"

"Do you? This all seems so strange, like a child dreaming she is Assipattle and will learn she is highborn with riches awaiting her. It simply cannot be true."

Patrick smiled. "In the Highlands, we call her Ashenputtle, but I ken well the tale, *mo chridhe,* and if I'm right about you, your uncle Angus kept you hidden in the hope that he could somehow win control of your sister's fortune . . . or, in the event of her death at a tender age, of your fortune."

Beth shook her head. "But I have none. Indeed, if I did, surely he would have used it to support me."

"Nay, for no one could lay hands on it. I do not know the details, but Molly was Maid of Dunsithe, Scotland's greatest heiress, and you would have inherited if she had died before she married. Now, of course, Angus cannot seize her fortune even if she dies, because it belongs to Kintail, but I believe she did mention once that Bessie would inherit something if she still lived and they could find her."

With a deep sigh, she said, "I find it hard to believe any of this. Surely, you will soon discover your error and be sorely disappointed."

The sad note in her voice made him want to deny it, but he did not want to lie to her. He was strongly attracted to her, and he wanted to protect her from Lady Farnsworth and Drusilla, but he did not yet understand his feelings well enough to know how he would react if he proved to be wrong about her identity.

He felt as if he had known her as long as he had known Molly, and he felt just as comfortable in her presence. In truth, he felt a mixture of emotions with her, but he could not honestly say yet that his feelings were anything more, and he knew her well enough to know she would see through any prevarication.

"I don't want you to marry me because you think I'm Molly's sister or because I may inherit something if you can persuade others to your thinking."

Her tone was calm, and thus the jolt of fury he felt surprised him. That she could believe such things of him was not surprising, so why did he feel such anger? Was he disappointed because he had found a woman who did not swoon at the thought of marrying him? Fin had often teased him about his easy triumphs with the gentle sex. Was he the sort of man who demanded conquests?

"Your fortune or lack of one is irrelevant to me," he said, forcing calm into his voice to match hers. "I am concerned only that Lady Farnsworth means you harm. If she speaks out about that gown, not to mention your jewelry, you will be hard-pressed to prove you did not steal it all. As my wife, you should be safe from such accusations, because no one but Kintail knows the extent of my fortune, and although many may suspect that it would not pay for such splendid attire, once we make it known that you are Molly's sister, all will be well."

"If you are right about who I am, perhaps you should just tell everyone. Would not the simple fact of her wealth put an end to all speculation about theft?"

"It might if we could prove who you are," he said, knowing that even then many might think she had stolen the things before learning she was Molly's sister.

She sighed. "I know of no way to prove such a connection. Indeed, sir, if I cannot make myself believe that one exists, how can we prove it to others?"

"We can certainly show that you two look alike, but that is not enough, particularly since no one ever called Angus a virtuous man. It was his example, after all, that resulted in Jamie's begetting a host of illegitimate children, for it was Angus who introduced him to the delights of the female form, and at quite a tender age."

"But you said that Angus is not my father," she reminded him.

"Others believe that he is, however, and there could be another explanation for your resemblance to Molly, who is known by many to be his niece."

"Oh, I see," she said, blushing. "You mean that, thanks to his licentious habits, there could be a hundred Border females who look like your Molly."

"Faith, lass, don't ever let Kintail hear you calling her my Molly," Patrick exclaimed. "You'd become a widow quicker than you became a wife."

When she chuckled, he caught her by the shoulders again and gave them a reassuring squeeze. "It will be well, *mo chridhe*. You will see, but you must let me protect you with my name whilst we seek the truth. You may believe me when I tell you that I think myself fortunate to be your husband."

He looked into her eyes, and what he saw there demolished his careful resolution. "Oh, lassie," he said, catching her close and bending to kiss her soft lips.

"Claud, they're coming! I can hear them, coming up the stairway!"

So fascinated had Claud been with the conversation in Sir Patrick's bedchamber that he had not noticed that Lucy had slipped out under the door, but now, returning, she caught his full attention.

"I doubt we can stop them," she said. "But come, I'll show ye!"

Following her into the corridor, he said urgently, "We must delay them! If Sir Patrick doesna consummate his union, they'll take the lass back!"

"But wha' can we do? Your mam said—"

"The door!" He gestured as he spoke, and the heavy door at the stairway end of the corridor slammed shut. "There," he said with satisfaction.

Lucy pointed her finger, and he heard a loud click. "Ye forgot tae lock it, ye great daffy, but that will hold them long enough for the man tae do his business."

Beth had become so confused that she wondered if she was right side up or otherwise, but the touch of Patrick's burning lips on hers steadied her chaotic world. She might not know who she was or how she had fallen into such a coil, but her body recognized its needs and desires perfectly well.

It took no thought to respond to his kisses, and she soon gave in to her hunger. His lips were hot but gentle, questing and soft, and his mouth was warm and welcoming when her tongue slipped inside. She sighed, and his arms eased around her, holding her gently and then more possessively. She opened her mouth to his thrusting tongue, gasping when one of his hands slid up alongside her right breast and fingers teased the bare skin above the lacy edge of her bodice.

When Patrick straightened, she moaned in protest.

"Sweetheart, I want to take you to bed, and since we are legally husband and wife, I have that right. 'Tis also the only way I know to protect you, but I won't take you unwillingly. If you truly want to be free of this odd union, you should know that I can arrange it. We need only apply to Cardinal Beaton for an annulment."

"Truly, you would do that?" For some reason, the suggestion lacked appeal.

"Truly," he said. "If that is what you want, I will still do what I can to protect you, but you should know that if you are not my wife, it will be difficult, because Sir Hector and his lady will have the right then to demand your return. For that matter, if we do not consummate our marriage, he can demand an annulment, and despite my relationship with Beaton, I may not be able to prevent it. The surest way is for us to consummate the union. What say you, lass? Will you trust me?"

A thudding on the corridor door sent Lucy swooping toward its keyhole. "Men-at-arms," she cried, peering through it. "Two big 'uns."

"That door will hold," Claud said confidently. "It be right stout."

Metallic rattling sounded on the other side.

"It willna hold against a key," Lucy said dryly.

Chapter 19

Beth's heart pounded so hard that she wondered if it might jump out of her chest. Her hands felt numb, and her breathing was raspy. She wanted to trust Patrick, and everything in her said that she could. She knew he cared for her, but that was not enough when she had followed her heart.

"Well, sweetheart?"

His hand touched her shoulder in a light, casual caress that flooded warmth through her to her toes. Her nipples pressed hard against the material of her bodice, tingling so that she could not think clearly.

She should say no.

She licked her lips, and he kissed her again as if he could not help himself. Then, with both hands lightly grasping her shoulders, he said, "Beth, love, tell me what you want. Don't torment me like this. I am not made of iron."

She swallowed, and then, trying to ignore her jumping nerves, she said, "I will do as you suggest, but may heaven help you if you are wrong about all this."

"Good lass," he said, scooping her into his arms and carrying her to the bed.

She lay tense and still, watching as he turned to stir the

fire, trying to ignore the fiery feelings in her body and the whirling confusion in her mind. He took a log from the basket and put it on the flames, then moved back to loom over her. With the golden firelight dancing behind him, he looked huge, dark, and shadowy.

She could barely see his face.

To her surprise, he stood looking down at her for several moments before he said ruefully, "It occurs to me that I have never before taken a maiden."

"Do you not know how?"

He chuckled. "I know how, but I am told that the first time for a lass is not pleasant, and I do not want to hurt you. My intention was to get it done quickly so you'd be safe from Lady Farnsworth and her family, but I think perhaps that would resemble a rape, and I'd liefer you believe your husband kind than cruel."

Realizing that he was truly apprehensive, she said quietly, "I know you would not hurt me a-purpose, sir. Show me what I must do."

The feelings coursing through her at the thought of coupling with him were similar to those she had whenever he touched her, albeit stronger and more intense. Her whole body vibrated its awareness of him and the nerves in her skin shouted for him to touch her again.

"You make me feel like a green lad, sweetheart," he said. "I scarcely know where to begin, but 'tis plain that we both have too many clothes on."

"I cannot take mine off by myself," she said, remembering that Drusilla and Jelyan expected to find her in their room when they returned. This time the thought failed to stir her to mention her duties.

"It does not surprise me that you cannot take off that dress by yourself," he said. "What I still want to know is how you got it on. Did you have help?"

"A little," she said. She did not think telling him that much would violate Maggie's rule, and even if it did, at this point she would not mind if her clothing vanished, leaving her in just her smock. It would simplify matters considerably.

He waited, clearly expecting her to say more, and she realized that he would next ask her to tell him who had helped her. She had promised that she would not do that, and she was risking much just by lingering. She would not risk more.

To divert him, she sat up and swung her feet over the side, saying, "I'll untie the laces in front, but you will have to undo the hooks at the back."

"Stand up, Beth."

His tone warned her that he was not going to give up so easily.

Watching him warily, she slid from the bed. He stood too close. Her breasts touched his doublet, making it feel as if he caressed her. She could feel his lower body move against hers. Looking up into his stern face, she dampened dry lips and put her hand on his arm.

"Ah, lassie," he muttered, kissing her hard as he caught her in his arms. His hands moved to the hooks in back, then dealt with her bodice laces and those of the smock beneath. She felt the cool touch of the air on her bare breasts, and then, more swiftly than she might have expected, Patrick's hands were warm against her flesh.

Not knowing what else to do with her hands, she put them at his waist, feeling the play of hard muscles there. Savoring the sensations that his hands on her breasts stirred through her body, she sought the fastenings of his doublet.

His lips took the place of his fingers on her breasts, making her gasp.

"Do you not want your clothes off?" she said, still breathless.

"Aye, lass, but you'll be too slow. I'll do it." His voice sounded ragged. He stepped away, and in moments, his doublet, shirt, and netherstocks were off and he was dealing with boots and hose. "Take off that damned French hood."

She gazed at him, fascinated, having never watched a man disrobe before.

The air was cold on her bare breasts, but she knew instinctively that he would object if she covered them. Instead, she lifted both arms to remove her headdress and cast it aside. Next, she unfastened her belt and dropped it onto the pile of clothing that he had flung to the floor, but when she moved to slip off her skirt and petticoats, he said, "Wait, let me. I want to undress you."

A dull thud sounded in the distance, and he glanced warily at the door.

The door at the end of the corridor swung hard against the wall, and two armed men in scarlet livery strode toward Sir Patrick's chamber.

With a gasp of consternation, Claud held up both hands.

The men froze in midstride.

"Claud, ye canna do that!" Lucy shrieked.

"Sir Patrick be busy," Claud said. "We'll give him more time."

"But that be against our rules, and they'll ken summat's amiss! What—?"

"Hush," he said, pulling her closer. "We can do as we please, just like Sir Patrick." She resisted, but confident that it would take little to persuade her, he claimed her lips and kissed her hard. When she responded, he sighed in relief.

Patrick stared at the door for a long moment, but all was silent.

"What was that?" Beth asked.

"Nothing, I guess. Still, we'd best not waste time."

"Do we not have all night?"

"I hope we may, but I've a notion we won't, so the sooner we attend to this the better. Do you still trust me?"

"I have not changed my mind, sir."

"Good lass." He cast his last garments aside and stood naked before her.

The firelight played over his body, turning his skin golden and highlighting the muscular planes of his chest, hips, and legs. If she had thought him handsome before— and she had—she thought him even more so now. And he was clearly ready to do what needed to be done.

He grinned. "Now for you, sweetheart." He loosened her hair first, and when it hung in a wavy curtain down her back, he said gruffly, "Let's have the rest of these clothes off you." It took only a moment, and then he picked her up and laid her on the bed, lying down beside her.

Lucy slid away from Claud, saying, "This willna do. Ye must release them! If anyone hears o' this, they'll hail us both afore the Circle!"

"They had keys, lass! What was I tae do?"

"But ye canna hold them! What if some'un else comes along?"

"But how did they come by keys tae doors in the King's House?"

"What does it matter?" Lucy snapped. "The rules, Claud! We're no tae interfere wi' mortals openly like this."

"I ha' interfered already, lass. We'll bide a wee bit longer."

Beth lay on the bed beside Patrick, delighting in the wondrous feelings he was stirring with his hands, his lips, and his tongue. When his tongue flicked one of her nipples, she sighed with pleasure and said, "You're sure we're truly married?"

"Aye, we are," he said, stroking her, his hand moving lower until his fingers reached the soft nest at the juncture of her legs. He paused. "Do you trust me, lass?"

"Aye." She would trust him with her life. Trusting him with her virtue seemed paltry by comparison. "What are you doing?"

"Easing the way, sweetheart, preparing you for what is to come."

"You are very large," she said, stroking him gently.

He chuckled. "I'll fit."

Then he eased himself over her, guiding himself carefully into her.

"Should I do anything in particular?" she asked.

"Just relax," he murmured. "I'll be as gentle as I can."

He began kissing her again, and she responded but found it hard to concentrate on anything but the odd, aching sensation of him inside her. There were moments when her body seemed to thrill to his possession, others when the ache increased and dulled the thrill, but although she could not help tensing then, it was not really unpleasant or painful, and she had no wish to be anywhere else. Had anyone told her she would be in Patrick's bed this night, his naked body hot against hers, she would not have believed it.

A new sensation startled her, and she gasped at its intensity.

"Now," he said, his lips warm against hers, "breathe deep, sweetheart."

She obeyed and felt a sharper pain when Patrick eased in all the way. It eased almost at once, and she took another breath. He seemed to fill her, and although her body ached whenever he moved, when he stopped, the ache eased again.

"Is that it?" she asked quietly.

With a sound in his throat like a moan, he muttered, "Not quite." He moved again, and then moved a little faster, thrusting now, and she bit her lip to keep from crying out. She could tell he was trying to be gentle, but the faster he moved the less gentle he was. There was pain but other sensations, too, and she savored those, wondering that she had never known such feelings could exist. Her breath came in sobs now, and his sounded the same. Then suddenly, it was over.

He relaxed, still in possession of her, and said, "You're my wife now, lass. No one can prove otherwise."

Filled with emotion, tears welling in her eyes, she touched his cheek.

"Claud, ye must let them go," Lucy pleaded. "Others will come."

"Aye, sure, I ken that fine," Claud said unhappily.

"Then . . ."

With a sigh, he flicked a finger, releasing the men.

Patrick saw Beth's tears, and remorse swept over him. He had tried hard not to hurt her, and now he felt a wave of tenderness such as he had never felt before.

"Don't cry, *mo chridhe*. The pain will pass."

"Kiss me again," she said.

He bent to obey, but a sudden pounding on the door startled them both.

Clutching him with one hand, Beth clapped the other hand over her mouth and looked at him, horrified.

Fear swept through him. It was too late for ordinary visitors, and now that his mission for Beaton was done, no one but Kintail commanded him, and Fin would have shouted his name as he knocked. He knew as certainly as he knew anything that whoever stood on the other side of the door represented danger to Beth.

"Who is it?" she whispered.

"I don't know. Friends identify themselves."

Another knock, loud enough this time to be the hilt of a sword, even a club, and a voice this time. "Open in the name of Cardinal Beaton!"

Beth gasped. "The cardinal! Oh, Patrick, what can it mean?"

"Danger," he said tersely, easing himself out of her.

"Open this door, or we'll break it down!"

"Hold on," Patrick shouted. "I'm coming!"

A body thudded hard against the door.

He got up, grabbed his netherstocks and hose, and started to scramble into them, but another thud changed his mind. "Hold patience!" he shouted. "You'll be lucky an I do not throttle you for interrupting my wedding night!"

Snatching a ring off his little finger, he gave it to Beth, saying under his breath, "Slip that on, lass, and do your best to cover yourself but no more. I don't want them gawking, but I do want them to know what we were doing."

Trembling now, as much from a reaction to her first coupling as from fear of what lay ahead, Beth obeyed him, sitting up and trying to cover herself.

As Patrick unbolted the door, her stomach clenched, and she feared that she would lose what little she had eaten that day. Then she remembered Maggie's warning that she could not answer for the consequences if Beth did not return to serve Drusilla and Jelyan, and the memory stirred fingers of ice along her spine. She was on her own now, come what may. Drawing a deep breath, she slid off the bed to stand beside it, clutching a blanket around her as Patrick opened the door. Two armed men in scarlet livery stood in the corridor.

"What the devil do you mean by creating such a disturbance?" Patrick demanded angrily. "If the cardinal sent you—"

"We ha' come for Elspeth Douglas," the larger of the two declared.

"There is no one here who answers any longer to that name," Patrick said, but Beth knew her gasp had given her away.

"That be her there," the second one said. "We ha' come tae arrest her."

"Rubbish," Patrick said. "What is the charge?"

"Witchcraft be the first one."

The first one! With a cry of horror, Beth reached for

Patrick, and he put his arm around her. She hugged the blanket tightly but it gave her no warmth.

"That charge is false," Patrick said with amazing calm. "What's the second?"

"Treason against James, High King o' Scots."

Beth's knees gave way. Only Patrick's strong arm held her upright.

Patrick fought cold terror and knew Beth felt the same, because her fingers gripped his arm as convulsively as Zeus's talons when the hawk was about to bate. Beaton's war against witchcraft was notorious. That he cared more about destroying witches than about learning if they were guilty of the charge was just as notorious.

"Stand aside, sir, or we've orders tae arrest ye as well," the taller man said.

"My wife is neither a witch nor a traitor," Patrick snapped, noting that Beth had recovered enough of her equilibrium to stand on her own.

"Then she can tell us how she came by all her finery," the spokesman said, gesturing toward the pile of clothing on the floor. "She's nowt but a baseborn maidservant, they say, but she were in the great hall dressed as fine as a princess."

"I've told you, she is my wife, and I am quite able to dress her in the style she deserves," Patrick said, controlling his temper with effort.

"Ye werena married afore tonight, though. Ye didna keep such finery here just in the event that ye might find yourself a wee wife, now, did ye, sir?"

Patrick was silent.

"Moreover, folks say the lass ha' been a-castin' spells

hereabouts, thereby endangering the King, his queen, and their two wee bairns. That be treason, sir, plain and simple."

Striving to collect his wits, Patrick said, "We will answer any questions we must, but since you lack the authority to accept or reject our answers, we will wait upon his eminence in the morning. I know him. I warrant he will hear me."

"Mayhap he will," the spokesman agreed with a shrug. "Ye'll find out in the morning, but me orders be tae arrest the lass now and lock her up till her trial."

Patrick glanced at his sword.

"Dinna try that," the spokesman said, touching his own sword hilt. "There be two o' us, sir, and ye'll unable tae speak for the lass if ye be dead or injured."

Beth stepped behind Patrick, as if his large body could protect her from the soldiers. He only wished it could. At least she had the sense to keep quiet.

Sternly, he said to the men, "I want your word that no harm will come to her before I have a chance to speak with his eminence."

"An he agrees tae hear ye," the second man muttered.

Patrick ignored him, saying to the spokesman, "This is naught but a charge laid by spiteful women, easily disproved. Do not forget that she is my wife, Lady MacRae, and treat her accordingly or I shall voice my complaints to the King."

The look the spokesman gave him said as clearly as words would have that the King's displeasure was insignificant compared to the cardinal's. And compared to either, Patrick knew the two men counted his fury small indeed. Never had he felt so helpless. Having to relinquish Beth to them felt worse than it had felt to watch Kintail taken hostage.

"We'll take her now, sir," the man said. "Come, mistress."

"Wait," Patrick said curtly. "You will allow her to dress properly. She cannot escape, for you stand in the only doorway. Stand outside until she is ready."

The second man said snidely, "Likely, the wee witch will conjure up a broomstick and fly off out yonder window an we did anything so daft."

"Oh, don't be stupid!" Beth snapped. "I just wish I *could* fly away."

Although he was glad to see she had not lost her spirit, Patrick feared she might suffer for it. He put his hand on her shoulder and gave it a warning squeeze as he said grimly, "You will speak to her courteously or answer to me."

The spokesman glanced at him, and Patrick held his gaze, still fighting to control his temper. He wanted to murder both men and get Beth away to safety.

Evidently, his fury impressed the spokesman, for he said, "I beg your pardon, sir. She'll no come tae harm wi' us. We canna go outside, but we'll turn our backs."

Not trusting either one, Patrick stood between the two and Beth while she scrambled into her skirt and bodice. When she picked up her belt, he said, "Leave it, *mo chridhe,* and your hood, too. I'll keep them safe. Give me your necklace, too. I'd say leave your shoes, but I don't want you walking barefoot. Art ready now?"

"Aye," she said quietly. "Will you come?"

"I wish I could, but I doubt they would allow it. In any event, I want to find his eminence." Turning to the men-at-arms, he said, "Is the cardinal still below?"

"Aye, sir, he were eating his supper just moments ago," the spokesman said.

Kissing Beth, Patrick said, "I'll come as soon as I can."

Her eyes were wide with fright, and he put his arms around her, holding her close, wanting to insist that they let him go with her but knowing he had accomplished as much as he could until he could get help. Even so, he hated watching her go away with them, looking so small and vulnerable.

She glanced back, and the attempt she made to smile wrung his heart. Throwing on his clothes, he exchanged boots for his court shoes, in case he had to leave the castle, strapped on his dirk and sword, and hurried to find the cardinal.

"All mortals be fools, Claud," Lucy Fittletrot said in disgust. "Your lass be nae more a witch than I be."

"Less," Claud said, wringing his hands. "There must be summat we can do."

"Mayhap me father will ken a way tae help her."

"I canna beg aid from your father till I can tell him his true name," Claud said. "But stay! Dinna ye ken what his true name be?"

"Nay, only Tom Tit Tot," she said. "Ye willna blame me an I canna help ye, Claud. That wouldna be fair when ye ken even less about your ain father."

"Dinna fash yourself, lass," Claud said with a sigh. "But me mam will flay me an I let ill befall our lass now. We must follow her."

"Oh, aye, we can do that. I want tae see what they'll do tae her. But first, me fine laddie, ye stirred a thirst in me earlier that keeps me from thinking straight, and we've this chamber all tae ourselves for a time."

Claud sighed, knowing that his mother would say he should put first things first. But his notion of "first" was rather different from Maggie's, and surely a few minutes more or less would not matter to anyone but him and his willing Lucy.

James wakened Nell, kissing her lips and her breasts, and then made her squirm with further attentions. Not until they lay back satiated did she remember seeing Patrick in the hall.

"Why is Sir Patrick here without Kintail?" she asked. When he did not answer, she said, "I should tell you I saw him in Cumberland, too, at Midgeholme."

"Indeed?"

"Aye," she said. "Surely, you know what he was doing there."

"I know that he trained a fine hawk and that he spent time in England, serving his king. What else I may know is no concern of yours."

"No, sire, but as to Kintail and his lady—"

"They are here, too," James said with a sigh.

"Faith, do you mean to tell me he is one of your Highland hostages?"

"Aye."

"I never dreamed . . . I heard that you had collected a few Highland chiefs and chieftains, but Kintail! James, his father gave his life in your service!"

"'Tis not a matter we need discuss now."

"I have been here three days," Nell said, struggling to keep from shouting the words at him. "You tell me now that my daughter has been here all that time?"

"Dinna be wroth with me, Nell," he said, turning to nuzzle her breasts again. "Kintail and his lass will still be here in the morning."

"But you should have told me."

"God's feet, madam, you should be flattered that I did not want to compete with your daughter for your attention. Now that the Queen is here and will remain for a fortnight, you may go to your daughter when I dismiss you."

Frustrated, knowing that like most men he would always put his needs before those of anyone else, Nell turned her attention to pleasing him.

Patrick soon learned that despite what the men-at-arms had said, the cardinal and his entourage had left the castle and the King had likewise retired for the night. Therefore, he hurried to the stables, ordered a horse, and rode down to the abbey.

A number of people strolled along the torchlit main streets, and he half expected to catch up to Beth and her escort but saw no sign of them. As he approached Stirling Bridge, he realized he had acquired a companion. Thunder loped alongside, matching strides with the horse. Patrick was not sure when the big dog had joined him, for he had left the lights of the town behind and despite the dog's size, his coloring made him nearly invisible.

"Hello, Thunder," he said. "Where have you been hiding?"

The dog wagged its tail, and Patrick felt oddly comforted by its presence. That feeling disappeared, however, when he reached Cambuskenneth only to be informed by the porter that his eminence had retired for the night.

Declaring that he would return at first light, Patrick remounted and, with Thunder again at his side, returned to the castle. This time, he headed for Kintail's chambers and, finding no guard on duty, tried the latch. The door was bolted, however, so he pounded on it as loudly as the cardinal's men had pounded on his.

"Fin, open up! It's Patrick!"

He heard the bolt slamming back, and then the door opened and Fin Mackenzie stood glowering at him, hair standing on end, a blanket carelessly wrapped around his waist, looking as wild as anyone had called him, "What's amiss?" he demanded curtly.

"Let me in," Patrick said, pushing past him. "Where's Molly?"

"Where do you think, damn you?"

"Call her."

"Devil take you, Patrick, you'd best have a good reason for this."

"What is it, Patrick?" Molly said from the bedchamber doorway. She wore her bedgown, and her hair was in its usual tumble, but she looked wide wake.

Reluctant to tell her what he suspected, now that he was face-to-face with her, he looked helplessly at Fin.

Kintail frowned. "Tell us," he said.

"Beaton has Bessie," Patrick said bluntly.

"Where?" they demanded, speaking as one.

Putting a protective arm around Molly, Fin added, "How do you know?"

"I didn't know at first," Patrick said, shoving a hand through his hair. "They called her Elspeth Douglas, but I'm as sure as I can be that she's your sister, Molly. I don't know how I failed to see it at once."

"See what, Patrick?" Molly's face was pale, her eyes wide, and the skin around her lips was white and drawn.

"You look just like her," he muttered. "That is, she looks like you." Seeing Fin's countenance harden, and recognizing the look all too well, he added hastily, "Her eyes are exactly like yours, although perhaps a trifle greener. She has the same long, thick, dark lashes. She is thinner than you, perhaps an inch taller, and her hair is flaxen but as straight as can be and as fine as silk. Doubtless, it was her hair that kept me from seeing how alike the two of you are, that and the fact that your clothing is more colorful and much more fashionable than hers."

"Is her clothing so drab?" Molly asked.

Both men looked at her.

Glancing from one to the other, she said defensively, "Well, perhaps it is not the most important detail, but it was an odd thing for you to say."

Gently, Patrick said, "She was not raised with the advantages you had, but she speaks like a gentlewoman and has a gentlewoman's quiet dignity."

Molly looked at Fin, and something in the look stirred Patrick's curiosity. "What is it?" he said.

Molly opened her mouth but shut it when Fin shook his head.

Before Patrick could repeat his demand, Fin said, "Do you honestly think this lass can be Bessie Gordon?"

"Bessie Gordon! You have found my Bessie?"

So engrossed had they been in their conversation that none of the three had noted the arrival of a fourth person in the still open doorway.

"Mother!" Molly cried, flinging herself into the arms of a smiling Nell Percy.

_____

Chapter 20

Despite knowing he could do nothing that night to free Beth, Patrick chafed at the few moments of reunion delight, as Molly and Nell hugged, exclaimed, and flung questions at each other.

"Where did you spring from?" Molly demanded. "You have not written since you left for England, and we feared the worst."

"Well, death would be the worst, but it was bad enough," Nell said dryly. "Angus would not let me leave or write to you. He was furious because his plan to ally his forces and Henry's with Donald the Grim had failed, and he blamed me for what he called the whole disaster."

"But it was not your fault," Molly said.

Nell had left the door open, and as Fin shut it, he said, "Did Angus tell you what really became of Bessie, madam?"

"He still insists that she is dead, but I did not believe him, and now . . . Did I not hear you say you have found her, Sir Patrick?"

"I believe so," Patrick said cautiously, looking from one to the other and trying to imagine if Nell's arrival affected the odds of rescuing Beth. He still wondered, too, what had made Fin and Molly look at each other so oddly. That there was a mystery was evident, but what it concerned was not.

With tears in her voice, Nell said, "Where is she, sir?"

He did not want to tell her. He wanted to rescue Beth first and bring her safely to them. Instead, the news he had would plunge her into the same abyss of terror that he inhabited, and there was nothing they could do to save her if he could not persuade Beaton to let her go. A cloud of pessimism settled in him as he looked at his two best friends and Beth's mother. Molly and Fin clearly wanted him to answer her question, and the silence had grown heavy.

Gathering himself, he said quietly, "Cardinal Beaton's men have her. I do not know where they took her. I did not think to ask, which was stupid of me."

Nell clutched her breast, bereft of speech.

"But *why* did they take her?" Molly demanded. "What can Bessie have done to attract the notice of such men?"

"She calls herself Beth now," he said. "She remembers dreams, she said, of a place where people called her 'Bethie.' "

"Merciful heaven, she really is our Bessie," Nell said, tears streaming down her face. "She called herself 'Bethie' from the start. She had the most adorable lisp." Her voice broke, and she looked helplessly at Patrick.

"But what did she do, Patrick?" Molly's voice revealed her rising temper.

Realizing that any answer he gave would be fraught with peril, he hesitated, uncertain how much to reveal about Beth's activities, and his own.

"Did they arrest her?" Fin asked bluntly.

"Aye," Patrick said, grateful for a direct question to answer.

"What are the charges?"

Not so grateful now, he drew a deep breath, and then said,

"They charged her with witchcraft and treason against the King."

Molly cried out, and Nell swayed. Fin caught her as her knees gave way.

"I'll carry her into the other room," he said. "You come, too, lass, so you can look after her."

"No," Nell said, clutching his arm. "I must hear all that Patrick has to say."

"I'm not leaving, either," Molly said with a speaking look at her husband. "How could they charge her with such crimes, Patrick? What could she possibly have done to make them think her either a witch or a traitor?"

"She did nothing, and they did not explain," he replied harshly. "They came, they banged on the door, and they arrested her. I could do nothing to prevent it."

"What door?" Fin asked as he steadied Nell on her feet again and kept a firm hand under her elbow.

"My door," Patrick said curtly. "Do you not want to sit down, madam?"

"No," Nell said.

All three of them regarded him with intense curiosity.

Molly's eyes narrowed, but she said with commendable calm, "Perhaps you had better begin at the beginning, Patrick. How did you find her?'

He looked at Fin. "I was on the run," he said. "You all know how I nearly came to grief at Midgeholme."

When Nell smiled ruefully, he knew that she was recovering her poise.

"You also told us that you stayed with Sir Hector Farnsworth," Molly said.

"Aye, and that is when I met her. They called her Elspeth."

Nell frowned. "Elspeth. Now, why does that name tug at my memory?"

"She believes she is Angus's daughter," Patrick said,

watching her to see if that information would help. "They told her that her mother was a serving maid."

"Angus's daughter," Nell murmured. "One of his 'accidents.' That is what I said she was." Looking at Patrick with dawning horror, she said, "A large woman, common as dirt, with outrageous wigs and a strident voice. She's got two homely daughters and talks incessantly."

"Aye, that would be Lady Farnsworth right enough," Patrick said. "One of those daughters has the voice of an eldritch. How do you know her?"

Nell's chin was trembling, and she clutched one hand with the other. "I met her here at Stirling when I came in search of Molly, but that woman cannot have known the truth," she added in a choked voice. "No one could be so cruel."

"What are you talking about?" Molly demanded, touching Nell's arm.

But Nell was looking at Patrick. "The girl was their maidservant, pale and thin. That horrid woman even sent her to me with a message, bidding me farewell as I was leaving for the Highlands. That wretched woman said she was Angus's bastard child, that he had given her to them to raise. Why did I not see it then?"

"You thought she was dead," Molly reminded her. "We all thought so then, because Angus told everyone she was." She looked at Fin, and Patrick saw the same awareness flash between them that he had seen before.

"But I never believed that," Nell said with a sob. "And I should have known my own daughter!"

"Do you remember visiting us at Dunsithe, madam?" Molly asked gently in what seemed a non sequitur to Patrick.

Nell frowned, clearly thinking the same. "When you and Kintail went there to inspect the estates you inherited?"

Molly nodded, but Patrick saw her cast another look at Fin.

"Of course, I remember," Nell said. "That was shortly before I rode back to Cumberland to rejoin Angus and tell him his erstwhile ally, Donald the Grim, had died before I reached the Highlands. Not that Angus cared a straw. He cared only that I had failed."

Molly bit her lower lip, looking ruefully at Patrick.

Fin said, "Tell us more about this lass, Patrick. Persuade me that she is who you believe her to be."

Irritation gnawed at Patrick, but habit and duty kept his tone even. "She is no witch, Fin, nor has she committed treason."

"But just how well do you know her, my friend? Did I misunderstand you, or did they arrest her in your chamber?"

"You did not misunderstand me," Patrick said, avoiding Molly's sharp gaze.

She said grimly, "I expect you thought she was just another maidservant to add to your collection."

It was close enough to the truth of how he had felt at first about Beth that he felt heat firing his cheeks, but he faced Molly, knowing he could delay no longer before speaking the whole truth. "She has become much more than that," he said, and emotion welled within him as he said it, telling him that he was speaking more truth than even he had known. "She is my wife, Molly."

Stunned silence greeted him.

"Thank God," Nell said, recovering first.

But Patrick watched Kintail, and when that gentleman frowned heavily, he braced himself.

Molly spoke before Fin did, saying, "How? Where?"

"By declaration, at the ball," Patrick replied, still watching Kintail.

"Explain yourself," he snapped.

Patrick did, and to his surprise and relief, no one interrupted. He began at the beginning and told them everything. Molly and Nell exclaimed aloud when he told them Beth had run away from Farnsworth to follow him, but Fin merely gestured for him to continue. And when he lingered too long on his description of Jock and his companions, and the training of Zeus, another impatient gesture recalled him hastily. When he described the King's ball, he told them only that she had borrowed a gown and attended, that he had danced with her, and that Lady Farnsworth had recognized her and had reported to Beaton's men that Beth had bewitched him.

When he finished, Fin said, "That's all?"

"Aye, most of it," Patrick said glibly. "I doubt I've left out anything of importance." With the one small exception, of course, that his Beth never explained where she got her fine clothing and jewelry.

Molly and Fin exchanged another look.

She said, "Are you sure, Patrick? Did Beth never say anything about—"

"Molly," Fin said warningly.

She looked at him, nibbled her lip, then looked at Patrick again. "Did she never do things or ask you questions that struck you as being odd?"

Patrick tried to think of anything that fit the description, but he could think of nothing other than that the lass might be a thief, a detail he would reveal to no one until he learned the truth. He shook his head. "We talked of many things," he said, "but I don't recall anything especially peculiar."

Molly persisted. "Then, is there aught about her that seems unusual?"

He shrugged. "She has a deft hand with birds of prey—with all animals, come to that. She told me that none had ever bitten or scratched her. Why do you keep looking at each other like that?" he demanded when they exchanged yet another of those odd looks.

Molly ignored his question, saying, "You said she speaks well, Patrick. Did she seem educated?"

"Aye, she said Sir Hector taught her when he taught his daughters."

Molly nodded.

"Does she speak only broad Scot?"

He stared at her. "I'd forgotten," he said. "When I said . . . a Gaelic phrase, she understood it. She said she must have heard it before."

"That may be true, of course," Fin said.

"Dancing," Patrick said. "That's another thing. She danced the galliard tonight as if she'd been taking lessons since birth. That's devilish peculiar, now that I come to think about it."

Nell had been watching them, silently looking from one to the other. "Why are you quizzing him like this?" she asked. "Everyone dances, but Gaelic is spoken only in the Highlands. Bessie must have met a Highlander, that's all."

Patrick found himself rejecting that notion out of hand. He could not accept the idea that another man, let alone another Highlander, had called her his heart.

Molly said, "We've got to tell him, Fin. There is something else. I know it."

"Aye," Fin said, "I see that much for myself, but we'll not do it together, lass. You remember what she said would happen if we talk of this. Mayhap if only one of us does, the other will continue to remember."

She frowned. "I don't know," she said. "We discussed no rules."

"Only the one," he said.

Frustrated, and feeling his temper stir, Patrick said, "What the devil are you talking about?"

Fin glanced at him, and the look reminded Patrick that he was not the only one there with a temper, but he no longer cared. "Tell me," he said.

"We must," Molly agreed.

Fin said, "Take your mother into the other room, lass. I'll tell him everything I can remember."

"But—"

"Don't argue with me. I'll also get out of him whatever it is he's been concealing from us."

A twinge of guilt stirred in Patrick, and he avoided Molly's gaze.

She said quietly to her husband, "It is true that he is more likely to tell you than me. Come, madam, we will leave them to talk."

"But I want to know what they say!"

"They will tell us later," Molly promised. "Presently, we must put our heads together and think how to help Bessie, although I suppose we must call her Beth now. There must be something we can do."

"I'll talk to Jamie," Nell said bluntly. "He will listen to me if he will listen to anyone, and cardinal or no cardinal, Jamie is still King."

"We'll discuss that," Molly said, firmly leading her from the room.

When the door had shut behind them, Patrick drew a deep breath and turned to face Kintail. He expected a blunt, angry demand to reveal everything he had left out, so it was with surprise that he saw Fin smile ruefully.

"This is a mess," he said.

"Aye," Patrick agreed warily. He said no more, deciding his best course was to let Fin take the lead until he saw where things were going.

Fin cleared his throat, looking oddly reluctant to proceed. Then, with a grimace, he said, "Doubtless, you've heard tales about the gift of second sight."

"Aye, I've heard the legends," Patrick said, truly bewildered now. "Some even say the lairds of Kintail were once blessed with the gift."

"Cursed with it would be a more apt description," Fin said. "It certainly did my father no good if he possessed it."

"He did not," Patrick said firmly. "Had he possessed it, surely he would have known of the trap Donald laid for him and his men, and he would have survived, but I don't see what the devil this has to do with Beth."

"I know you don't, but if you think you can take that tone with me—"

"I'll apologize for the tone, but for God's sake, man, if you've an explanation to make, make it!"

"Faith, you're in love with the lass!"

It was on the tip of Patrick's tongue to deny it, but he did not. Instead, he said, "She is my wife, Fin, in every sense of the word."

"Aye, but marriage and love do not always go hand in hand."

"Fin, for the love of God—"

"Aye, you're right, but this is not easy for me, either. It is not just a matter of the sight, Patrick, but concerns the wee people, as well."

"If you don't cease talking nonsense—"

"But it is not nonsense. I once thought it was, but I learned my error, and a good thing, too. Do you recall how skilled Molly is with a bow and arrow?"

"Aye," Patrick said.

"And with animals?"

"Aye, she can ride any horse she's ever thrown her leg across."

"Is it your belief that she killed Donald the Grim?"

"She did. She shot him with an arrow when he attacked Eilean Donan."

"Then you will doubtless think me demented when I tell you that things did not happen the way you and everyone else thinks. Molly had help, just as I have help whenever I beat you at chess."

Patrick's patience was spent. "What the devil has chess to do with this?"

"When Molly lived with Mackinnon, he was said to be unbeatable at chess. Now, I have that same reputation, and he no longer does. Think about that."

"Damnation, Fin, I'm ripe for murder, so if you are trying to tell me that wee people help you win at chess, I must tell you th—"

"Just one wee person," Fin said. "I'll not tell you her name, because that is forbidden and at the moment, I cannot recall it, anyway. But she and her son have watched over Molly since Angus abducted her from Dunsithe when she was a child. I believe they watch over Bessie, too."

"Nonsense. If they were watching Beth, Beaton would not have her."

"I don't think they work that way," Fin said. "I've little notion of how they do work, mind you, but Bessie's . . . Beth's . . . skill with hawks, her knowledge of Gaelic, and other things you have said, would suggest that unnatural forces are at work. I can see them when they are near me, you know."

"See who?"

"The wee people."

"You're daft!"

"I thought so," Fin said with a chuckle. "I don't know if I'll lose the gift by speaking of it, but she did say that the more we speak about our experience, the more quickly we'll forget the details. Nevertheless, you need to know that they exist, and that somehow Molly's protectors lost Bessie after Angus took the girls away. They've been searching for her, though, and if they've found her . . ."

He let the silence linger suggestively, but although certain images were flashing through Patrick's mind, he did not speak.

Fin said, "There's something you did not tell us, something you held back."

"What makes you think so?"

"I know you as I know myself, Patrick. You are protecting her somehow, or trying to protect her. But we need to know what you left out."

Patrick hesitated only a moment. "I'll tell you," he said, "but you must not tell Molly or Nell, because I do not yet know if it is true. Beth swears it is not, and I believe her, but I must know the truth before we tell anyone else."

"Agreed," Fin said. "Now, tell me."

"When Beth appeared at the ball, she wore a gown more splendid than any I have ever seen," Patrick said. "Jewelry, too. One of the biggest diamonds I've ever seen on a solid gold leaf pendant, a jeweled hood, belt, and pomander, even jewels on the heels of her shoes. And Jock . . . do you remember young Jock?"

"Aye, what of him?"

"He was dressed like her page, but when I walked toward her, he melted into the crowd, just disappeared, and he was not in my chamber when we went there after I declared our marriage."

"Just as well he wasn't," Fin said dryly. "I warrant the clothing and jewelry had as much to do with Lady Farnsworth's insistence that Beth had bewitched you as anything else did. If she had noticed Jock, the fat would really be in the fire."

"Aye," Patrick admitted, pushing away thoughts of witches and fire. "Beth swore she did not steal anything, Fin, and the cardinal's men did not accuse her of theft, so I'd venture to guess that no one reported anything missing."

"No one will," Fin said. "Unless I miss my guess, what you

just said does more to prove her identity than all you said before. I believe the wee folk provided her finery. Indeed, for all I know, she may have been wearing her own jewelry."

"Her own—"

"Aye, because Nell said that Bessie's inheritance consists mostly of jewelry. We discovered Molly's inheritance but not Bessie's, so we've never seen it."

"Discovered? She was the Maid of Dunsithe. Everyone knew of her wealth."

"Aye, but its whereabouts was a mystery, and I cannot tell you the details, because I promised I never would," Fin said. "But unless I forget everything as a result of telling you what little I have, perhaps I can help you find Beth's treasure after we win her freedom. If not, then perhaps Molly can." He hesitated. "Now that I think about it, though, Molly had to find hers, so likely Beth will, too."

Patrick was still trying to cope with the idea that wee folk might be involved. "If wee people got Beth into this mess, they should get her out," he said.

"I don't know if they can," Fin said. "They tend to keep away from any doings of the Kirk, and they have rules of their own, or so I was told."

"You have truly talked with this . . . this creature."

"Aye."

"Sakes, Fin, if I did not know you as well as I do—"

"I know."

Patrick fell silent, thinking, and Fin did not interrupt him, which was as odd as all the rest, he thought. Fin's patience was even more limited than his.

That thought drew another.

"I expected you to be annoyed about my marriage," he said bluntly.

The rueful smile reappeared as Fin said, "In a sense I bear responsibility for both of you. I should have had a say in who Bessie marries, since there is no one other than Molly, Nell, and me to claim kinship with her. As for you . . ." He paused, adding, "You owe me fealty, my friend, so you should have apprised me of your intentions beforehand."

"Aye, and I would have, had there been time," Patrick admitted.

Fin chuckled. "I'll agree your time was short."

Patrick was grateful for Fin's good mood, but he saw no humor in the situation, so he said nothing.

With a wry look, Fin said, "Have you given any thought to what we can do?"

"I mean to speak with Beaton first thing in the morning."

"I'll go with you," Molly said from the doorway. With a glance at her husband, she added, "I trust you two have finished your private talk, because Mother and I have been going mad waiting to learn how we can help."

"You will not go with Patrick," Fin said flatly.

"Yes, I must," she said. "Beth is my sister, and the cardinal has always been courteous to me. If I tell him who she is—"

"He will simply believe you are doing all you can to help Patrick," Fin said. "Since you cannot tell his eminence that you can identify her absolutely—"

"Why should I not tell him that?" Molly demanded.

"Would you lie to the man who stands in the Pope's place in Scotland?"

She bit her lower lip.

"Just so," Fin said. "You will remain here—you and Nell both," he added as Nell appeared beside her.

"I shall speak to James," Nell said. "He has a tenderness for me, and it cannot hurt us to have his ear. He feels little love for Davy Beaton."

"Perhaps," Patrick said. "But neither does he dare to thwart Beaton."

"Faith, sir, Jamie is still King, and if he could stand

against Angus and defeat him at the age of sixteen, he can stand against Beaton now. See if he does not."

Patrick looked at Fin, but for once, that gentleman declined to take the lead, saying, "Until Jamie releases me, I can do little to help, so Beth's fate lies in your hands, but I am at your service if you need to discuss any tactics or strategies."

Patrick nodded, feeling a chill at the thought that Beth's future, if she was to have one, lay primarily in his hands. He did not know if she was safe, even now.

"Patrick," Molly said gently.

He looked at her blindly.

"Where is Bab?"

"Bab?"

"Aye, your sister. Where is she?"

He shook his head. He had not spared a thought for her in hours.

"We'll find her," Nell said. "Come, Molly, and put on some clothes. You'll have to come with me, for I do not know her."

"I'll come straightaway," Molly said, turning to her husband. "Don't say that I must not, Fin. This is something that I *can* do."

"Aye, lass, and tell that baggage that if she's done anything she should not have done, she will answer to me."

Patrick felt only relief that he would not have to deal with Bab, too, and he remembered then where he had last seen her. "She was with Alex Chisholm, Molly, so she is still with him, because he would not abandon her until he had restored her to me or to you. You'll find her in the great hall, dancing her shoes to shreds."

Chapter 21———————————————

Beth struggled to retain her wits and her composure, but it was not easy.

Her jeweled, silk slippers were made for dancing, not for walking on cobblestones, and the cardinal's men had made her walk halfway down the steep hill to the Tolbooth. Inside that bleak stone building, they locked her in a drab cell furnished only with a bench along one wall and a bucket to which they pointed when she gathered enough courage to ask where she was to relieve herself.

At first, because total darkness enveloped her after they took their torch away, she thought she was alone. Her body and mind ached for Patrick, and she wondered how soon he would come. Then a female voice said, "Who be ye, then?"

Startled, she replied, "My name is Beth. Who are you?"

"Och, she be one o' the gentry," another voice sneered.

She nearly told them she was no gentlewoman, only a commoner like themselves, but remembering she was supposedly married to Patrick, and thus a lady, she said bluntly, "I am accused of witchcraft and treason."

"Aye, well, they say we all be witches, too," the first voice said. "I'm Ellen, and I be here 'cause me husband's mother says I've bewitched him and made him unable tae get sons. The fool thinks he be Henry o' England and can cast off any wife wha' doesna get lads for him."

"Will we all be tried together?" Beth asked.

"Sakes, mistress, we been tried and found guilty already," Ellen said. "Ye'll ha' your trial in the morning, soon as his eminence drags hisself out o' bed. Least, he seemed tae be still half asleep when they tried me."

"Me, too," a new voice declared.

"How many of you are there?" Beth asked.

"There be six o' us."

Beth sighed. It should have given her comfort to have companions, she thought, but having them seemed to be creating the opposite effect.

After a silence, one of them said, "D'ye ken anyone wi' power, mistress?"

"Dinna be daft," another said sharply. "There be none so powerful as Davy Beaton, and he wants a grand show, does Davy."

"What sort of a grand show?" Beth asked, knowing even as she asked that she did not want to know.

"A great witch burning," Ellen said. "He means tae do it the day afore Easter, tae cleanse his precious Kirk for the grand day."

Beth's throat seemed to close. She could scarcely breathe. "Oh, Patrick, I need you," she murmured, hugging herself. "Come to me soon."

Perched together on the stone sill of the little arched window, Claud and Lucy stared at each other in helpless dismay.

"What will me mam say o' this? I dinna want tae think about it!"

"I think ye mun find her, though," Lucy said in a worried tone. "They did say the cardinal will try the lass tomorrow."

"Aye," Claud said, "but our lot doesna muck about wi' the Kirk or the cardinal. Theirs be a world we dinna enter, and since they has the lass . . . Och, but the Circle will ha' much tae say about this, and I dinna want tae hear it."

"Find your mam, Claud," Lucy said firmly.

With a heavy sigh, he agreed.

She was inside the castle, although she did not know how she had managed to get in. And he was with her, right beside her, as they walked down a long carpeted corridor. There were no doors, but as they reached the wall at the end, it disappeared, and a chest stood before her. But the corridor was cold now and sounded as if rats ran hither and yon, and when she reached for her key . . .

Chilled to the bone, Beth awoke to noisy sniffing and snuffling above her. Everything else was still, and she could make out the dull gray light of dawn in the high, arched, heavily barred window. Standing, she looked up, listening, stiff from lying in the only position the narrow bench allowed.

The snuffling sound came again, followed by a low *woof.*

"Thunder!"

The dog's furry gray snout and black nose poked through the bars.

"Oh, Thunder, fetch Patrick. Go! Find him!"

The dog's nose disappeared, and she heard rapid footsteps. Keeping her voice low, so only he would hear, she called, "Patrick! I'm down here!"

"Mistress Beth!"

Disappointment surged through her. "Jock?"

"Aye, it be me," the boy said. "What be ye a-doing down there?"

"The cardinal's men arrested me last night. How did you find me?"

"Thunder must ha' followed ye, 'cause he come and fetched me afore the sky got light. He wouldna leave me be till I followed him."

"I'm glad you came," Beth said, trying hard to suppress her disappointment. "You must find Patrick and bring him here to me."

"I'll find him, mistress, but I dinna think they'll let him in. When I were at the gate, a man asked tae see his wife, and they said nae one sees prisoners now."

"Then how did you and Thunder get in?"

"I could see it wouldna be wise tae say me dog brung me, so I asked m'self what Sir Patrick would do, and it come tae me tae say me dad were a guard and I needed tae find him. They let me and Thunder in staightaway."

"That was clever," she said. "Jock, tell Patrick I think they mean to try me straightaway."

"Aye, I'll tell 'im," he said. "Ha' fortitude, mistress."

Hearing Patrick's watchword on the boy's lips comforted her briefly, but when he had gone, she felt bereft again, and terrified.

A golden glow at the edge of the eastern hills showed that the sun would soon be up as Patrick rode across the castle's timber bridge. Although he was preoccupied with thoughts of what he would say to the cardinal, he recognized Jock running up the hill toward him with Thunder loping alongside.

"Where the devil have you been?" Patrick demanded when the boy was close enough to hear him.

"I might ask the same," Jock retorted. "Did ye nae go back tae your room last night after ye flung your pretty clothes about?"

"My actions are no concern of yours," Patrick informed him harshly. "Yours, on the other hand, if you want to continue serving me, are very much my concern."

"Aye, sure," the boy said, brushing a hand across his brow to push his hair out of his eyes. "Mistress Beth says ye're tae come and get her straightaway, but she's in the Tolbooth, so I dinna think they'll let ye."

"How did you learn where she is?"

"Thunder came and pulled me out o' me bed and took me tae her window, and she said I should tell ye they mean tae try her straightaway."

"We'll see about that," Patrick said, fighting a wave of chilling fear. "I am going to the abbey now to see his eminence and arrange her release."

"D'ye think the cardinal gets up afore the sun shows its face?"

"I do not care when he gets up," Patrick said curtly. "I will be there."

"Aye, I'll go wi' ye then," Jock said. "Thunder, too."

"I don't know if that's wise," Patrick said, tousling his hair, "but I own, I'll be grateful for your company."

"Aye, for we ha' fortitude and tae spare, the both o' us."

A full hour passed after Patrick and his companions arrived at the abbey before the porter showed Patrick to his eminence's audience chamber.

As Patrick knelt to kiss the ring, Beaton said, "I have urged Kintail's release, but Oliver Sinclair still insists that the hostages are less troublesome here than they would be if allowed to return home."

"I know you will do all you can," Patrick said quietly. "I have come on another matter—one even more urgent to me."

"You need only tell me what it is," Beaton said. "I am greatly in your debt, for Henry's armies are gathering now in the English east march, but thanks to you, our men will be in place to thwart his intended invasion. So, how can I help you?"

"Last night your men arrested my wife."

"I know of only one arrest last night," Beaton said. "Surely, you cannot have married a traitorous witch, Sir Patrick."

Grimly, Patrick said, "I did no such thing. A spiteful woman and her equally spiteful daughters lodged those spurious charges, my lord. Lady MacRae had the misfortune to grow up in their home, and they are displeased that she married me without their approval, but it was she who protected me when the English were searching for me—at the risk of her own life, I might add."

"Then perhaps you were not aware that she is the daughter of the traitorous Earl of Angus, and like many of that wicked tribe, dabbles in the occult."

"I am aware of no such dabbling," Patrick declared, striving to control his temper. "I do know that Angus told them she was his baseborn daughter, but in fact, he abducted her from Dunsithe Castle. In truth, she is Lady Mackenzie's sister, Elizabeth Gordon, the younger daughter of Lord Gordon of Dunsithe, so you see how imperative it is that she be released. She is kin to the Earl of Huntly, your staunch ally, and to Mackenzie of Kintail. And, I— And she is my lady, sir."

"I would like to help, Sir Patrick," Beaton said, "But you must realize the charges are ones I cannot overlook. I have worked too hard to rid the Scottish Kirk of such evils. You yourself are suspicious of Farnsworth, and the woman helped you train that hawk he gave to his grace, did she not?"

"Aye, but the hawk has naught to do with the charges against her."

"Does it not? James has told everyone who will listen how tame it is. It is hardly beyond belief that the wench cast a spell over it and over you, too."

Fists clenched, Patrick said, "With respect, my lord, that is absurd."

"She must be properly tried. If she is innocent, we will soon learn as much."

"But—"

"That is all, sir," Beaton said, picking up an ivory-handled silver bell near his right hand and ringing it.

"I have heard they will try her today," Patrick said. "I want to be there."

"It is more likely that her trial will take place tomorrow or the next day, but if you are indeed her husband, you may not attend. We try witches by religious tribunal and allow few spectators—and no family members, who are too likely to let emotion interfere with good sense. I will represent your interest, never fear."

The door opened, and the porter stood waiting.

Patrick would have liked to haul Beaton out of his fancy, carved chair and force him to change his mind, but he knew that if he took even a step in that direction, the porter would summon armed guards. Soon after that, he would find himself behind bars, helpless to aid Beth in any way.

Therefore, with a curt bow, he turned on his heel and went out. In the courtyard, he found Jock waiting but barely paused long enough to order the boy to look after his horse before striding on toward Stirling Bridge. Thinking only of burning off his fury before he had to face anyone else, he crossed the bridge and walked mindlessly until he realized he had come to the gates of the Tolbooth.

His luck there proved no better than at Cambuskenneth, for when he gave his name and demanded entry, the guards informed him that witches did not receive visitors, no matter who those visitors might be.

More furious than ever, he returned to the castle, crossed the outer close, and was about to enter the inner, when Francis Dalcross stepped in front of him, saying with the haughty arrogance of a popular young court gentleman, "One moment, Sir Patrick, if you please. I would speak with you about your beautiful sister, Barbara."

"Don't let me hear *Mistress MacRae's* name on your lips again, you insolent puppy," Patrick snapped, lashing out with a powerful fist.

Without breaking stride, he continued toward the palace entrance, paying no heed to the fact that he had knocked the insolent puppy flat.

Claud paced the parlor floor, his small store of patience depleting rapidly, but certain she would come. He wrung his hands, knowing that every moment he spent waiting for his mother, the lass spent dreading what lay ahead. He had failed, but the lass landing in the Tolbooth was not his fault. It was Maggie's.

Maggie had dressed her and sent her to the ball. She had broken the rules, interfered in a way that mortals had noticed, and the clan's rules did not allow that. It was one thing to assist with chores and learning, and to provide skills to help with those endeavors. It was quite another to shift a mortal from one social class to another right in front of the King and much of his nobility and gentry.

"Just see the result," he muttered to himself. "Ruin, likely!"

Dust motes swirled in front of him and began to form into a solid shape.

"At last!" he exclaimed in relief. "Where ha' ye been, Mam?"

But as the motes solidified, they lengthened, growing into a tall, muscular body, quite unlike that of Maggie Malloch. A shock of green hair appeared even before the apparition's long, thin face took form.

"Good day tae ye, lad," Tom Tit Tot said. "Where ha' ye mislaid me Lucy?"

"What be ye doing here?" Claud demanded in dismay.

"Why, I thought ye'd be glad tae see me, but ye be as glum as a drizzle." His eyes twinkled, and Claud saw that their pupils were whirling green and red lines, like spinning archery targets. "Ha' ye no learned me true name yet?" Tom asked.

"I have not," Claud snapped. "I ha' other matters on me mind."

"Aye, sure, laddie, but none so important as this." He tucked the fiddle under his other arm in order to scratch his head. "It did occur tae me that I neglected tae mention one small detail when last we spoke."

Warily Claud said, "What did ye forget?"

"Tae tell ye how much time ye ha' tae solve me wee puzzle."

Claud swallowed. "How much?"

"Till the next meeting o' the Circle," Tom Tit Tot said blandly.

"But the meetings be secret! How will ye ken, yourself, when it is?"

"I ha' friends in high places, lad, a fact ye should bear in mind whilst ye bend your mind tae me puzzle. Naught else should distract ye till ye earn the right tae wed me sweet Lucy. See ye remember!"

And with a popping sound, Tom Tit Tot vanished.

Smashing his fist into Francis Dalcross had done nothing to calm Patrick, and by the time he reached Fin and Molly's chambers, his fury threatened to consume him. He snatched open the door, strode through the anteroom without pause, and stopped in the center of the sitting room to glower at its lone occupant.

Fin looked up from a table where he was writing letters. His right eyebrow crooked upward, but he did not speak.

"Although bloody Beaton claims to be much in my debt, he will not help, and the guards at the Tolbooth refuse to let me see her," Patrick snapped.

Fin said quietly, "You will accomplish little by barking at me, however."

For once, Fin's displeasure did not faze him. "I must *do* something!"

Setting aside his quill and frowning heavily, Fin stood up. "First," he said, "I would advise you to control your temper."

Patrick straightened, thrusting his shoulders back. "This is no time to fling duty at me, Fin. I've spent the past year serving you and his bloody eminence in ways I could never have imagined before last August. I did it not only because I believed it was my duty but also because I believed I had failed to protect you from Jamie just as my father failed to protect yours at Kinlochewe. I would have given my life to win your freedom."

"Patrick—"

"Nay, let me finish. I probably perjured my soul in your service, and the only good thing to come out of it was my sweet, unpredictable Beth. If you have aught to say that will help me rescue her, say it. Otherwise, keep your thoughts to yourself."

Black silence loomed between them, and Patrick realized he was braced for battle, that he would in fact welcome it.

"Does Beaton ask anything more of you?" Fin asked, his tone deadly calm.

"If he does, he will demand it in vain," Patrick retorted. "Loyalty, I have discovered, is for fools. It avails an honest man nothing good."

"By heaven," Kintail growled, "you go too far."

The two men faced each other, with Patrick aware of nothing but that he was about to vent the fury that had filled him for the past hour and more. Since Kintail wore no sword, he unbuckled his and cast it onto an upholstered bench by the wall.

They circled, eyeing each other warily. They had frequently pitted their mettle against each other but had not fought in earnest since boyhood.

Kintail made a slight gesture, as if he were beckoning Patrick on, and Patrick leaped to answer the challenge, closing and grappling with him.

"Fin! Patrick!"

"Mercy, what are you doing?"

Neither man took heed. It was as if birds chirped, nothing more.

It felt good to fight, to have someone fighting back who was his equal or better, but although they fought hard, neither seemed able to overpower the other. They knew each other too well, had wrestled too often. Each could anticipate the other's moves and counter them, but Patrick welcomed the challenge.

This time he would win. He turned, managed to thrust a hip into Fin's side, and braced himself to throw him.

A flood of cold water put a sputtering end to the battle.

Gasping and dripping, both men straightened abruptly and glared at Molly, who glared right back, her left hand on her hip, the other holding a large silver pitcher, the contents of which she had just emptied over them.

Beside her, Barbara MacRae said, "Have you lost your mind, Patrick?"

"Where the devil have you been?" he demanded.

"Right here," she said. "Molly and Lady Percy collected me from Sir Alex Chisholm last night and brought me here to sleep. I must say I was glad to see them," she added bitterly. "You disappeared without a word, and Sir Alex insisted it was his duty to keep me with him until you returned to collect me. He was horrid!"

Molly said, "Never mind that, Bab. He is leaving for home in the morning, so you won't see him again whilst you remain at Stirling."

"Good," Barbara said flatly.

A thought struck Patrick. "Is Alex leaving alone," he asked, "or is the entire family returning to the Highlands?"

Barbara gasped. "Patrick, you wouldn't!"

Molly's lips twitched. "The whole family, of course," she said. "But what on earth have you and Fin been—?"

"You will go with them, Bab," Patrick interjected. "You had no business staying here without our mother, and you know it. I doubt you even spared a thought for how you'd get home if Fin and Molly spent the winter here."

"But we knew you would return," she said. "Don't make me go, Patrick, please. I'll be good, I promise, and you can take me home when you go."

Anger filled him again, but before he could reply, Molly said hastily, "Leave us now, Bab. I'll come to you as soon as I can."

The look Molly gave her told Patrick as clearly as it told his sister that Molly meant to intercede for her, but it was Fin's stern look and his own, he was sure, that sent Bab away with no more than a martyr's sniff.

When she was gone, he said to Molly, "Don't badger me. She is going home. I can trust Alex to keep her safe, something I can't do myself until Beth is safe."

"So you did not succeed with Cardinal Beaton," Molly said. Glancing speculatively at her husband, she added, "Perhaps you would like to fetch some towels, sir, so that you and Patrick can dry yourselves."

Fin held her gaze. "Perhaps you will fetch those towels, sweetheart, and a few more to clean up this mess you made. And then, *perhaps,* I will overlook the impertinence of a wife who dashes cold water over her husband."

"You deserved it," she said, meeting his gaze calmly. Then, to Patrick, she added, "Both of you deserved it for behaving like a pair of naughty bairns."

"We'll discuss that later," Fin said. "Now, go and get some towels, lass, and whilst you're about it, tell that baggage Bab that she is not to pester Patrick about staying here. She will obey him without protest if she knows what's good for her."

She looked from one to the other. "I do not like to leave you alone when I don't even know why you were fighting."

"It was nothing," Fin said, adding with a direct look at Patrick, "I did not realize how overset he was, and I took umbrage when I should not."

Molly hesitated, watching Patrick. Realizing she still did not trust him to behave himself, he said ruefully, "It was my fault, Molly. I came here seeking help, and instead I let my devilish temper get the best of me."

"But surely Fin did not refuse to help!"

"I never got the chance," Fin said, his eyes twinkling now. "You've a strange way of seeking help, my friend."

"I'll get the towels," Molly said, "and I'll speak to Bab, too."

Relieved, Patrick watched her go. Then he turned ruefully to Fin.

"*Pax,*" he said, holding out his hand.

"*Pax,*" Fin agreed, gripping it hard with both of his.

By the time Maggie Malloch entered her parlor, Claud was beside himself.

"What's amiss?" she demanded when he practically flung himself at her.

"They've arrested our lass and be charging her wi' witchcraft!"

"Witchcraft!"

"Aye, it were them clothes and the jewels, Mam, and the auld besom what raised her told the cardinal's men our lass bewitched Sir Patrick!"

Maggie frowned. "What a pity that mortals ha' so little brain," she said. "'Tis all a body can do tae adjust her mental abilities and comprehend their thinking."

"But ye caused it, Mam. Ye gave her yon baubles and such."

"Aye, and what if I did? What is it wi' them? They dinna notice when one o' us cleans a kitchen, or keeps evil spirits from the door, or when a man's arrows fly truer than he ever shot 'em afore. But put a few baubles on a pretty lass, and—"

"But ye said I shouldna do things that they can see," Claud protested. "Why, when I froze two men in their tracks last night, Lucy said ye'd be vexed."

"Aye, and so I am if ye did such a thing. Ye canna interfere wi' men's actions, lad. That be the one rule o' the Circle we mustna break."

"But ye turned back history," Claud protested. "Ye undid a host o' actions."

"Aye, and the Circle called me tae account," she said calmly. "That time, laddie mine, 'twas your interference wi' a man's death that forced me tae do as I did. If I never said that tae the Circle, 'tis because ye're my son, Claud."

"I stopped his blood flowing, is all. We ha' always done that."

"Aye, but for our own. Ye did it for an enemy. D'ye no see the difference?"

Her voice was gentle, and although he thought he understood her point, he decided he'd be wise to change the subject. "D'ye ken Tom Tit Tot?" he asked.

Maggie's expression altered ludicrously. "Why d'ye ask about him?"

Not wanting to admit he was in another scrape, he said, "He seems a bit strange, is all, and he goes by another name, too, so if ye ken what it be—"

"I dinna ken any other name, but Tom Tit Tot's a right scoundrel, and ye'll do better no tae listen tae him or tae his fiendish music. Ye've nae time for such, any road, 'cause ye mun keep watch over our lass. Now, be off!"

He went.

Chapter 22

Beth's morning did not begin well, for the guard admitted two stiff-necked women who stripped her of her clothing and examined her body from tip to toe. Although they helped her dress again afterward, the ordeal was humiliating.

Afterward, two guards took her to a room two floors above her cell with rows of benches, like pews, flanking a narrow aisle. At the front, a carpeted dais held three high-backed chairs behind a long, polished table. The chairs were empty, and although a few men sat scattered on the benches, she recognized none of them.

No sooner did her escorts show her where she was to sit than everyone stood and three men in long robes entered, followed by men-at-arms. She recognized one of the three by his splendid red garments. Apparently, Cardinal Beaton himself was to preside over her trial. Briefly, hope stirred. Perhaps Patrick had spoken to him, and her ordeal would end quickly.

As the cardinal took his seat, a man-at-arms bent to speak to him. Beth thought the man looked familiar, but she did not know him. Beaton glanced at her and then said evenly, "The crier will read the commission convening this assize."

A round little man stepped up to the dais and began to read

in a thin, reedy voice. Beth understood little more of the legal phrasing than her name and that she was accused of casting spells and consorting with the devil. There was much more, and she heard the word "treason," but none of it seemed real.

When he finished reading, the crier declared, "If any man can say aught of Elspeth Douglas or these charges, let him step forward and be heard."

A distinguished-looking man carrying a sheaf of documents said, "Your eminence, I am Thomas Craig, advocate for his grace the King. I hold numerous depositions charging Elspeth Douglas with bewitchment, dealings with the devil, and treasonable attempts on his grace's life. She has likewise been examined and found to bear the devil's mark on her right foot."

Beth could not think. What devil's mark? And where was Patrick?

Beaton said, "Is there no one to speak for Elspeth Douglas?"

"Aye, your eminence." Another man, who looked like a member of the gentry, stepped forward, adding, "I am William Hart."

"We know you well as a great legal expert, Sir William," Beaton said. "The accused could have no better advocate."

One who knew her might be better, Beth thought. She had never seen Sir William before, nor did he seem interested in her. He did not even glance her way.

"Pray, present your depositions," the crier commanded.

Sir William apparently had none, but the King's advocate handed his to the judge at Beaton's right, who glanced briefly at them and passed them to Beaton. The cardinal took longer to look them over, then passed them to the man at his left.

It did not seem to Beth as if any of them read more than a sentence or two, but the third man said, "These are quite clear, I think."

She glanced at her so-called advocate. His hands were

clasped behind his back, and he looked straight ahead, somber and silent.

"Is there no witness to speak for the accused?" Beaton asked.

Sir William replied, "No one, your eminence."

"But that cannot be!" Beth exclaimed, leaping to her feet. A heavy hand bit into her shoulder as one of her guards sought to force her back to her seat.

"Let her speak," Beaton said. "What witness can you provide, mistress?"

"I . . . I am sure Sir Patrick MacRae will speak for me."

"He is not here."

"Then he must not know that this trial is taking place," she said desperately. "Cannot someone send for him? My advocate, perhaps?"

Beaton shifted his gaze. "Sir William?"

Still without looking at her, Sir William said, "As you know from your own conversation with Sir Patrick, your eminence, although he would like to vouch for the accused, he can cast no factual light on the charges before you today."

"What charges?" Beth cried. "I have heard only nonsense about devil's marks, bewitchment, and casting spells. Unless I am mistaken, the so-called devil's mark is naught but where a rooster pecked my foot three days ago. I've cast no spells, nor have I ever communicated with the devil."

The King's advocate said, "We are told you are a maidservant, mistress, yet you stand before us today clad in fine clothing, your headdress and heels glittering with valuable gemstones. How do you account for that if not by witchcraft?"

"They were lent to me," Beth said, striving to retain her dignity. She knew if she revealed the source of the clothing, they would not believe her. Moreover, she would be left standing in her smock, which would surely confirm all they believed of her. She added desperately, "Those jewels must be only bits of colored glass!"

"Easily proved," Sir William said. "Pull off a shoe, lass, and hand it to me."

Eagerly, certain that she had made a point at last, she obeyed, prying off one of the larger jewels and handing it to him. He put it on the floor and stepped hard on it with his heel. The piece shattered.

"There, you see!" she exclaimed.

"Your eminence, the wench has proved the case against herself," Thomas Craig said. "These depositions clearly state that the jewels she wore last night were genuine. Since she has had no visitors, the only way they can be glass now is if she turned them into glass herself!"

"But I did no such thing! They were glass last night, too!"

Beaton said, "I fear that in your foolishness you have given Mr. Craig all the evidence he requires. There is one more who wishes to speak, however." He nodded to the man-at-arms who had spoken to him earlier.

The man said clearly, "When my men and I met that wench on the road a few days past, she were some'un else, some'un called Lady Elizabeth Douglas. She carried a falcon, and the great dog named as her familiar were with her, too."

Beth struggled to maintain her calm, trying to imagine what Patrick would do. She could imagine him scolding, but beyond that . . . Then, as if he whispered in her ear, she could hear him say that if one had to lie, one should do it with fortitude.

The thought of lying made her feel sick, but she said firmly, "That was not I. They do say that there are hundreds in Scotland that look like me, however."

"It is your word against his then," Beaton said, "but God will sort it out. In the meantime, I believe we are in agreement."

"No," she cried, collapsing to her stool when her knees failed her.

"Elspeth Douglas," Beaton intoned, "we find you guilty of witchcraft and treason, and sentence you to death by burning, in the yard between the Tolbooth and the Marykirk at noon on Saturday next."

"But I am innocent!"

"Then you have nothing to fear," Beaton said. "God watches over innocents, and since Saturday is the day before Easter, if you are innocent, I warrant He will allow you, too, to rise again on Easter Sunday."

Claud stared at Lucy in dismay. "That surely didna go as I'd hoped."

"He said if the jewels were real, she mun be a witch."

"Aye, so I turned them tae glass," Claud said.

"And he said that could happen only an she were a witch."

Claud sighed. "I dinna understand mortals, and that be plain fact."

"Aye," Lucy agreed. "But what will we do now?"

"I dinna ken," Claud said as they watched the guards take Beth back to her cell. "Me mam said I ha' tae fix it, and here she's gone off again."

"I think we should ask me dad," Lucy said. "He's right clever, is me dad."

"Nay," Claud said. "I told ye, I willna go tae the man till I ken his true name. D'ye no ken summat that could help me?"

"I might," Lucy said. "Let me think a bit."

"Well, dinna think long. She'll be burnt tae a crisp in three days' time."

"Oh, Claud," Lucy said, "dinna be vexed." She leaned

closer, moving her hands expertly over his body. "Let me show ye summat new that I learned."

"Lass, I canna rest till we ha' a plan and I learn your father's true name!"

Lucy sagged, her chin on her chest. "I'll think then," she muttered grumpily.

"Aye, that's good," said Claud.

Patrick, Fin, and Molly spent the latter part of the morning discussing Beth's predicament, but although they talked over many ideas, no plan seemed feasible.

"In truth," Molly said, "until we learn whether Mother can persuade the King to help, there is little we can do." Wistfully, she added, "If only Fin were free to gather the Mackenzies and MacRaes. *Then* we could rescue her!"

Patrick exchanged a look with Fin and said, "Even if he could, most of them are in the Highlands. We'd do better to talk to Huntly. He is one of the most powerful lords in Scotland, and he is your cousin, Molly, and therefore Beth's as well. Moreover, he is here in Stirling for the festivities."

"Aye, but he supports Beaton," Fin reminded him. "I doubt he would do anything the cardinal might perceive as undermining to his power."

Patrick suspected Fin was right, but it seemed foolhardy to dismiss the powerful chief of the Gordons without even consulting him.

Looking worried, Molly said, "Beaton clearly does not think himself bound by his debt to you, Patrick. Do you think he'll keep his word about Fin's release?"

"I don't know," Patrick said honestly. When a single rap at the door heralded Jock's hasty entrance, he relieved part of his frustration by snapping, "What do you mean by entering without awaiting proper leave?"

"Sorry," Jock said, "but they've sentenced Mistress Beth tae burn on Saturday! How'll we stop 'em?"

Stunned silence greeted his words.

Patrick could not breathe, let alone speak.

Kintail recovered first. "I thought you told us Beaton said the trial would not take place until tomorrow or Thursday."

"That's what he told me," Patrick said grimly. "He must have known even then that her trial was but an hour away. By heaven, if one spends an eternity in hell for murdering a cardinal, then I—"

"Murdering him would not help Beth," Molly snapped. "Think, Patrick!"

He took a deep breath. "Did you see her, Jock?"

"Aye."

"H-how is she?"

Jock shrugged, clearly not sure, for once, what to say. He muttered, "One o' them louts what brought her back tae her cell tried tae take liberties, but Thunder growled at him, and the lout snatched his hand back straightaway."

Speechless again, Patrick yearned to have one moment alone with the lout.

Fin said curiously, "Do you mean to say that dog was there, Jock, the one that came with the three of you to Stirling?"

"Aye," Jock said. "He waited on the ground outside o' her window wi' me after they took her away."

"I am glad he prevented the guard from harming her," Molly said. "But why would the man pay him any heed if Thunder was outside a barred window?"

"I dunno," Jock replied, "but he snatched his hand back as if Mistress Beth was red-hot. Thunder be gey big, ye ken, and he looks fierce when he growls."

Patrick collected his wits. "Where is he now?"

"He wouldna come away, and Mistress Beth said I shouldna try tae drag him," Jock said. "Them guards will find a way tae shoo him off afore long, though."

The three adults looked helplessly at one another.

Frustrated, Patrick said, "I cannot even think. My mind fails to focus."

"I know how it is," Fin said, looking at Molly, who was visibly holding back tears. "I've felt that way myself. Making decisions and acting on them is easier when failure does not mean the death of the one you love."

The last words struck Patrick hard. "Beth must *not* die," he said.

From the doorway, Nell said, "She won't. You will speak to the King."

Molly ran to her. "You talked with his grace! What did he say?"

"Thank you," Patrick said fervently.

Nell hugged Molly but looked over her shoulder at Patrick. "I think you owe your thanks to that splendid hawk you trained. Jamie is quite taken with him, and has agreed to speak with you and Fin after supper. I am to take you to him."

"Not sooner?" Patrick said. "Did you not tell him how urgent this is? Beth is locked in a filthy cell, probably terrified out of her wits. I want her out, madam!"

"Pray, sir, calm yourself. I did not try to argue her case to him because I do not know exactly what they have accused her of doing, what laws may apply, or what evidence they have. Nor would Jamie have heeded such argument from me," she added with a wry smile as she and Molly sat together on an oak settle nearby.

"Then what *did* you say?" Patrick asked.

Arranging her skirts, Nell said, "I told him she is my daughter and the wife of the man who not only trained his precious hawk but risked his life to prevent an invasion of

Scotland. Do calm yourself now, for you will gain nothing by making angry demands of his grace. We must all scheme a little beforehand, I think."

"I could be calmer if I could see Beth," Patrick said.

"Well, you cannot," Nell said. "They won't let anyone visit a condemned witch or traitor."

"Mayhap they will," Jock said thoughtfully.

"How?" Patick demanded.

"I ha' been watching the guards, ye ken," the boy said. "They think I come tae see me dad, so they pay me little heed, and I ha' seen them let other men in when they bring messages for the warden."

"Do they not send a guard to show them the way?" Molly asked.

"Nay," Jock said. "Only if the chap asks how he should go. Since ye dinna ken her window, I could tell 'em I'll take ye tae the warden."

"What of Bab, Patrick?" Molly asked. "You should talk to Lord and Lady Chisholm, and arrange for her to accompany them tomorrow."

"I'll do it," Fin said. "I'll send a message to Chisholm to come to me here."

"You've my thanks then," Patrick said. "Tell the lass I'll get to her as soon as I can, but that in the meantime she is to behave herself as if I were with her."

"Oh, aye," Fin said with a chuckle. "I'll tell her."

Knowing he could leave Bab in Fin's capable hands, Patrick turned to the boy. "Let's go, Jock. I mean to see my lass."

Beth sat on the hard bench in her bleak cell, trying hard not to think about the great burning. The other women seemed resigned to their fate, and their conversation did not help.

She wanted to speak to Maggie Malloch, to ask her for help, but she feared Maggie would refuse. After all, if she had returned to the Farnsworth chambers, as she was supposed to, she would not have been with Patrick when the cardinal's men came. Of course, if she had not gone to the ball, none of it would have happened—nor, she realized, would she be Patrick's wife now.

Tears welled in her eyes, but whatever happened and strange though it seemed, she *was* his wife. No one had mentioned her marriage at the trial, and she wondered if it would have done any good to shout her new name at them. Perhaps they simply would have accused her—as Lady Farnsworth had—of bewitching Patrick. Indeed, that charge was probably in one of their horrid depositions.

"Beth!"

With a cry of joy she looked up and saw Patrick's face at the window.

"You came!"

"Aye, sweetheart, I'm here, for all the good it will do you."

"But why must you peer down at me from up there? Will they not let you in to speak to me?" She wanted his arms around her, holding her tight.

"Nay, lass," he said. "You can have no visitors. Beaton's orders, I suspect."

"I thought he was your friend!"

"He is not," Patrick growled, adding, "I cannot stay long, sweetheart, for someone will soon demand to know why I am here. Jock is keeping watch with Thunder, so we should have a few moments. Are you all right?"

"Aye," she said, valiantly trying to look as if that were true and knowing that she failed miserably. She wanted him to kiss her.

"Oh, lassie, I want to hold you," he murmured, putting his hand between the bars and reaching down.

She jumped onto the bench. By stretching, she could reach him.

Squeezing her hand hard, he said, "I'll do all I can. You know I will."

"Why did you not come to my trial?"

"Beaton told me it would not be until tomorrow or Thursday. He lied."

"They said you wanted to vouch for me but could not give any facts to contradict the charges."

"That is true enough," he muttered.

"Oh, Patrick, I would tell you everything if I could!"

"That is not necessary, sweetheart. I know you did not make any pact with the devil or betray the King."

She wanted him to believe in her, but she could not help asking, "How can you be sure of that?"

"I just am," he said with a gentle smile. "Apparently, you have something in common with your sister besides your looks."

"What?"

"We should not discuss that now," he said. "I don't know what consequences may result, and I won't take the chance that they may be disastrous."

He seemed to be trying to tell her something without putting it into words, and she had a feeling that somehow he knew about Maggie. But she dared not ask if he did. The thought that he might know gave her an odd sense of comfort, but when she heard Jock calling to him, she wanted to cry.

"Don't go yet."

"I must," he said, "but I'll think of something, sweetheart. Have fortitude."

"How can you say that to me at such a time?" she asked.

"'Tis the watchword I live by, lass. It has seen me

through much, and if there were ever a time to trust it, this is that time. I'll say one other thing, too, though, because whatever happens, you should know. I love you, Beth, now and forever."

With one last warm squeeze, he let go of her hand.

"Oh, Patrick . . ." Tears choked her voice, but when she swallowed them, he was gone. She collapsed to the bench, buried her face in her hands, and wept until she could weep no more. The murmur of voices from the other cells had stopped when she first spoke to him. No one offered comfort now, for they had none to offer, and she was afraid that she had no fortitude left.

After Patrick and Jock returned to the castle, there were still several hours left before Fin and Patrick's appointment with the King, but when Patrick suggested that they discuss their options, his oldest and best friend ordered him to sleep.

"I cannot. We must think of a plan."

"Don't be an ass," Fin said. "You'll think better if you sleep, and you'll be much less likely to offend his grace. We need his help. Now, go."

Jock woke him in good time, bringing a tray of food, which he set now on the table under the window.

"Good lad," Patrick said, tousling his curls.

"Aye, well, it be nae cause for messin' me hair," Jock said indignantly. Twenty minutes later, Patrick met Nell and Fin and went with them to the King's private chamber. When they entered, they found James sitting in his favorite armchair, and to Patrick's surprise, Zeus was on a perch beside him.

"Come in, come in," the King said heartily. "Sir Patrick,

my thanks earlier for training this amazing creature were insufficient. Look what he can do now."

James reached out a gloved fist, and when the hawk stepped onto it, he stroked its wings and back for a moment before he murmured, "Watch this."

To Patrick's astonishment, James turned the hawk gently onto its back, and it lay in his lap, letting him stroke its soft belly.

"Have you ever seen the like?" James demanded.

"Never," Patrick replied, as delighted as James. "I've heard of less aggressive birds allowing such liberties, but never a gos."

"This one is certainly extraordinary," James said. "But I am told you want to speak to me about a particular matter. I do not know if I can help, but mayhap we will think of something."

Nell said quietly, "Will you permit me to remain, sire? She is my daughter."

"I know that you say she is, madam."

"I am sure that she is," Nell said.

"If the gentlemen do not object, you may stay. It is good to see you again, too, Kintail. I trust your accommodations remain satisfactory."

"As to that, sire," Patrick said, seizing the opportunity, "I know that his eminence has spoken to you about the agreement we made. I had hoped we might have heard good news by now."

James looked bewildered. Continuing to stroke the hawk's belly, he said, "What agreement is this? I know of none concerning Kintail. Davy Beaton has not mentioned his name to me."

Chapter 23

Patrick's sense of betrayal was stunning. He felt as if a void had opened inside where once he had known who he was and what he believed.

"What is it, sir?"

"Sir Patrick, are you ill?"

"Patrick."

He heard Nell and James as if from a great distance, but when Fin spoke his name in that particular tone, he turned automatically, albeit blindly, toward him.

"I know exactly what you feel, but you must set it aside," Fin said.

"You do *not* know how I feel."

"Look at me."

Patrick blinked, focused, saw the anxiety in his friend's eyes, and forced his mind to focus. "You cannot know," he said, wanting to shout the words but somehow lacking the energy.

Fin glanced at James, then met Patrick's angry gaze. "You feel betrayed clear down to your soul," he said. "You gave your loyalty to a man, believing in him, knowing he trusted you and believing you could trust him, but he failed you."

Again, Fin looked pointedly at James, and Patrick realized that his friend did indeed understand at least part of what he was feeling.

James said, "You speak of Davy Beaton, do you not?"

"Aye," Fin said, holding the royal gaze. "I believe you are aware that Sir Patrick spent the past eight months in England at considerable risk to himself."

"I know that," James turned to Patrick. "But how does it concern Kintail?"

"I became a spy only because Beaton promised Kintail's release in return," Patrick said. "Since my return he has continually sworn that he was doing all he could to persuade you but that others impeded his progress."

"I see." James shot Kintail a shrewd look, adding, "I warrant you were not speaking only of Beaton, though, were you, sir?"

Fin returned the look steadily. "No, your grace."

"The people of Kintail have ever remained loyal to the Crown."

"We have."

"And you believe the Crown owes you something in return for that fealty."

"The Crown does as it sees fit," Fin said.

James looked at Patrick. "Do you believe that, sir?"

"What I believe is of no consequence," Patrick said bitterly. "My dispute is with Beaton, and clearly he does not count the cost of betraying loyalty. Nor does he care that he has condemned an innocent lass to death so he can make a grand pretense of cleansing the Scottish Kirk of evil and corruption."

"Do you not believe he means to reform the Kirk?"

"I believe that Davy Beaton cares only for the fortunes of

Davy Beaton," Patrick said savagely. "His so-called reforms are laughable—or would be if they did not serve disaster to so many. He claims to fight witchcraft yet holds his trials in secret so that none may hear how weak the evidence is. He discards loyalty as if it were dust, and despite learning that Beth is neither a true maidservant nor Angus's baseborn daughter, he is bent on burning her as part of his grand conflagration."

Nell's gasp diverted him, and he said grimly, "Forgive me, madam. To say that without thought for your presence was needlessly cruel."

She shook her head but turned to James, her expression sadly eloquent.

James grimaced. "I would like to help," he said, "but like it or not, Beaton stands as the Pope in Scotland. His word in matters of faith is the word of the Holy Father, and I cannot countermand it without jeopardizing the entire Scottish Kirk."

"Surely, you can do something, sire," Nell said. "You are King."

"Aye," he said, looking ruefully at Kintail and Patrick. "I am King, and yet I command no army without the consent of my nobles. In truth, though, I have not treated those most loyal to me well. All you said of Beaton, Kintail, holds true for me, and clearly do I see that now. I ask you to forgive me if you can, sir."

"Always, your grace," Kintail said instantly.

"And you, Sir Patrick, will you likewise forgive?"

Patrick hesitated, automatically glancing at Kintail, but that gentleman returned his look without comment, his expression wooden but readable to one who knew him well. The decision was Patrick's.

He said, "I can forgive a man who admits his mistake,

sire, but as to offering him my full faith and trust after he has demolished them . . . that is not so easy."

"You are honest, sir, and I take your meaning well," James said. "Trust, once broken, must be rebuilt, and that takes time and effort. I do ask for forgiveness, but I will strive to make amends."

"How, sire?" Nell asked.

"As of this moment, I declare the Laird of Kintail a free man with all his rights of position and title restored. Moreover, despite Beaton, I still have great influence in many quarters. Have you perchance broached this matter with Huntly?"

"No," Patrick said, glancing at Kintail. "He supports Beaton, does he not?"

"Few amongst the nobles now in Stirling would act against me even if they do tend to support Davy Beaton," James said. "I believe that if I speak personally to Huntly and others who came here with large escorts, I can at least persuade them not to interfere if you attempt to rescue the lass on Saturday."

Nell said unhappily, "Not until Saturday?"

"Aye, madam," Patrick said. "It would take an army to rescue her from the Tolbooth, and we do not have an army. If we have a chance, it will be when we have a great crowd and much confusion."

"In the meantime," James said, "you and Kintail should enlist the aid of any friends you have here who have not already departed, and we must not meet again over this. Beaton has spies everywhere, as you know."

"I can carry messages, if necessary," Nell said.

The King smiled. "No, madam, you cannot. With her grace here, I'd be in greater danger if you did than if Beaton should learn that I support this endeavor."

"True enough, sire," Patrick said, "but we must have

some way to know if you succeed in persuading Huntly and the others to stay out of it."

The King grinned wryly. "Beaton has demanded my presence there despite my disapproval, and I'd already decided to dampen the effect by organizing a hunt to take place afterward. You," he added to Nell, "are welcome to join us then, because other ladies of the court will do so. If I am successful, Sir Patrick, I will take Zeus with me. You will recognize him even at a distance, will you not?"

"Easily, sire," Patrick said. "He will serve as an excellent signal."

The interview was over, and the three hurried back to tell Molly.

The next two days were busy, and since they had decided it would better serve their plan if Kintail continued to act as a hostage, lest Beaton realize the King had intervened, they arranged for some friends to meet with him at the castle, and Patrick visited others himself. He spoke to Sir Alex Chisholm first.

"I'll stay, of course, with as many men as I can spare from my parents' entourage," Sir Alex said, "but I want my family out of harm's way."

"I understand," Patrick said. "Indeed, I'd still like Bab to go with them. It is one thing for Lady Kintail to stay with her husband, quite another for Bab to stay."

With a droll look, Alex said, "You'd need to hire a keeper."

"She needs a husband," Patrick said suggestively.

With a lazy smile and twinkling eyes, his friend shook his head, and Patrick bade him adieu, setting off for St. Mary's

Wynd. He had put off calling on Sir Hector, because he feared he would lose his temper, but it had occurred to him that Sir Hector might not know of Beth's fate, and might even know a way to help her.

"Inform Sir Hector that Sir Patrick MacRae desires to have speech with him," he told the maidservant who answered the door at Farnsworth House.

Having no idea what Lady Farnsworth or her daughters might have said, Patrick did not know what sort of reception to expect, but it was all he could do to wait patiently until the maid returned.

"This way, sir," she said, leading him to the chamber where he had first spoken with Oscar Farnsworth.

When Patrick entered, Sir Hector was alone. He stood, saying, "You are a man of many surprises, sir."

"I suppose I am," Patrick said. "May I ask, sir, if you are aware of the events that took place late Monday night, and their consequences?"

"I know only that you claimed to have married Elspeth, sir, and that your behavior put my wife into a frenzy. She insisted it could not be true, and I do not know if you meant to make such a declaration, but when she assured me Elspeth had not countered it, I was forced to explain what you must have just discovered. Marriage by declaration is legal, I'm afraid. You would do better to apply to your cardinal for an annulment."

"He is not my cardinal," Patrick said grimly. "Nor is my lady wife baseborn. I collect that Lady Farnsworth did not say anything else about Monday night."

"Why no, and how can Elspeth not be baseborn? Angus himself admitted that she is his daughter by a common maidservant."

"Have you always found the Earl of Angus trustworthy, sir?"

"No, I have not," Sir Hector said with a sigh. "Sit down, Sir Patrick, and tell me what you know that I do not."

Patrick did so, adding that Lady Farnsworth and Drusilla had accused Beth of witchcraft. That the news came as a terrible shock to Sir Hector was clear.

"May God have mercy on them for such wickedness, for I shall not," he exclaimed. "They know that she is no witch. If there were ever a child with less inclination toward the dark arts, I don't know her."

"I do not know if you can help her, but if you can . . ."

Sir Hector shook his head. "If she is in Beaton's hands, I can do nothing. I *would* like to call my wife and daughters, however, to confront them in your presence with what they have done." He did so at once, and Lady Farnsworth entered a few minutes later, with Drusilla.

"What's he doing here?" Lady Farnsworth demanded.

"Where is Jelyan?"

"She went to the shops with our aunt," Drusilla said. "Why is Patrick here?"

"He is *Sir* Patrick to you, my girl, and he has told me a shocking tale of wickedness perpetrated upon an innocent lass who never did us any harm."

Indignantly, Lady Farnsworth said, "If you mean Elspeth—"

"Be silent," Sir Hector said sharply. "I collect, however, that you did make an accusation of witchcraft against the poor girl."

"Poor girl, indeed!"

"Aye, Father, you did not see her, but—"

"Not another word, Drusilla! That my own wife and daughters could do such a dreadful thing appalls me. You will return to Farnsworth Tower at once, all of you, to contemplate the evil you have done."

Lady Farnsworth snapped, "Ridiculous!"

"We only just arrived!" Drusilla protested.

"Does either of you realize that if Elspeth dies, you will have murdered her?"

Both women were silent, but Patrick doubted that either understood the gravity of her offense.

Sir Hector said sternly, "It is small punishment for what you have done, but you will leave this afternoon. I'll provide an escort, but I cannot accompany you as I still have business here. You will keep to your chambers until you depart. I do not want to see you before then. Order Jelyan's things packed, too, of course."

"Jelyan had naught to do with it," Drusilla said, nearly weeping.

"Nevertheless, she will go, too. You can explain to her why she goes."

Patrick took his leave, feeling that Lady Farnsworth and Drusilla had gotten off much too easily.

"Bethie, this way."

She could hear the whisper, although it was little more than movement of air in the long, dark corridor. The path she followed glowed dimly, so she could see the way ahead, but she did not know where she was going, and she was bone weary. The way lightened a bit more. She could see a golden glow ahead, perhaps firelight, perhaps something else, and she hurried toward it.

She was alone, although she had a sense of someone hovering nearby, watching and waiting—whether friend or enemy she did not know. The glow was nearer, and she saw something dark in the center, a chest. As she drew nearer

*and reached for the key, the sense of watchers nearby turned
ominous.*

"Wake up, lass."

*Despite the danger, she needed to see what was in the
chest, but the voice—a different one now and familiar—
pulled her away.*

Blinking, Beth opened her eyes and looked around the
bleak cell. She did not recall ever having slept during the
day except when she was ill, but she had not been sleeping
well at night.

"I am here," the voice said quietly.

"Maggie!"

"Aye, 'tis me," the little woman said. She stood on the
floor near the window wall, looking smaller than usual, and
tired.

"I'd nearly lost hope that you would come," Beth exclaimed. Guiltily, and in a lower tone, she added, "I know
we should not let the others hear us talk—"

"Pish tush, lass, ye needna fret about them," Maggie said
with a dismissive gesture. "They canna hear us."

"Then why did you not come sooner? It was the clothes
and the jewelry, you know, that made them think me guilty,
but I could hardly tell them the wee folk had provided them.
What are we going to do?"

"I dinna ken, lass, I wish I did."

"But surely you can winkle me out of this! I am *not* a
witch!"

"I canna do it, lass, for 'tis the Kirk, and I canna work me
spells against it or against men o' the Kirk. We o' the Secret
Clan ha' nae place in such doings."

Horrified, Beth said, "*Are* you aligned with the powers of
darkness, then?"

"Nay, nay, we fit betwixt good and evil, just as the mortal world does, only separate from it. Our world were cre-

ated when the heavens opened to cast out the Evil One. A few others fell out through the opening, sithee, and they were the beginning o' our clan. We ha' nae power against the Evil One or against the Kirk. Each time ye call on Him wha' the Kirk espouses, ye'll note that if I be wi' ye, I disappear. The same would happen were ye the sort tae call on the Evil One, too."

"But did you not know this could happen if you dressed me in such splendor for the King's ball?"

"Nay, I—" Maggie paused, frowning. She shook herself a little, then harder, shutting her eyes tight and shaking her head until her hair stood on end.

Beth opened her mouth to ask what she was doing, but Maggie shook her head harder, as if she sensed that Beth would speak and wanted her to keep silent. Then she drew a breath so deep that it puffed her up, making her rounder and rounder until Beth feared she would pop.

At last, with a great whooshing sound, Maggie exhaled until her face turned white as snow and she shriveled up like a prune.

Beth watched, fascinated.

A moment later, Maggie looked normal again, and angry.

"What is it?" Beth asked. "What's amiss?"

"Plenty," Maggie said angrily. "Here I were thinking it were Jonah Bonewits, but there be another wi' a more mischievous nature who bewitched me once afore, and I should ha' felt his touch. Claud even said his name but I didna suspect his mischief in this. He'll pay now, though, blast his whirling eyes!"

Maggie vanished, and Beth stared at the empty space in shock. She had no idea where Patrick was, and her only hope had just disappeared, leaving only a puff of white smoke behind.

She heard a rattle of keys. The guards had come to fetch her.

"Claud, where are ye?"

"Here, Mam," he said, hurrying to meet her in the parlor. "What's amiss?"

"Why were ye asking about Tom Tit Tot?"

Claud hesitated, but when she glared, he said, "He set me a puzzle, Mam. I'm tae tell him his true name, or . . ."

"Or, what?"

"Or I canna marry Lucy, but I dinna want tae marry her, only he says I must, 'cause I bedded her, but—"

"What is Lucy Fittletrot to Tom?"

"Why, dinna ye ken? She's his daughter."

To his dismay, Maggie's bosom swelled in fury. In a deadly calm voice, she said, "D'ye recall I said that Tom Tit Tot be a mischief maker?"

"Aye," Claud said warily.

"Well, ye canna marry his Lucy."

"But he said—"

"Dinna heed anything he says! Tom Tit Tot's your father, Claud."

He gaped at her, thundershuck. "Then Lucy—"

"Ye ha' the same father, so ye canna marry wi' her. He ha' been making a game o' ye, just as he did wi' me afore ye were born."

The woodpile in the center of the great square between the Tolbooth and the Marykirk stood ten feet high. Around it, at intervals, seven stout stakes were stuck in the ground, and nearby stood loads of coal, a barrel of tar, and kindling. Men stood guard over these items, lest someone should try to interfere with God's plan to burn the witches, but the general atmosphere was much like a holiday fair.

The crowd was enormous, growing larger and noisier by the minute.

The sight of the great pyre made Patrick feel sick, and he knew his companions felt the same, as by sheer force of size and determination, he and Fin made a path to the front for themselves and Molly. Molly's face was as white as a sheet, and her lips pressed tightly together. Under her cloak, he knew she carried her bow and a quiver of arrows, but what good they would do, he did not know. There were too many people, too many guards wearing the cardinal's scarlet livery, and although he and Fin had exercised their persuasive powers over the past days, he had little faith that the few who had promised them aid would be any help.

Molly walked between them, and Fin kept an arm around

her, his sharp gaze scanning the increasingly boisterous crowd. "The King and his party are yonder," he said, jerking a nod.

Patrick saw Jamie on a fine bay gelding, accompanied by his banner carrier on a dappled gray beside him. The other men and women with him were mounted and dressed for hunting, their birds gaily hooded and jessed.

Most carried their birds on gloved fists, but the King's hawk perched calmly on his shoulder, the red plume on its black hood standing out clearly. At any other time, Patrick would have felt proud to recognize Zeus and to see the young hawk so calm amidst such furor. Now he felt only added tension, but at least some of the King's powerful nobles had agreed to keep out of any action that erupted.

"Perhaps we should be mounted, too," Molly said, her voice barely loud enough for her two companions to hear.

Patrick muttered, "We don't want to draw unnecessary attention, but we'll need to be nearer the horses when they bring out the women. Even then, I'm wondering if we can get to her through this mob. I just can't seem to think."

Fear had never before interfered with his ability to do battle, but never had the stakes been so high. The thought of stakes turned his gaze back to the pyre. Seven women were about to lose their lives in a terrible way, and at least one of them had been falsely accused and convicted. What of the others? He knew nothing about them, but since Beth was innocent, he doubted their guilt, too. The God he believed in, the one that had created Beth and his magnificent Highlands, would never demand such a terrible price from an innocent person.

All the women had been imprisoned at the Tolbooth, and it was thus from the north end of the square that the procession would come. Doubtless, Beaton and his lads were forming up to lead the way with pomp and circumstance.

Beside him, Molly said, "Fin, do you see her?"

Thinking she was asking about Beth, Patrick frowned,

because from where they were, in front of the Marykirk near the pyre, surely they would hear the crowd react to the procession's approach long before they could see anyone in it.

Oddly, Fin said, "I doubt that I could see her in this crowd, lass, or any of them. Faith, unless I saw a familiar face, I'd not know them, because they'd look like anyone else to me, just smaller."

"Who?" Patrick demanded.

"The little—"

"Hush, Molly," Fin said sharply, his eyes scanning the crowd as they would before a battle, seeking enemies and possible allies.

Nodding, Molly moved closer to Patrick and said in a voice that would not carry beyond his ears, "Recall that Fin has the gift of second sight, Patrick. He does not speak of it, for I think it embarrasses him that he can see the wee folk when most other mortals cannot. I don't know how much I'm allowed to tell you, but I did hope some of them might be here today to help Beth."

"Considering that they are most likely responsible for her predicament—"

"We'd best not discuss that here," Molly interjected warningly, "lest we find ourselves bound up beside her, facing the blaze. I will say, though, that I've tried to communicate with the one I once knew."

"I am glad you and Fin are here with me," he said with a sigh, scanning the crowd in the same experienced way that Kintail did. "Fin should not have lingered after Jamie agreed to his leaving, though."

"Neither of us would abandon you," Molly said flatly, "and thanks to Jamie, Fin is not in much danger. We'll return home soon enough."

A roar erupted from the crowd, and peering over heads in front of him, Patrick saw the procession slowly approaching.

"I'll get my horse," he said. "You and Fin will do what suits you best, lass, but seek any way you can to help her. And, Molly," he added, nearly choking on what he was about to say, "if we fail and they start that fire without strangling the women first, for the love of God, let your aim be true."

Grimly, Molly nodded, and satisfied that rather than let her younger sister burn to death, she would use her great skill to put an arrow through Beth's heart, Patrick pushed his way through the crowd to where Jock held the horses.

They were behind the old jail, but Patrick knew that even if he could reach Beth on horseback, he would have little chance for escape, because routes leading out of the city were anything but clear. There were really only two, and to get to either one, he would have to ride up or down Spittal Street, along the north edge of the square, because on the south side, the Marykirk backed against the town wall.

Spittal Street teemed with people, and there would be guards at the town gates. Never had he felt so little confidence. Where, he wondered, was his fortitude?

He found Jock and the four horses easily enough. There was none for Beth, but Patrick's stallion could easily carry two, and an extra mount would only slow them at the outset. Patrick had worried that the lad would not be able to hold all four, but despite the din, they seemed quiet enough.

Patrick mounted a magnificent black, the larger of two stallions that James had provided. Shifting his sword into place, he made sure his pistol was ready to fire and his dirk easy to grab. From the look of things, no weapon would help much, but having them handy made him feel better. Whatever happened, he was going to save Beth if he could. If he could not, he would die with her, because there would be no turning back. If the crowd or Davy Beaton's guards did not slaughter him, Beaton would hang him at the first opportunity.

But that would not matter, not if Beth died.

He could see the procession clearly now, and he urged the stallion forward, glowering at anyone who even looked as if he might dare object to a mounted horseman pressing his way through the crowd. His fierce looks quelled many, but he paid little heed, his attention firmly fixed on the procession.

The seven women, draped in black, stumbled awkwardly along with heads bowed low, each led on a chain by a soldier of the Kirk.

He knew he would have little time to act once they reached the pyre, because in Scotland, unlike England, folks did not think it necessary to cause the actual death of a witch by fire, so in most cases the authorities mercifully ordered her strangled at the stake before incineration. However, since the cardinal's purpose was to produce a grand spectacle, Patrick doubted that Beaton would allow any of his victims to die mercifully.

Warily, he glanced around, certain that he must be drawing unwanted attention, but he saw other riders now, clearly gentry, who obviously thought themselves too grand to stand amidst the rabble in the square.

The condemned women were much nearer, and to his horror, he saw that each of them was heavily hooded and draped. Moreover, the chains were attached to witches' bridles, heavy iron rings that closed about the necks of the condemned women. Each had a spike in front, directed upward and inward, that pierced her black hood and filled her mouth, the whole horrible device acting as a painful gag.

Covered as each face was by both hood and steel, they all looked the same. He could not tell which one was Beth.

The noise was deafening. People shouted, shrieked, and roared at the witches, and Beth could see nothing through the hood covering her face. The awful steel spike poked her with every movement, hurting her mouth, and the collar around her neck rubbed the coarse material, bruising her. She could hear some of the women moaning and keening, even over the roar of the crowd, but although she had never been so frightened in her life, she would not weep. She would not give Cardinal David Beaton that satisfaction.

He had not even questioned those who had accused her. Nor had he let her face or question them. He had accepted her guilt and declared her penalty as if the accusation alone were sufficient. Doubtless, the other six women had suffered similar trials. Surely, God did not condemn people that easily.

She tried to pretend she was elsewhere, but her imagination failed.

Thanks to the bridle, she could not have talked if she tried, but the soldiers had tauntingly said that the bridles would not prevent the women's screams. The cardinal, they said, wanted the crowd to hear them and know that even by shrieking to their evil master, the witches could not prevent God's will.

How she longed to hear Maggie Malloch's voice through the din, to hear her say that she had discovered new powers against the Kirk, that the magic that had so splendidly clothed Beth and decked her with magnificent jewels was after all strong enough to save her. But she had already heard Maggie's voice for the last time. Even an army of wee folk could not help her now.

The toe of her right shoe caught the edge of a cobblestone, and she tripped again, but a strong hand caught her just as it had the other times she had stumbled. They would not let her fall in the street, because they wanted to execute her without any unnecessary delay.

It was hard to maintain any dignity with her hands tied behind her and the heavy, hooded robe tangling her legs. The urge to whimper and moan like the others was nearly overwhelming, but she would have fortitude. She was sure that Patrick was in the crowd somewhere, and she would not shame him or herself. She would go to her death in a manner that befitted Lady MacRae.

She wished she could speak with Patrick just one last time to tell him how much she loved him. She had scolded herself repeatedly since their last meeting for failing to say the words when he did, but she had been so shocked then and so unsure that he had meant them that she had said nothing. Even now, she feared he had said he loved her only because he was terrified for her. Still, it was enough that he cared as a friend. He was the best friend she had ever had.

The chain connected to the ring around her neck jerked her forward, and two strong hands caught her by her upper arms. She had to press her lips to the horrid spike to keep from gagging on it, and only fierce control kept her from struggling against the bruising grip on her arms. Her legs would not hold her.

"Stand still, damn ye," a harsh voice growled. "Ye'll meet your Maker soon enough. Dinna give me trouble afore then."

The collar felt tighter around her throat. Could he be going to strangle her?

She did not want to die. She had only just begun to live.

Tears pricking his eyes, Patrick watched from his saddle as the men leading the witches stood them before their stakes, lifted them, and then slipped the iron rings over the stake tops, holding the women in place as securely as if each were bound from head to toe. He had been sure that he would know Beth despite the hood and robe, that he would recognize her shape or know her walk, or just instinctively know her from the others. But he did not.

The men stepped away, and the roar of the crowd faded as Cardinal Beaton stepped forward, looking magnificent in his red robes and gold miter. Pressing his palms together in a prayerful way, he waited for the din to fade to silence. Then he waited a moment longer.

When he had everyone's attention, he said in a clarion voice, "Hear me, one and all. As God hath made covenant with His Kirk, binding Himself to be our God and requiring of us both faith and obedience, so does Satan align with his subjects. They agree to obey his rules, and he promises to grant their desires. Each of these women has made compact with the devil, agreeing to use his help in the working of wonders. Because witchcraft is the most detestable sin in the sight of God, because fire is His only certain purification, and because, by Moses' law, no witch may continue to live, death is the witch's portion, justly assigned by God."

Automatically steadying his horse, Patrick stared at the hooded figures, but he could still see no difference, nothing to tell him which one was Beth. Realizing that all hope was dying, he decided he had to let her know that he was there.

The crowd was silent, still listening to the cardinal's oration.

"Today you will see plain evidence of God's will," Beaton declared. "Watch closely, that you may witness what comes to those who doubt His power."

Shutting his eyes instead and thinking only of Beth, Patrick whistled the signal he had used to call Zeus, certain that she would recognize it as easily as the hawk would. Zeus might bate when he heard it, but he was jessed and the King would calm him. And Beth would at least know she had friends nearby. She would guess they were helpless, but it would reassure her to know they were there.

To his astonishment, a matching whistle answered his.

He opened his eyes. Surely, it could not have been Beth, not with the witch's bridle gagging her. Although he had heard that such bridles did not prevent victims from screaming, no one could whistle with a sharp metal bit pressing on her tongue.

Beaton's hand shot up to signal the lighting of the fire, and Patrick realized that the cardinal meant to burn them alive. Frantic now, he glanced at Molly, expecting to see her set an arrow to her bow, but she stared straight ahead.

Following her intent gaze, he saw Zeus spread his powerful wings. The King reached to stop him, but it was too late. Having snatched off his hood and somehow slipped his jesses, Zeus swooped to one of the witches and landed on her shoulder.

Without a thought for the people blocking his way, Patrick gave spur to the stallion, and a path somehow opened before him to the single, black-hooded figure with the hawk on her shoulder. He charged toward her, and for all the attention he paid his surroundings, he and she might have been alone in the square.

As he drew near, a man-at-arms leaped toward her, his dirk raised to stab, but just as Patrick recognized the man's intent, Zeus screamed and raised his wings threateningly, giving the soldier pause, and a gray streak hurled itself forward, teeth bared, knocking the man to the ground.

Reining in and reaching down as the fiery stallion reared and pawed the air, Patrick slipped an arm around the figure with the still screaming hawk on its shoulder. Zeus shot skyward and away, and as he did, Patrick lifted the slender black-robed woman, who seemed weightless now, and held her easily as he flipped the iron ring over the top of the stake. Then, holding her tightly, he spurred the plunging stallion. He could do nothing about the iron ring around Beth's neck, her bound hands, or the terrible witch's bridle, but she was free, and he held her close.

How the stallion made it through the crowd, he would never know. He saw people flee before the maddened beast's flashing, iron-shod hooves, but he knew the cardinal's men would risk life and limb to keep one of Beaton's witches from escaping. Nevertheless, as the horse plunged forward, the way continued to clear until no one stood in its path. No one challenged him even at the town gate. Even so, Patrick rode hard until he was sure that no one followed closely enough to catch them. Then, at last, he slowed to make Beth more comfortable.

Beth felt enormous relief when the horse began to slow. She had known at once that the rider was Patrick, and he held her as he rode, but she felt battered and bruised nonetheless. The hood was so stifling she could hardly breathe, but at least she was alive. When the horse stopped, the hard, muscular arm that clamped her close to the rider's body eased its hold, and he shifted her to sit before him. The heavy ring around her neck opened, and he pulled off the hood.

"Thank God," he murmured, wrapping his arms around her and lightly kissing her forehead. They were the first words she had heard since the bird's sharp talons had spasmodically clutched her shoulder.

She hugged him tightly, not wanting ever to let go, but after a few moments, Patrick held her a little away and looked searchingly into her face. "You're really all right," he said. "Can you talk?"

She nodded. "I think so. My tongue is sore, but it works."

"That bridle must have been faulty. The spike seems to have fallen off."

"Did it? It was horrid, but when Zeus came to me, I forgot about it."

"Did you not whistle to him?"

"I heard you whistle," she said, smiling weakly. "I tried to answer, but I did not think I had made a sound. The noise around me was awful, but I did hear you."

He hugged her again and kissed her on the mouth. She responded at once, astonished that she felt no pain after enduring the horrid bridle for so long. Even her tongue did not hurt anymore, as she soon discovered. Moments passed, during which she did her best to forget the past days and the terror of that day, and to remember the feeling of Patrick's body beneath her hands and that of his hands on her, but when the stallion moved nervously, Patrick chuckled.

"We dare not linger, much as I want to," he murmured against her lips. "I don't have a mount for you, sweetheart, but the black will carry us both easily."

She sighed when he straightened. "Where are we going?"

"To the Highlands," he said.

"Nay," she heard another familiar voice say. "That'll be the first place they'll search for ye, so tell him ye'll be safer d'ye head south tae Dunsithe."

Beth saw that Patrick had not heard, because his expression did not change. He was still waiting for her to comment.

"Tell him," Maggie said sharply, taking form on his shoulder.

Wide-eyed, Beth nodded.

"What is it?" Patrick asked, glancing around warily.

"We must go to Dunsithe," Beth said.

"And tell him no tae stop for anything along the way," Maggie ordered.

Patrick looked into Beth's eyes. "Dunsithe?"

"Aye," she said, "and we're not to stop until we get there."

Patrick's eyes narrowed. "But why do you want to go there?"

Beth hesitated.

"Tell him," Maggie said.

"We must go there," Beth said. "Maggie Malloch says we must."

"Tell him Molly and Kintail will meet ye there—and your mother, too."

Beth obeyed, and Patrick looked sternly at her, but to her surprise, he did not instantly accuse her of having lost her mind.

"Something strange happened in that square, too," he said at last. "I won't pretend to understand, but I won't question any of it now, either. The only thing that matters now is that you are with me."

Grinning, Maggie said, "Tell him the crowd in the square freed them other women after he took you. They thought the hawk were a messenger from above, declaring heavenly opposition tae the cardinal's will. Tell him, too, that your cousin Huntly and others prevented the cardinal's men from following you. Pandemonium reigns in Stirling yet."

When Beth relayed the information, Patrick frowned. "I will ask one question," he said. "Just who is telling you all this?"

"She is," Beth said, pointing at his shoulder, only to see that Maggie had vanished again. "She's gone now. I know you don't believe in her, but—"

"Look," Patrick said, gesturing.

Beth obeyed and smiled when she saw Thunder loping toward them. Then, hearing a mewing sound, she looked up and saw a hawk circling overhead.

Patrick said, "I think I'll just accept that you're safe, sweetheart, and leave it at that for now."

Relieved but exhausted, she soon slept in his embrace, and

continued to sleep as they rode through the night without stopping any longer than to let the stallion drink from a brook or river. They arrived at Dunsithe late the following afternoon.

In the cobbled courtyard of the huge castle, Beth gazed about her in awe as two pretty women and a tall, well-built man came running out to welcome them.

The older woman stared at Beth as if she could not believe her eyes.

"How did you know we'd come here, Fin?" Patrick asked as he slid down from the saddle to shake hands with the man and to hug the younger woman.

"We just knew," she said, hugging him back and grinning. The grin faded as she stepped back, looked up at Beth, and said, "You must be my little sister."

Tears welled in Beth's eyes, and an ache of longing filled her. "Am I truly? Are you sure?"

"Oh, my dear, there can be no doubt now!" the older woman exclaimed, tears streaming down her cheeks. "Lift her down, Patrick. I want to hold my daughter!"

Beth gasped in astonishment. "Mother?"

Still tearful, the woman nodded. "Yes, my darling, and that is your sister, Molly, and her husband, the Laird of Kintail."

As Patrick lifted Beth down, he held her close for a moment, murmuring, "You have a family now, my love. I hope you like them."

"I will," she said, savoring the endearment as she turned to her mother and said, "I never expected you to be so beautiful."

Laughing and crying at the same time, they threw their arms around each other and hugged as if they would never let go.

A good deal of time passed before anyone mentioned the treasure.

They had finished eating a tasty supper in the splendid great hall, during which Beth had listened happily to her mother and sister chat about the family she had not known she had, and gazed about at the hall's magnificent furnishings.

Patrick gently touched her arm. "I nearly forgot," he said, reaching into his doublet as she turned to him, and withdrawing the chain with the gold leaf pendant that she had worn to the ball. "I brought this along for you, although I left the pomander and your belt at Stirling with the other trinkets."

"You need not have brought it," she said. "I am sure it is mere trumpery, because the jewels in my shoes proved to be only colored glass, you know."

"Don't be too certain of that," Molly said, glancing at Fin as Patrick fastened the chain around Beth's neck. "We should show her the chest, should we not?"

Fin nodded and said to Patrick, "You should come, too. If you are not meant to be there, I warrant we'll soon know as much."

Bewildered by their comments, Beth saw that Patrick was, too.

"Don't think you are going without me," Nell said firmly.

"Come along, then," Molly said as she and Beth followed the men. "As Fin told Patrick, if you are not wanted, we'll know."

Beth gave up trying to understand them, but when Patrick smiled at her, she relaxed. He trusted them, so she would, too. He took her hand, and they followed the others down a corridor with splendid carpets, and colorful arrases on the walls.

At the end, Fin grabbed hold of what looked like a stone slab and pulled, and to Beth's amazement, the whole thing opened like a door, revealing a dark tunnel beyond. When they entered, the stone slab swung shut behind them.

For a moment, she was frightened and clutched Patrick's hand tightly. Then, astonishingly, a silver glow lit the way ahead just as it had in her dreams. Involuntarily, she clutched the gold leaf and went on with the others.

As they rounded a curve, she saw the chest ahead, sitting just as it had in her dream. A sense of dread touched her just then, and a man leaped out of the shadows near the chest, a drawn sword gleaming threateningly before him.

Shrieking, "No, Angus, no!" Nell crumpled to the floor.

"Step forward, lass," the man growled, looking at Beth. "I ha' waited long for this. Open yon box and hand me all that lies inside. Then I'll leave ye in peace."

Patrick and Fin were unarmed, and when Fin, who was in the lead, leaped toward the intruder, a swift thrust of the sword felled him. Molly screamed, but with his free arm, the man knocked her hard into the wall, and she, too, collapsed.

Patrick stepped protectively in front of Beth, but the villain leaped toward him, sword slashing, and the unarmed Patrick was no match for him. As he fell, an eldritch screech echoed through the tunnel, and the villain stopped in his tracks.

Briefly, Beth thought she was hearing her own screams, but when the man whirled, a huge black bear loomed over him out of the shadows. The man raised his sword, but the bear knocked it aside as it charged. To Beth's astonishment, the man vanished and Thunder appeared in his place, barking and growling. When the bear paused, the dog leaped for its throat, but the bear stepped aside and Thunder ran into the wall. The dog shook its head and glanced at Beth.

Music suddenly filled the tunnel—eerie, haunting, and magically beautiful. Despite her terror and every horrible thing that had happened, it made her smile, and her feet twitched as if at any moment she would begin to dance.

"Plague take ye, ye peevish, white-livered, hag-born runagate! Ye might as well show yourself properly now. Ye've won the day." Astonishingly, the bear spoke but with

Maggie Malloch's voice, and as it did, the huge dog seemed to grin and stood upright.

Its shape shifted and changed before Beth's eyes. To her shock, in place of the huge gray deerhound stood a man with bristling green hair, a fiddle in his right hand and a bow in his left. The pupils of his eyes whirled in red and green spirals, and Beth counted six fingers on each of his hands.

She could not move or think straight. Tears streamed down her face, and her throat ached as she realized she had survived the cardinal's witch burning and found her family only to lose everything. And here Maggie Malloch was playing tricks with a dog and a bear. To be sure, the dog—or the man that had taken its place—was grinning, and Maggie was angry, but—

"Tom Tit Tot," Maggie exclaimed. "I hoped I'd never see your rascally face again, yet here ye be, making your mischief and ruining everything."

"Ye might show yourself properly, too, lass," the odd-looking man said. "I ha' missed ye summat fierce."

"Mam," a new voice said, "he has six fingers on each hand!"

"Silence, you!" shrieked the man, whipping fiddle and bow behind him.

"Aye, so he does," Maggie said in a deceptively even tone. "I suspected as much when I realized some'un had cast a spell tae encourage me tae overstep the mark, helping the lass. There be few powerful enough tae do that, but this villain ha' done it twice now. I didna count his fingers afore now, though."

"I ken his true name!" the new voice exclaimed triumphantly.

"Say it out loud, Claud, quick!"

"Jonah Bonewits be your name, ye bastard!"

"He canna shift now ye've solved his riddle," Maggie exclaimed.

The green-haired man shrieked, and his shape and coloring changed again, his hair standing out like rays of the sun and turning from green to red with fair tips. His face narrowed, and Beth saw that his cheeks bore multicolored streaks, but his eyes had lost their whirling colors and glittered darkly now with fury. Raising both hands high, he bellowed, "Show yourself properly, ye vixen queen o' curds!"

"Afore I do," Maggie said tautly, "ye should ken that the lass has seen everything ye've done here today."

Hands still raised, the man froze in place, clearly horrified.

The bear vanished then, and Maggie appeared in its place. Facing the odd man with her hands on her plump hips, she said calmly, "Ye'll do nowt tae harm her, Jonah Bonewits, for although ye hid her from us, ye ha' protected her, and having protected her, ye canna harm her now."

"I do serve Angus," he said.

"Ye serve nae one but yourself," Maggie said scornfully. "Ye'll no force my Claud tae marry your Lucy, neither—and he is *my* Claud, ye hollow-eyed wretch. Ye're tae leave him be."

"Aye, well, Lucy Fittletrot isna *my* Lucy," the man said. "She were just helping me wi' a bit o' mischief."

"I'll be taking this up wi' the Circle," Maggie said grimly.

"Ye do that, lass," the man said, eyes narrowing again. "If ye want tae pit your powers against mine again, ye just do that." With that, he vanished.

Maggie turned to Beth. "Ye'll be safe now, lass. Nae one will harm ye."

"But what of the others?" Beth asked, her voice choked with her tears.

"They be only sleeping," Maggie said. "I stopped the blood where it flowed, and the women are no hurt at all. Ye'll see when they waken."

Rushing to kneel beside Patrick, Beth saw that Maggie was right. He breathed normally, and she could find no sign of blood despite having seen the man stab him with the sword.

"Thunder and the man with the sword were the same person, and you were the bear!" she exclaimed. "The others will never believe it. I can scarcely believe it, myself, though I saw it with my own eyes."

"Ye'll no be telling them," Maggie said. "Until they stand they'll no waken entirely, and when they do, they'll remember only that ye were about tae open yon chest wi' your key. 'Tis your fortune inside, and none but ye can open it. They'll see nowt amiss, I promise ye, and your own memory o' this will fade at once."

As she spoke, her voice faded, and Patrick stirred.

Beth's attention instantly shifted to him. "Oh, my love," she murmured, helping him up, "hold me tight."

He obeyed as the others stood, and Kintail said, "Have you your key, Beth?"

Without thinking, she put her hand to the chain and found that her gold leaf had turned into a golden key. A moment later, the chest was open, and even in the dim light of the tunnel, the magnificent jewelry inside glittered brightly.

Chapter 25

The woods near Dunsithe

The woodland was eerily dark and silent. No breeze stirred, no leaf twitched. It was as if the wee folk had cast a spell over every creature, so quiet that walking beneath the trees, Patrick could hear only his footsteps crunching through dead leaves, and when he paused, he could hear himself breathing. Drawing his cloak around him, he stood until he heard rustling in the shrubbery and the distant cry of a night bird, enough to reassure him that no mischief was afoot.

But where was Beth? She had gone upstairs to get ready for bed soon after they returned to the great hall after finding her inheritance, but when he had gone up a bit later, she was not in their room. He had searched briefly before a hunch stirred, suggesting that she had somehow slipped out and gone into the woods.

As he remembered that disconcerting thought, he saw a silvery glow ahead, and soon came upon a glade where the moon cast silvery light on the familiar figure standing quite still on the grass in the center.

Barefoot, clad only in a white, clinging nightdress, she

stood with her face tilted toward the heavens, her lovely, slender profile etched against the dark woodland beyond. Even her hair looked white as it spilled down her back in a silken sheet. Her eyes were closed, their long, thick lashes casting shadows on her cheeks. The sight reminded him briefly of the day he had seen her step out of the cave, and he wondered what she was thinking.

The air was cool and a little damp amidst the lush greenery of the woods. He inhaled deeply, wanting to go to her, to take her in his arms and hold her close.

At the thought, he could almost feel her so, could easily imagine her soft flesh pressing against his. Aware of the warm cloak he wore, he wondered if she noticed the chill, or if she had lost herself in her thoughts, as she had once told him she had done since childhood whenever she wanted to escape an unhappy moment in favor of a happier one.

Was she unhappy now? She had been through a great deal, for her world had turned upside down during the past sennight. What normal person would not be bewildered? He yearned to help, but even so, he hesitated to interrupt her now.

Instead, he watched, and as he did, he sighed with the pleasure he derived simply by being near her. Had anyone told him that such a feeling could come from nothing more than the awareness of a woman's presence, he would have laughed as he had laughed at so many things in his life. For years, he had cast off the notion of letting life surprise him. Even before his father's death, experience had taught him that life was brief and unpredictable, and he had resolved after his mother's death never to let life's unpredictability disturb him so terribly again. But he knew now that he had misled himself and underestimated the power of love. He knew now that he would have sacrificed his life and all he held dear to save Beth. He knew, too, that he would never see the world in the same light again now that she was his.

She opened her eyes, and his body stirred when she inhaled and her soft breasts rose beneath the thin gown she wore. He held his breath, wondering if she sensed his presence. She stood still, though, a young Diana, worshipping the moon.

Then, as it occurred to him that he might startle the liver and lights out of her if he moved now or called to her, she said softly but nonetheless clearly, "I suppose you have come to take me back."

For a moment, he was uncertain that she had spoken to him, because she still gazed at the moon, but then she turned her head and smiled at him.

"How did you know I was here?" he asked.

"You may think you move through the woods with stealth, sir, but in this stillness, you sounded like an army on the march. How did you find me?"

"You were not in our chamber, so I came out here."

"But why here, to this place? These woods are vast, and I might have gone elsewhere, might I not?"

He did not remember moving toward her, but he stood facing her now. Quietly, savoring the sweetness of being with her, of feeling his body stir in response to her, he said, "It felt as if I should come this way, and so I did."

She nodded. "I knew you would. Do you suppose the wee folk are managing things for us again?"

"I doubt it," he said, smiling and reaching out to shift an errant strand of her silky hair back over her shoulder. "I choose to believe that I knew where you were because I love you and could sense your presence. And you knew I was coming, not because I was as loud as an army on the march, but because you are attuned to my senses in the same way and for the same reason that I am attuned to yours."

She smiled. "Truly, Patrick?"

"Truly, *mo chridhe*," he said, putting both hands on her shoulders and bending to kiss her.

She met him halfway, stretching upward, leaning into him, and letting her body press against his, just as he had imagined feeling it only moments before. He inhaled deeply, enjoying the familiar flowery fragrance of her hair and moving his hands from her shoulders, down her arms, and around her, holding her close. Her lips felt soft and yielding beneath his, her body pliable and warm.

His body stirred again, and he yearned to possess her.

Slipping off his cloak, he spread it on the ground, then lifted her and knelt to lay her down upon it. She gazed serenely up into his eyes, making no protest.

"I want you," he murmured.

"Now, Patrick? Here?"

"Aye, lass, now and at once."

"But what if someone comes?"

"I'll shoot them," he said matter-of-factly, unbuckling his belt and setting pistol and sword aside.

Beth started to chuckle, but his hand moved to her breast, and the chuckle turned into a gasp of pleasure.

"Oh, Patrick."

"Damnation," he murmured.

"What?"

"This blasted gown of yours fastens in the back."

"You'll think of something," she said with a teasing smile.

Lying on one side, he gathered her close and kissed her neck, sending feathery ripples of pleasure through her. Then his lips found hers, crushing them, and his passion warmed her, making her tremble as her body leaped to his touch.

She could no longer keep both hands still, and her right one slipped beneath his doublet, pulling his shirt free of his breeks and then moving to explore the tight bare skin beneath it, caressing the hard lines of his ribs and the muscular planes of his flat stomach.

Elbow crooked now, he rested his head on his left hand, but his right one stayed busy, caressing her breasts, kneading them, and teasing her nipples through the thin fabric of her gown. He paused, smiling and gazing deeply into her eyes.

She reached up and stroked his cheek. Then, with one finger, she traced a line up to the corner of his eye, moving her fingertip gently across his eyelid so that he shut his eyes, and then stroking along the line of his eyebrow, back down to his cheek again. She touched his lips with two fingers, lightly, teasingly.

Patrick groaned. Never had he felt such sensations. Flames roared through his body, flames that she had stirred to life with no more than the touch of her fingertip. It was no wonder Davy Beaton and the others had believed her to be a witch. She certainly had bewitched him. And if God willed it, she would continue to do so for as long as they both lived.

Her fingers still teased his lips, and impulsively, he caught one of them and sucked on it, savoring the taste of her skin.

She smiled, and yearning swept through him. He wanted her with a passion that he had never felt for anyone before. Holding her, he rolled to his back, pulling her atop him and reaching for nightdress ties. They succumbed swiftly to his eager fingers, and in moments, he stripped the gown from her body and flung it aside. As his hands caressed her naked back, the fact that she had worn so little both delighted and angered him in a mixture of overwhelming emotion.

"You should not have come out so scantily clad, lass. Don't do it again."

"Or?" Her voice sounded lazy, teasing.

He rolled again, this time pinning her beneath him and looking down into her eyes. Sternly he said, "Or I'll smack that pretty backside of yours until you learn to take more care. What if you had come upon an enemy out here, with you barefoot and wearing only that thin gown?"

"No one is here but you," she murmured, "and you still have your clothes on." Now both of her hands were under his shirt, feeling cool on his skin but stirring heat through his body. "Take off your clothes, Patrick," she added, still in that teasing murmur. "I would see you naked in the moonlight, my love. Or would you have me act as your handmaiden?"

The thought of her undressing him excited him, but he was too impatient, so although she helped unlace his doublet, he did not wait for help with his shirt, yanking that garment off over his head and sending it after her gown.

Her nimble fingers were busy at his belt, and his breeks, boots, and netherstocks soon went the way of their other clothing.

Maggie Malloch watched with a fond smile.

"They'll be safe now, I warrant," Claud said, joining her.

"Aye, for now," she said.

"Must you leave again, Mam?"

"Aye, a storm's brewing in the north, and we've folk involved, so I'm tae look after things there." Her tone was bitter. "Jonah Bonewits were at fault and thus ha' been banished from the Circle, but I overstepped, too, they say, and must prove m'self again tae keep me own place there."

"Ye'll do it, Mam. I ken fine that ye will."

"Aye, laddie, but your feckless father made a vile kettle o' stew this time, so I mean tae put him out o' the stew-making business for good—one way or another."

Claud shivered, but when she waved her pipe and disappeared, he followed, leaving the lovers in sole possession of the little glade.

Patrick was magnificent by moonlight, Beth thought, looking lovingly up at him. In truth, he was magnificent in any light. The sight of him made her forget everything but her desire. The grass was like a soft bed beneath his cloak, and if it was damp, the dampness did not touch them.

"I want to kiss you, Patrick."

"Kiss me then, lass. Kiss me everywhere."

"Everywhere?"

"Aye, everywhere," he said, stretching out beside her on his back and adding with a lazy smile, "if you dare."

Beth felt her nipples harden at the thought of what he wanted her to do. She continued to gaze at him for a long minute more, enjoying the way the moonlight played on the hard muscles of his chest and other interesting bits of his anatomy, one of which was standing at attention, begging for her notice.

"I dare," she said, rolling to her side and stretching to kiss him lightly on the nose, the way he had so often kissed her.

"That's a start," he said.

"Aye, and there's your mouth, too." She lingered over his mouth, tasting his lips and, when he parted them, thrusting her tongue inside. But when it quickly became apparent that his patience and lust would soon overwhelm his delight in what she was doing, she ceased her exploration of his mouth and kissed his chin as lightly as she had earlier kissed his nose.

From there, she kissed a path to his chest, lingering occasionally to taste him, then moving to his nipples. When he gasped, she knew he was enjoying her attentions, but although she teased his nipples a bit, she did not linger there long. Moving lower, caressing him with her hands, then with her lips, never giving him an indication of where she meant to kiss him next, she tormented him the way she knew he would delight in tormenting her, until the tip of her tongue began to trace a line along his inner thigh. She felt his body tense then, and when she grasped him, she felt his flesh pulse beneath her fingers and heard his breath quicken.

She kissed the pulsing flesh, then stroked upward with her tongue, amazing herself with such wanton daring, delighting in his reactions.

"Oh, lass." He reached for her with both hands and pulled her upward, caressing her spine with one hand as his lips possessed hers and his tongue parted them to enter her mouth.

Her tongue teased his for some moments, and then he kissed her neck and shoulders, pausing to tease her nipples briefly as he worked his way down her body. She shivered, and he warmed her by stroking her, one hand moving to her breasts, full now and demanding his touch. His free hand moved to her legs, and when he stroked the inside of one thigh, her body began to move, urging him on. His mouth claimed hers, and she responded with a moan, moving a hand to guide him inside.

He eased his way into her, and her body welcomed him. When he paused for a moment, she held her breath, savoring the sensations that he stirred in her. Then he kissed her more possessively, and the waves of pleasure heightened. He began to move, gently at first, then more demandingly, and her body leaped in response to his. When he thrust his tongue into her mouth, it was as if he possessed her from the top of her head to the tips of her toes. The world around them had vanished, and there was no one left but the two of them. The fiery sensations increased, sending rivers of heat coursing through her until she thought she could stand no more. But there was more, and more, until her body seemed to explode.

But he did not stop, even then, moving faster and faster until she could not seem to breathe, and then at last, gasping, he collapsed atop her.

He was still after that for a long moment, although his breath was hot against her neck, tickling her. He was heavy, but she did not mind.

"Speak to me, sweetheart, or I'll think I've crushed you," he murmured.

"You haven't," she said, "but you are a bit heavy."

He eased to one side, and she drew in a long, deep breath of contentment.

"Beth, Patrick, are you out here?"

Molly's voice, sounding annoyed, carried easily to their ears.

"Faith," Beth muttered, "she sounds just like Drusilla did the day we met."

"Nay, lass, Molly could never produce a screech to match that shrew's. Nevertheless, I expect we should go back before she turns all Dunsithe out in search of us. Where did you put your gown?"

"*I* did not put it anywhere," she reminded him. "You threw it over there somewhere. Where are your breeks and boots?"

"With your gown," he said, rolling over to collect them. "Here, slip it on quickly. She's nearly upon us."

Beth chuckled. "Art shy, sir?"

"Nay, lass, but I'd not want to shock Molly."

"Or Kintail," she said, still grinning.

Patrick laughed. "Now, you have the right of it. I don't want to think about what he'd do if he found me naked in his wife's presence. Hurry up!"

Still chuckling, Beth scrambled into her gown and let him tie the laces. When Molly called to them again, she shouted, "Over here!"

By the time Molly appeared at the edge of the glade, they were decently clad and standing to greet her.

His arm across Beth's shoulders, Patrick said, "Did you fear we'd been taken by the enemy?"

"We did not know what to think," Molly said as her large husband appeared behind her.

"I told you so," Patrick said to Beth with a grin.

Fin said grumpily, "What the devil brought you two out here?"

"It certainly was not the devil," Patrick said, still grinning, his arm still possessively around Beth. "'Twas the moon that enticed us, laird, only the moon."

"Aye, you've been moon mad all your life," Kintail said. "But I expected Beth to show better sense."

"Oh, no," Beth said without a blush. "I am as moonstruck as Patrick, I fear."

Kintail shook his head and put an arm around his wife, urging her to turn away as he said, "I think, my love, that we are very much in the way here."

"Molly!" Nell's voice floated through the night.

"Sir Patrick, are ye out here?"

"Ho, Sir Patrick!"

"Faith," Patrick exclaimed. "Did you turn out the whole castle?"

Beth grinned at him, but Molly said, "We'll head them off." Slipping free of Kintail's arm, she pushed him ahead of her. "Tell them all to go back inside, sir," she commanded. "They are more like to heed you than me."

"I do not know why they should; you never do," Kintail said loudly enough for Patrick and Beth to hear.

Laughing, Patrick drew Beth close and hugged her. "Do you like having your own family, sweetheart?"

"Aye, sir, very much, although it seems strange to know they were there all along, whilst I've had no idea that they existed."

"You had your dreams," he reminded her.

"It wasn't the same, though. I thought they were just dreams."

"Is it all right now—that we're married, I mean?"

"Aye, sir," she said, looking into his eyes. "It is right and true, I think."

He smiled, and they stood looking at each other for a long moment.

"Ah, sweet Beth," he murmured. "You have become my very life to me."

He kissed her again, but she soon made him stop. "This place has become too public," she said. "Perhaps we can find some privacy in our own room, although with wee folk keeping watch, one never knows."

Laughing, clearly not intimidated by any wee folk, he scooped her up in his arms and walked with her back through the woods to Dunsithe.

Dear Reader, ———————————————

I hope you enjoyed *The Secret Clan: Hidden Heiress.* Those of you with further interest in the period may enjoy reading *The James V Trilogy* by Nigel Tranter (Coronet Books, 1995), while those who are interested in the wee folk will enjoy *An Encyclopedia of Fairies, Hobgoblins, Brownies, Bogies, and Other Supernatural Creatures* by Katharine Briggs (Pantheon Books, New York, 1976).

Although the Scottish Reformation came years after its European and English equivalents, in 1560, the reasons for its occurrence are similar, and although Cardinal David Beaton strongly resisted reform, he contributed much to the process. The great corruption of the Kirk from the top down was the main reason the reformers prevailed in the end. Priests enjoyed carnal relationships, and many married. Almost any blessing or benevolence was up for sale, and the good fathers were up to their ears in political corruption as well. David Beaton controlled the Scottish Crown through his influence on James V, and the burning of an innocent for political reasons resulted in Beaton's assassination in 1546.

Arthur and James, the two sons of James V, died of a mysterious illness not long after Arthur was born, and thus it was that James V's heir was Mary Queen of Scots. She was born 7/8 December 1542, seven days before the death of her father.

Witchcraft, in and of itself, did not become a capital offense in Scotland until 1563, but witches were shunned and punished, and treason *was* a capital offense. Thus, too often, persons charged with witchcraft were found guilty of treason as well. Janet Douglas was burned for witchcraft amounting to treason in 1539.

Once again I want to express my heartfelt thanks to Pam Hessey of the California Hawking Club for helping me learn about hawking and falconry, and even more particularly for her anecdotes about training hawks, two of which I used in this book. Any errors are mine (but do remember that Sir Patrick had help from the wee folk, so perhaps you can just blame Maggie Malloch).

Many thanks also to my agent, Aaron Priest, and his wonderful assistant Lucy Childs, and to my editors, Beth de Guzman and Karen Kosztolnyik. All four of these amazing people are constantly swamped with work, yet somehow always have a moment to spare, and I want them to know I appreciate that.

As for Maggie Malloch, you will meet her again in the story of Sir Patrick MacRae's sister Barbara and the tangle she creates when she attempts to deal with an unscrupulous Highland sheriff and the legendary hero who dares to challenge him. Look for *The Secret Clan: HIGHLAND BRIDE* at your favorite bookstore in early 2003. In the meantime, happy reading!

Sincerely,

Amanda Scott

http://home.att.net/~amandascott